PAPER WAR

SYMBIOSIS

RYAN LEKODAK

Symbiosis
Published by RandallVision Publishing.
San Diego, California

ISBN: 979-8-9896545-2-9 (Paperback), 979-8-9896545-3-6 (Hardcover)
FICTION / Thrillers / Technological

Cover and Interior design by Victoria Wolf, wolfdesignandmarketing.com. Copyright owned by Ryan LeKodak

RandallVision
PUBLISHING

BLACKOUTS

OCTOBER 2043
THE WHITE HOUSE,
WASHINGTON, DC

DEBI WILLINGHAM came back to herself with a gasp.

A few of the other aides spared her a glance but quickly looked away, unable to meet her eyes. Debi rubbed the bridge of her nose, holding in a sigh.

Had she blacked out again? For how long?

A few steps away, President Mary Pastore addressed the press about the change in curfew. That was something at least—Debi's episode had lasted only a few minutes. Still, she wasn't reassured. The blackouts had become more frequent. Some were relatively short-lived, but once, she went dark for an entire day. That time, Debi had come to at her desk, a stack of memos in front of her. The weird part: None of her colleagues had noticed anything wrong with her behavior that day. Most of her daily tasks had already been taken care of. But Debi had no memory of completing them, or even getting to work that day.

Scared of what that meant, she then locked herself in her room for several days. After a week without a blackout, she'd returned to work.

And now this.

She caught Sarah glancing at her with a slight smirk on her face. Debi lifted her chin and made a point to meet the woman's eyes. Sarah probably thought she'd fallen asleep. Where did she get off, judging her when Debi could smell her perfume all the way over here? Debi let out a small laugh at the thought. The bitch wanted everyone to think the perfume covered up a glandular problem, yet almost all the aides knew she wore it to mask the chlamydia she'd contracted from Matt.

As if she could read Debi's thoughts, Sarah looked away. Good. Debi had no intention of letting anyone question her professionalism; she had earned her stripes and would not be undermined. She was the chief aide in the White House. Naturally, others wanted her position. Few could have endured what she had to get it. Other aides had gone missing or died during Mayday, and most of those remaining simply resigned afterward. Debi was one of the few who stayed. Newer aides assumed she'd just taken advantage of a national crisis. In reality, she'd been the one to hold everything down while the world went to hell. She'd been the one to rally the remaining aides and staff so the entire White House didn't break down. And she did it while grieving over the death of her husband, Albert.

But none of them saw that. Debi would not have expected them to. People had proved increasingly adept at ignoring truths that didn't favor them.

Debi pushed the thought from her mind. Aides like Sarah had to be put in their place once in a while. This was something that Debi was getting increasingly good at. She glanced around once more. Everyone else was staring straight ahead, pretending to listen to the speech. Debi focused on it as well, though there was no need to. She had written every word of the speech and knew what it contained.

" …cooperate with police departments. It is for the safety of you and yours. Medical teams will also be set up along major …"

Medical teams, Debi scoffed internally.

Mary had specifically asked Debi to put that in, though Debi herself didn't see the point. What are they going to do? The official reason for the curfew was a rising pandemic. But unofficially, no one knew why hundreds of thousands of people had been disappearing recently—or why the ones who returned had … changed.

It had started with those missing after Mayday suddenly reappearing with little or no explanation. Then others had disappeared and returned. It was never for longer than two days—not enough time for people to truly start getting worried and organizing search parties. But all the same, no one was the same when they came back, no matter how long they were gone. Debi had heard of a teenager beating his father almost to death with his bare hands.

But that had been several months ago. Back then it was relatively easy to know when someone was infected: memory loss, rigidity when walking, behavioral changes. But as with everything important, people wisened up too late. Now the signs weren't as obvious. The infected showed no changes until they attacked.

That, more than anything, terrified Debi. They hadn't yet been able to study those infected before they attacked. If they had, would they have found the victims had experienced random blackouts? Maybe Debi should get checked. Wouldn't that be safer? The blackouts could be a symptom of something else.

Debi felt a fog settle over her mind. The world slowed as her thoughts moved at a crawl. She felt pressure on her brain, a vague feeling that lasted a moment and was gone.

Debi came back to reality with a gasp. What had she been thinking? And, God, why did her head hurt so much?

A few feet away, President Pastore was finishing her speech.

Thank goodness.

Debi needed to lie down. She'd spent the last few days on her feet setting up the press conference. Now the stress was catching up with her. A few hours' sleep, and she should be back to normal.

Her phone vibrated, and Debi flipped it open. With any luck, it was the secretary of defense replying to her email.

Tyra Chityothin: The extraction is set for two weeks.

Debi stared at the text for a moment. And another. Who was Tyra Chityothin? What was she extracting, and why did she feel the need to inform her about it?

Debi's thumbs hovered over the keyboard. But before she could respond, a fog settled over her mind, wiping her thoughts. By the time Debi came to, Mary Pastore, the president of the United States, was heading toward her. The press conference was over.

v

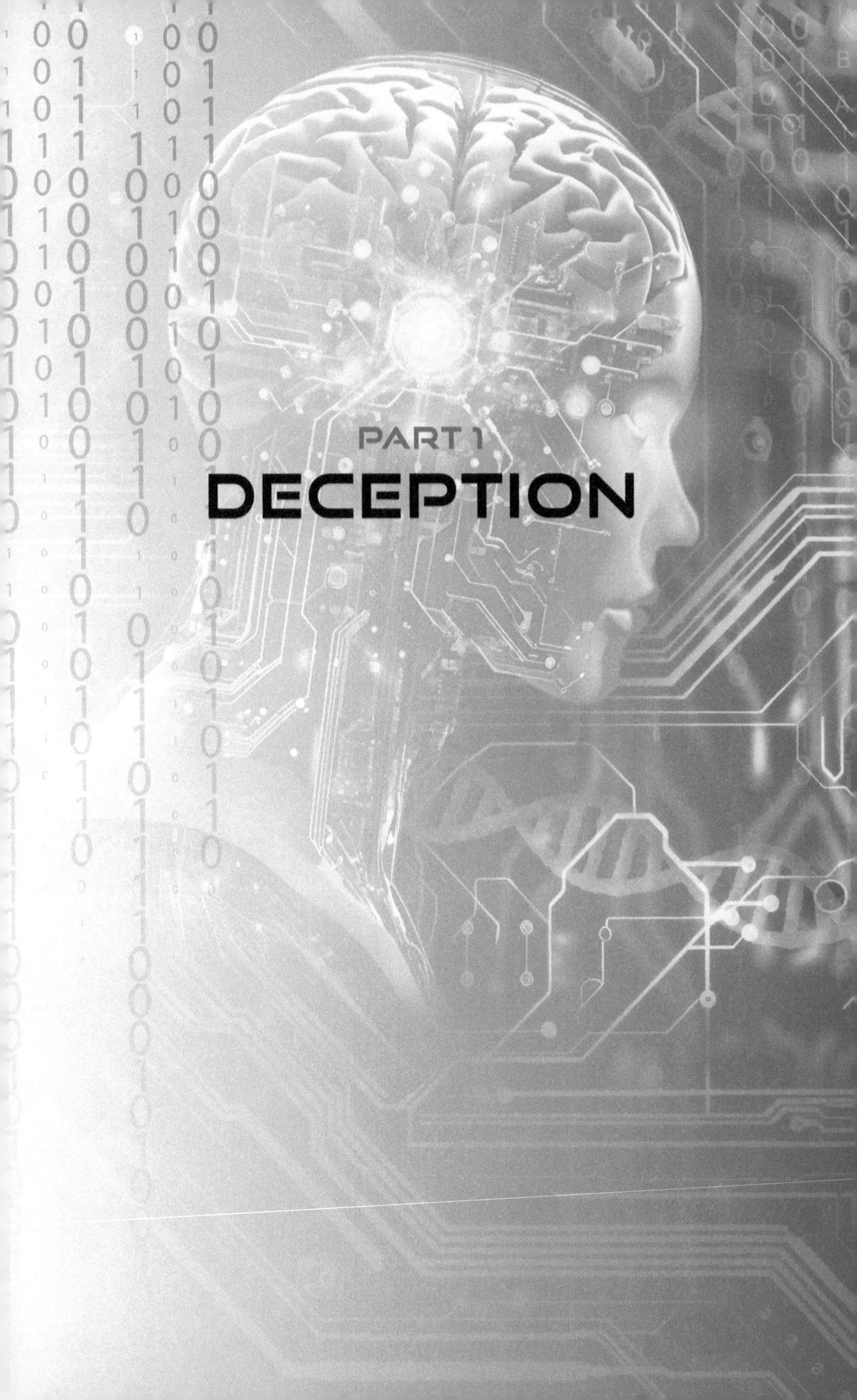

PART 1
DECEPTION

CHAPTER

1

OCTOBER 2043

JOHN F. KENNEDY AIRPORT,
NEW YORK

DJ DIDN'T LIKE PLANES. He hadn't liked them as a kid, and he didn't like them now. It was hard to trust something you had no control over and no way to escape from. It was even harder to trust something that you'd watched fall out of the sky like birds with their wings clipped. In fact, the only thing DJ hated more than planes was trains. That was a whole other thing.

Naturally his distaste for airplanes extended to airports, though for a slightly different reason. Whenever DJ was in an airport, he felt like he was a minute away from getting bombed, tackled, or randomly violated by TSA agents under the guise of a drug search. The place was noisy, smelled weirdly of jet fuel and burned coffee, and always seemed to have armrests covered in snot. For DJ, the best part of an airport was the exit.

"Can you stop that?" Christy said beside him.

"Stop what?" DJ asked, glancing around the gate.

"That," Christy hissed again, following her words with a jab. "You're looking around like you're going to get robbed or something."

"I'll take that over TSA," DJ muttered.

"What?"

"What?" DJ asked back, scanning the area again before focusing on Christy. "What's the delay here anyway? What's taking so long?"

Christy rolled her eyes. "Hermione is still trying to convince her to stay."

DJ blew out a breath and finally forced himself to face the sight he'd been avoiding. Several feet away, Manar, Ndidi, Pratima, and Hermione stood as a separate group. Manar's expression was as inscrutable as ever. However, DJ could almost feel the impatience wafting off him. In contrast, Pratima was like a mountain stuffed in a sensible suit. She looked like she could wait for years as long as Ndidi asked her to. Ndidi and Hermione stood next to each other, whispering furiously. Several times, Ndidi glanced in his direction, which told DJ all he needed to know about their discussion.

It had been a week since Manar and CJ had returned from defeating the AI Helene in the depths of the Internet. After Manar had debriefed everyone, driving home the point that Helene was no longer a problem, the team spent the next few days deciding on their next step. Ndidi immediately wanted to start reverse engineering the picospores to create a permanent cure for autism, one they could administer en masse. While DJ agreed about the value of a cure, he'd figured it would be wiser to first ensure there wasn't a way for Helene to reappear and screw everything up again. But even then, he'd wondered about forcing a cure on individuals on the autism spectrum who might not want it. Ndidi had lacked such doubt, and surprisingly, CJ had taken her side.

When the discussions had turned into a screaming match, Manar had suggested that he and Ndidi take a break in Nigeria, giving everyone a chance to cool down. DJ thought that was a bullshit idea, but at least their break would give him, Christy, and Olsen the chance to tie up whatever loose ends Helene had left behind.

Especially that bomb, DJ thought.

They'd stumbled on it while trying to rescue Ndidi in the maze underneath the steel factory. But since the goal then had been to rescue Ndidi, DJ had left it alone. By the time Olsen had checked in again with a full SEAL team and bomb squad, the whole thing was gone—poofed into thin air! A part of him seriously regretted that they hadn't just left Ndidi and taken care of the bomb then and there.

"We're not going on vacation, Hermione," Ndidi said, throwing her hands up in exasperation. "I've been away from the Okafor Corporation for too long. I need to make sure everything's running smoothly."

"Sounds like they're about done if Ndidi is repeating excuses," Christy noted.

DJ grunted, going through his mental to-do list. The first step should be contacting Olsen so they could run another sweep of the factory in case they'd missed anything the first time. Then DJ would try to find the dealers that Manar had contacted on the dark web. He'd need Manar's help with that, so DJ would probably delay that so the man could enjoy what Ndidi insisted wasn't a vacation. He needed to address several minor things at Sparta, but that wasn't urgent.

Most practically, he needed to get an apartment for himself and CJ.

Most of the team had been living within Sparta for the past year because it had been convenient. But with Helene taken care of, everyone would have to go their separate ways.

He wasn't looking forward to apartment hunting.

In the end, it took about ten more minutes for them to gather up, and it only happened because Ndidi and Manar's flight was called. Half an hour later, the rest of them were back in Sparta. DJ was following Hermione to her lab in order to tick something off his list.

He closed the laboratory door behind him and immediately scrunched up his nose. Because Hermione worked with picospores, she constantly cleaned the whole place with bleach. The sharp chlorine smell made DJ want to sneeze.

He rubbed his nose. "How's it coming with our would-be spies?" he asked. That's what DJ had started calling the hostages they'd rescued from the steel factory. Most of them had been kidnapped and controlled by Helene since Mayday. Ndidi had freed them—several hundreds of them. However, when they'd become separated, the former hostages had gone their own way; Helene had taken control of them again. A week or so later, the AI had sent several dozens of the group to Sparta, presumably to meet with Ndidi, but almost definitely to extract info on the Synaptic Pulse, the device that Hermione developed to neutralize the picospores and remove them from Helene's control. With the help of some of his buddies in Sparta security, DJ had detained them in Sparta's isolation chamber until Hermione could remove the spores from them so they'd be free of Helene's control.

"I finished with the last one a week ago," Hermione replied, turning to him with concern in her eyes. "But, DJ, these people need help. Several of them just keep staring into space, never saying a word. Most of them are too terrified to go out because they're afraid that Helene's just going to take control of them again. Honestly, I don't blame them."

DJ sighed. He'd spent as much time as he could with the former victims, but his efforts alone could never undo the years of trauma that Helene had inflicted on them. DJ had already expended most of the goodwill he had with Sparta by asking them to take care of the former captives for so long. If he pushed for anything more, they'd push back. Fortunately, since Hermione was done extracting the spores, he could start contacting the families of the hostages and hand them off. It felt like passing on the problem, but DJ didn't see anything else he could do.

"I'll handle it," he told Hermione. He and Christy could spend an hour going around to collect contact details verbally. For those who couldn't talk, Olsen could help him dig up their backgrounds.

"How's Bethany doing?" he asked softly.

Hermione's expression fell. She turned her back on him, arranging some notebooks on her lab bench.

Now I feel like a dick.

Bethany, by herself, had extracted the picospores infecting her. DJ didn't think he'd ever seen Hermione so angry. She'd yelled for over an hour, raving about how Bethany had given up the cure for her autism. Although DJ had needed to separate Hermione from Bethany, Ndidi's face stayed twisted in confusion as if she couldn't understand why Bethany wouldn't want to be stuffed full of the things responsible for her trauma.

For her part, Bethany had met both of their reactions with fierce determination. Without the spores, she faced the same difficulty with facial expressions as CJ. Nonetheless, her resolve was clear for anyone to see, and that more than anything finally calmed Hermione down. She didn't really accept the choice, just decided to drop it for the moment. DJ could see that on her face. Unfortunately, so could Bethany.

Hermione sighed. "She still hasn't left the isolation chamber." Bethany had been among the former captives while they'd been under Helene's control. Now she spent most of her time talking to them, giving them the honest time and attention no one else would. She was a key reason extracting the spores had gone so smoothly.

"Do you plan on talking to her?" DJ asked.

Hermione's head whipped toward him, and DJ's eyebrows rose. "And say what, DJ? 'Hey sis! I'm sorry that you felt so misunderstood by me that you decided to undergo a dangerous procedure just to prove a point.' Would that help?"

"Actually, yeah." DJ shrugged. "I think the whole point was to demonstrate that she's capable of making her own choices."

"But what she demonstrated," Hermione hissed, "was that she's not yet well enough to avoid making stupid choices." She took a step closer, eyes wide. "DJ, I don't want to say this about my own sister, but Bethany isn't well. Like, not just the trauma. She's mentally not well. Her brain's chemistry is scrambled like a freakin' *egg*. Helene and those picospores were the only things that were keeping it together. But Bethany doesn't understand that. She *can't* understand that, because she's traumatized. It's a vicious circle, and I don't know what to do. I don't know how to fix it."

By the last point, Hermione was sobbing onto his shirt. DJ was standing awkwardly with his arms around her.

How come any time I come here, she always cries? he wondered.

"It could just be because of everything she's been through, Hermione. What she needs now is time to heal. She needs you to be there for her, now more than ever."

Hermione took a step back, trying her best to compose herself. "I'm trying to. But it hurts to see my sister like that, to watch her be in so much pain."

DJ leaned down to meet Hermione's eyes. In his gentlest voice, he said, "This isn't about you, Hermione. Get your head out of your ass."

CHAPTER

2

OCTOBER 2043
SPARTA HEADQUARTERS, NEW YORK

DJ HADN'T TAKEN MORE THAN A FEW steps out of Hermione's lab before he found the next problem he had to solve—rather, the problem found him.

"Hey, DJ! Wait up," someone called from behind him.

DJ sighed. He could turn around and deal with whatever this new crisis was, or he could sprint to the elevator and check off the next thing on his list. He knew what he wanted to do, but recently he'd found that what he wanted didn't really matter.

When did I become so self-sacrificing? he wondered.

Surprisingly, an answer immediately popped into his head. It had started when Ndidi had put CJ—the most self-sacrificing person DJ knew—in a coma for several months. Meaning, it was Ndidi's fault. That figured. Lately, he'd found out that almost all of his problems could be traced back to Ndidi.

"DJ!"

He turned back. *Albert, huh?* He should have sprinted. Albert was effectively the leader of the former captives when they were freed from Helene's control. Middle-aged, he had a scraggly beard that was not past redemption. "Thanks for waiting up, man," he said finally, wiping sweat off with a face towel. "I've been looking all over. I need to talk to you."

DJ forced a smile and continued to the elevator. "Well, I'm kinda on my way to something, but if you don't mind walking and talking, I'm all ears."

"That's fine," Albert replied, entering the waiting elevator car. DJ punched the elevator button. "I don't plan on taking much of your time anyway. I just wanted to inform you that I need to leave."

"Oh?" DJ said absentmindedly, his eyes on the floor marker. "You've contacted your family?"

"Contacted? No," Albert replied, shaking his head. "That's why I have to leave: to meet her." He chuckled grimly. "Honestly, she probably thought I was dead and moved on. But it's not like I can blame her. It's been three years since Mayday, and I thought she was dead too. Still, what am I going to do if she's moved on?"

DJ glanced at him. "How did you find out she was alive?"

Albert's eyes brightened. "She was on the news."

DJ had added a TV set to the isolation chamber, which he called the IC, a week ago in his efforts to make the place more comfortable and less prison-like. He'd tried to deck the place out as much as he could, adding couches, "liberated" vending machines from Sparta's rec room, and an "acquired" pool table. Giving the former captives something to distract themselves with eased DJ's conscience about keeping dozens of people in forced isolation.

Still, one of them finding his wife on TV wasn't something he'd expected. But he'd take the win.

"She's not the hot weather woman on Channel 7, is she?" DJ chuckled. "I gotta tell you, man, if she is, I have some things to confess."

"Come on, man. The girl's like twenty." Albert laughed. "But no. Debi has worked as a presidential aide for several years. Before Mayday, you wouldn't have seen her within a hundred steps of Mary Pastore. But she must have been promoted or something because she was basically standing next to President Pastore during the press conference yesterday." He stared at his hands and chuckled wryly. "I'm ashamed to say that I barely recognized her. It's been so long."

The elevator dinged on their floor. DJ cleared his throat. "Well, man, I'm sure it'll work out," he said as both of them stepped into the hallway. "But an aide to the president? Doesn't that mean she's in Washington? That's a little far out, don't you think? I mean you're free to go, of course. That's basically what I'm coming to tell you guys. You're all free to go at any time. But Washington's quite a distance, isn't it?"

"It is, isn't it?" Albert muttered, almost deflating.

Wonderful, DJ thought, *I feel like a dick again.*

"And she probably thinks I'm dead," Albert continued. "I can't just go to her after all this time."

"That's not necessarily a terrible idea," DJ said, turning into another hallway. "I'm guessing you lived in Washington originally, right? You'll probably have to go there eventually to sort out your house, bank, and all that stuff. I just think it'd be a good idea to contact your wife first."

Albert stared at his hands, looking lost. "Where would I even start?"

DJ opened his mouth and then closed it. *Where the hell is Chloe when you need her?* "You can probably get her contact info online. Finding and taking advantage of private information about people is basically what the internet was made for anyway. But you're the one who will know best what to say. I'll be happy to spot you for whatever you need: bus money, a train ticket—you name it."

Albert nodded, though his eyes were still glazed. "Yeah, I appreciate that, man. Thanks for understanding."

"There's nothing to understand," DJ replied. He turned into another hallway, then a few steps later, he pushed open the door to the IC. Immediately, several eyes turned to him.

With the addition of the furniture and games, the IC looked like a rec room lounge, but it felt like a prison. Unlike a true lounge, there was no music playing, and the scant conversation going on was whispered or muttered crazily. Barely anyone used the couches. Most sat on the floor, holding their knees. In the corner, one guy was lying in a fetal position, staring blankly at the wall.

DJ sighed. He'd added more lights and games, but the heaviness in the air pressed in on him in an almost suffocating way, sucking away what little joy he had left.

How the hell did Bethany stand it?

She was at the other end of the room, trying to calm a woman who was muttering to herself and angrily scratching at her wrists. DJ's heart clenched at the scene. It hadn't always been this bad, of course. Some of them, including Albert, had taken Hermione's extraction reasonably well, coming out with their minds and personality intact. But for others, it was as if Helene and the picospores had been the ones holding their minds together. Once Hermione had broken the connection, their minds had broken with it.

The latter group was a subset of the former. Those who had come out with their minds intact after the spores were extracted then lost it when Helene was defeated. DJ wouldn't have believed that if Bethany hadn't been there to confirm it. According to her, several of them—slightly more than half a dozen—had just spontaneously screamed at the same time and clutched their heads. When DJ had checked the time stamp on the camera, it was a few minutes before Manar's transmission came in of Helene's defeat.

There were probably several reasons to explain that, but DJ didn't want to explore any of them. With Helene destroyed, Hermione was working on synthesizing a completely new batch of picospores. The new spores would be used in the worst cases, and hopefully that would fix everything that had messed up their heads.

Albert wandered off, and DJ headed toward Bethany. It didn't take long for him to explain what he wanted. Soon, they were going around, collecting what details they could from each person. Some were responsive enough to answer DJ's questions, while others needed a little prodding. More than a few had completely forgotten their identities. That led to a mild panic in DJ. The last couple didn't respond, no matter how many times DJ poked them. Eventually, he just settled on taking their picture so Olsen could figure it out.

Even with Bethany's help, the whole thing took the better part of two hours and succeeded in sucking out the rest of DJ's joy. He met Bethany at the door and added her to his list.

"What … what happens to them now?" Bethany asked softly.

DJ blew out a breath. "Now Olsen and I go through the list and find their families, who will hopefully be overjoyed. Then we send them off. With a little luck, their families will give them the help they need. The worst cases will have to be chipped so they can be monitored more, at least until Hermione is done with her experiment. But we can't afford to keep them here."

Bethany nodded slowly. "And, um, what … happens to us?"

DJ grimaced. That was a slightly more complicated question. "That depends on everyone, Bethany. But the way I see it, first we have to clean up the mess Helene made. The former captives are easy, but there are probably thousands or even hundreds of thousands of people left in the wild without her control—and maybe without their minds.

"It'll take a shitload of time and effort though … which is why I intend to leave it to the proper authorities to handle. I figure that we've busted our asses enough about this while they've done jack shit. It's their turn."

He threw a grin at her. While Bethany's expression didn't change, a twinkle in her eye showed her amusement.

After a moment, his thoughts went to the nanites, and his smile fell. He stared at his hands. "After that, I'll probably need to figure out what's going on with this stuff moving around inside me. According to Martin, it's not going to just go away by itself. I'll probably need to stay in touch with the Murder Twins for a bit for training and all that."

"And … after that?" Bethany whispered.

"After that, CJ and I will probably get an apartment somewhere, get a job, and probably grieve for our parents. It's been long overdue, I think." He knew, of course, what Bethany wanted to hear. Something along the lines of how the team would stay together. If they disbanded, Bethany would be left with Hermione and Ndidi, and both of them had shown several times that they couldn't accept the girl for who she wanted to be. DJ could have told her that. However, despite her appearance, Bethany wasn't a child, and she wasn't an idiot. DJ wouldn't treat her as either.

The next things out of her weren't subtle pleas or hints. Instead, she asked the question he hoped she wouldn't: "How … um, how is CJ?"

3

OCTOBER 2043
SPARTA HEADQUARTERS,
NEW YORK

CJ WAS SITTING AT THE COMPUTER when DJ entered. The light from the monitor was the only illumination, leaving most of the room encased in shadow. CJ's fingers kept clicking away at the keyboard as DJ closed the door behind him, struggling to ignore the familiar heaviness that wrapped around his shoulders.

It was the exact scene that he'd left six hours ago. Once again, CJ had stayed in the same spot the entire day. No. That wasn't right. At some point, he must have gotten up to turn off the lights and draw the blinds, plunging the room into a gloom that felt suffocating. The space seemed to amplify the isolation. The room was certainly empty enough—just a bed and a table, leaving plenty of room for DJ to wander aimlessly or collapse into despair without bumping into anything.

DJ threw himself on the bed, lying face up. He took a deep breath and regretted it immediately. His brother hadn't moved from the chair all day, and there'd been no circulation since the blinds had been closed. Thus, the whole room smelled like hot cat piss.

DJ closed his eyes, and did his best to ignore it. It'd just been a couple of hours since he'd seen Ndidi and the rest off at the airport, yet he felt like he'd aged several years since then. And it sucked that it was now a familiar feeling. DJ let his mind wander, not dwelling on anything specific.

Not thinking used to be easy. Now, after just a few seconds, responsibilities pecked at his mind. It took Herculean effort to force them away. He had to use a technique to do so: a technique that he'd learned from a book he'd read.

What happened to me? DJ thought in disgust.

He pushed that thought away, and every other that followed it. Eventually his mind settled, and his breathing evened out. His body pulled at him to sleep, but DJ resisted, basking in the calm. Waiting.

Eventually, CJ spoke. "Was … um … was Ndidi angry?"

"No, she wasn't," DJ said. CJ didn't reply, so DJ opened one eye to glance at him. "But … if you'd been there, you could probably have convinced her to stay."

"You would have … um … have been in the best pos-position to do that," CJ replied, his mouse clicking still furious.

"Why do you say that?" DJ asked.

"You … uh … know why," CJ replied.

DJ did know why, of course. Despite whatever bullshit Ndidi might claim, the main reason she and Manar had left for Nigeria was DJ couldn't stand looking at Ndidi's face. He made no effort to hide it. DJ didn't think he would ever forgive her for what she'd almost done to CJ—even if CJ seemed to have already done so. That wasn't surprising though: CJ had always had a soft heart.

The truly mind-blowing part was that even Manar seemed to have completely overlooked the fact that she had attempted to kill him. Even though Ndidi had failed, she'd still put him in a coma for several months and left him stranded in a situation where he could have easily ended up brain-dead.

To her credit, Ndidi had apologized. Several times, and mostly while weeping. But then DJ would remember CJ's unconscious body or picture what his brother had been through while in the Virtual Realm. He'd remember the determination on Ndidi's face when she spoke about "curing" Bethany, despite the girl's wishes.

And then, DJ always thought to himself, *The bitch would do it again.*

If there was a chance to do everything again, if there was a giant red Redo button, DJ was sure, without a shadow of a doubt, that Ndidi would make the same choice. She would betray them again, endangering her lover and DJ's brother, just to ease her own guilt about what had happened to Bethany.

That was something DJ couldn't forgive. He made no effort to hide it. This was why Manar had suggested that they leave. If DJ had said he'd play nice, they probably would have stayed. CJ was right. DJ knew it. But saying that would have defeated the whole purpose of the conversation.

He tried another tack. "Do you think I should forgive her?" he asked softly.

CJ was silent for a moment, though his fingers never stopped moving. Why did that piss DJ off so much?

"I … I do not understand why … um … why it is an issue, honestly," he replied finally.

"It's an issue because of what she did to you," DJ said, his voice tight.

"It was … um … my decision, DJ."

"First of all, it was a decision she forced you to make," DJ growled. He sat up. "Second, you know that's not what I'm talking about, CJ."

CJ sighed and finally turned to DJ. "Then … then … um … what *are* you talking about?"

Is he really going to make me say it? DJ thought, glaring at his brother. More to the point, CJ glared back, holding DJ's stare.

"Fuck it," DJ snapped. He counted down. "What I'm talking about is the fact that you've barely said two sentences to anyone, including me, in the last two weeks. I mean, I had to hear what you went through from Manar." He raised another finger. "You refuse to leave your computer and don't even say goodbye to Ndidi, a woman you've idolized since childhood and whom you claim to have forgiven.

"And finally, this nonsense." He gestured around the room. "Shutting off the lights? Closing the blinds in the middle of the day? Look, you haven't moved from that chair all day, not even to take a damn bath, CJ. The whole room smells like cat piss. But you're just clicking away at your damn keyboard.

"What I'm talking about is the fact that you're obviously depressed, and I don't know how to help you because you won't talk to me—your brother, the guy who's always had your back. Now, I've tried to be patient, and I've tried to be understanding. But you of all people know that isn't my strong suit. So are you going to tell me what the hell happened to you over there, or am I going to have to beat it out of you like when we were kids?"

DJ was breathing hard at the end, glaring at his brother. A part of him was worried that he'd gone too far, but the greater part of him was just pissed off. CJ glared back just as fiercely.

And then, as if he couldn't hold it back anymore, CJ snickered. The sound was so sudden that, at first, DJ didn't know how to react. It cut through the silence like a knife and dispelled whatever pressure there was. DJ tried to keep up his glare. CJ just snickered again. This made DJ snicker. And then it went downhill from there. Soon both brothers were howling with laughter. CJ leaned back in the chair while DJ rolled on the bed, both of them clutching their stomachs.

"Papa … um …" CJ started, and then broke into chuckles. He tried again, "Papa always … um … he always said that violence is never the answer."

"Not true," DJ replied, wiping a tear. "There are a lot of idiots out there who respond to strength faster than reason. Violence helps to cut through the bullshit."

"What … uh … does that mean?"

"It means," DJ explained, "violence is sometimes the answer."

CJ thought about that. DJ briefly wondered if he was remembering something about the Virtual Realm. *This brings us back to the crux of it*, he thought. "So, are you going to tell me?"

"Tell … you what?"

DJ narrowed his eyes.

CJ grinned—or at least he tried to. His face tensed. The smile came out as more of a grimace. Just like that, the amusement faded from CJ's eyes. He regained the same haunted look he'd had for the last few days. DJ's grin fell as well. He was about to give up this attempt when CJ spoke.

"I … um … felt normal," he started softly, staring at his hands. "There, I mean … um … in the Virtual Realm. My avatar was digital … which, um, meant that I had a new body: one that wasn't on the autism spectrum. I didn't have problems remembering basic information or focusing and staying on topic and didn't … didn't, um, have so much trouble just speaking. I could smile when I wanted to.

"Basically, for the first time in my life, I felt what it was, um … what it was like to be normal, to be like everyone else. And it was amazing." CJ's voice cracked on the last line. He took a breath. DJ noticed his hands were shaking. "For the first time in my life, I … I felt like I was in control of my own body—free in a way I hadn't experienced before. And now that … that I'm back—"

"You're constantly reminded about what could be possible," DJ finished for him. He understood where his brother was coming from. He'd never experienced that, of course—not even close. But he understood in the way a nonartist could appreciate a painting.

CJ had always hated being on the autism spectrum, even as a child. Especially as a child. He would be so angry every time he had an episode, and then he'd retreat within himself and stay in a corner of the house as if afraid to be a burden. When they discovered Ndidi and the techniques from the Okafor Autism Centre, CJ took to them with a vengeance. He'd spent days going over each technique over and over again—and he'd punish himself twice as harshly whenever he made a mistake. This would sometimes lead to another episode and another cycle of punishment, which used to drive their dads mad with worry. They almost considered ending Ndidi's mentorship.

But eventually, CJ mastered the techniques, and his episodes happened less frequently. He communicated better, could access his memory more easily, and figured out how to keep himself grounded. Self-hatred still occasionally flashed in CJ's eyes whenever he stuttered or when he stalled while looking for a word, but on the whole, he'd improved greatly. DJ just wished he didn't notice those moments, but maybe he was just being overly critical.

The fact was that, all his life, CJ had chased after being normal—or at least what he considered normal. He'd gotten a taste of it for a few months before being yanked back to his own "abnormal" body. Who wouldn't be depressed after that?

And more to the point, how the hell could DJ help? He always saw himself in that role, but this time he couldn't play the hero. This was something his brother would have to come to terms with himself.

"Now you … um … you understand why I didn't say anything?" CJ said after a few minutes.

"Yeah," DJ replied softly.

"Yeah."

WHEN NDIDI WAS YOUNG, after weeks of begging, her father took her on a tour of the Okafor Corporation. It had taken the whole day, of course, because of her father's thoroughness—never mind that Ndidi had fallen asleep halfway through and didn't wake up until the tail end of the tour. She'd try again more than a few times.

As she grew older, her tours of the Okafor Corporation became routine inspections. Every inspection still took her several hours to complete despite the conveyor belts the company installed to help employees get around faster. The place would always feel huge, she thought.

"It's small," Manar said, wheeling their bags through the bedroom doors.

Ndidi jolted out of her daydream. "What?"

Manar shrugged. "You compared it to Sparta," he explained, "so I expected it to be bigger."

"It *is* like Sparta," Ndidi said. "How can you not see that?"

"Because you're wrong?" Manar glanced at her with amusement.

"It's my fault," Ndidi said. She took the bags from him and placed them in the closet before starting to undress. Manar sprawled across the bed, exhaling deeply. "I shouldn't have taken you through one of the side entrances," Ndidi continued. "Maybe after walking for an hour, you'd understand how large this place is."

Manar opened an eye. "Just an hour?"

Ndidi threw her panties at him. "My point is, the Okafor Corporation is massive, but not in the same way as the Sparta Headquarters. Maybe that's why you don't see it."

"What do you mean?" Manar asked, propping himself up on one arm. Ndidi saw that he still had her panties in his hands, so she bent a little and shimmed out of her bra. Her chest swayed with the motion and Manar's eyes followed her breasts as if unable to help himself.

Ndidi grinned, pretending not to notice his stare as she searched for a change of clothes. "What I mean is that Sparta Headquarters was built all at once, with all of its departments in a single towering building. But the Okafor Corporation started small and expanded as my father grew the business and branched out into new fields. The end result is a dozen buildings revolving around a central hub." She glanced up at him. "But you missed all of that because I was being considerate and took a shortcut. So, I can only blame myself."

Manar snorted. "You were being considerate to yourself. You almost fell down twice on the way out of the airport."

Ndidi paused in the middle of putting on a shirt to glare at him. "It was an eighteen-hour flight, Manar, with no layovers. If anything, you're the odd one for being able to walk straight after that."

Manar scoffed and reclined on the bed without replying. A moment later, Ndidi joined him, resting her head on his chest. Automatically, his arms wrapped around her as he pulled her closer.

His heartbeat was slow. Ndidi didn't know why she noticed that, but she did. Her heart felt like it was going to burst out of her chest at any point. It'd been that way for the last several weeks because, well, as near as Ndidi could figure, she still didn't believe that this was real—that any of it was real.

She'd expected Manar to hate her after he'd awakened. She'd prepared herself for it—had even packed her bags and everything. Ndidi suspected that a part of her had even wanted him to reject her, that his admittance of her guilt would ease the burden of what she'd done. She didn't regret saving Bethany, though she recognized she had betrayed the group to do so, Manar specifically. She'd wanted him to hate her, to never forgive her. That would have made sense.

But instead, the moment he'd awakened, he'd kissed her.

DJ hadn't told Manar about what she'd done. Maybe he wanted to punish her further by making her come clean, or maybe he just hadn't wanted Manar to be distracted while facing Helene. Whatever the reason, at that moment, Ndidi was extremely grateful for DJ. Even after Manar had learned what she'd done, he hadn't left. Moreover, he'd defended her.

Several weeks later, she still didn't know how to feel about that. Their time together had been a dream. Ndidi was constantly afraid that, one day, she'd wake up.

"What's your itinerary like?" Manar asked, breaking into her thoughts.

Manar had suggested going on a vacation to create space between her and the rest of the team. Ndidi, however, had been the one to suggest they go to Nigeria. She had to eventually. Helene's defeat meant that she no longer had an excuse to stay away. But now that she was here, Ndidi was already regretting it.

She sighed. "I have a meeting with Uncle Abaeze in the morning. He's acting as the deputy chairman since he was one of my parents' closest friends. He basically raised me, so my first challenge will be to get him to see me as a grown woman and not as the child who hid behind his legs when she got her mother angry."

Manar chuckled. "And after that?"

"After that, I'll have to read through several years' worth of reports and updates to get caught up. After *that*, I'll have to audit the files to be sure no one has been stealing from the company during all the chaos. Most of the management teams were handpicked by my father, but now that he isn't around—"

"They would not be able to contain their greed. Humans will become greedy," Manar finished.

Ndidi nodded. "How about you? What will you be doing?"

"Me?" he asked, rubbing her head. "I'm sure I can find something to keep me busy."

She glanced up at him. Reflecting the sunlight, his eyes almost looked like burnished gold.

CONSUMED BY THE LOGISTICS of getting the former hostages to their homes, DJ hadn't been to the warehouse in weeks. The last time he'd contacted the Murder Team was to tell them about Helene's defeat, but in his defense, this was the first time he'd cleared up enough work to be able to come over. *Clear up enough work?* DJ thought, slightly disgusted. *Is this my life now?*

The warehouse hadn't changed. Although at least twice as large as the average building of its type, most of that space was covered by a maze of discarded boxes and broken-down machines from decades past when the building was still in use. With a building as old as this one was, there were bound to be weird sounds, and so DJ tried to ignore the faint clanging sound of metal rods hitting against each other repeatedly. Navigating the maze, he headed to the medical ward—a small space cleared of boxes with a light fixture. For some reason, though, most of the medical equipment had been taken away, leaving just a bed and a small bedside table. Although the space already stretched the definition of *ward*, it nailed *depressing*.

He found Martin staring off into space, his brow furrowed in deep thought, his lips pressed together as if he were wrestling with something unspoken. DJ paused for a moment. On a good day, Martin looked like the cliché of a kindly old man but with some muscle, probably from rolling his wheelchair everywhere. For some reason, whenever he saw the man, DJ was always reminded of his grandfather. Strange since DJ had never met his grandfather.

He cleared his throat lightly, causing the older man to jump. "My God, DJ! You scared me," Martin said, adjusting his wheelchair until it faced DJ. He pulled a handkerchief from somewhere and rubbed his face. "Please forgive my appearance. I didn't expect to have guests. What brings you?"

DJ pretended not to see the old man's attempt to clean himself. Instead, he leaned against the pile of boxes that made up the wall. "I had some free time, so I thought I'd drop by." He nodded to the empty bed. "What happened to your patient?"

Martin put away the handkerchief and finally met DJ's eyes. "He got better," he replied. "Isn't that the dream of every doctor?"

But Martin didn't look particularly happy. DJ couldn't blame him—not with *this* patient at least. "Where is he now?" DJ asked.

Martin adjusted his glasses and pointed deeper into the warehouse toward the source of the clanging metal sound. "I'm surprised you didn't hear them. They've been at it for most of the morning."

DJ raised his brows. "That's *them*? I thought it was the pipes or something. What the hell are they doing?"

STARING AT THE SCENE IN FRONT OF HIM, DJ understood: They were sparring in a makeshift ring half a dozen yards wide. DJ had bad memories of this place. Although they had built the ring so the twins wouldn't get rusty, training usually consisted of Karla and Chloe violently ironing out an argument or using DJ and Christy as punching bags.

At that moment, however, Karla and Liz were working together to attack José. Every collision, the source of the metal-on-metal clanging DJ had heard when he entered the building, sent shock waves toward DJ dozens of feet away at the end of the ring.

"Good!" José bellowed, deflecting a strike from Liz. He countered with a blow that knocked her flat on her back. The impact created foot-long spider-web cracks in the concrete. José stared down at her. He'd once been human. DJ knew that. He'd *seen* the man as a human. But that was before his body had been disintegrated by a laser as he tried to save his daughters. Unfortunately for him, Helene hadn't been willing to let him go. After several months, José had reappeared—ten feet tall. His head was intact, but his body was now entirely made of titanium as if he wore a suit of armor. DJ had once described him as Terminator meets Robocop. The comparison was still fitting.

"But you can be better," José continued. "You can be faster. You can be stronger. And you," he said to Karla as he spun around to catch her flying kick aimed at his head. He held her foot firmly and pulled at it until Karla dangled futilely in his grasp. And then he slammed her into the ground. "You will need to learn control."

Karla stood up immediately but retreated to her sister's side. It was difficult to differentiate between them. They had the same blood-red hair and wore matching tight black leather jumpsuits. Together, they stared down their father for a moment before exploding into action. Although there was no word between them, their every step was perfectly in sync, every attack perfectly coordinated. At moments like this, it wasn't difficult for DJ to picture how the girls must have operated as conjoined twins, sharing the same body but having different heads. DJ had only pieced together snippets, but he knew that they'd been born that way. Karla controlled the left side of the body, and Liz controlled the right. To even walk, the girls had needed to be in perfect sync. Under Chloe's and José's training, they'd become what was probably the most deadly pair of assassins in the US.

"It's almost like he never left," Chloe said from beside DJ, resting her elbow on his shoulder.

DJ jumped. "Motherfu—" he cursed, glaring at her. He hadn't even heard a whiff of her until she'd spoken. She smirked, irritating DJ more. "Yeah, yeah, you're sneaky and shit. Want a prize?"

"Oh, come on, DJ. Don't pout." Chloe laughed, pulling away. "You'll just encourage me." She was dressed in a pair of tight leather pants and a blouse, but she'd undone her ponytail, so her brunette hair fell freely over her shoulder. She tsked. "You should know better by now. Looking also encourages me."

DJ sighed. He'd only *glanced*, but even that hadn't escaped her notice. He ignored her statement, nodding toward the ring. "What's with that?"

José caught Karla by the throat and threw her toward her sister. Liz simply caught Karla, spun her around, and launched her back. José dodged the kick, caught Karla's foot once more, and slammed her again into the ground. This created another web of cracks. "They're catching up," Chloe replied.

That's catching up, huh? DJ thought. Eventually he noticed that, although the girls had been taking constant hits, neither of them looked hurt. That could have been because of their bionics, of course. However, DJ didn't think so. As huge as he was, José definitely had more than enough strength to cause lasting damage if he wanted to. He must have been holding back, but that didn't fit into what DJ knew of the man.

The girls finally landed a punch on José. Instead of getting angry, the man's laughter boomed throughout the space. Liz's expressions had always been hard to read, but now she was smiling openly as she was decked across the face and then smashed into the ground. Karla was the only exception. Her lips were pulled into a snarl, and her eyes showed her intense concentration.

"When CJ and I catch up," DJ said, unable to take his eyes away from the scene, "we usually just talk over coffee or something."

"What're you talking about?" Chloe asked. "They're talking." And they were. Though it was mostly José criticizing the girls' technique. Every once in a while, Karla told him where he could shove it.

"Anyway," Chloe continued, turning to face him, "what brings you here?"

"I'll get to that," DJ replied, finally peeling his eyes away. "First, you wanna fill me in on how this touching scene came to be? I came here thinking José would still be in a coma."

"Well …" Chloe drawled. "After I got your message about Helene, I asked Martin to wake him up."

DJ raised his brows. "Just like that? What if I'd been lying, or wrong?"

"We've been through enough together," the brunette said softly, looking at DJ through her thick lashes. "I decided that I could trust you."

DJ snorted.

Even Chloe couldn't hold the expression for more than a moment before she chuckled. "I mean, I *did* trust you," she said, "but I also put José inside a reinforced cage and had Martin monitor the situation every step of the way." She glanced toward the ring. "We didn't let him out until the old man had done every test he could think of. It took days."

DJ nodded. That made sense. Martin had been the one to originally develop the nanites that Helene used to take control of José in the first place. Helene had upgraded the nanites, of course. However, if anything was wrong, Martin should have been able to detect it.

"So," Chloe continued, "why are you here, DJ?"

He shrugged. "I had some free time," he said, repeating the same thing he'd told Martin. "I thought I'd drop by."

Now it was Chloe's turn to snort.

DJ grinned. "Snort all you want! It's the truth." Chloe raised a brow, putting an arm on her waist. He continued. "*But* it's also possible that I came in to find out what your plan was moving forward."

"Since our lives are basically purposeless without Helene?" Chloe asked, grinning as well. "Afraid we'd go back to our old murder-y ways?"

"Well, I wouldn't put it *that* way," DJ drawled. *But yeah, that's exactly what it is,* he thought. From what he'd pieced together, the Murder Team had started with José working for the CIA—that is, until he'd been framed and Chloe had been sent to kill him. By then, José had already adopted the twins and started to train them in his murderous ways.

Chloe was captured, fell in love with José—or whatever the fuck they had going on—and somehow got José his job back at the CIA. Years passed, and the Murder Twins grew into psychotic hit men for the Agency. Eventually, the family got Helene's attention. The AI contacted José, promising him a way to separate his conjoined daughters. José accepted, betraying the CIA and basically the nation by extension.

Things kind of spiraled down from there. But with Helene dead, the Murder Team practically had no job. And that was terrifying, seeing as the only skill they shared seemed to be the very one that had earned them their nickname.

"Well, no need to worry your pretty little head," Chloe assured him. "We're probably going to lie low for a while, get some R and R or something."

"And you think Karla will be okay with that?"

"We know how to handle our girls," Chloe said. "It's about time that Karla learned to calm down anyway."

DJ nodded slowly. That sounded way better than he expected. Honestly, a part of him was wary of just letting them go, knowing what he did about their temperament. But even if she'd been joking, Chloe was right: They'd been through some chaos together. On some level, DJ felt he could give them the benefit of the doubt. Plus, it wasn't like he could capture them anyway. Even if Olsen mobilized an entire navy base, DJ was sure they'd find a way to slip away. And then he'd be screwed.

At least now they were still on reasonably good terms. DJ could keep tabs on them, even give Olsen their contact information in case the admiral needed their help at some point. The CIA wasn't the only one with problems that needed to quietly disappear.

"All right, then," DJ said finally. "One last thing: the favor you insist I owe you. Am I off the hook?" Martin had given DJ the nanites he'd extracted from the twins. Chloe resented it, and since then, it'd been like a noose around his neck. He wanted that noose off as soon as possible.

Chloe didn't say anything for a minute as she stared toward the ring. *No*, DJ realized, *she's staring at José*. "Yeah. You're off the hook. For now, at least. Who knows what the future might bring?"

DJ groaned. "Can you at least tell me what it's about?"

"Where's the fun in that?" Chloe turned to him and grinned. "At least this will force you to keep thinking about me."

DJ grinned, despite himself.

"Good!" a voice boomed from behind DJ. He spun around with a curse, meeting José's gaze staring back at him. That was when DJ noticed the sudden silence. Somehow he'd been so engrossed in his conversation with Chloe that he hadn't noticed the end of the spar.

When did I become so unguarded around these people? Probably when I realized that being on your guard isn't going to mean shit if they decide to attack me.

He took a step back so he didn't have to strain his neck looking up at the giant of a man. Coincidentally, this put him beside Chloe. It almost looked like he stood beside her for protection.

"It is nice that you are getting along," José continued loudly. "Chloe has told me about what your team and my family have been up to while I was …"

A thrall of a psychotic artificial intelligence, DJ thought.

" … indisposed," José finished. "It seems I owe you a debt of gratitude, Darren Kojak."

"That's, uh, that's not really necessary, man." DJ chuckled. "All in a day's work. Plus, it was Hermione's tech anyway …"

"I am not one to leave my debts unpaid," José said. "For that, I could help you control the nanites that you stole from my daughters." His eyes pierced through DJ as if he could see the nanites swimming inside DJ's body.

"Look, man," DJ said, sighing. "We've already hashed all of that out. If you want the damn things so much, you're welcome to take them. As long as, y'know, the process does not involve cutting me open or some nonsense."

He was tired of them holding this burden over his head. It wasn't like the nanites had really *done* something for him. He hadn't felt anything since that one time he'd landed a punch on Karla. If they were going to keep harping on about the damn things, DJ would rather they just take them back. It was a headache anyway.

Surprisingly, José shook his head. "No. I will respect Martin's choice. What I'm offering is a way to train the nanites in your body, to guide their growth in a way that suits you best."

"Training?" DJ thought back to the spar he'd witnessed a minute ago, and he unconsciously retreated several steps. "I'm good. Thanks."

"Coward," a voice hissed in his ear. For the *third* time, DJ jumped. A moment later, Karla walked into view, sneering at him as she headed toward José. DJ wanted to scream.

What the hell is up with these people?

He looked around for Liz and saw her beside her father, silently staring back.

"It's not cowardice to want to avoid a beating," DJ bit out, glaring at Karla. He retook his place beside Chloe, ignoring the amusement in her eyes. "Call it me being sensible—though I understand if that's a hard concept for you to grasp."

Karla's eyes widened with rage. One of her hands reached for her dagger. But José placed a hand on her shoulder, and her hand froze. His eyes had never left DJ. Under his gaze, DJ felt his anger bleed out. "You will apologize to my daughter, Darren Kojak," José stated.

A stubborn part of him wanted to refuse. But a larger part was just exhausted. He sighed. "Look," he said. "I take back what I said, but I'm still gonna pass on your training, José."

The man ignored him, turning to Karla, "Apologize."

Karla snarled at her father. "No."

José's gaze turned cold. It was as if the temperature of the room dropped by several degrees. Liz shifted, but she didn't leave her father's side. DJ thought he could see actual sparks flying as Karla met her father's glare.

And then, Karla disappeared.

At first, DJ thought that she'd started attacking, but then a tower of boxes crashed several feet away. DJ saw Karla sprawled on top of the pile, knocked out. *Oh crap.* DJ's eyes widened. *Did this dude just—fuck! I didn't even see his hand move!*

Chloe sighed, but it was Liz who went to help her sister up. Karla had already awakened and was clutching her head. DJ knew the exact moment she realized what had happened because her eyes basically *burned*. Her face twisted into the most intense, hateful expression DJ had ever seen—or ever wanted to see, honestly. If someone had pointed that look at him, he'd probably dig himself a grave. It was literally a look that could kill.

And then, Karla turned it on him.

"Motherfucker," DJ swore, dropping into a guard stance. It was instinctive, like putting your arms up when someone was swinging at you.

"Enough," José said, stepping up beside him. Something about the motion seemed to make Karla snap. She disappeared once more. DJ's gun was in his hands at the same moment, pointed in the direction where she was. He pulled the trigger—

The bullet stopped two inches away from the barrel of the gun, blocked by José's open palm. DJ adjusted his aim without missing a beat. He was about to shoot when he noticed Karla, held up by her neck by José's other arm.

"I said enough," José repeated. DJ whistled, impressed despite himself. He replaced his gun but kept his hand hovering over it, just in case. José continued, addressing his daughter. "I blame myself for allowing you to run wild. At the time, I thought your nature would make you stronger. But"—his gaze turned cold once more, and this time, DJ was sure the temperature had dropped—"you *will* learn control, Karla."

"I would rather die," Karla choked out, "than follow you for another day."

"Now, now," Chloe chided, yawning. "Let's not say something we'll regret."

"You have taken everything from me," Karla continued. Her voice was strained. Every word was bitten and rasped out, but she didn't seem to care. "You have taken my childhood from me, and even my sister." Liz was staring back at her, confusion in her eyes. But she didn't leave José's side and didn't ask her father to let Karla down.

That's gotta hurt, DJ thought.

"You might have been fine being Helene's dog," Karla spat. "But I would rather die than let you take away my freedom."

Well, now she's done it, DJ winced inwardly, taking a step back.

José narrowed his eyes. "It does not matter what you wish. You are *my* daughter, and you will listen to me."

Karla spat in his face, her expression full of defiance. "Then kill me now."

José stared at her without saying a word. DJ could guess what was going on in his mind. He was still holding Karla by the neck. He'd already proven that he was far stronger than she was. It'd probably just take a thought to kill her.

But then, how could he? No matter how dysfunctional and messed up their family was, José had already proven that he loved his daughters. How the hell could he kill her? The alternative, though, would be to give up control.

And José didn't strike DJ as the kind of person to do that.

The few moments while the stare-down lasted were some of the longest of DJ's life. During that time, he tried his best not to breathe too loudly, just in case he set something off or called attention to himself. For some reason, he felt he was intruding on a private moment. More, he felt the private moment was somehow *his* fault. But that was crazy, right?

Chloe stood beside DJ. Her whole body was tense, as if ready to spring into action at any moment. This made sense since she was basically the girls' mother. DJ didn't think she was going to let José kill Karla.

As for Liz …

DJ could read a thousand emotions in her eyes, all of them fighting for dominance. Her head swung from her father to her sister as if she could not understand what was happening. For all their lives, she and Karla had always been together, always in sync. But now, one way or another, she was going to lose her sister. DJ honestly couldn't imagine what she was going through. And he never wanted to. He didn't know what he'd do with himself if he was ever put in the same position with CJ.

"I have raised you," José said finally, "I have cared for you, and when it mattered, I gave my life, my pride, and my freedom for both you and your sister. But now you insult me to my face, spitting on everything I have given you. I do not care about your hatred or disgust, but I will not be disrespected by my own daughter. You want your freedom? You can have it." He released her neck, and Karla fell to the ground. José crossed his arms, glaring down at her. "We shall see what you can achieve without me."

Damn! DJ thought. *That escalated quickly.*

6

OCTOBER 2043
SPARTA HEADQUARTERS,
NEW YORK

DJ WOULD HAVE BEEN SURPRISED if any of them had noticed his exit over all the shouting. A part of him had wanted to stay and play peacemaker. However, with all the fists flying around, he was more likely to have been killed completely by accident—or maybe even deliberately if they decided the family drama was his fault.

Isn't it though? a part of him wondered. *If you hadn't gone there, none of it would have happened.*

DJ told that part where to shove it. He'd gone there with the reasonable intention of finding out their plans. How the fuck was it his fault that everyone decided to go batshit crazy while he was there? If anything, that tension had probably been building up for a while. DJ's presence just happened to set it off.

DJ refused to dwell on it, rubbing his arms in the cool October breeze. Others were out walking as well, all of them were hurrying somewhere. Like DJ, most were holding their arms for warmth, but others were holding … *Shit, are those weapons?* Several people held pipes at their sides, while others held baseball bats and other threatening household objects. DJ even noted a knife stuffed down someone's pants.

He turned a corner. Now that he'd noticed it, there was an oppressive feeling in the air—a subtle pressure that weighed down on everyone. Nobody else walked alone. Most people were in groups of three or more. At least one of them carried a weapon openly. Each group gave considerable distance whenever they passed each other, glaring at the other warily.

Damn, DJ thought. The news about the picospores had gotten out several months ago. People took it as a disease and not for what it was. Naturally, the fact that most victims turned violent made several people wary—DJ just hadn't realized how wary. It had been several weeks since Helene's defeat, so there should have been no cases of the disease after that. Shouldn't things have calmed down by now? Or were people pissed off about the curfew?

A droning sound blared, sending DJ's gaze upward. He couldn't find its source. Still, the sound persisted, drawing the attention of several other people. They were glaring at the sky as if they wanted to personally attack it.

What is up with that?

He glanced up one final time and then pulled the thought from his head. A couple of people were starting to look at him. DJ quickened his steps, focusing on getting to his destination and turning regularly to ensure he wasn't followed. He arrived at the Sparta Headquarters in a little over a quarter of an hour.

He nodded to Mark, the receptionist, and made his way to the elevator. About half of the captives had been reunited with their families over the last few days, but several had no families or families that had died or gone missing during Mayday. And there was still a subset of people from whom DJ hadn't been able to get their information at all. He'd forwarded that list to Olsen, but he hadn't heard back yet. He'd give the old man a few more days before following up.

Should I also tell Olsen about the fallout that went down with the Murder Team? DJ cleared the thought from his head. He could decide on that later. The important thing now was checking in on Hermione to find out her progress with the spores. With any luck, they'd be able to bring the traumatized back to their senses, get their contact info, and then get them on their way to their families.

"Wow," DJ muttered to himself as he came out of the elevator. "I've turned into a complete asshole."

"Hey, DJ!" Albert was jogging toward him.

Shouldn't you be in Washington right now? DJ thought as Albert stopped in front of him and bent over to catch his breath.

Albert straightened. He'd cleaned up since DJ last saw him; he'd cleaned his beard and gotten clothes that fit him better. DJ figured he'd been trying to look presentable when he met his wife. Except he was here, sweating profusely. His face was twisted into the most intense expression of urgency DJ had ever seen. "I'm sorry to ask you for this, DJ, but I need your help."

"Sure thing, man," DJ said, extending his hand. "Not gonna lie. I didn't expect to see you so soon."

"I didn't expect to be back so soon either," Albert replied, returning the handshake. "Or at all honestly. I figured even if Debi had moved on that I'd just start all over there, maybe go back to carpentry."

DJ made way for someone to enter the elevator and kept walking, realizing they were literally just standing in the middle of the hallway. He didn't know how long the conversation would take, so he couldn't go to Hermione's lab directly. He headed to the isolation chamber instead, Albert walking beside him. "Guessing that didn't work out?" DJ asked.

Albert chuckled grimly. "That's what I'm trying to figure out. I thought it was going great. I met up with Debi, who's the freaking chief aide to the president by the way," Albert grinned proudly. But then his expression darkened. "Anyway, we're having a nice dinner and catching up, when suddenly her phone pings. Her eyes get all glazed, and she cuts off in the middle of her sentence and starts scrolling. Personally, I think it's kind of rude because we used to have a no-phone-at-the-dining-table rule. But we haven't seen each other in several years, so I just chalked it up to something that's changed."

"It could have been an emergency call from work or something," DJ suggested.

"Exactly," Albert agreed easily. "So, I asked about it. Not like specifics or anything, but just like in general, if there was a problem or something. And she completely ignored me. She didn't even look up."

DJ's eyebrows rose. He shifted to the side to allow someone to pass and then turned a corner into another passage. "That's … kinda weird."

"We haven't even gotten to the weird part yet," Albert said. "A few minutes after some furious texting, she dropped her phone. And then her eyes lost that weird glazed look, and she continued eating like nothing had happened."

DJ started to get a strange feeling in his gut.

"I gently probed with a joke about how the president must have fallen in love with her organizational skills, just like I had. Y'know, for the president to have been texting her so late."

"Terrible joke, but all right," DJ said, pushing the door to the isolation chamber.

"But she looked at me like she had no idea what I was talking about," Albert continued as if he hadn't heard DJ. This was entirely possible. The man was completely in his head, staring down and gesticulating while talking. "So, I nodded to her phone, but she still looked so confused, like she had no clue that she'd been texting for several minutes."

Both of them took a seat on one of the lounges. DJ's strange feeling became stronger.

"Anyway, this went on for a few seconds or so before I decided to just drop it, in case it turned into a fight or something. She brought up another topic and I leaned into it. We enjoyed the rest of the dinner."

"The end?" DJ asked hopefully.

"I wish." Albert chuckled. "If that was the end, I'd still be snuggled in bed with my wife. The rest of the night was amazing. Like, really amazing." Albert wiggled his eyebrows suggestively. But then his expression darkened with confusion. "Anyway, the thing with the phone happened several times over the next few days. She'd get a text, look at it, her eyes would glaze over, and when she was done, she'd have no memory of it. Sometimes she wouldn't even be using her phone. We'd be talking, and suddenly her eyes would glaze over and she'd be gone."

He shifted in his chair, an intense look on his face. "But the truly weird part is that this didn't happen every time. Sometimes she would get a text or a call and answer it normally. A few times, she'd even explain what was going on, that she's working on a campaign or something."

"Did she ever give an explanation for the other—"

"No," Albert said, meeting DJ's eyes. "She didn't. It was like she lost all memory of it when she dropped her phone."

DJ pondered for several moments. Albert didn't have to say why he needed DJ's help. In fact, DJ didn't *want* him to say it. He preferred not to even think about why his gut was screaming at him right now. They were supposed to be done, weren't they? They were supposed to have been done with this bullshit several weeks back when Manar and CJ had sent the message that Helene was defeated. That was supposed to have been the end. All that was left was the cleanup. That's what DJ had been busting his ass over for the past couple of days.

So what the fuck is this then? DJ screamed in his mind.

The rage came out of nowhere. It surged through his blood like a flood. *Why the hell does it sound like Albert's wife is a goddamn Dead Eye? What is this? A fail-safe? One of her plans that's running on auto? Or did the psychotic bitch come back from the grave just to fuck with me?*

There was another possibility, of course, but DJ's mind shied from even considering it. Manar and CJ had assured him that Helene was dead. That was it. He wasn't going to think further about that.

But what the hell was happening with Albert's wife? Albert was staring at him, and DJ knew the man was expecting him to say something. Of course, he didn't know what to say; he just knew he couldn't assume the issue would resolve itself, even if it was most likely something that Helene had put into motion before. Just because the AI was no longer around didn't mean DJ could just let its plans keep running.

He cursed again. The anger went as quickly as it had come, leaving DJ suddenly weak. He gave Albert a tired smile. "Up for a road trip?"

CHAPTER

7

OCTOBER 2043
WASHINGTON, DC

IT WAS ALREADY LATE, so DJ figured it'd be better to get an early start the next morning. Albert gave Debi a bullshit excuse for returning home the next day, and DJ went off to his room. CJ was sitting at the desk, and thankfully the room didn't smell like three-day-old cat piss. At least he'd taken the time to clean up.

DJ almost didn't tell him. On his walk back to the room, DJ had come up with several reasons why he shouldn't tell CJ about what Albert had said. Chief among them was the fact that, ever since their talk, CJ had been doing better, so it would have been counterproductive to tell CJ something that'd make him start doubting himself, or even make him feel guilty. The other points were variations of that. But they were really good arguments—all perfectly justifiable.

In the end, DJ decided to tell him for one simple reason: CJ was his brother, and he told him everything. Plus, DJ didn't know how long this whole thing was going to take. It wasn't like he could just leave without saying anything. But the first reason sounded better, so that was the one he was going with.

Surprisingly, CJ took the news well. Naturally, he came to the same conclusions that DJ had but agreed with DJ that it was probably something that Helene had put in motion before her demise.

The fact that his brother was thinking along the same lines went a long way to easing DJ's mind.

So, the next day, DJ, Christy, and Albert were on a road to the capital. He would have preferred for it to just have been him and Albert, but as with his brother, DJ couldn't just pack up and leave without telling Christy. Naturally, when he told her, she wanted to come to watch his back. DJ had told her that there'd be no back-watching necessary since it was a simple in and out—maybe an abduction, depending on how difficult Debi was going to be. She'd narrowed her eyes at him.

DJ had wisely shut up after that. He'd only argued for the sake of it anyway, to convince himself that it was going to be a simple operation. Christy was the only combat member of the team that was still available. Scratch that, she was the *only* member of the team still available. Manar and Ndidi were rekindling their fire in Nigeria, and Hermione was working on the new batch of spores. The Murder Team had their own problems going on. When shit hit the fan, DJ would be glad to have Christy watching his back.

No, DJ thought, *if shit the fan. If.*

"EVENING," DJ SAID SEVERAL HOURS LATER at the threshold of Albert's house.

"You must be DJ and Christy, right?" Debi said. She was in her midforties, but her round, freckled face and small stature made her seem younger than she was. She opened the door wider, stepping to the side. "Come in, come in. You must be freezing."

"Thank you kindly," DJ said, as both he and Christy entered the house. The place was comfortably heated, making DJ sigh in relief. Debi took Christy's coat, but DJ held on to his. Albert, who they had dropped off before they checked into their hotel, was coming from somewhere in the house just as Debi led them to the living room.

"Hey, man," DJ greeted, extending his hand. "Thanks for the invite. Your home is lovely."

Albert waved him off, gesturing them toward a chair in the living room. "Please, after everything you've done for me?"

"Bert told me that you were the ones who found him," Debi said, taking a seat beside her husband. She rested her cheek against his shoulder, placing a hand on his chest. DJ and Christy took adjacent chairs.

"Saying *found* gives us more credit than we're due." DJ chuckled. "We basically stumbled into him by accident."

"No need to be so humble," Debi said. "Even if you stumbled into him, you could have just left him there. Bert told me that you both took care of him for weeks until he got over his trauma."

"Again, you're giving us too much credit, Debi. We just did what anyone else would have done in our shoes."

"Not everyone." Debi shook her head. "Not even most people. Not these days. Everyone is far too afraid now. If someone else had found my Bert wandering around like that, he might never have made his way to me." Debi gazed at DJ and Christy, her eyes serious. "So, no, I'm not giving you too much credit. You two are heroes for what you did, and I'm incredibly grateful to both of you."

Well shit, DJ thought, squirming in his seat. *Way to make this so much harder than it needed to be, Debi.*

"Let's head to the dining room," Albert suggested, looking vaguely uncomfortable.

The four of them made their way to the table, but the conversation stalled. The plates were already set, and Christy helped Debi bring out the food. Within a few minutes, they were digging in.

"So, Debi," DJ asked, "what do you do?"

"I'm the chief aide to the president," she replied, a hint of pride in her voice.

DJ raised his brows in feigned surprise. "Very impressive," he said. "What's that like, getting to meet the president on a daily basis?"

"It was a little difficult at first," Debi started, "but that was because of my own admiration of her and the pressure not to screw anything up. But I've been doing this for years now, so I'm more used to it. Plus, Mary is really easy to work with. That makes everything run much more smoothly."

"Mary, huh?" DJ chuckled, taking a bite of his food. "Must be nice to be on a first-name basis with the leader of the most powerful nation in the world."

Debi laughed as well. "It has its moments," she replied.

"And its disadvantages, I'm sure," DJ added casually. Albert's eyes widened. Christy raised a brow at that, but she didn't even look up from her food. At Debi's confused look, DJ explained. "I've worked security once or twice for some high-profile clients before," he said, "so as chief aide, I'm sure you get a lot of crazies that want a piece of you."

Debi nodded in understanding, but then she shook her head. "I haven't really faced anything like that." She considered. "I mean, there's the occasional person who wants to get close to me to get access to the president, but most times Secret Service gets to them before it ever becomes a problem."

"Most times?" Albert asked, worry in his voice, just as DJ had coached him.

"Yeah. Lately there've been some signs …" Her voice trailed off, and she stared into space, her eyes glazed. The moment lasted a few seconds, then she snapped back into focus. Debi smiled, in embarrassment. "I'm sorry," she apologized. "What was I saying?"

DJ's lips turned into a thin line. *Crap.* A part of him had been hoping that Albert had been mistaken, that he'd exaggerated a couple of weird instances out of nervousness or stress or some other nonsense. But now that he'd seen it himself, that part of him was silenced. But another thought rose up.

It's different, he thought. When Albert had explained the whole thing back at Sparta, DJ had assumed Debi was a Dead Eye. But that was obviously not the case. Dead Eyes had eyes that were … well … dead. That wasn't the case with Debi. Even while under Helene's influence—because there was no denying that it was Helene's influence now—her eyes weren't dead. They were just … clouded, like the eyes of someone under a bunch of medication.

That's probably what's causing the memory loss, DJ thought. *It's probably Helene wiping her tracks.*

"What?" Debi asked when the room remained silent. "Did I say something wrong? Bert, are you all right?"

DJ's grin was back in record time. "Not at all," he said, drawing her attention to him. "You were talking about people who get close to you because of your connection to the president."

"Yeah …" she said, looking worriedly at her husband. DJ made a gesture to the man, snapping him out of his thoughts enough for him to hurriedly compose himself. "There've been some issues once or twice. But the Secret Service usually handles those cases."

"And when they can't?" DJ pressed.

"Then I handle it myself," Debi replied firmly, confidently. She was about to continue when her phone dinged with a text. DJ's hand reached into his coat pocket. "Please excuse me," she muttered. "It's probably work." She picked it up, and her eyes started to glaze again.

Immediately, DJ jerked up from his seat, the Synaptic Pulse in hand. There was a flash of light, and Christy reflexively caught Debi before her head hit the table. DJ was already reaching for her phone. From start to finish, the whole thing hadn't taken three seconds.

"Christy, can you bring the car over to the front?" DJ asked, scrolling through the phone. Christy headed to the door. "Albert, please calm down. Debi's fine."

"What the hell did you do to my wife, DJ?" Albert yelled, raising Debi's head. He calmed down slightly when he saw her chest still moving, but there was still anger in his eyes when he stared at DJ.

"I knocked her out," DJ responded absentmindedly. He tossed the Pulse to him. "With this."

"What is this?" Albert asked, holding it between two fingers as if afraid to set it off. "Why didn't it work on us too?"

"Because," DJ replied, finally looking up from the phone, "it's programmed to affect only people with picospores running through their veins. The rest of us were clean." He snatched the Pulse from him and placed it in his coat pocket. "But evidently, your wife isn't."

"How long is she going to stay unconscious?" he asked.

"Oh, the Pulse lasts only about an hour," DJ said. "But we're going to *keep* her unconscious for about four hours."

"Why?"

DJ stared at him like he was an idiot. "Because that's how long it takes to drive back to New York, Albert. I'd recommend you pack a few things for her and then call her office with a bullshit excuse about why she won't be at work for the rest of the week. Better move fast. We should be out of here in fifteen if we're going to beat that midnight traffic."

"I THOUGHT WE WERE DONE with this," Hermione said, staring at the unconscious form of Debi hooked up to a machine and lying on a cot. Hermione punched a few codes into the device, and it came to life.

"You and me both," DJ replied.

"You realize what this means, don't you?"

"No," DJ said firmly. "And I don't want to. All I wanna know is if you can extract the spores from her or not."

Hermione looked at him in surprise. "DJ, we have to talk about this. We can't just ignore the problem." DJ met her eyes. That was all, but it was enough to make her pause. "Fine," she said, turning to the device. She pushed a couple of buttons and connected a cable from the machine to her computer. "But I'll do you one better. I've figured out how to read every command given to the spores."

"What does that mean exactly?"

Hermione sighed, but she didn't stop clicking away at her computer. "You already know that Helene modified the original designs of the spores, making them more efficient." DJ nodded. "Well, I was afraid that if the new spores I synthesized didn't meet that quality, then the victims' bodies would reject them, maybe making everything even worse. To avoid that, I spent the better part of last week studying the spores I'd extracted from Helene's former hostages."

"Oh, *that* was why," DJ said dryly. "You sure it wasn't because you just couldn't resist?"

"And a few days ago," Hermione continued as if she hadn't heard him, "I finally figured out a way to hack into the spores without them self-destructing. This means that I can access their history and read through the commands that they were given."

"Get to the point, Hermione," DJ drawled.

Hermione glared at him over her shoulder. "*That* means that we can figure out what exactly Helene was manipulating Debi to do for her." She straightened from the computer, adjusting the monitor so that it faced DJ. He could make out a bunch of text, but it was all gibberish to him.

He looked at Hermione. "Can we figure out Helene's plan from that?"

"Part of it, at least," Hermione replied. "I doubt Debi was her only tool in whatever this was."

"Still, at least now we have a lead," DJ stated.

CHAPTER

9

OCTOBER 2043
SPARTA HEADQUARTERS,
NEW YORK

"SO, CAN YOU DO IT?" DJ asked.

"I'm, uh, I'm still not sure what exactly you … you want me to do," CJ responded, turning the phone in his hands."

"That's Debi's phone," DJ explained. "According to Albert, Helene takes over whenever Debi gets a message or something. But I've gone through all her messages, her emails, everything, and I can't find anything that's even remotely shady. That makes me believe that the texts are deleted as soon as Debi reads them. But we need those, which is where you come in. Can you do it?"

"I have … um … some questions," CJ said. He connected the phone to the computer and punched in a few keys.

"Shoot."

"First … do we … uh … do we know who's on the other side of the texts?" he asked, clicking away at the computer. Several tabs opened one after the other, closed, and then were replaced by even more tabs.

"No, we do not," DJ replied. "That's part of what I'd like you to figure out when you retrieve the messages. Next question."

"Okay … um … do we know how Helene is … is taking over Debi's mind without a processor to program the spores?" DJ had been wondering the same thing, but he didn't have an answer. Helene had transferred her core to the internet, so when CJ and Manar had defeated her, for all intents and purposes, they'd destroyed the AI's central processing, basically wiping her mind. But if Helene was really behind Debi's blackouts, even if through an automatic process, then there was a tiny bit of the AI still running around somewhere. And that was scary.

DJ shook his head in answer to CJ's question.

"Do we … uh … do we know why Helene needs Debi to read the text in the first place? Why does she not just hack into the … the phone directly? It should be possible if she can somehow still program the spores."

"CJ, I have no fucking idea, all right?" DJ said, in exasperation. "At this point, you know as much as I do. But we can both learn more *together* if you retrieve the messages from the phone."

CJ leaned back in his chair and adjusted his monitor so DJ could read the screen. "I am done."

DJ swallowed what he was about to say. "Wait, seriously?"

"It is not a difficult thing to … to do, DJ," CJ said. He frowned. "That is … uh … surprising, considering it involves Helene."

DJ scanned the text on the dialogue boxes. Most of it was messages that he'd already seen on the phone, but the retrieved ones had been highlighted in a different color. DJ focused on those. "Who the fuck is Tyra Chityothin?"

"That is … uh … that is not what you should be worried about, DJ." CJ pointed to a part on the screen. "Look at the date."

Shit, DJ cursed. Whatever it was that Helene had planned, it was going down tomorrow.

10

DURING DJ'S CHILDHOOD, his family had been coming back from a trip, and his dads had decided to make it a road trip so that the "fun didn't end," or something like that. It was supposed to be a relatively easy drive, but they'd miscalculated how difficult it would be to get two kids packed, especially when those two kids did not want to be packed. Because of that, they ended up leaving relatively late in the day and had to drive through the night.

CJ conked out pretty early, but for some reason, young DJ decided that he'd stay up throughout the trip. For the first part of the journey, staying awake proved easy, since he could stare at the trees passing by and let his imagination run wild. When he got bored, he'd listen to his dads' conversations—not understanding much of what they were saying, of course, but their voices were familiar. And then night fell: the trees were no longer visible, and both dads were too tired for idle conversation.

Still, DJ had refused to sleep. When his eyes had grown too heavy to stay open, he held them wide with his fingers until they burned. It was by far the most miserable night of his life, but he did it. He stayed awake.

DJ was reminded of that night when, an hour after he spoke to CJ, he was behind the wheel once more.

"Care to fill me in on why we're going back to Washington?" Christy asked lightly.

"Because we need to know what Debi had planned to do tomorrow," DJ replied.

"You mean what Helene has planned?"

DJ shook his head. "CJ is still sifting through the data. There's no saying when he'll find something. What we're going to do is check her calendar and notes at the house to see what we can find about her upcoming tasks. Apparently, Debi is the kind of person who writes down appointments." DJ glanced in the rearview mirror. "Isn't that right, Albert?"

"Is my wife going to be all right?" Albert asked from the backseat.

"Come on, man." DJ sighed. "Don't let the fear win. You've gone through the process yourself. You know it's perfectly safe."

"I also know that the process doesn't always work perfectly," Albert retorted. "I just don't want my wife to be part of the statistics."

From what Hermione had told him, the extraction process by itself was pretty straightforward and completely safe. If it wasn't, Bethany wouldn't have been able to use it on herself without frying her brain. The problem wasn't the extraction itself but how deeply the spores had integrated with a person's brain. The more integration, the more the mind had to handle when the spores were suddenly removed.

So far, there wasn't a way to gauge the reaction until after the fact.

But how much of a dick would I be if I said that?

"Debi will be fine," he said as confidently as he could. "We'll have this sorted out in a day, and she can be back at work by Monday, tops."

A few hours later, DJ glanced around the house. Surprisingly, it was exactly as they'd left it. At this point, Debi would have been missing for roughly twenty-four hours, give or take. Considering her position, DJ had expected Secret Service agents to have swarmed the place for clues.

"Lucky us," he muttered to himself. Christy threw him a questioning glance, which he ignored. He turned to Albert, who still had a dazed look on his face.

He clapped his hands twice, jolting Albert from his thoughts. "All right, man, we're looking for your wife's appointment book, dairy, or calendar—basically whatever the hell she uses to keep track of her appointments and tasks. You take upstairs while Christy and I take down here."

When Albert still remained in the same spot, DJ let out a bit of the impatience he'd been keeping caged. He stepped in front of the man, getting in his face until Albert was forced to meet his eyes. "Look, man," he barked. "I know you're worried about your wife. But every second you waste is a second you're putting her in danger. Helene obviously wanted to use her for something. Now I don't know what, but if it pans out, you'd best believe that Debi is going to be in a lot of trouble. And it's going to be *your* fault because you couldn't get your act together when your wife needed you. Think you can live with that? Think she would be able to live with you when she finds out?"

Albert's eyes narrowed in anger, and he swung at DJ. The move was so slow that by the time he threw the punch, DJ had already stepped to the side. "The anger's good," DJ continued casually, "but it's misplaced. Instead, direct it to where you can help Debi." He gave Albert a small push that forced him toward the stairs.

That, at least, seemed to pierce the haze in Albert's mind because the anger in his eyes dissipated as quickly as it had come. He gave DJ a nod before finally heading up the stairs.

Only when he was gone did DJ finally turn to meet Christy's stare. "Something to say?"

Christy scoffed. "Don't look so smug," she muttered. She looked at him from the corner of her eye. "Now why did you actually send him upstairs?"

"Because," DJ drawled, bringing out his phone and punching in a number, "it's better if he isn't involved in this next part."

"So the stuff about Debi's appointment book and Albert being his wife's only hope?"

"Bullshit," DJ stated plainly. "There's only one reason why Helene would need Debi."

"The president?" Christy guessed immediately. DJ nodded. "That still doesn't explain why Albert had to be sent on a wild goose chase."

"It's for his own good," DJ said, bringing the phone to his ear. "It's best that he have plausible deniability for this next part."

She raised a brow. "And I don't need plausible deniability?"

"No one would believe you didn't know anyway," he said absently, "but you're welcome to join him upstairs."

Christy scowled. "Who're you calling anyway?"

DJ was about to answer, but the person on the other line finally picked up. "Wake up, old man," he said into the phone. "We got shit to do."

OCTOBER 2043
THE WHITE HOUSE,
WASHINGTON, DC

THE NEXT MORNING, DJ pulled up outside a White House security checkpoint. Despite the cold, there was a lot of foot traffic: some people clearly passing through, others gathering for a glimpse at the White House. When one of them revealed a picket sign, DJ wasn't surprised. But he *was* surprised when he noted another one clutching a steel rod. DJ rolled his eyes. How dumb did you have to be to bring a weapon to the White House?

With his survey done, DJ turned to the other people in the car. "Everyone clear on the plan?"

"I'm not," Albert said immediately.

"You sure this is the best way, D?" Christy asked, a hint of trepidation in her voice. Christy had been with him since the first day of navy orientation and had experienced nearly all the missions, fights, explosions, and near-death situations

DJ had. But through all this, DJ could only count three times when she'd seriously been worried about what they were getting themselves into.

Who could blame her? This was the White House, the motherfucking capital of the country, arguably the modern world. If they screwed up here, the consequences would be unimaginable—not just for them but for their families. Everything they'd worked so hard for in the last several years would be gone. Poof! Up in smoke. Anyone would feel pressure when they thought about it.

DJ met her eyes. "No, I'm not," he said. "But I don't have any other ideas. I wish we could have just called Manar and had him figure out this shit. But whatever Helene's planned, it's going to go down today. This means we're out of time. I don't know if this is the right move, but I do know that we need to do *something*."

DJ looked at Albert so the man knew that he was addressing him. "Obviously, I can't force you to stay for this. Albert, this isn't your fight. And Christy, you've already busted your ass for far too long. If either of you wants to pass on this, you can just walk away. No hard feelings."

Albert leaned back in the seat, his gaze distant. But DJ's attention was back on Christy. What was she going to choose? He fixated on the question so much that he didn't see the slap to the side of his head coming. "Damn, Christy," DJ muttered, rubbing the impact zone.

Christy glared at him. "Didn't you say we were in a hurry? Why are you wasting time saying stupid stuff?"

DJ's face stretched into a grin. "Hey, can't a guy make sure?" He turned to Albert and saw the determination in the man's eyes. "Seems like we're all on the same page. Let's get this done then."

The three of them got out of the car and made their way to the White House. DJ was in the lead while Christy and Albert took up positions beside him. DJ suppressed a shiver and tightened his jacket. Very soon, the three of them reached the visitors' checkpoint.

"Names?" the attendant asked. He wore his full uniform and openly displayed a Glock—an effective first layer of security, DJ figured. He answered for all of them, and the attendant glanced down at a list. "I'm sorry, but I don't see you scheduled for a tour today. Please reconfirm your dates and come back."

"Please, check again." DJ grinned. He brought out a document from his jacket and placed his ID on top. The soldier rolled his eyes when he saw this but still made a show of scanning it when DJ passed it over. A few seconds later, the attendant's expression became more serious.

"I apologize for the confusion. Please wait here for a few minutes while we arrange a tour guide for you."

Christy raised a brow and threw a sideways glance at DJ. Albert looked far too nervous to be capable of speech. As long as no one did anything stupid, the document that Olsen sent over should get them through the first couple of hurdles. After that, though, they were on their own.

True to his word, the attendant returned only a few minutes later. They were quickly ushered through the visitors' entrance into a room with a high ceiling, marble floors, and decorative moldings. The carpet wasn't as opulent as DJ would have imagined, but it was still plush enough that his feet sank slightly with every step. He lightened his footfalls, and the sound disappeared entirely. *Cool*, he thought. There were five cameras scattered around the room that he could see, and probably double that number that he wasn't supposed to see. He tried to find the hidden second entrance—because there had to be a hidden second entrance—but gave up when his second casual glance didn't reveal it.

Instead, he focused on the woman waiting for them. DJ was sure her bright smile and sensible suit were meant to convince people she was a tour guide—if a person didn't already know that most tour guides for the White House were Secret Service agents.

"Hey, guys, I'm Maya," she said, showing off her pearly whites. DJ pretended not to notice, "I'm sorry about the wait. There was a mix-up with your appointment that had to be cleared up."

Yeah, DJ thought, *the appointment didn't exist until five this morning.* He was insanely curious about how Olsen had pulled that off. But DJ didn't think he wanted to know the answer. "Don't mention it, Maya." DJ grinned back at her. "My friends and I are in your hands."

"Thank you for your understanding," Maya responded, giving a smile that was somehow brighter than all the rest. "Let's start then?"

"About that," DJ said. "You can just link us to one of the other tours going on right now. There's no need for you to cater to just us three, right?"

"Your appointment was for a private tour."

"It was," DJ agreed easily, even though he'd had no idea, "but that's because I'd planned to have a bigger group. But since only the three of us could make it today, it wouldn't make sense for us to take up your time when we could easily join another group. That's not a problem, is it?"

Maya's smile wavered. She glanced at the document in her hand before replying. "No, that's not a problem."

Damn, DJ thought. *What the hell did Olsen put inside that thing?*

Outwardly, though, DJ's face showed no change, even as Maya took several minutes to explain the rules of the place, including the long list of things they were not supposed to do. DJ listened with half an ear because, well, what was the point?

Once Maya had exhausted herself, she led them through a connecting hallway into the White House proper. DJ checked his watch, then realized that it was the third time he had done that in the past minute. He made a mental note not to do it again.

Debi's calendar hadn't revealed any urgent appointments with the president, but that could have been because Helene erased any thought of her writing it down. The closest he'd gotten to anything useful was a note that the president would be having a meeting of some kind. Debi hadn't planned to attend, so the note had been to remind one of the other aides to be present. That at least gave him a sense of direction, but it didn't change the fact that DJ was basically walking in blind. He knew things were going to hit the fan at some point, but the nature of that chaos and the time it would happen remained a mystery. He just had to pray that they would get into position before it did and that their infiltration wouldn't end up with him in orange at the end of it all.

They met with the other group at the East Room, where Maya handed off the three of them to the other tour guide. There were about a dozen other people in the group, which DJ thought was a fair size. After a brief pause, New Maya continued her speech about the history of the East Room, its significance, and its use. Albert looked away, too nervous to be paying attention, while Christy looked surprisingly interested. For his part, DJ recalled the floor plan that he'd memorized earlier that morning. How Olsen had gotten his hand on *that* little gem, he didn't know, and he certainly was never going to ask about it.

DJ charted their course in his head—twice to be sure that he had it down. It was a hastily made plan, so it was bound to fail, but it was all he had. He still had several minutes before the tour reached his target, so DJ tried to focus—for the cameras if nothing else.

Eventually the tour moved on to the State Dining Room, and the tour guide gave the usual spiel about when it was commissioned, by what president, its historical significance, and all of that. DJ felt Christy and Albert look at him several times. He understood their impatience—he felt it too—but he couldn't hurry the tour, could he?

They spent what felt like an eternity at the State Dining Room before moving on to the Red Room, Green Room, and Blue Room. By the time they were leaving, Christy jabbed DJ with her elbow, obviously unable to hold in her impatience. "How long do you plan on leaving us in the dark, D?" she whispered.

About ten more minutes, give or take, DJ answered inwardly. He imitated her tone when he replied, "It's not really intentional, Christy. I'm basically making this shit up as I go."

"You don't have a plan?" she hissed in a low tone.

Still, it was enough to draw the attention of several people. DJ flashed all of them a grin that faltered when he met Christy's glare and Albert's panicked look.

"I *do* have a plan," DJ said.

Most of one, at least.

"Tell. Me," she bit out.

I can't do that, DJ groaned inwardly. "Look," he said, "it'll take too long to go over it, but the gist of it is that I'm going to slip out soon, and I need you and Albert to create a distraction when you get the signal. Something to draw attention and keep you in the building, but not something so wild that you'll get thrown in jail."

Christy narrowed her eyes as though she didn't believe that DJ had a plan. "What's the signal?"

DJ winked at her with more confidence than he felt. "Trust me. You'll know when it comes." That was bullshit, of course. There was no way DJ was involving them in this. He couldn't have stopped Christy from coming, but he could stop her from getting implicated with him—more implicated, at least.

Christy tried to get more out of him, but DJ shushed her so he could listen to the tour guide. "Usually," New Maya said, "the Oval Office would be next on our list, but unfortunately, it isn't available for viewing today, so we'll be moving to the Roosevelt Room for the next part of the tour. As we do, you'll be able to see—"

Despite what New Maya had said, DJ doubted that the Oval Office was available very often, if at all, with the public sentiment these days. It'd be too easy for a shoulder-chipped nut job to make a fool of themselves in the president's office. Still, the Oval Office wasn't really what DJ was concerned about.

"How about the Cabinet Room?" someone asked.

DJ didn't know who said it, but he could have kissed him.

"Unfortunately, the Cabinet Room isn't available either," New Maya replied.

"Why?" DJ asked, throwing his voice so it sounded like it'd come from somewhere else.

New Maya's smile faltered. "The room is currently being used for a meeting."

Jackpot, he thought. He signaled Christy to let her know that he'd be gone soon, and he got a nod in return. Unfortunately, as if to make up for the abbreviated tour, several members of the group decided to take pictures of as many things as they could. Because of that, DJ's *soon* ended up being several minutes later when the tour was finally ready to move on. The hallways all followed the same basic theme: high ceilings, marble floors covered by thick carpets, and walls painted with soft, neutral colors. Paintings dotted the walls periodically, some were obviously placed there for aesthetics, while others were of notable figures in history. New Maya stopped in front of a couple to give some information about the person and their significance in history. DJ tried to force himself to listen, but he couldn't stop his thoughts from drifting.

For most of his life, DJ wasn't one to think too deeply about things. He depended on his gut to make his decisions. Whether it worked out or it didn't, DJ was always ready to bear the consequences. Because of this, he'd been in a lot of tough situations. Like, a lot. Disregarding the mayhem of his childhood, DJ's brief career in the Marines put him in more tough situations than most people would ever face in a lifetime. He'd been shot at more times than he could count, survived explosions, several attacks by swarms of drones, and even a laser that one time. Sure, in the beginning, he had his fair share of nervousness, but he'd reached the point that he was largely unfazed by such things. Even more, his nervousness became largely overshadowed by excitement. And that excitement acted like a shield whenever he was in a tough spot.

Now there was none of the excitement—and all of the nervousness. But it wasn't *constant* nervousness. It only snuck up on him whenever he thought about where he was and what he was about to do.

DJ didn't know what to make of that, which was perfectly fine since he saw his chance to slip away coming up ahead. He rubbed his ear. "You ready?" he whispered into the air, ignoring Christy's curious glance.

"*Yes*," CJ replied a moment later, his voice coming through the small earpiece that DJ wore.

He hadn't expected his brother to insist on coming along when he'd explained the situation to him the night before. He would have refused—partly because he wouldn't want to implicate CJ, but mostly because CJ's only job would have been to hack into the White House security systems, and DJ didn't want to take that risk.

He'd told CJ that. His brother had spent the next hour assuring DJ he wouldn't be caught. It was more words than DJ had heard him speak since he'd returned, and frankly DJ hadn't had the heart to refuse. So CJ had tailed them in a separate car all the way to Washington and then to the White House. And since he was already being stupid, DJ decided to go all in and have his brother be his eyes through the White House cameras. DJ wouldn't be totally blind throughout.

"Good, do it now," DJ said, as the group approached a hallway with two exits. The group went through one, while DJ surreptitiously slipped into the other. He felt his companions' gazes on his back, but at this point, the die had been cast. "Did you do it?" he asked in a low tone.

"*Yes*," CJ replied.

"You looped the feed?"

"*Yes.*"

"And you made sure not to record anyone passing or walking?" DJ confirmed.

"*Yes.*"

"Because you know that's how they always screw up in the movies," DJ continued. "The security sees a guy walking with the same interval, and then they notice their feed has been looped."

"*I know, DJ.*" His brother sighed. "*I made sure that there is nobody in the loop.*"

"Good, good," DJ said, glad that the hallways were empty so no one could see him talking to himself. "Final question then: Are you sure that this can't be traced back to you?"

CJ sighed again, deeper this time. "*Is there anything … uh, that I can say that will convince you that I am perfectly safe?*"

No, not really, no. "Saying it one more time would help," DJ answered as he finally reached the Cross Hall. The hall served as a central axis for most places in the White House, and so it had several passages connected to it. DJ paused for a moment to orient himself before picking a passage.

"*I'm perfectly safe, DJ.*"

"I mean, you *say* that," DJ said. "But how can I believe you? Like, I know I don't know jack shit about this, but isn't it common sense to know that the White House has a ton of security? They probably have guys whose only job is to continuously monitor, update, and reinforce their defenses. And here you are, calmly telling me—"

"*DJ,*" CJ cut in sharply. "*Do you … do you think that Manar could have done it without, uh, being discovered?*"

DJ considered it. "Honestly, I figure that it'd be easy for him, considering the things you've told me about him."

"*Then I can do it as well.*"

It was the silent confidence in his voice that made DJ stop right there in the middle of the passage. DJ didn't doubt his brother's skills. He never had. But it'd been CJ himself who'd told him that Manar was miles above him when it came to programming. More to the point, most of the information DJ had learned about Manar had come from his brother gushing about the man.

And now CJ was basically saying he was as good as Manar?

"All right then," DJ said. CJ wasn't the type to exaggerate his skills out of pride or ego. If he said he was just as good, then DJ was going to take it. Plus, it wasn't hard to believe. From what both he and Manar had told DJ about the Virtual Realm, DJ figured the place was practically a mecca for programmers. CJ had spent several months there, so of course his skills had improved. "What's in front of me?"

"*There should be … uh … a checkpoint at the end of the passage,*" CJ said. DJ turned a corner. For some reason, he'd expected a turnstile metal gate, like those used in train stations, but it was only a large door with an electronic access control panel by the side. "*Pause for a few seconds when you get there and I will … will unlock it for you.*"

DJ hesitated. "You have control over their security systems?"

"*Only the outer ones,*" his brother replied, far too calmly in DJ's opinion. "*All the cameras are … uh … on the same server, but the inner … inner security is on another server, and I am not … um … not confident I can break through their defenses without being detected.*"

And true enough, when DJ got to the access panel, its light switched and the door opened into another hallway. DJ passed through, fully aware he was committing a crime. The hallway was narrower, with only enough room for three people to stand side by side. He learned this while passing several people, most of them wearing suits. He boldly strode past a second group—staff members, DJ assumed, based on their uniforms—and kept his eyes forward, as if he were too busy to notice them.

Espionage hadn't been part of DJ's job description during his time in the Marines, but he'd picked up a few things while sneaking through his fair share of terrorist dens. He could boil it down to two essential skills: act natural and think on your feet.

It was incredibly difficult to break into the White House, to the point that only idiots or heavily armed groups would attempt it. Because of that, once you were already in, most people would assume you belonged there and wouldn't question your presence. If you built on that and acted as if you had somewhere important to be, people would be less likely to even notice you because, after all, *they* have important things to do. You would blend right in.

DJ had been using that trick since he split up from Christy and Albert. He ignored every person he passed as if he was too busy to notice them—because he *was* too busy to notice them. And they in turn ignored him because they had places to be. This let him travel relatively uncontested.

DJ rounded the corner and nearly collided with two Secret Service agents. One had an afro that added height, while the other had a buzz cut so close it practically revealed his scalp. Both wore fitted suits, dark glasses, and earpieces in one ear.

He narrowly avoided crashing into Afro Man by stepping back just in time—his first mistake. For a split second, both agents looked startled, their eyes widening behind their shades. DJ's heart raced as he wondered if he'd moved too quickly, too smoothly. Did they notice? Were they piecing it together? He could feel their surprise, but was it genuine or just a facade to throw him off?

He began to overthink. Why hadn't they reacted sooner? Had he caught them off guard, or had they been waiting for him to slip up? The silence in the hallway, the way the carpet masked his steps—he realized he'd been walking quietly, too quietly. That was his second mistake. His stomach knotted as he imagined them analyzing him, just as he was doing to them, wondering whether they'd already decided he didn't belong.

It would have flown for someone smaller, but DJ's size meant that his footsteps should have been loud enough for them to hear him coming. They probably didn't realize that yet. Hopefully by the time that they did, DJ would be long gone.

"My apologies, sir," Afro Man said, finally taking his own step back. "I didn't hear you coming."

DJ threw him the most harmless grin in his arsenal. "Nah, don't mention it, man." He chuckled. "It was an honest mistake, and it's partly my fault. I didn't notice you either."

"Thank you for understanding, sir," Afro Man said. He didn't do anything as absurd as smile, but his expression lost some of its initial tension. However, that was a marginal thing. From the slight scrunching of his brows, he wasn't going to let DJ off just like that. As if to prove him right, Afro Man continued. "However, this is a restricted area. May I see your identification, please?"

Buzz Cut stood by the side, watching DJ intensely. He pretended not to notice and kept the grin on his face. "Sure," he agreed easily and handed over his Marine ID. It was no longer valid since he'd been kicked out over a year ago, but it wasn't like that fact was written on it. Still, before the agent could look too closely at it, DJ continued. "I have a message to deliver to the chief aide for the president."

Afro Man glanced up at that, his expression becoming more confused and wary at the same time. "What's the message?"

DJ chuckled wryly. "Look, man! I understand it's for security and all, and I can't do anything if you insist. But my orders are to give it to the chief aide personally. This was assigned to me as a punishment, so I'd rather my ass not get chewed up more than it already would be. You know how it is, right?" It was a rhetorical question of course. What person working for the federal government didn't understand how fucked up orders could be?

Afro Man nodded in understanding, but Buzz Cut still didn't seem convinced. "Do you have the orders with you?" he asked.

"Nah! Just the message," DJ replied, but as he did that, he reached into his jacket and brought out the copy of Olsen's document. "But I have this."

Buzz Cut collected the document. While Afro Man just skimmed through it within a few seconds, Buzz Cut seriously seemed like he was reading it. Who *was* this guy? DJ had gone through the file several times, but he hadn't figured out which part made the external security react the way they had. And he couldn't have these agents finding a problem with it.

"Don't mean to rush you, guys." DJ chuckled again, drawing both of their attention back to him. "But the order's kind of time-sensitive. So, if there's no problem …"

"Yeah, there's no problem, sir," Afro Man said. Buzz Cut seemed like he wanted to say something more. But Afro Man collected the document from him and returned it to DJ, along with his ID. "Sorry for taking up your time, and for the earlier accident. Have a good day."

"Hey, man, don't mention it." DJ grinned. "I get that you're just doing your jobs." He gave a nod to each of them and then continued down the hallway as if he didn't have a care in the world. He could feel Buzz Cut's eyes on him. DJ kept his pace measured and casual until he could no longer feel the man's attention.

"*That was … uh … nicely done,*" CJ commented quietly.

"That was only the first," DJ replied grimly. "Let's hope the other ones go as well."

CHAPTER

12

THE WHITE HOUSE, one of the most significant buildings in the world, had survived hurricanes, earthquakes, protests, and attacks. In fact, it had even been set on fire. But it had never faltered as a representation of US power and influence or as a symbol of hope, change, and triumph over adversity. Indeed, its strong walls were fortified by the American spirit.

That's what people tended to focus on when they spoke about the White House. Or at least that's what New Maya had harped on about in her speech. But what New Maya, and everyone else tended to forget was that despite everything it represented, the White House was still just a building—an incredibly important building, yeah, but also just an old building.

Because of this, it underwent constant and regular repairs and maintenance just to keep it standing. More to the point, every few years, a president would come into power and decide to renovate the building. One of the earliest renovations was the Truman Balcony added in 1948, but there have been several additions since then, adding to the building's cultural significance and making it, well, ridiculously huge.

That's what they should have been talking about. DJ passed the State Dining Room an eternity ago. He'd entered the West Wing Lobby and the countless hallways that it connected. For several minutes, he had been surrounded by doors on each side of the passage. That confirmed he was in the area that housed the president's offices as well as the administrative spaces.

It also explained the sharp increase in foot traffic.

In this hallway alone, DJ had passed two groups of what had to be aides. Their movement reminded DJ of interns working in a firm: young people filled with awe and well-earned terror. It was refreshing in a way DJ couldn't quite put his fingers on. A group of interns were rushing to complete a task that was probably unfair and below their expertise. When was the last time DJ had seen panic in a "normal" workplace?

Interns were the least of those DJ interacted with. More and more, he passed access control panels or Secret Service agents standing at checkpoints. With CJ's help, the access control panels weren't much of a problem, though DJ felt a small amount of guilt every time he bypassed one. Unfortunately, the agents weren't so easy to deal with. So far, the combination of his bullshit reason about delivering a message and Olsen's document had been enough to quell any suspicions, but he couldn't exactly rely on it.

"*You are … uh … approaching another checkpoint,*" CJ said in his ear.

"Roger that," DJ replied. He was approaching the Oval Office, and in front of the door were two Secret Service agents, complete with fitted suits, shaded glasses, and sticks up their asses. This wasn't DJ's destination, so he upped his pace slightly to avoid interacting with them, but he couldn't fully ignore their presence. Both were relatively tall. The one on the left had dark-brown hair and muscles that were barely contained by his suit. In contrast, the one on the right had blond hair and a lean build, though DJ didn't doubt he packed a fair bit of power. Their attention had focused on him the moment he'd stepped into view, but DJ kept up the pace he'd set for himself: slightly fast, but not so fast that it was in any way threatening.

With a few steps, he was within talking distance of them. Their eyes followed him, but DJ simply gave a nod to each of them and turned into an adjacent hallway. He could feel their stares on his back, but as long as that was all they did, they could stare all they wanted. According to the map in his head, the Cabinet Room was practically a hallway away. DJ checked his watch. *Just in time*, he thought. According to Debi's calendar, the meeting would start by noon—that is, in twenty-five minutes. DJ was surprised he was going to make it. The tour had taken up most of an hour, and he was certain his meanderings about the endless corridors had taken another hour. Still, it worked out. There was no point to complain—

"Sir?" a voice called. DJ kept walking. He just needed a little more to get to the end of the passage. Just a little—

"Sir." the voice called louder and carried a hint of a threat.

DJ sighed and turned around. He didn't bother with the grin. Instead, his tensed jaw showed his impatience. "Yes?"

The agents hesitated, obviously taken aback by his tone. Now they were unsure. Should they have stopped him? He couldn't be lost. He'd had to have passed the other checkpoints, which meant he probably had clearance to be in this area. Had they pissed off someone important? They were trained to hide it, of course, but DJ was sure he could read every one of Muscle Man's and Blondie's thoughts.

To their credit, they didn't back down. But then they faced the next obstacle. DJ had already gone well into the passage by the time they had called, so there were several feet between them. DJ obviously wasn't willing to go meet them. They couldn't very well leave their post—interrogating him across the distance would diminish their authority and intimidating aura. The two agents shared a brief look before Blondie finally came over.

"This is a restricted area, sir," he started. "I'm afraid I have to see some confirmation that you're cleared to be here." DJ handed over his ID and the document, and the man started making his way back toward his partner. Now DJ would have to follow him if he wanted to collect his documentation afterward. It was nicely done, DJ had to admit. "This doesn't say what your purpose is for being in this area of the White House."

"I have a message to deliver to the chief aide to the president," DJ replied, deliberately checking his watch. "Look, man! I understand that you're just doing your job. But I'm kinda on a time crunch here, so if we could hurry this up—"

"It'll just take a minute, sir." This time it was Muscle Man who spoke. He leaned over to look through the paperwork as well. DJ glanced at his watch again. So much for making it in time. Muscle Man looked up once more. "This doesn't state that you have clearance to access this part of the White House, sir."

"Well, I don't know, man," DJ said, blowing out a breath in exasperation. He didn't even try to keep the impatience out of his tone. "None of the other agents had a problem with it. And listen, this was assigned to me as a punishment, and I'm already going to be in trouble for cutting it so close. But if I deliver it late, my superior's going to chew my ass."

"It'll only take a minute, sir," Blondie said, not even glancing up from the document. "We have to follow procedure. We advise that you be patient, sir."

DJ rubbed the bridge of his nose. He'd been so close. Obviously, they weren't going to let him pass. It could have been that they'd found something wrong with Olsen's document, or they just didn't like the fact that he'd brushed past them initially. Whatever it was, they'd confirmed he wasn't some big shot who could cost them their jobs. *But he was so close.* Just a few more steps and he would have gotten to the Cabinet Room without causing a national incident.

"Can you provide the name of your White House contact or sponsor?" one of them asked.

"I don't have a contact here," DJ replied calmly. Olsen could technically have been considered his sponsor, but it wasn't like DJ was going to rat him out. "I told you, I just have orders."

"Well, I'm sorry, sir," Blondie started, "but without a sponsor and appropriate clearance, you cannot be in this restricted space. I've already called one of my colleagues to escort you out. It should just take a minute."

DJ met the agent's eyes and saw the small hint of amusement that the man tried and failed to bury. They weren't sending him back because they thought he was a threat or that he didn't actually have clearance to be there. They were stopping him because he'd hurt their pride. DJ's eyes narrowed. "It's like that?"

"*DJ …*" CJ warned.

"It's like what?" Blondie asked.

"I have orders to deliver a message to the chief aide in the Cabinet Room, which is basically a hundred steps that way," he pointed. "I've been wandering through these bullshit hallways for over an hour now. But you're not going to let me finish the last few steps so I can complete my task and get on with my life? It's like that?"

"*Calm down, DJ.*"

"I'm afraid it's not up to me," Blondie said. His tone was perfectly flat and calm, which *really* pissed DJ off. "I have to follow procedure, and your paperwork does not give you the clearance to be in this restricted area. Also, I'm going to have to ask you to watch your tone, sir."

"My tone isn't the problem," DJ gritted out. "The *problem* is that you think I'd drive four hours all the way from New York and then spend another hour and a half of my life getting lost in these bullshit passages for something that isn't incredibly important." He took a step toward them.

"I'm going to have to ask you to stay where you are, sir," Blondie said, reaching his holstered gun.

Muscle Man took a step forward. "If you come any closer, it'll be taken as hostile intent."

"*DJ. You … you need to calm down,*" CJ said.

"How am I being hostile, man?" DJ asked, but he stayed where he was. "I just want to collect my ID."

"Unfortunately, both documents will be kept for the time being, and they'll be returned to you after they've been processed."

DJ sighed. "I guess it *is* like that," he said. Blondie started to talk, but DJ waved a hand to shut him up. "Where are Christy and Albert right now?" he said, looking away from the agents.

"*They are … uh … almost at the end of the tour,*" CJ replied. "*But DJ … you have to calm down.*"

"Cool your tits, bro. I'm calm," he said. And he was. Whatever anger he'd been feeling was gone. Now he was just resigned. "But you understand what needs to happen, right? It's not even on me now. You understand that, right?"

"Who're you talking to, sir?" Blondie asked, his voice tense. Both agents had taken a step back, with their hands firmly on their guns.

DJ cut them off, raising his finger in the universal sign for *just a minute*. On the other end of the comm, CJ sighed. "*I … um … understand,*" he replied. "*But DJ … make it quick. We are … uh … almost out of time.*"

"Will do," DJ nodded, dropping his finger and fully facing the two agents. Now DJ didn't know what they saw on his face, but whatever it was, it made them take another step back and fully unholster their guns.

"There's no reason to be rash, sir," Blondie said. "Stay right where you are, and you'll be escorted out shortly."

DJ opened his mouth to speak but then thought better of it when he saw Muscle Man calling for backup.

DJ lunged.

And the world froze. Or it seemed to, at least from DJ's perspective. His legs were tensed, and in the middle of uncoiling for a tackle, but both agents were completely frozen. One of Blondie's feet was suspended in the air, in the middle of taking a step back, while Muscle Man stood motionless, one finger pressed to his ear. His mouth was open, but his lips weren't moving.

No, DJ realized. His lips *were* moving, just very, very slowly. *What the hell is going on right now?* But even as he thought that, the answer was pretty obvious. There was supernatural bullshit running inside his veins—and it was tired of DJ ignoring it.

After an eternity, DJ's feet left the ground and launched him toward the agents. But even though he knew he was moving much faster, it felt like he was swimming, as if the air had become water and he was pushing against it. Within a second, DJ was in front of Blondie with his arms opened up to tackle him. At the last moment, DJ changed his mind and twisted out of the way. He'd seen the way the Murder Twins moved. If DJ was moving anywhere close to that speed, then a tackle might end up breaking Blondie's spine.

DJ landed in a crouch several feet away and to the side of the agents. He straightened, and the world returned to normal. The agents hadn't been able to keep up with his speed. They still stared in the direction that he'd originally been in. And naturally, when they finally noticed him at their side, their faces twisted in panic. Fortunately for DJ, these were trained professionals who didn't do something as stupid as accidentally firing at him. Unfortunately for them, since there were no bullets to keep him away, DJ closed the distance within a second. This time, he'd regulated his speed so that there was no fear of accidentally killing one of them. Since he was moving slower, the agents were still able to react, but not even close to fast enough to impede him.

By the time DJ was in front of him, Blondie's eyebrows were still lifting in surprise. A second later, he doubled over, clutching his stomach. In another second, he was on the floor as DJ released his chokehold. It had all taken less than three seconds, but that was enough time for Muscle Man to recover from the shock and aim his gun at DJ.

However, with DJ crouched over Blondie, Muscle Man couldn't risk a clear shot. He hesitated for a split second, then swiftly holstered his weapon, choosing to engage hand-to-hand. But that moment of indecision was all DJ needed. He caught the movement, spun around, and before Muscle Man could land a blow, DJ struck hard. A second later, Muscle Man crumpled to the floor beside his partner, a fresh bump forming on the back of his head.

DJ stood over the two agents. For the first time, he understood why he'd never stood a chance against Karla whenever they sparred. He also understood why she'd been so angry the one time DJ had managed to land a punch on her. But even at his fastest, he wasn't even close to matching her top speed. Still, it would have been downright insulting if either agent had been able to land a punch on him.

He was breathing hard, but it wasn't because he'd done something particularly tasking, rather because of the massive amounts of adrenaline pumping through him.

"*Well,*" CJ said, "*that was … uh … something.*"

"You caught that, huh?"

"*Barely, but yes,*" CJ replied. "*Your … um … nanites?*"

DJ shrugged. "That's my guess too. It's the only thing that makes sense."

"*Will you … um … take José's offer then? It did not … uh … look like you had much control.*"

"Y'know," DJ said, "as tempting as it is to be disemboweled by Karla in my sleep, I figure it's probably better if I leave the Murder Family out of this one. I've always been good at figuring shit out by myself anyway." He waited a second for CJ to overthink his last statement, but he couldn't hold back anymore. "Hey, bro, any chance you managed to record it?"

"It … um … re-records automatically."

"Sweet," DJ said. He was sure that his brother could see his grin. The last ten seconds played on a loop in his mind. "Christy is never going to believe me without proof."

13

OCTOBER 2043
THE WHITE HOUSE, WASHINGTON, DC

THERE WAS A PAUSE for a few seconds before CJ spoke again. *"You … uh … you know what this means, right?"*

Of course he did. He'd attacked two Secret Service agents in front of the Oval Office. That was basically the worst crime someone could commit short of stabbing the president in her sleep. And it was *exactly* what DJ had been afraid of. But he didn't see how he had a choice. Stopping Helene's plan was far more important than DJ breaking the law.

Yeah, that'll keep the insanity away when you're rotting away as a class 1 felon. It was for the greater good.

He pushed the thought away with a force of will and instead focused on something else. "Is there somewhere I can put these guys?"

CJ hesitated. *"Do you mean like a … uh … supply closet or something?"*

DJ scratched his head. "I mean, in the movies, there's always one placed conveniently close by for the heroes to stash the body of his opponents."

"*There is … uh … nothing on the feed,*" CJ replied.

DJ looked around for ideas. Eventually, his eyes landed on the Oval Office. "Do you think … "

"*No, DJ,*" his brother said immediately. "*That is … uh … a mon-monumentally stupid idea.*"

"Do you have any better ones?"

Silence.

DJ grinned. "Guess we're doing it my way then."

The keys to the office were in Blondie's pocket, but DJ hesitated at the huge door. Somehow breaking into the office seemed far more of a crime than anything he'd done, and that was after considering he was about to stash unconscious Secret Service agents inside. DJ pushed through his misgivings and threw open the door.

DJ had seen several movie depictions of the Oval Office over the years, but all of them paled in comparison to the real thing. It wasn't that the Oval Office was significantly bigger or more luxurious than those shown on TV. But to DJ, it seemed more real somehow. Probably because it was. Every other depiction was just that: a representation. DJ was staring at the real deal, a room that screamed its authority in a way that few places could have. The Resolute Desk stood dead in the center of the room, flanked by several chairs and sofas that were probably used for presidential meetings and discussions. Most parts of the walls were adorned with portraits of former presidents or paintings of historically significant periods. There were a lot of those, as well as a few knick-knacks on the desk and other decorations, like vases on shelves, and even a small bust of … Roosevelt? DJ couldn't tell.

"*Is there a problem?*" CJ asked in concern. "*Why … uh … are you just standing there?*"

DJ jumped. "Oh, shit, right." He quickly dragged the unconscious agents inside and placed them out of the way in one of the corners of the room. He took back his ID and documentation as well as their comms but left them with everything else. With any luck, by the time they came to, DJ would be far outside their jurisdiction. He took one last look at the office before leaving and locking the office behind him. He glanced at his watch. "I can still make it in time—"

"You!" a voice shouted from down the hall. "Don't move!"

DJ sighed. *They come one after the other like ants.* There were two of them running down the passage, both with their guns out. One of them pointed the weapon and shot at him, the sound reverberating in the small space as the bullet whizzed past his ear. DJ felt the air of its passage, which had nearly engraved a line in his skull. Then the man lined up another shot.

For the most part, DJ was a pretty chill guy. He'd put a lot of effort into cultivating that attitude while growing up: the ability to take things in stride. But that didn't mean he didn't get mad. It just meant that when he *did*, he was good at brushing it off. Most times. But everyone had their limit.

Apparently, DJ's was getting shot at when he was trying to do the right thing.

Because they'd shot at him. They'd *actually* shot at him. Him. They saw *him* as a threat. He, who'd been busting his ass for the last three-plus years running around and dealing with Helene, while the idiots who *should* have been doing something sat on their asses and waited for the problem to solve itself. Even after it was supposed to have been done and Helene was supposed to be dead, DJ was still here, risking his goddamn freedom to put out the fire. And these idiots had fucking shot at him.

The rage DJ felt was familiar—he had felt it several times in the past three years. Sometimes it was when he was running around in one of Helene's facilities, outmanned and outgunned but putting his life at risk while everyone else in the government ignored the AI's threat. Several times, it was slipping into their booth in Coronado and staring at an obviously sleep-deprived and severely stressed Olsen, a man he'd started to view as a father figure. Most recently, though, he'd felt that rage while looking down on CJ lying in a coma. DJ had felt the anger, and he'd brushed it off time and time again. It didn't matter what everyone else was doing, right? It only mattered that he was aware that he was doing the right thing. Right?

Right?

Wrong. Because, when there was no recognition for one's actions, it gave dickheads like the fool shooting at him the leeway to act on their misunderstanding of the situation. On any other day, DJ might have brushed it off. But he was tired of all of it. Why should he be the one putting his life on the line time and time again? Why should he be the one sacrificing all the time? He'd tried to be patient. He'd tried to be tolerant. He'd tried to brush off the anger.

But fuck that.

Time to try something else.

"YOU … UM … *need to calm down, DJ,*" CJ told him several seconds later. DJ stood over the unconscious bodies of the two Secret Service agents. He'd already stripped them of their comms and guns and was in the process of dragging them into the Oval Office to meet their colleagues.

"No," DJ countered. "*You* need to tell me why I didn't get a heads-up about these guys. What the hell, CJ?"

"*I … uh … was distracted.*"

"Distracted?" DJ scoffed. "That's your excuse, that you were distracted? By what? Your job is literally to sit in the car and warn me if there are threats I need to—"

"*I was dis-distracted,*" CJ interjected, his tone hard. "*Because the … uh … the program I was running on Debi's phone finished running and … and I was going through the result.*"

Crap. DJ grimaced, feeling like someone had dumped a bucket of cold water on him. That was actually a good reason, and he'd completely lost his cool. The fact that he'd gotten pissed at his brother should have been his first clue that he was wrong. "Crap, I'm sorry, bro." He sighed. He stopped pulling the two agents and brought out the key to the Oval Office. "I don't know what got into me."

"*It is fine,*" CJ said easily, his tone going back to normal, "*but you … uh … you need to calm down.*"

"Lesson learned," DJ replied, picking up the agents again. "So, what'd the stuff say? Do we know the point of all this?"

Finally, CJ said, "*It is … um … basically what we feared.*"

DJ arranged the agents carefully against another corner of the room, and then straightened. He sighed. "Do we know how?"

"*No,*" CJ responded. "*At least not yet. I am … uh … running another program.*"

"Not yet, huh?" DJ repeated to himself. There was really only one reason why Helene would target the president, and it was probably the same reason why she'd targeted Admiral Austin ages ago. DJ had explained his suspicion to his brother, and CJ had agreed that it seemed likely. And it became even more likely when he'd learned that the president would be in a meeting with other cabinet members by noon, the same time that whatever Helene had planned was supposed to happen.

Still, DJ had wanted to be wrong.

He wasn't. In a few minutes, Helene might make puppets out of the country's leaders.

CHAPTER

14

OCTOBER 2043
OKAFOR CORPORATION,
ABUJA, NIGERIA

NDIDI ZIPPED UP HER OUTFIT. She'd planned to wear one of her suits before she realized that the only reason she'd picked it out was her father: Whenever he'd had a meeting, he'd worn a suit. But Ndidi wasn't her father, and as it'd taken several days for her to arrange the board meeting, it wouldn't do for her to give the impression she should be treated like her father.

But then again, Ndidi was far too old to deliberately wear something provocative just to prove a point. She settled on a sensible jumpsuit: formal enough to be worn to a meeting, but stylish enough that there were no doubts about her gender. She gave herself another once-over in the mirror and smoothed out the wrinkles. And then her gaze went to Manar, lying on the bed.

"You're sleeping again?" she asked. "You've been doing that a lot lately. Are you sure you're not ill?"

"I'm not ill," Manar replied softly, "and I'm not sleeping either."

"Then what are you doing?"

"Meditating," he said as if his thoughts were a thousand miles away. "I'm working on something, and it's in its final stages. But there are a few bugs that are proving difficult to get rid of."

Ndidi's brows went up in surprise. From what she knew, Manar hadn't worked on anything new since Helene had been destroyed. She glanced at her watch and tsked in annoyance. It was already late afternoon. If she didn't leave now, she'd be later than she'd planned to be. She would have to drill him for more information when she returned.

"Go," he said, as if reading her mind. "Go and take back your company. We can talk more when you return."

Ndidi grinned without knowing why. It would be an exaggeration to say she was going to take back her company. However, with how difficult it'd been to set up this meeting, she hoped that Manar's words didn't end up becoming a premonition.

Either way, Manar was right. They could talk more when she got back. Ndidi just hoped he wouldn't be too bored with her gone.

"IN-INCOMING," SAID CJ through DJ's earpiece.

"Shit, seriously?" DJ turned. Sure enough, another set of Secret Service agents—six this time—was just turning the corner. Something about DJ standing in front of the Oval Office must have pissed them off because they all brought out their guns at the same time and pointed them at him.

"*Ignore them, and … um … head to the Cabinet Room,*" CJ advised. "*The … um … meeting should have … have already started.*"

DJ tamped down the flicker of disappointment and nodded. The Cabinet Room was basically in front of him, and time was running out. It would be stupid to get bogged down in a drawn-out fight. Although, with his new speed, it wouldn't be drawn out at all. He'd need a minute tops—

And in that minute, Helene could dose the cabinet members and turn them into puppets. With that thought, the last part of him that wanted to fight died out. DJ finally calmed down. Unfortunately, in the time he hesitated, the agents had already crossed half the distance to him. Their guns were pointed, but none of them were stupid enough to shoot. DJ slowly raised his hands. The agents, probably thinking he was surrendering, slowed their pace slightly. But DJ quickly dropped his hands and threw something toward the group.

Immediately the agents dove to the floor. DJ seized the opportunity and sprinted toward his destination. He expected the world to slow down like it had the last time, but nothing happened—he was moving at his normal speed. Whatever boost the nanites had given him seemed to have worn off. Now DJ was even more relieved that he had trusted his instincts and avoided a direct fight.

Footsteps echoed behind him soon after. Apparently the agents had figured out that DJ had thrown keys at them, not a grenade. By then, DJ had already reached the end of the passage and turned into another one. He sighed but kept his pace steady, cursing under his breath as he passed door after door. He was confident he was heading toward the Cabinet Room, knowing it should be at the end of this corridor.

It wouldn't take long now.

Naturally, that was the moment the agents started firing at him.

"You should … uh … probably run faster," CJ suggested helpfully.

"Master of the fucking obvious right here!" DJ yelled, pumping his legs as hard as he could. Adrenaline flooded his veins. DJ crossed his fingers, hoping the nanites would activate again. But no dice. His speed was still firmly below supernatural. Bullets whizzed past him like flies, lodging themselves in doors and walls. DJ focused on evading as best as he could while maintaining his pace. Even though he didn't have catlike reflexes and wasn't running with super-speed, he was still faster than the agents. Significantly faster from the fact that it was more and more difficult to hear their footsteps. The bullets were also coming far less often, which he assumed meant they had fallen behind.

"Incoming from the front," CJ reported, like the buzzkill he was.

"How are they finding me?" DJ growled. Having to zigzag to force a missed shot pissed him off just a little bit more.

"Uh … the ones behind are … are radioing in your position and direction. Plus, there are … uh … cameras all over the White House."

"Cameras?" DJ asked. "I thought you controlled the cameras."

"I did"—CJ stressed the past tense—*"but it is … uh … inevitable that they would pay more attention to the camera feeds at this time, and if they are … uh … are not able to find you where you should be—"*

"Then they would know they've been hacked and would try to trace it back to you," DJ finished. "Well, can you stop the radio stuff?"

"Not in a short … period of time, no," CJ answered. *"And not without … uh … without risking getting detected."*

A few seconds later, a pair of Secret Service agents came into view in front of him, guns already pointed. "Fuck me," he groaned. He ducked into a roll just as two bullets passed over his head, and straightened in the middle of the pair, his arms swinging. DJ was vaguely aware of the amount of training that Secret Service agents undertook, but he'd trained as a Marine. DJ knew what he was capable of, and pound for pound, he was fully confident he could floor the two agents, given enough time. His fear was that, if he took too long, the agents behind him would catch up. Then he'd be screwed.

Fortunately, DJ discovered that he didn't really need much time. His punches landed faster and harder than they normally did, and attacks that might have been difficult for him to dodge before were suddenly easier. DJ didn't think that he was moving any quicker than normal. Rather, he was able to process the fight a lot better than he normally could, meaning he could react to every attack faster than they could react to his.

It made DJ almost feel sorry for the agents—until he remembered that they'd shot at him.

It was a more subtle enhancement than full-on supernatural speed, but the nanites obviously were still going to work on his body. Normally, he'd find something like that extremely weird, but since it was currently keeping him alive, DJ found he didn't mind that much.

Within a minute, DJ moved on, leaving both agents unconscious on the ground.

By then, the agents behind him had caught up enough to keep firing, but it didn't matter since DJ could see large mahogany doors at the end of the passage. The agents must have understood that was his destination as well because although their shots came less often, they were better aimed and closer to hitting their target. DJ ducked and weaved as best as he could until he was a few feet away from the doors. Then he placed his arms in front of him and bulldozed into the room—and found nothing. The room was empty. An imposing king-style oak table dominated the center of the room, polished until its surface gleamed. Surrounding the table were several high-backed chairs. DJ recognized the president's chair at the end of the table from the intricate carvings etched into the wood and the high-quality leather, obvious from just a glance. Just as in the Oval Office, several historical paintings hung on the walls of the room, but there were also several shelves lined with leather-bound volumes that DJ figured were the records of past meetings and decisions.

He took all this at a glance, but his gaze kept returning to the chairs around the table. The *empty* chairs.

Why the was the room empty?

"Why the fuck is the room empty, CJ?" DJ asked, panting slightly as he checked his watch. "It's past noon. Shouldn't the meeting have started by now?"

"*I ... um ... don't know,*" CJ stammered, clearly confused. "*There are two possible explanations. One, the president ... um ... and all the officials were moved the moment you started causing chaos. Two, we have ... um ... the wrong venue for the meeting.*"

DJ shook his head, speaking quickly. "No way we can eliminate the first one. I haven't used a gun, but they've already fired at me, and several agents are down. That's more than enough to escalate the threat level. They would've at least moved the president by now. Hell, they could be locking down the whole place and calling in more backup."

"*So we ... uh ... have the wrong venue,*" CJ concluded, his voice tense with the realization.

"It can't be that either," DJ refuted. "New Maya said that the Cabinet Room wasn't available because of a meeting." A bullet drilled into the door beside him, reminding him of how screwed he was. DJ ducked fully into the room, closed the large doors, and picked up one of the high-backed chairs to use as a wedge.

"*She … um … could have lied,*" CJ said.

"She could have—what? No! She couldn't have," DJ said. "There was no reason for her to. What would have been the point?"

"*What would have been the point … um … in her saying the truth?*" CJ countered. "*The more I … uh … I think about it, DJ, the more it makes sense. New Maya said … uh … said that it was unavailable for a meeting, but the Cabinet Room is used only by the president for official reasons. So … uh … her giving you that information was the same thing as giving you, or any other hostile party, the exact position of the president.*"

"That bitch!" DJ muttered.

"*She was … um … only doing her job, DJ,*" his brother reminded him.

"Of course, she was doing her job," DJ yelled, pacing around the room. By now the agents had reached the door and were attempting to batter it down. "But while she's getting a promotion, I'll be put in isolation for beating someone up."

The sound of cracking wood became louder. DJ hadn't thought they'd destroy the doors to the room, but he'd been wrong more than once already today.

"*Let us think,*" CJ said. His tone was tense, which told DJ he was suppressing whatever he was feeling so he didn't get overwhelmed and spiral into an episode. "*Re-regardless of your actions here, Helene is not … uh … she is not going to let the meeting be canceled. If the meeting was not held here, then … uh … then it is held somewhere else in the White House.*"

DJ thought about the layout he'd memorized. "The Roosevelt Room? It's the only place that makes sense."

"*There are … uh … lots of places that make sense, actually,*" CJ said, "*but most of them are used for emergencies, so … um … I agree with you.*"

"All right then. So I just have to find a way to get there," DJ said.

"*Without … um … getting caught by the group of Secret Service agents outside the door,*" CJ added.

DJ stared at the door. They'd stopped shouting for his surrender a while back, but now the banging had become deafening. From the way the door vibrated,

DJ figured that they'd brought in a battering ram or something similar. He had a minute tops.

"Should be a piece of cake."

CJ was silent for a long while. "*Re-remember all those times when we were … uh … younger and I had an episode and you … always tried to make it better, but … uh … instead you made it worse and got scolded by Dad and Papa?*"

What the fuck? "Why the hell would you bring that up right now?"

"*I am just … uh … starting to notice a trend,*" CJ replied. "*You … you always try to help, and you always mess it up.*"

DJ felt a spark of anger. "What are you doing, CJ?"

"*It happened … um … when we were younger. And … uh … when you joined the Marines, you took responsibility for your team, and … and you basically ruined their careers, DJ. Kyle might be able to fix the mess you made, but … but you have basically ruined Christy's life.*"

DJ growled. "I'm going to assume that there's a point to all this, CJ, but stop it. You're starting to make me mad."

"*Um … even now,*" CJ continued as if he hadn't heard him, "*this was supposed to be a … uh … relatively simple mission, but you messed it up and probably implicated both Christy and Albert. Christy probably … uh … expected something like this to happen and can deal with it, but Albert cannot … uh … not easily walk away. Even if he does not end up in jail, he definitely can no longer live in Washington, much less work here. He … uh … he would be forced to leave after just re-reuniting with his wife, DJ. Because you messed up his life, like you always do.*"

DJ lost it. "What the absolute fuck, bro? You don't understand shit."

The door finally caved in at that moment, creating a hole large enough for half a dozen Secret Service agents to pour in. None of them had guns, but DJ saw a mixture of Tasers, batons, and knuckledusters. They had him cornered now, so they wanted to capture him for interrogation instead of straight up killing him.

DJ rushed them.

The world slowed down around him, but DJ was far too pissed off to care. He crashed into the group like a wrecking ball. There was no iota of skill in his movements, just pure power. He wasn't so far gone that he'd accidentally kill anyone, but his punches were still hard enough to leave bruises. The ones that hit anyway. It was six against one. Despite his significantly enhanced speed and power, DJ quickly found himself losing the upper hand against the coordination of the agents. They'd surrounded him. Whenever he went in to attack one, he was interrupted by three others coming at him, all from different directions, and all targeting different places. DJ could easily take punches and kicks, but the batons hurt enough for him to notice, and the Tasers were even worse. Without the nanites, he would been fried by the voltage.

Eventually the pain pierced his anger. DJ realized how stupid he was being. He retreated. The agents tried to stop him, of course. But he gritted his teeth and pushed back until he was out of the scrum. His back was against a wall so it wouldn't happen again. The six of them were forced to come at him from the front, and only in pairs so they didn't get in each other's way. That was significantly easier for DJ to manage—especially when he regained enough of himself to start using the techniques drilled into him in his years of military training.

The agents came as a wave, trying to overwhelm him. But their numbers didn't mean much now. DJ was more than fast enough to react to any surprises. The first pair came at him. DJ broke their rhythm with ease. Rage still burned in his veins. DJ poured it out on them. He found gaps he was sure that he wouldn't have noticed normally and then punished them for it. By this point, all the agents had lost their weapons, so DJ was sure he could have forced his way through them. But this was similar to the time he'd fought Karla at the Sparta gym. He'd been holding on to his rage too long—ever since Albert had informed him about this bullshit. Now he needed to let loose or he'd explode.

Karla wasn't here so, this time, the agents would have to serve as his training dummies.

A minute went by before the agents finally realized that two at a time weren't going to cut it. They adjusted their position and came at him in threes, switching out in a seemingly random way to avoid becoming predictable. DJ calmly increased his speed and doubled down on his technique. He'd been controlling his strength all this time. But that became harder to do when he sped up. He was forced to pull back his punches too much. This disrupted his rhythm and opened him up despite his speed. The agents took advantage of each opening and punished him for it. Individually each punch didn't do much to him, but together, they started to add up.

DJ switched to the techniques that Karla had beaten into him. And from the first hit, something in him clicked.

Since his first training session with her, DJ had seen through Karla's facade: that of a mindless brute. She *was* still batshit crazy, but not when she fought. Unlike her sister, who focused on dismantling her opponent's techniques step by step, Karla focused on breaking through everything in her way, and she did that by basically bullying her opponent with her incredible strength and speed. This made her style of fighting perfect for DJ in this case.

He still had to hold his strength back, but not so much anymore. And since he didn't have to dedicate so much of his attention to that, it was easier for him to focus on breaking through. The agents were forced to switch out constantly, clutching their sides, heads, or arms. DJ had started hitting hard enough to break bones. They kept coming at him, but they were slower, more hesitant, and full of openings.

DJ tore through them all.

Within a minute, three of the men were groaning on the floor, while the others were knocked out cold. By this time, more agents had come through the door. They stared at him like he was a monster. He couldn't blame them. Something in him was changing. He could feel it. He didn't know if it was the nanites or if he'd just hit the wall for the last time. But something was different. DJ pushed the thought out of his mind. He'd figure it out later. The fight had taken the edge off his anger, but he was still pretty pissed off.

This next set switched out their Tasers and batons for guns and shields.

DJ cracked his knuckles and then rushed to meet them.

OCTOBER 2043
THE WHITE HOUSE,
WASHINGTON, DC

DJ WALKED OUT OF THE CABINET ROOM, leaving over a dozen men in various forms of distress. His clothes were torn, evidence of where he'd just barely dodged bullets. He was breathing hard, which made sense since he'd just soloed over a dozen highly trained Secret Service agents. But DJ didn't feel like he'd reached his limit yet.

Fortunately, he didn't have to find it. At the latter end of the fight, his anger had dulled, and so did his power-up. A slow alarm rang through the building, along with a prerecorded voice calling for an evacuation. From there, DJ knew that they'd started taking him seriously. He mentally perused the map he'd memorized and started jogging toward the Roosevelt Room.

"*That was … uh … very impressive,*" CJ said.

"I'm not talking to you right now."

"*Do you … um … know why I said all those things?*" he asked.

"You figured out that the nanites reacted to my anger. And you realized that using their enhancement was the only way I would get past the agents without getting caught."

"*You … um … you understand then,*" his brother said, sounding relieved.

"Just because I understand doesn't mean it wasn't the absolute dickest move that you could have played, CJ. And it doesn't mean I should just brush it off. You could have told me what you figured out, and I could have gotten angry over the fact that they shot at me, or that I'd probably have to do this bullshit with Helene all over again. Point is, of all the ways you could have pissed me off, you chose this one. Seriously? Fuck you, bro."

CJ sighed. "*You are right. I … um … am sorry.*"

DJ grunted but didn't respond. Of course, he knew that his brother had just been trying to keep him alive by whatever means necessary. But did that mean DJ was suddenly going to be okay having his biggest insecurities thrown in his face? Hell no. It might not be soon, but he'd get over it. For now, he'd just focus on completing the bullshit mission.

It was an easy enough thing for him to retrace his steps from the Cabinet Room back to the Oval Office, and then from the Oval Office, he just followed his mental map to the Roosevelt Room. But when he got to the final passage before his destination, he faced a dozen men standing behind a makeshift fence, dressed in full riot gear and clutching batons. Both sides saw the other the moment DJ turned into the passage. DJ slowed to a walk, but he didn't stop despite their warnings. From their uniforms, DJ could tell these weren't cops, but they weren't run-of-the-mill Secret Service agents either. This was an elite squad of some kind but not actual reinforcements from the local precinct. Good. That was the balance DJ needed.

Did they seriously bring in just a dozen men? DJ wondered. *Didn't they see what I did to the last group?* He was about to push the question out of his mind when something clicked. "You still have eyes in the building?" he asked his brother.

"*Yes.*"

"What's Christy doing?"

CJ hesitated. "*What … uh … you asked her to.*"

Fuck, DJ cursed inwardly. That was why his brother had brought up DJ implicating Christy and Albert. They'd probably noticed the increased activity and taken that as DJ's sign to cause a distraction. It took actual effort, but DJ pushed the thought out of his mind. The best thing he could do for them was wrap up here as fast as possible and then go help them out. And for that, he needed his full focus. "Have they moved the president yet?"

"*Cannot say,*" CJ replied. "*The cameras for … um … important places are on a separate server.*"

That made sense, or CJ would have known that the Cabinet Room was a dead end. He changed the question. "Well, have you seen the president running around the hallways?"

"*No.*"

"Tell me when that changes." DJ stopped when he was within talking distance of the men. "Any chance you'd believe me if I told you that I come in peace?"

"You're under arrest!"

"On the ground!"

"Stop right there!"

"Surrender now!"

DJ sighed. It had been a long shot anyway. With the nanites, he could easily get through the blockade, but that'd mean getting angry, and DJ was done with that. Plus, he didn't need to get angry every time he wanted to activate his nanites. Sure, Karla was basically a compressed ball of rage, but Liz was always composed, and she easily kept up with her sister. Just standing there, he felt stronger and faster than he had ten minutes ago. That meant the nanites could still enhance him even when he wasn't emotional. His anger just spurred it on and accelerated the process, leaving DJ with the benefits after he'd calmed down. That might explain why, at baseline, Karla was slightly stronger than her sister. With her anger issues, her nanites were probably constantly working at an accelerated pace.

Because of that, DJ was confident he could get through the blockade, with or without his nanites. But he had to at least *try* to be diplomatic. "Look," he started again, silencing them. "I'm not here to start a fight or anything. I'm sorry about your colleagues and stuff, but they're the ones that came after me. And from their example, I think both of us know that you guys aren't enough to stop me."

There were a few scoffs at that. But DJ focused on their body language: their fidgeting, the way they licked their lips, and how they constantly adjusted their grip on their weapons.

"But like I said," he continued. "I'm not here to fight. But I *do* need to get into that room." He pointed behind them. "I need to speak to the people in there. Now I don't have a lot of time. If it'll hurry your decision, I can allow one of you to come over and search me to prove that I'm unarmed. That way, you know I'm not here to endanger anyone inside. And if it makes you feel better, it's a matter of national security." DJ thought about it. "Actually, scratch that, it's a matter of *global* security."

The group hesitated, casting sidelong looks at each other and muttering. DJ waited patiently. They didn't believe him, not fully. But they knew as well as he did that a fight would be a bad idea. That made them more inclined to listen. Of course, they could be stalling for time, but if that happened, DJ would just tear through them.

One of the agents, a man with so much muscle his body armor looked like a T-shirt, met DJ's eyes. "This is above our pay grade, man. We're going to have to pass it up." He jerked a thumb at the closed door behind him to show what he meant.

DJ didn't have a problem with that. He shrugged. "Sure, but like I said, I don't have a lot of time." And then, just to screw with them, he stared them down and threw on his most confident grin. "Not to be mean or anything, but if you're trying to bullshit me or stall for time or something, then we might as well get this show on the road right now." His expression showed that he didn't give a fuck about whatever they were planning, that he was confident enough to break through everything they could think of. And since there was no visible reason for him to be so confident, it'd make them wonder what he had up his sleeve.

The agent stared at him for another few seconds to probe DJ's seriousness. For his part, DJ channeled José as he met the other man's eyes. Without warning, the agent broke the stare, turned on his heels, and went into the Roosevelt Room. He was there for a couple of minutes—during which time, DJ could faintly make out several voices shouting—before coming back out. The man's expression was one of resignation and a hint of relief, which told DJ what he needed to know.

"Captain Barnes," the man said, stretching out a hand. DJ took it firmly but didn't offer his name. Doubtless they knew it already. "The president has agreed to a meeting. But first I have to pat you down to ensure you aren't carrying any weapons, sir." DJ almost chuckled but let the man keep pretending that it had been *his* idea.

When the fuck did I become so cocky? DJ wondered.

He'd stood in front of an armed blockade and confidently threatened to mess them all up if they didn't let him through. That wasn't the kind of risk DJ would have taken before. *But that was because I was weak before.* That morbid thought could have come from José. But that didn't mean it was wrong.

Before this, DJ *had* been weak. Physically, he was a capable fighter, but even as a Marine, several dozen people could have wiped the floor with him. DJ was averagely ranked. That was why Admiral Austin could screw with him as much as he'd liked without DJ being able to do anything about it. Even in terms of resources, DJ had to depend on Olsen for most of his equipment because he didn't have enough authority or connections to source for them himself.

But now DJ doubted anyone would take him in a fight so casually. He didn't plan on throwing his new powers around, of course. Someone like José, for example, didn't need to punch someone in the face for them to respect him. There was something in the way the man carried himself that practically screamed he wasn't one to fuck with.

That was strength.

And DJ emitted the same aura, considering how the agents stared at him.

"Sure," DJ shrugged, granting the unspoken request for permission. He stretched his arms to the sides. To his credit, Barnes showed no discomfort as he patted DJ down, briskly starting from his sleeves, down to his pants, and back again. The only hesitation came when he reached DJ's jacket. DJ stopped him before the man could bring it out.

"I'm afraid I'll have to know what it is before I can clear you, sir," he said.

"It's classified, bro," DJ responded.

"I'll have to insist, sir."

"Does it feel like a gun?" DJ asked.

"No, but—"

"Does it feel like a grenade or any explosive that you know of?"

"No, it doesn't, but—"

DJ continued speaking over him. "I know you have a device to detect explosives. Is it going off?"

The man grimaced but conceded the point. He stepped back and gave a signal to the rest of the men. Immediately, their tension eased, and they stepped to the side as DJ passed through the blockade and into the Roosevelt Room where the most powerful people in the country were waiting for him.

OCTOBER 2043
ROOSEVELT ROOM,
WHITE HOUSE, WASHINGTON, DC

JUST LIKE IN THE OVAL OFFICE, the walls of the Roosevelt Room were decorated with historical paintings and photographs, these ones primarily of former President Franklin D. Roosevelt. There was a large oval table in the center of the room, surrounded by a dozen chairs, each occupied by one of the most powerful people in the country. DJ noted the Speaker of the House of Representatives, the secretary of state, the director of national intelligence, and several others that he couldn't recognize.

The only truly familiar face was Admiral William Austin, who was probably representing someone higher up the chain. DJ would have felt a measure of assurance if Austin's glare wasn't like a sword being run through him. Every other person stared at him with a mixture of anger, expectation, arrogance, and bored curiosity. But no fear. That was reserved for the aides standing behind them. From their expressions, DJ confirmed that everyone in the room had been informed of his exploits in the last hour.

He counted more than a dozen Secret Service agents stationed around the room, which, when combined with the other group stationed outside the room, could account for their confidence. DJ would be fucked if it came to a fight, and he was doubly relieved that he hadn't fought his way in. A pair guarded each of the two exits within the room, and another stood close to the president. They undoubtedly were ready to end him within a moment's notice.

DJ's attention was forcefully arrested by the woman sitting at the head of the oval table. Like almost everyone in the country, DJ had only seen President Mary Pastore on the news, but true to what he knew about her, she looked a couple of decades younger than most presidents before her. She wore a sensible black suit that contrasted wildly with her flowing white hair, though the outfit did nothing to hide how tall the woman was. She was sitting down, of course, but DJ didn't think she was an inch over five foot six. Nevertheless, the woman practically screamed power. She exuded self-assuredness despite her stature, an aura that came from knowing your every word had to be obeyed. She fixed DJ with a piercing look.

"Well, I'm here. What do you want?"

DJ knew he should salute—the commander in chief deserved that respect. He gave a sharp, respectful salute before lowering his hand and meeting her eyes. "Permission to speak freely, ma'am?" he asked, his tone direct.

That got him a raised brow from the president and even more glares from the Secret Service agents. Several of them looked as if they wanted to shoot him on the spot. DJ ignored them. It didn't matter what they thought, just what the president thought. She stared at him with an unreadable expression for several seconds.

And then she nodded.

DJ hid his relief. It would have been such a pain if he'd had to watch his words every step of the way. "Look, I'm sorry for just barging in here and all, but I have no idea what the usual procedure is." *Nor do I care,* he wisely kept it to himself. "But my team and I intercepted a plan from Helene a day ago, and we had to act fast." Everyone except the president and Austin stared at him blankly, so DJ clarified. "Helene? The artificial intelligence? Threat to the world?"

"We know who Helene is … Darren Kojak, right?" a balding man with a prominent paunch spoke up. "And we'll get to the threat you believe she poses in a moment, but first … you mentioned a team. It's my understanding that your team disbanded over a year ago when you departed from the Marines."

DJ's eyes narrowed at that. "I was referring to a different team, sir, one working outside the government. We recognized the threat that Helene posed and have been trying to stop her since Mayday."

The man grunted. "I don't suppose the woman who was just apprehended for causing a disturbance in the White House is also part of this … team?"

Damn, DJ grimaced. "She is, and she was working under my orders, so I request that any punishment be put on me."

"That'll depend on the outcome of this meeting," President Pastore said. She threw a look at the balding man. "I trust that the director of national intelligence will allow our guest to finish his report before interrupting." The man—who was apparently the director of national intelligence—nodded in acknowledgment and stared at DJ expectantly.

With both his and Christy's freedom on the line, DJ gave a full breakdown of everything he and the rest of the team had been involved in concerning Helene since Mayday. Initially, he wouldn't have mentioned it as he hadn't thought it was necessary. There was no way the president didn't know what was happening under her nose, right? But since it seemed that even the fucking director of national intelligence was unaware, or at least pretending to be unaware, DJ figured it best to bring the full situation to their attention while he had the chance. He glossed over everything concerning Olsen and Admiral Austin, and he'd have done the same for the Murder Team, but they were too involved for him to overlook them.

He didn't know how long he'd be allowed to keep talking, so he tried to be as concise as possible, without any embellishments or exaggerations. Still, he was talking about several years of history and more than a few near-death situations. The only time the president interrupted was when DJ got to the part about Manar and CJ uploading themselves to the Virtual Realm. DJ tried his best to explain, but even he hadn't fully understood when his brother had explained it to him. Eventually, DJ got to Albert coming to find him and everything that had happened after that.

The room was silent when he was done, with the exception of the aides scribbling furiously in their notepads. DJ stayed silent while those in the room processed everything he'd said. It was difficult since his life hung in the balance. But he'd already said everything he could to defend himself and his actions. It would be enough or it wouldn't.

Eventually, President Pastore cleared her throat. "That is quite a tale," she said, "with several very alarming elements, if it's true. The most reasonable question is, Do you have proof for any of it?"

Most of the proof was at Sparta Headquarters, either in the isolation chamber or strapped to Hermione's table. However, DJ had expected this question, so he was reasonably prepared for it. "As I said, the reason I'm here is that I believe Helene is planning to use the picospores on most if not all of you here and completely take over the country's leadership. But because none of you knew about this, then she most likely has already integrated herself into the government to some extent and probably has control of at least one of you right now." DJ deliberately didn't look at Admiral Austin when he said that, but he thought he saw the man grimace.

"That's absurd," someone said. DJ didn't know who he was, but he noted his face, along with the four other people who protested alongside him. "You think everyone here is a fool and we wouldn't notice if someone among our number wasn't himself?"

DJ ignored him to focus on President Pastore. "I have a way to confirm it, ma'am." At her nod, DJ reached into his jacket and took out the Synaptic Pulse. It was what Captain Barnes had felt earlier, but DJ hadn't wanted to reveal it then. His motion had been fast enough that the Secret Service agents hadn't been able to react in time, so there was a frantic moment when they all pulled their guns at him all at once.

DJ sighed. One of the agents close to him took a step forward to take the device from him. DJ stared at the man until he realized how stupid he was being and returned to his position. President Pastore cleared her throat. "I assume that's the device you mentioned? The … Synaptic Pulse?"

"Yes, ma'am," DJ replied. "The best way to check would be for Hermione to run a couple of tests back at Sparta, but it's pretty much the same thing if we just take whoever falls unconscious from this back there."

"This is idiotic," someone said. It was the same man who had spoken up earlier. "You can't seriously be considering this, Madam President. For all we know, that's a bomb and he's willing to sacrifice himself to destabilize the nation."

"Suicide bombers rarely ask for permission before they blow themselves up, Morgan," President Pastore said dryly. "And I think we're all aware that if sergeant Darren Kojak wanted to harm us, after coming this far, there's precious little any of us could do to stop him." The glance she threw at him when she said the last part made it clear she was only saying that. There had been *plenty* they could have done to stop him. Once again, DJ was glad that he hadn't decided to force his way in.

Morgan wasn't deterred. "We've already humored the boy for close to an hour—"

"Meaning a few more minutes wouldn't hurt," President Pastore interrupted smoothly.

The man seemed prepared to say more, but President Pastore nodded at DJ, which was all the permission he needed. He turned the Pulse toward the room, increased the intensity the way Hermione had shown him, and activated it.

Immediately, the room lit up in white.

It lasted for only a moment. But when the glare ended, there were a little more than half a dozen people on the ground. DJ resisted the urge to roll his eyes when he saw Morgan was one of those. The aide behind him was still standing, staring blankly at the unconscious form of his boss. And was that satisfaction in his gaze? DJ shrugged but didn't dwell on it.

Apart from Morgan, only three other cabinet members were unconscious. DJ had honestly expected more. But it made sense. If Helene had had control of most of the cabinet members, then she would have had a straight path to turn the president and the rest of the members. With a unanimous vote, she could do basically whatever she wanted for the country. Three aides had also been affected by the Pulse and knocked out, along with the two Secret Service agents guarding the exit.

DJ cocked his head at that.

For the first time, everyone had the same expression of shock on their faces—except Austin, who just sighed while looking around. More than likely, most of them had hoped DJ had been lying or exaggerating to save his skin. Now that he'd been proven right that Helene *had* taken over part of the leadership of the country, they didn't rightly know what to do.

President Pastore scanned the room, looking as though she had aged several years in mere moments. Frankly, DJ wouldn't want to be in her shoes. To her credit, however, it took only a minute before she regained her composure. She turned to one of the aides still standing. "Please, get some people to clear the room and secure the ministers somewhere safe."

The aide ran out, looking relieved to have been sent.

Next, President Pastore focused on DJ. He met her eyes squarely. "On behalf of the entire United States of America, I'd like to personally thank you for bringing this threat to my attention. In light of it, and your obvious expertise in dealing with Helene, I also extend a formal request for you and your team to work officially with the US government."

DJ hesitated. "Do I still have permission to speak freely, ma'am?"

President Pastore raised a brow at that but nodded. "Now more than ever."

"Two things then. First, can I assume that, since you understand why it was so important, my actions today—as well as those of my teammates—won't be held against me?"

President Pastore's eyes narrowed. But she nodded. "I can agree to that," she said. "Especially since there appears to be no permanent damage done." DJ wondered if broken bones counted, but he wisely decided to keep that to himself. "And the second?"

DJ had wanted to say there was no threat to get rid of, but people were still lying unconscious on the ground, knocked out because they were still under Helene's influence—an influence that should no longer exist if Helene were truly gone.

And yet, here we are. DJ could no longer deny the possibility that Manar and his brother had been somehow wrong, that Helene *hadn't* truly been destroyed, at least not permanently. It wasn't over yet.

DJ rubbed the bridge of his nose, sighing. "I appreciate the offer, Madam President, but if I'm going to do this again, I'd prefer to work with my team." President Pastore started to protest, but DJ continued speaking. "With all due respect, my team has been suppressing Helene for several years. That comes with a level of experience that'll take too long to teach to someone else. And again, with all due respect, we can't afford the time it'll take. This is the most overt that Helene has ever been. She no longer cares about hiding in the shadows. What I mean by that is"—DJ met her eyes—"when Helene strikes next, it's probably going to be open war."

"And you think your team can handle it by yourselves?"

"Ma'am, we've already *been* handling it," DJ replied. "But if you're willing to back us up, then we're not going to turn down some resources."

"You'll have them," President Pastore assured him.

DJ finally relaxed. He'd have to call back Manar and Ndidi, but he'd give them a few more days to enjoy their time away. DJ doubted José and Chloe would be willing to help them again. But if he could find Karla, he might be able to persuade her. They'd have to track down where Helene was hiding this time and draw her out. And for the first time, Helene had made a mistake and left them a lead: Tyra Chityothin.

CHAPTER

18

NDIDI PAUSED AT THE DOOR, one hand on the knob. The wall shook with the sound of something crashing into it. She frowned, glancing back in the direction of the main building. The labs were too far away for an explosion to reach them.

Should I go back and check?

The walls shook again. This time there was no mistaking it. The crash had come from *inside* the room. Ndidi charged in. How could an intruder have reached so deeply—

She paused, frozen in the doorway.

The room was completely trashed. Several chairs had been reduced to splinters. The television was broken. There were several cracks on the dresser, presumably from where the chairs had crashed against it. But where Ndidi had expected to see a thief ransacking the place, Manar stood in the middle of the room, holding half of the broken table. Feathers drifted down through the room, sticking to his clothes in clumps, giving the impression of some sort of bird costume. In another lifetime, Ndidi might have found that funny. But there was nothing comical about the look of absolute rage on his face.

Ndidi had seen Manar angry before. She'd seen him fly into moods that could have rivaled her father's. But she'd never seen this. *This* was something else. Even in his worst moods, Manar didn't break things. He was far too in control of himself for that. Now it seemed he'd completely given in to the emotion and let it rage, perhaps for hours.

That wasn't the Manar she knew.

Ndidi grew cold. How much had he changed when he'd been in the Virtual Realm? Was she the one who'd done this to him?

He looked up at her entrance, freezing in the middle of throwing the table at the wall. Sunlight streamed into the room, catching his eyes and making them gleam like burnished gold.

Ndidi could see the moment he registered her because his rage retreated. It wasn't an immediate shift, more of a slow realization of what he'd done. Ndidi had expected horror. For a minute, Manar looked around the room, his gaze distant. Ndidi didn't say anything. She simply closed the door and locked it.

Manar's knees buckled, and he curled up on the bed, his elbows on his knees. Ndidi took a seat beside him and placed a hand on his shoulder.

"DJ and Christy attacked the White House," Manar said eventually as a way of an explanation.

Ndidi's eyes widened. "What?"

"The *White House*, Ndidi," he repeated, heat in his voice. "Those *idiots* attacked the president of the United States. From what I heard, DJ tore through the Secret Service like they weren't even there."

Ndidi tensed while she tried to wrap her head around it. Of all the possible things she'd expected Manar to say, this hadn't even been on the list. It didn't make sense. Why would DJ attack the president? How would he have gotten far enough into the White House to have become any sort of threat? And he took out the Secret Service? Just DJ and Christy?

None of it made any sense. She said as much to Manar.

"I don't understand it either." He sighed. "I'm still getting more information. He doesn't look like he's in trouble. But he put the entire team at risk—the entire company. It was reckless, and it was stupid and—"

"Wait," Ndidi cut in, frowning. She and DJ hadn't seen eye to eye since she'd been captured by Helene. But she was confident he wouldn't do something like this without a monumentally good reason. Although the ex-Marine was reckless, there was always some logic behind his actions. And Manar had said Christy had been with him. This confirmed it. DJ wouldn't have risked Christy unless it had been important. "Why did they attack the president?"

"Does it matter?" Manar asked, turning to look at her. His eyes had gone back to green, but they still held their usual piercing intensity. "They can't be left to their own devices for long. We have to go back to New York and—"

"No, Manar," Ndidi said quickly. Manar's eyes flashed, but she continued before he could say anything. "We can't leave. I just started taking back my company, and I can't stop halfway. The board meeting went fine, but there's still a lot that I need to do." Manar still didn't look convinced. Ndidi planted a soft kiss on his lips. "Plus, this is also supposed to be for *us*, remember? To make up for all the time that we missed."

Manar stared at her, but he wasn't looking at her; he was running her words through his mind and trying to make a decision. "Okay," he said, finally. "How long do you think it will take to be done here?"

At least nine months, she thought, unconsciously placing a hand on her stomach. But no, saying that would only scare him. "Not too long."

There was no need to rush anyway. With Helene gone, she and Manar had all the time in the world to be together.

CHAPTER

19

OCTOBER 2043

SPARTA HEADQUARTERS,
NEW YORK

DJ COLLAPSED ONTO THE BED with a soulful groan. Every cell in his body was drained—it was a miracle they hadn't crashed during the drive back. The president had offered them a ride, but DJ had turned her down. Having the resources of the entire US government would make his life a hell lot easier, but also much more convoluted. He'd have to deal with political bullshit, which was bound to be hell on earth. A small price to pay if it meant getting rid of Helene for good.

For good, huh? DJ sighed, adjusting his position on the bed. How many times had he had that thought? How many times had they believed that they'd finally finished her off, that she'd been completely destroyed, only to discover that it'd been a trap all along?

For years, they'd been getting rid of her for good. And where had that gotten them? Even the president hadn't known of the threat that Helene posed, not even when Helene had drones flying over the skies and people being manipulated like puppets to do her bidding. There was a goddamn bomb being built somewhere. And no one in power had been aware of it.

What did that say about the depths of Helene's influence?

What did it say about their chances of "getting rid of her for good"?

And even if they *did* somehow eliminate all traces of the AI, what about the picospores? Hermione, as well as the rest of Helene's hostages, had proved the spores could be used for good. But without Helene, the spores were useless. And if the AI wasn't there to maintain the spores, everyone she'd infected could very well end up mentally broken permanently.

Do I really want that on my conscience?

If he failed, Helene would take over the world. If he succeeded, thousands—if not hundreds of thousands—of people would have their minds broken beyond repair. Either way, he'd lose. And if that was the case, what was the point in fighting?

DJ groaned into his pillow. *This is why people shouldn't think.* He turned to lie on his back just as the footsteps he'd heard stopped at the door. A moment later, his brother came into the room.

"Update?" DJ asked when CJ just stood there.

"I am … um … sorry."

DJ closed his eyes. He wasn't angry, not anymore. But it was going to take more than a day for him to completely get over it. He understood why CJ had said the things that he had, but they'd struck a little too close to home. With how tired he was, he just didn't have the strength to deal with this right now.

"Update?" he repeated, feeling CJ's eyes on him as he waited for a response.

"Um … I have recovered all the lost messages, and … uh … my program should be done tracing the hack back to its source within the hour."

DJ nodded, his eyes still closed. He needed to get started finding everything he could on Tyra Chityothin. It should be easier with the president's help, but DJ didn't want contact with President Pastore—or anyone she'd recommend—directly. Maybe he could rope Olsen into doing it. The admiral was more versed in these kinds of things, and his position would give him more leeway than DJ could ever hope to have.

More importantly, though, DJ trusted Olsen. He knew the man wouldn't stand for bureaucratic bullshit.

Olsen it is. He nodded to himself.

"How … um … how long are you going to give me the silent treatment?" CJ asked. He'd moved to the desk but was still staring at DJ. The only light in the room came from the open window. DJ knew his brother couldn't see his face, but he could make out CJ's clearly in the moonlight. It wore his worry. CJ was genuinely anxious that DJ wasn't going to forgive him. "You said … uh … you understood why I did it."

"I'm not giving you the silent treatment, bro," DJ replied. "I'm just too tired to get into it right now." But as he said that, he realized it was a lie. He *was* tired, but this brief amount of lying down had already helped him recover. He'd welcome a nap, but he no longer felt at the edge of death's door.

DJ took a deep breath and then raised himself until he sat at the edge of the bed. Although his muscles groaned in protest DJ ignored them and methodically peeled off his clothes, revealing the map of bruises covering his body. Seeing them brought attention to the pain DJ had buried.

DJ winced as agony spread through every part of him. His body had been put through the Secret Service meat tenderizer. Although he could feel the nanites working on his wounds, that only brought more pain. Maybe he wasn't feeling as good as—

He blacked out.

WHEN HE CAME TO, CJ WAS KNEELING beside him, holding a bowl of water. CJ dipped a cloth in the water and brought it to a cut on DJ's arm.

"Fuck," DJ hissed. He gritted his teeth against the pain as CJ dressed his wounds. The room was silent for a while. DJ had his eyes closed while his brother moved from one wound to the other to clean them.

"What … um … happens now?" CJ asked, breaking the silence.

"What happens now?" DJ repeated, opening his eyes. "We can't pretend that Helene isn't still around. I know you and Manar believe you destroyed her in the

Virtual Realm, but we have to accept that she tricked you guys somehow. She tricked all of us. She's still around, and she's no longer content to remain in the shadows. The evidence today proved that." He let that sink in before continuing. "We have to change the way we work too. But apart from that, it's the same routine as before. We keep kicking her ass until she stays dead."

CJ nodded but didn't say anything more. There was nothing more to say. He'd been wrong to think they would lose whether or not they defeated Helene. If Helene won, everyone in the world would become her puppet. But even then, they still had a chance to find a cure for the picospores and help everyone who had been infected.

As long as there was a shot at victory, DJ was going to take it.

CHAPTER

20

OCTOBER 2043

SPARTA HEADQUARTERS,
NEW YORK

"IT WAS RISKY, RECKLESS, *not to mention incredibly stupid, DJ. I don't care if you rot in jail, but your actions also put your brother and Christy at risk. For that, I ought to tie you to a chair and ..."* Olsen's voice blasted over the phone.

DJ winced and stretched the phone away from his ear, glad CJ wasn't there to hear this verbal lashing. His body was still a map of bruises, but he'd recovered enough to at least take a shower.

"Cool your jets, old man," he interrupted, taking a chance when the admiral paused to take a breath. "What're you putting all the blame on me for? You're the one who gave me the credentials and map of the place."

"*It was* supposed *to be a simple infiltration,*" Olsen said through gritted teeth. "*The credentials were meant to get you past everyone except a captain, and you had an order to explain as much as you could and call me or Austin if that wasn't enough. At no point did I authorize you to run around the White House and inca-pacitate Secret Service agents!"*

DJ held the phone away from him until the shouting stopped. "Well, shit hit the fan sooner than I expected, okay?" he replied. He forced a cheerfulness that he didn't feel. "But it all worked out in the end, didn't it?"

DJ could vaguely make out a *whooshing* sound, like someone was blowing air into the speakers. This lasted for ten seconds before Olsen finally responded.

"Why did you call me, DJ?" His tone was deceptively calm—a frightening reality because DJ knew Olsen got that way only when he'd almost been pushed too far. DJ knew the admiral would be pissed, but he hadn't thought too deeply about it. Probably part of the problem.

But DJ, too, was right. He'd fucked up—big time even. But it had all worked out in the end. And now it was time to move on. But to do that …

"I need your help," DJ said.

"You ungrateful little shit," Olsen growled, but there was no heat in it. *"Well, what are you waiting for, you brat? Should I die before you speak up?"*

DJ grinned the first real smile since he'd returned. "We have a lead. CJ traced the hack on Debi's phone, and we got a name and a location. This could be our one shot to finally get something on Helene. We're going to need to know every-thing we can about her so we don't blow it."

"Why don't you just ask the CIA?" Olsen asked dryly. *"Sounds as though you have the president's blessing."*

DJ grimaced. "I thought of that," he said, choosing his words carefully, "and I was thinking that's where *you* would come in." DJ quickly held the phone away from his ear in anticipation of another tirade. When none came after a few seconds, he tentatively brought the phone closer.

"I wasn't sure you'd be smart enough to realize you'd be chewed up and spat out if you'd approached them by yourself," Olsen said. *"It's good to know your brain is not totally useless."*

"So, you'll do it?"

"I was wrong. Maybe your brain is *useless after all if you need me to spell it out for you."*

Well, fuck you too, DJ thought. "One more thing—" he started.

"*I swear to God, you won't be satisfied until I'm wiping your ass for you. You're a leader. Now act like it*," Olsen spat. "*Brats these days*."

He hung up.

DJ stared at the phone for a moment, a smile creeping up his face. Somehow he found he'd missed the old man yelling at him. It was a level of normal that DJ hadn't felt in a while. It took him years back to when he'd sit in Olsen's office, scared to all hell but defiant enough to engage in screaming matches with the old man. It was a simpler time. His body was looser, and he felt refreshed.

He hadn't been able to ask for his second request. Getting the admiral to act as the middleman to the CIA—and the rest of the government eventually—had been DJ's major goal. With that amount of resources, Tyra Chityothin wouldn't have anywhere to hide.

That was one last thing to worry about.

"What's next?" DJ muttered, running through his mental list. With the ball rolling on Tyra, he could go to the gym to test out what exactly the nanites had done to him. Ideally, he'd have someone on the Murder Team give him some pointers. But DJ was extremely reluctant to go back to the warehouse. He couldn't even begin to imagine where Karla had gone. The rest of the Murder Team was a powder keg just waiting to go off, and DJ refused to be the fuse.

He also had to call Manar and Ndidi and catch them up. President Mary Pastore would definitely have suppressed all news about DJ's escapades in the White House, but DJ would still have to come clean.

With any luck, they'd come rushing back. DJ had given them enough time to themselves. They might do something stupid in the name of love, given more time.

TYRA CHITYOTHIN

OCTOBER 2043
NEW YORK CITY, NEW YORK

TYRA CHITYOTHIN SCOOPED UP another set of papers and tossed them into the fire. While she didn't hurry, her pace wasn't slow. Every movement was optimized for efficiency. There was no waste. It'd been several hours since Christopher Kojak had found the backdoor that she'd placed on Debi Willingham's phone. Naturally, Tyra had bounced the signal through relays all over the world. But for someone with Christopher's level of skill, that would only buy her a few hours before he traced the link back to her apartment. And a few hours after that, she was confident Darren Kojak would be breaking down her door.

Tyra couldn't be around at that time. But she also couldn't leave anything for them to find. She'd already planned her next steps, and although she didn't have long, she knew hurrying would only lead to sloppy mistakes. Tyra was above that.

But she *wasn't* above feeling excitement at the thought of the next few days. She'd been exposed and was confident that Darren wouldn't let the chance slip away. She would be chased; she would be pursued. Then she would kill them all.

Tyra felt her nanites vibrate at the thought. Helene had always viewed humans as little more than insects, even if she'd deny it. And so Helene always underestimated DJ and his team. Tyra was the opposite. Although their ideals conflicted harshly, Tyra respected DJ. She understood what he was capable of. And that was why she would kill him the first time she got the chance.

Her face split into a grin. It would be *glorious*. She would do what Helene had failed to do time and time again.

Tyra got wet just thinking about it.

CHAPTER

NOVEMBER 2043

OKAFOR CORPORATION,
ABUJA, NIGERIA

NDIDI DISCONNECTED THE CALL. DJ wasn't the type to shy away from difficult conversations, so Ndidi wasn't surprised when the ex-Marine tried to come clean about what had happened at the White House. Still, she found it odd that he'd called her and not Manar. While DJ and Manar didn't have a particularly close relationship, theirs was far better than his and Ndidi's, especially in the past few months. Why had he called her?

Does it matter? she thought. It didn't. She was just using that to distract herself from the other things DJ had said—specifically the reason why he'd raided the White House in the first place. Manar hadn't told her about Helene's backup plan to infect the leaders of the government with picospores. He probably hadn't known, and Ndidi certainly wasn't going to tell him. She knew he always blamed himself for everything Helene did, and she definitely wasn't going to be the one to cause him such pain, especially since it no longer mattered. DJ and the others had already taken care of the threat. The problem was solved, so she felt no need to cause Manar grief over it.

Of course, there was the other reason Ndidi didn't want to tell him. She was afraid Manar would leave her to go back to New York if he heard anything about Helene. He'd already hinted at it several times, but Ndidi had managed to deflect those conversations. So no, she wouldn't tell him about this or about the fact that DJ had asked for their help. Ndidi was confident the request was merely a politeness. DJ would rather run naked into a burning building than genuinely ask for her help.

That, Ndidi thought, narrowing her eyes, *would actually take him admitting that I'm useful.*

"Is everything okay?" Manar asked beside her, placing a hand on her shoulder. Ndidi blinked and focused. Manar stared at her in concern, his eyes searching her face for something. "You've been staring at the wall for several seconds. What did DJ want?" He frowned. "What'd he do now?"

Ndidi quickly smoothed her brows and forced a chuckle. "He didn't do anything. He basically just called to tell us about what happened in the White House. He said he wanted to keep us updated."

Manar's frown eased. "Did he mention why he did it?" he asked, staring at her intensely. He must have thought DJ had said something that had disturbed her.

"He sounded like he was in a rush," Ndidi replied, shaking her head.

Manar nodded, easily accepting the explanation. Ndidi bit her bottom lip and considered telling him the truth then and there. But when she opened her mouth, nothing came out. She turned away and tried to remember what they had been doing before DJ had called.

It clicked a second later. Manar had suggested that Ndidi give him a tour of the Okafor Corporation. She'd jumped at the chance because she'd always felt bad, leaving him in the room every day when she left. Manar had assured her he was never bored since he was working on a project that kept him busy. Ndidi had never actually seen him working on it, however, so his assurances didn't stop her from feeling bad.

Manar had teased her about the building when they'd first arrived weeks back, so Ndidi had been as thorough as her dad when she gave Manar a full tour.

She'd hoped that, several hours in, Manar would begin to get tired and acquire an appreciation for how large the building was. But that plan had failed spectacularly. Several hours later, Manar was still as interested in everything as he had been at the beginning of it. He hadn't even broken a sweat from the walking, which was honestly most surprising since Ndidi hadn't known the man to work out a day in his life.

Eventually, Ndidi had to throw out her original plan and focus only on the most important locations so they could be done before the end of the day. They'd already gone through some of the satellite buildings that held some of the corporation's factories and machines. She'd been taking him through the labs when DJ's call had come in. At the rate they were going, they might not even get through half of the campus before the end of the day.

So what though? Ndidi shook her head. The tour was simply a way to spend some quality time with Manar. It didn't really matter if they couldn't get there anyway. Worst-case scenario, they could pick up the next day from wherever they stopped. With that comfort, she directed him to labs and described what the rooms were for, aiming to be as quiet and as unobtrusive as possible when moving around.

Manar looked at most rooms with passing interest. Others he seemed invested in, leading to several minutes of back-and-forth as Manar asked questions and Ndidi described the work done there. She enjoyed seeing Manar's excitement on full display. She even started to look forward to seeking out rooms she thought would excite him.

"What are all these?" Manar asked several rooms later, pointing to equipment at the back of the lab. They were covered in a light layer of dust, with a piece of tarp hanging from the side where someone had haphazardly tried to cover them.

"This used to be the Cloneys' old lab," Ndidi explained. The lab had been repurposed for another project at some point, though the researchers weren't around for some reason. "I'm actually surprised all that hasn't been put in storage after all these years. It's not like anyone can operate it."

Manar crossed the room, staring intensely at the machines. "This is what was used to develop the picospores?"

Ndidi shook her head. "Not … exactly. By the time they worked here, the technology was still in its early stages. They *did* use the machines, but the technology eventually outgrew the machines."

"Outgrew?"

"The first picospores needed a lot of energy to work," she replied. "I mean, the final versions still do, but the initial prototypes were much worse—and a massive headache to finance. My dad always complained about them." She chuckled, nodding at the equipment. "These were custom-made for the spores, but even they struggled to keep up with the load. So we built better ones."

"If they were such a headache, why didn't your father just drop the project?"

"Because he saw something in them," Ndidi said softly. "I wasn't there when Hermione's father first pitched the idea." She shook her head, her gaze distant. "My dad was on it immediately. He didn't care about the cost, or even how much such a technology would make the company. He just saw what it could be used to do—and the people it could help. Everything else was secondary to him."

"He sounds like a good man," Manar said, matching her tone.

Ndidi nodded. "He was the best." For a moment, she lost herself in her thoughts as memories of her father flashed before her eyes.

"Do they work?" Manar asked suddenly.

Ndidi blinked. "Come again?"

He tapped the machines, creating a ringing sound. "Do they still work?" Ndidi nodded, confused. He continued. "Wouldn't it have been better to just upgrade these ones instead of building others from scratch?"

Ndidi chuckled, finally understanding what he was getting at. "I see your point, but no. Cloney thought the same thing, but these machines were designed for an initial concept of the spores. Later picospore designs were different enough that a full rebuild made more sense."

Manar looked skeptical.

Ndidi chuckled again. "Come on," she said. "It's easier to just show you."

A few minutes later, Ndidi and Manar were in another part of the building, standing in the middle of a laboratory that had been abandoned for several years. A light layer of dust covered the surfaces, including several machines that were arranged like the ones in Hermione's Sparta lab. Ndidi pointed to a few of them. "See the difference?"

Manar nodded absently. He walked between the machines, running his hands along them as if he could learn something from touching them. Some of them he spent more time on, even blowing away the dust in one case. Ndidi watched silently. She was happy to see him so interested in something, though something about the whole scene felt odd. Ndidi just couldn't put her finger on why.

"All of these work, right?" he asked.

"They haven't been used in years, so they probably need to be serviced. But apart from that, they should be able to work, yeah. Why do you keep asking that?"

Manar turned and met her eyes. "Because you should start producing pico-spores again."

CHAPTER

22

NOVEMBER 2043
SPARTA HEADQUARTERS,
NEW YORK

DJ PACED AT THE FRONT of the conference table. "What do we know about Tyra Chityothin?"

"We know her name." Christy yawned from her spot at the table, her head was propped up by her hand. She stared at DJ with half-lidded eyes. How could she already be bored when they'd just started?

"Valuable input, Christy," he said, his lips pressed into a line. She gave him a mock salute. "Anyone else?"

CJ gingerly raised a hand and DJ almost face-palmed. "We … um … we know where she was when … uh … when she hacked into Debi's phone."

"We can cross that out," he said dismissively. "She probably noticed when you started tracing the signal back to her, so there's no way she's still there."

"I think it's worth looking into," Hermione muttered from the other end of the table. She was slouched over the table, her eyes heavy with exhaustion. Her lab coat was wrinkled and stained, and her hair, usually tied back in a neat bun, cascaded around her shoulders in disarray.

When was the last time she slept? DJ thought. *Or took a shower?*

"She was probably in a rush when she left. Maybe she left something that could help us."

"You could be right," DJ said, pointing at her with a pencil, "if you weren't so wrong."

Hermione rubbed her eyes.

"Helene chose her for a reason," Christy explained. "This means that she has to be halfway competent."

"*Christy is correct.*" Olsen's voice rumbled through the conference call mic. "*Tyra Chityothin is more than just a random goon Helene picked from the street. Before her abduction during Mayday—where her trail ends—she occupied a high-ranking position in GeneTech. She worked and specialized in cybersecurity and AI development, with a specific focus on social engineering. There were also rumors that she was involved in genetic manipulation, but we haven't been able to dig up anything concrete yet.*"

CJ tensed, and Hermione sat up straight, looking wide awake for the first time. Only DJ and Christy still had blank expressions. "Anyone care to translate?" DJ asked when no one offered.

"*It means,*" Olsen growled, "*that Miss Chityothin was actively involved in securing computer networks against cyberthreats. And she did this by developing AI technologies similar to Helene, as well as exploiting human psychology for security purposes.*"

"And the stuff about genetic manipulation?" Christy asked.

"*Nowadays every corporation is working on genetic manipulation,*" Olsen said. "*It's possible that Miss Chityothin brushed against the field, especially considering the position that she held. That might have been what gave birth to the rumors, but like I said, we haven't found anything concrete yet. It would be counterproductive to jump at shadows that might not exist.*"

"It depends on how bad these shadows are though, right?" DJ said. "How bad are we talking here? Minus the genetic manipulation stuff, how much shit are we in?"

"It's not really something we can measure, DJ," Hermione answered. "But it does mean that, at a basic level, Tyra is incredibly smart, analytical, and adept at strategic planning."

"Plus," Christy said, "if she was really into genetic manipulation, then she wouldn't have a problem with morals or ethics."

CJ spoke up. "And … um … even before her abduction, she would have been used to working with artificial intelligence. This means that … uh … there would be no conflict with Helene that we might have exploited."

"Damn!" DJ said, blowing out a breath. "It sounds like Helene couldn't have picked a better henchwoman if she'd tried."

The intercom crackled. "*That's truer than you realize, son,*" Olsen said. "*There have been reports that, before her abduction, Tyra showed signs of mental instability. In fact, according to her previous coworkers—those we were able to get in touch with—the company had ordered her to several meetings with a psychologist, all of which she missed. She was about to be laid off when Mayday happened.*"

"Let me see if I have this right," DJ said. He raised a finger, beginning to count. "We're dealing with a cybersecurity expert, which means we probably won't be able to spy on her without her noticing." Raising another finger, he continued, "And even if we do decide to take that risk, she's so incredibly smart that she'd probably use the information we get against us and set a trap that'll screw us over." He raised a third finger. "Plus, she's used to working with AI, so she and Helene are probably on the same wavelength. This is without considering the picospores, which basically makes her a puppet of the AI." He raised a fourth finger. "And because that isn't enough, she's probably mental enough to not have any moral qualms with dooming the human race just for shits and giggles."

He looked around the table. "Is that right? Did I get it all?"

"Yeah, pretty much," Christy replied after considering it momentarily.

"If you're both done," Hermione said, glaring at both DJ and Christy, "where do we go from here?"

No one said anything for a moment—even Olsen, which DJ found surprising. He expected the old man to take this opportunity to unveil a nugget of wisdom that would both provide a path and insult DJ at the same time.

"*DJ,*" Olsen said, "*This is your mission, son, and your teammate has asked you a question. What's your plan?*"

DJ glared at the speaker. *Are you kidding me? You're using* this *as a training moment. Really? Of all the bullshit …*

DJ blew out a breath. Fortunately, he did have a plan, so he wasn't totally caught with his pants down.

That didn't mean it hadn't been a dick move though.

Every eye was on him, so DJ pushed down his annoyance. "Hermione," he started, "you said you were able to gain a measure of control over the spores you managed to extract? Is it possible to trace their signal back to its source?"

Hermione frowned. "Theoretically it might be possible, but how would that help us get Tyra? Wouldn't it be better to put our efforts into finding her?"

DJ shook his head. He turned to his brother instead of answering her. "CJ, how long did it take you to trace Tyra's hack? And how would you rate her skills based on that?"

"It took … uh … multiple days of several of my programs working concurrently to triangulate her location. Not … um … not a long list of people can do that." His brother wasn't boasting when he said that. It was simply a fact. DJ didn't understand most of it when he tried to explain, but CJ had reached a whole new level of skill after returning from the Virtual Realm.

DJ faced Hermione again. "Well, there you have it," he said, gesturing at his brother.

"There you have what?" Hermione asked, confused. "Was there supposed to be a point in that?"

"I swear to God, D, if you don't take this seriously …" Christy added, leaning over the table toward him.

DJ sighed. He knew he was being a dick. But he was tired and he was frustrated. He needed to vent. But this wasn't the right way to do it. Everyone was just as tired and just as frustrated. It didn't make sense for him to make it worse just because he was irritated. Maybe he could head to the gym and spar to work out his frustrations.

"I'm sorry, Hermione," he said after a moment, rubbing his eyes. "What I meant was that, if it took my brother so much time and effort to perform what should have been a relatively simple trace from Debi's phone, then Tyra Chityothin can probably counter him to some extent. We *could* find her if we put our minds to it, but it would be better to make her come to us."

"And how do you plan on doing that?" Christy asked.

"By forcing her to defend something that neither she nor Helene can risk losing," Hermione answered in his place. She stared at DJ with wide eyes as she realized what he intended. "You want to attack the picospore production facility."

DJ gave a sharp nod.

THE ENTIRE ROOM WENT SILENT, which was a better reaction than DJ had predicted. He'd expected most of them to immediately protest. The fact that they didn't, suggested that no one had any other ideas, not even Olsen.

That was worrisome, especially since attacking the spore production facility was a half-cocked idea he'd thought of while trying to fight off sleep during the drive back from Washington. He hadn't worked out any of the details. In fact, he hadn't been sure the idea was even feasible. Only Hermione would know, but first she'd have to come out of her shock.

CJ was the first to speak up. "How … uh … did you come up with the idea?"

"Before we left for Washington, Hermione mentioned that she'd figured out a way to hack into the picospores without them self-destructing like they did every other time that we'd tried," DJ explained. "That means she could access the spores' history and read through the command that Helene—or maybe Chityothin, depending—programmed into them."

That brought an outcry from CJ and Olsen. They immediately realized the potential of that discovery. Both started throwing questions at Hermione, who looked taken aback by the attention. She threw accusatory glances at DJ, making him realize that he probably could have broken the news of the discovery in a better way. However, Hermione's fatigue seemed to retreat slightly as she answered the questions. This told him that she didn't strictly mind the attention.

He rolled his eyes at that.

"Anyway," he said when he recognized the impromptu interview wasn't going to end anytime soon. Fortunately, his tone was enough to make both Olsen and CJ realize that that was probably not the right time for their questions and they fell silent. "This got me thinking: If we had even a bit of control over the spores, then we might be able to trace their signals back to where they were programmed."

"Is that even possible?" Christy asked.

"I don't know." DJ shrugged. He turned to Hermione. "Is it?"

Hermione returned his stare as she considered the question. "Theoretically, it *might* be possible. But it would probably require far more than the peripheral control I have over the spores right now. But DJ"—she gave him a helpless look—"hacking … tracing back signals—that's outside of my specialty. I was only able to achieve this much because Helene's versions of the spores are still somewhat similar to my father's original version, even if on a significantly higher level. I was able to determine enough similarities to provide a direction for my analysis. But I've reached my limit with that."

Her voice had gone softer, and tears welled up in her eyes. That admission had obviously been difficult for her, but she clearly didn't want to give the team false hope. It was admirable. DJ felt guilty for putting her in that position. But at least now he knew that his idea wasn't feasible. They'd have to think about something—

"Um … I could help," CJ said. Everyone turned to him, and he wilted under the attention. But only for a second. DJ watched as CJ forced himself to meet all of their eyes before continuing. "Hermione's … uh … specialty might not be in programming, but … um … mine is. And … uh … apart from Manar, I am probably the most knowledgeable person in the world about Helene's programming."

DJ grinned. He was used to such confidence from his brother while they were alone, but CJ had always been uncomfortable in the spotlight. He tended to undersell himself in the presence of others unless DJ forced him to speak up. But this time he'd done it on his own, which was huge in ways that words couldn't properly explain.

Guess he couldn't spend all that time with Manar in the Virtual Realm without something rubbing off the arrogant bastard.

DJ wanted to rush over and grab his brother, but he knew that would only embarrass him. He limited himself to leaning over for a fist bump. "All right then," he said, clapping his hands. "Hermione and my brother will track the spores back to their source. And when they do … we raid!"

"We're still not sure it's poss—" Hermione started.

"We would have to … um … have to test …" CJ protested.

But DJ wasn't listening at that point. His mind was already planning how they were going to storm what was definitely a heavily defended facility with only two combat-trained members and an old man.

DJ could think of only one option and it made him sigh. *I guess I've put it off long enough,* he thought.

CHAPTER

23

NOVEMBER 2043
OKAFOR CORPORATION,
ABUJA, NIGERIA

"RESTART THE PRODUCTION of the picospores?" Ndidi recoiled.

"I know," Manar said, taking a step toward her, his eyes never leaving hers and his hands raised halfway up in a gesture of peace. "You're revolted. You're disgusted at the thought after everything that Helene has used the picospores for. I know that you're going to say that it was a stupid idea for me to have suggested it, to have said it out loud, even as a joke—especially as a joke. You're probably going to insult me—not out loud, of course, but in your head—for even thinking about it. I understand all of that." He put her hands in his.

Ndidi wanted to pull away or push him away. But she let him hold her.

"I understand why every part of you would reject it. Helene has used the picospores to do terrible things to a lot of people, and you've been there to witness all of those atrocities—especially with Bethany. Anyone in your shoes would react the same way. But Helene is *dead*, Ndidi."

"Manar—"

"Listen to me," Manar said, piercing her with his gaze. Under the light, his eyes took on a golden luster that rooted her to the spot. "Helene is dead," he repeated softly. "I don't know what DJ told you, but I saw her corpse with my own eyes. I even dismantled her code so CJ and I could return. She's *dead*."

Manar's words washed over her like a tsunami. There wasn't a shred of doubt in his tone. He was fully confident in himself. But then again, Manar was always confident. That complete self-assurance was one of the things that had drawn her to him in the first place. It still drew her to him, years later.

"Hermione and her father created something beautiful with the picospores," Manar continued, speaking softly. "Helene subverted their purpose, but that doesn't mean that the spores themselves were the problem. Now that Helene is gone, they can be used for their original purpose: to transform billions of lives. It won't change the things that Helene did with the spores, but it would be a step in the right direction, wouldn't it?"

Ndidi's mind flashed to every moment she'd witnessed a Dead Eye being controlled by Helene. She remembered the first moments she'd been kidnapped, when Bethany and the other hostages had marched like robots unable to control their own bodies, their own *minds,* all because of Helene's control. She pictured the isolation chamber back at Sparta that held dozens of people whose minds had been broken by the picospore extraction. She pictured Bethany, who was so traumatized that, despite knowing the danger, had taken the risk to remove the spores from her body because she couldn't bear having them in her.

But that's just one side of it, isn't it? Ndidi thought.

Her mind went back several decades to when she was a child, watching her father and Dr. Cloney talking about the potential of the spores and their potential applications for the world in general. She remembered Dr. Cloney and a younger Hermione working on the project together late in the night, all to make their vision come true. Ndidi hadn't been there for most of the process, but she knew how much the picospore technology had meant to Dr. Cloney.

Finally, Ndidi pictured her children at the Okafor Centre. She'd invested most of her adult life in trying to help individuals of all ages on the autism spectrum. With Bethany, Helene had already proven for a fact that the picospores could cure them permanently. And it wasn't only autism. The picospores could help hundreds of millions of people suffering from mental conditions all over the world. It would revolutionize medicine entirely.

She focused once more on Manar. His eyes had never left hers. He hadn't spoken, allowing her to work through her thoughts. Ndidi knew she'd already been swayed, and in no small part because of the person who had suggested the idea. If it had been anyone else, she didn't know how she would have acted. But it hadn't been anyone else.

It had been Manar, and Ndidi found that she agreed with him.

Her father had believed in the potential of the picospores. He'd been willing to pay any price to see it succeed, just because of the good that it could do. Of course, Ndidi had had a vastly different experience with the technology. But why should she let that stop her? Because of a threat that no longer existed?

"You're right," she murmured finally. "Helene is gone. We shouldn't let the fear of her limit our actions."

"Exactly," Manar said, pulling her closer. "Although the last few years have been traumatic for all of us, we can't keep living in the past. We have to move forward. More to the point, we have to start undoing the destruction Helene caused." The excitement in his eyes dimmed slightly when he said that, and Ndidi's heart broke. When was he going to stop blaming himself for Helene?

"You're right," she said to pull him out of his thoughts. "But how are we going to do that?"

"You've mentioned several times that you've been having problems winning the respect of the board of directors, right? They don't trust that you'd be able to lead the company successfully and grow it?" he asked. Ndidi nodded. "Well, if you restart picospore production here and launch it as a branch of the company … " he trailed off.

But Ndidi immediately understood, and her eyes widened as she carried the thought to its end. "Even if we sell them at a discounted price, we would still make *billions* while still helping those who need it."

Manar grinned. "I'm betting that you won't have much problem with the directors after that."

Ndidi started to join him. Then something occurred to her. "There's only one problem though," she said. "Hermione is the only one who can produce the spores."

Manar leaned in and kissed her softly. "I've studied Hermione's notes extensively since she started working at Sparta," he said, full of confidence. "I'm sure that I can recreate the technology."

He was piercing her with his eyes. "All I need are your resources."

CHAPTER

24

NOVEMBER 2043
SPARTA HEADQUARTERS,
NEW YORK

HERMIONE SHUFFLED OUT of the conference room and to the elevator after the meeting. CJ followed behind her, but he didn't say anything. Hermione wasn't present enough to hold a conversation, so they walked in silence.

A part of her was angry at DJ for forcing her to admit that she'd hit a wall in researching the picospores. But he hadn't really forced her, had he? He'd asked her a question because he'd needed to know whether his plan was feasible. Hermione had decided to come clean. Despite how exposed she'd felt at that moment, she still stood by her decision. It was better that she knew her limits instead of promising a miracle she couldn't live up to.

And it would have been a miracle to do what DJ wanted, at least if Hermione had been working on it alone. Helene's version of the picospores was leagues beyond what Hermione and her father had originally designed. It was above anything Hermione had thought was even possible.

The AI had taken what should have been a relatively straightforward technology aimed at supporting the immune system in fighting infections and made it something that could affect the body both chemically and neurologically. She used it to control her victims *genetically.*

That was a level that Hermione couldn't even begin to grasp. She'd tried. Hermione chuckled dryly. Oh, she'd tried. But the only progress she'd made over the last few weeks was in pulling her hair out. She'd given up, then had to admit it during the meeting. Now she was going to have to get back into it.

Hermione sighed and glanced at CJ out of the corner of her eye. She had to admit that her task might not be so impossible with his help. DJ's plan required the help of a programmer, and from what she'd heard, CJ was one of the most talented ones around. Even better, the months he'd spent in the Virtual Realm must have given him insights that would be invaluable.

Their success, though, would depend on how much of the picospore technology he could grasp. *But that's not going to be today*, Hermione thought. She was in no shape to begin what would probably be another few weeks of torture. Her eyes could barely stay open as it was, and even she avoided taking deep breaths because of her smell.

She needed a hot shower and a nap on a surface that wasn't a lab bench. Only after she would step into her lab. She told CJ as much. He nodded without a word. They agreed to meet the next day to start. Hermione went off to her room, already thinking of what bath soaps she'd use.

HERMIONE TOOK CJ FOR A TOUR around the lab—at least, as much as she could, considering the entire space was about nine hundred square feet. It was functional and large enough to contain all of her equipment. But there wasn't much leg room, especially for two people.

They made it work. Within a few minutes, Hermione had breezed through the standard equipment—the ones that would probably be found in any lab. After that, she moved on to those specialized to the picospores.

"That's the spore extraction tank," she said, gesturing to the large tank at the back of the room, after noticing CJ's gaze on it for the third time. "The most recent version, at least." She tapped it twice, producing a metallic *clang*. "Take a good look. We're going to be working with it a lot."

CJ made his way to the machine while Hermione stared. Orange liquid filled the inside of the tank to keep the spores from degrading.

"What do you mean by … um … recent?" CJ asked.

"It's the most recent version of the tank, made specifically to hold Helene's latest version of the picospores." CJ turned to her. Nothing about his expression showed it, but Hermione could feel the confusion flowing off him.

"There have been several different versions of the spores over the years," she explained. "The first were the ones my dad and I designed." She pointed toward the other end of the room where a smaller tank leaned against the wall. "Helene took that version and upgraded it into the ones you guys first encountered." She gestured to another tank beside the first. "*That* version took over the victim's minds completely, killing their personalities so thoroughly that they became little more than robots."

Hermione tucked her hair behind her ear. "That characteristic made them easily recognizable as puppets. When we exploited that, Helene upgraded the spores once more to make the Dead Eyes." She pointed to another tank. "That version reduced the robot-like behaviors into something more manageable. However, it also left them with distinctively lifeless eyes, which we exploited once again.

"She's upgraded it several times after that, improving on something every time," Hermione continued. CJ listened silently, following her finger every time she gestured at another tank. "Sometimes it was in reaction to a feature we exploited, but other times, it was just to improve on the design and make it better. She's done this for years. Until the latest version," Hermione said, gesturing toward the tank. She sighed, suddenly feeling tired once more. "These are the spores taken from the hostages from the underground factory. As far as I've been able to determine, they're Helene's upgraded version of the spores."

CJ hadn't said anything for a while. Hermione wondered if he felt the same helplessness she did. It was difficult not to feel a sense of impotence when looking at the tanks. It had taken her and her father over a decade to design and create the original version of the spores, but Helene churned out a new version every few months. Depressing.

"You … um … you have studied all of these?" CJ said finally, gesturing to the different tanks.

Hermione shrugged. "They were easy to study at the beginning. The upgrades were relatively straightforward. Eventually, though, the gaps between them became so big that their designs were almost completely unrecognizable from the original version. That's where I'm at right now."

"You … uh … mentioned that you have managed to read and hack into the spores. How?"

Hermione led him to one of the lab desks where she'd set up her laptop. The device was connected to a miniature version of the tank. It held a few million spores—a sample for easier to study. Hermione gestured to the computer screen displaying a bunch of readings.

She understood part of it. Others were pure gibberish to her. She glanced at CJ, about to ask if he'd had more luck, but the look in his eyes, roving about the screen like he was reading a novel, made the question moot.

Huh, Hermione thought, *we might actually be able to do this.*

DJ FOUND THE MURDER TEAM, sans Karla, in the warehouse training area. Liz sat crossed-legged in the corner of the room, while José and Chloe were at the center in the middle of a conversation. Rather, José was speaking while Chloe listened, slowly running a rag over her gun. She didn't frown. Nothing in her body language expressed frustration about being lectured, but DJ could feel an almost palpable sense of danger radiating off her. It was like he was standing next to a bomb about to go off.

None of them had turned at his entrance. They knew he was there. They just didn't care, which didn't bode well.

Maybe I should have waited a bit more before coming here, DJ thought. But that ship had already sailed. He felt that if he turned back, he'd be immediately cut down. So he did the opposite and took a step forward.

"I wasn't sure you guys would still be here."

"Unfortunately, we cannot help you today, DJ," José said, not looking up.

"Yeah. You guys look real busy," DJ drawled. "I just thought I should update you. Apparently, we were wrong. Helene isn't actually dead." Chloe stopped cleaning her gun, Liz opened her eyes, and José turned to meet him. Tension built within the room. DJ almost took a step back under the weight of their attention. "I figured that you guys would want to know."

Chloe stood in one smooth motion and crossed the room until she was all up in his face. "Explain. Now."

DJ did. That was the whole point of his coming anyway. He needed more combat-ready people for when they raided the spore production facility. But the Murder Team would never join him out of the goodness of their hearts. They had to believe it was in their best interests. Fortunately for DJ, helping him stop Helene *was* in their best interest. He skimmed over the part with Albert and Debi and focused more on Tyra Chityothin. He was about to get to the part about the White House when José stood.

"Enough," the man said. Despite his large size, he moved with the same grace as Chloe.

"We should hear him out, José," Chloe said, glancing back at him.

"What is there to listen about?" José questioned, striding toward him. Liz also stood and made her way over. Pretty soon, the three of them stood in a half circle around DJ. While none of them showed the slightest hostility, José stared down at him like a lion looking at a deer. DJ didn't like that. "He obviously seeks to draw us to his cause, but we have already spoken on this matter. We will no longer involve ourselves in matters involving the AI."

"That was when we thought that Helene was dead and the only thing left was to clean up her mess," Chloe countered. "DJ's story changes that."

"I also doubt you'd have much choice in whether or not you're involved," DJ added.

José stared at Chloe. "His story changes nothing. We will defend ourselves if necessary, but we are not going to involve ourselves with the AI. I will no longer hear of this." He held Chloe's gaze for a moment, as if daring her to protest. Then he turned around and started to walk back.

That was it? He'd spoken, and so it was done? Just like that?

Chloe stared at his retreating figure, but she didn't say anything. Neither did Liz. In fact, Liz's expression hadn't changed throughout the conversation, although that was to be expected. DJ had noticed Liz's near worship of her father. He suspected that was part of why Karla had left. But Chloe? The brunette obviously disagreed with José, but she hadn't even tried to fight.

What the hell was that?

And why was José so against this anyway? DJ hadn't tried to hide the fact that he needed them. He wasn't good with subtlety anyway. But it didn't take a genius to know that with or without DJ, Helene wasn't just going to leave their family alone. No one, not even an AI, likes to see their investment wither and go to waste.

"Karla was right," DJ found himself saying. "You really have become Helene's dog."

José stopped.

Whelp, I've done it this time. DJ grimaced, though he didn't let it show on his face. *CJ always said my mouth was going to be the death of me. But damn! That had been fun to say.*

DJ had never liked José. The man had always been a dick, except for that moment when he'd sacrificed himself to save his daughters. That had earned him a bit of respect in DJ's eyes. When José had come back as a cyborg, it'd earned him a bit of pity. No one deserved to live like that. Both of those feelings had disappeared when DJ saw how the giant handled parenting. Right now? It slid into negative.

Still, none of that explained why DJ had insulted him. He was blunt, sure, and he'd always had a low tolerance for dicks. But he rarely went out of his way to be deliberately provocative.

Then DJ recognized it: He was *pissed*. But why? He'd known he had a fifty-fifty chance of enlisting the Murder Team, and José's initial refusal had been expected. That wasn't what had pissed DJ off. It was the *way* the man had refused. He'd completely shut down Chloe—a veritable psycho, sure, but also one of the most headstrong women that DJ knew. The man had tamed her so completely that he'd taken for granted the fact that she would listen to his orders as if they were law. And for what? Because he was scared?

That rubbed him the wrong way, sure, but it didn't really explain why he was so angry. His blood was boiling, pushing him to do *something*. It wasn't the first time DJ had experienced this—and he'd learned long ago how to handle it.

But why was he reacting so strongly this time?

DJ couldn't figure it out. He didn't have much time to think about it anyway because José turned and strode back until he towered over him. Chloe took a step to stand beside DJ as if to protect him. That didn't go unnoticed by José. Surprisingly enough, the Terminator remake didn't seem angry. Instead, he sighed. "You call me Helene's dog because I have no wish to involve myself or my family in a pointless battle?"

"How's it pointless? She's trying to take over the world, man."

"And how has your defiance done anything to change that?" José asked. He'd spoken softly, but his size made every word sound as if it'd come from a speaker. "You have fought against the AI for years. Where has that gotten you? How many times has she outsmarted you and trapped you? How many times have you thought that you'd defeated her to have discovered you were wrong? How much have you lost in the process?"

DJ wanted to refute him, but unbidden, he thought of Kyle and Christy. Neither of them was dead. Nevertheless, he'd lost Kyle as a teammate and brother when he'd left the navy base, and Christy's insistence on following him out had cost her a once-promising career. CJ also popped in his head. DJ felt guilty, but it was true, wasn't it? His brother hadn't really been the same after coming back from the Virtual Realm. There was a distance between them that hadn't been there before.

"Do you realize it now?" José asked. "I have lost my body and one of my daughters. I will lose no more in this pointless battle."

"Helene didn't take your daughter," DJ retorted. "She left because you are a coward and a shitty dad."

José's eyes widened. Suddenly, DJ went flying. He crashed into a pile of boxes several feet away, splintering them. His chest hurt. However, it hadn't been broken, which told him that José had been holding back. DJ lay there for a moment while rage burned through his veins. He felt the now-familiar rush of power as his nanites activated.

"Why are you even listening to him, José?" Chloe asked. "You know it's the nanites messing with his hormones."

Well, that solves that mystery, DJ thought. He raised his head at the sounds of footsteps approaching him. Instantly, he was back on his feet. José looked down at him. Once again, DJ's blood thudded in his ears, urging him to move. DJ pushed down the impulse, but not too far.

"First my daughter, and now you," José said, glaring at him. "I must have been gone for too long if people believe they can disrespect me in such a way. What gives you such confidence?" He leaned, getting all up in DJ's face. "An ant enhanced by all the nanites in the world is still an ant."

DJ smirked. "How much do you want to bet that this ant can knock you on your Terminator ass?"

Chloe pinched the bridge of her nose as José roared with laughter. It didn't sound fake—José genuinely found the thought of DJ beating him hilarious. But why wouldn't he? DJ was talking out of his ass.

"You have done a great service for my family," José said when he regained his composure. "Chloe seems to have taken a liking to you. For these reasons, I will not kill you." His presence filled the room, heavy with authority. "I offered to train you once, something that would have helped you take control of the nanites you have stolen. You refused. Yet I will teach you a lesson while still giving you a chance to fulfill your mission here."

"What're you talking about?"

"Land just one punch on me," José said, "and my family and I will join your cause."

CHAPTER

26

NDIDI'S HEELS CLICKED on the hallway's tile floor. The noise annoyed her, but she'd gone for a ruffled blouse and pencil skirt today. Flat shoes wouldn't have paired well with that—plus Manar loved it when she wore heels.

Today was for him.

It had taken a couple of meetings to get the board of directors to agree to the picospore production. That was only after she'd shown them videos of Hermione's experiments and her report about its potential, using Bethany as a case study. The fact that they'd taken Hermione's words over hers didn't bode well and proved that Manar had been right: Using her father's name and authority to win back the company wouldn't work. The board had respected her father because he'd earned that respect. Ndidi would have to do the same, and the picospores were the answer.

The lab was a hive of activity. Manar stood in the middle of it, directing everyone. For the most part, they were reusing the same equipment that Hermione and her father had used. A few, however, had new designs and needed to be built from scratch. Approving each one provoked a minor battle with the board, but Ndidi had convinced them, and now they were being installed.

Manar grinned at her. He started coming over, but something called his attention. "Hey! Be careful with that, would you? That costs more than every organ in your body put together. If you damage it, even selling you wouldn't recoup our losses. And you—" He turned to another technician. "Do you want to kill us all? If you didn't know how to install it, you should have said so."

Ndidi strolled to his side. "Problem?"

"It's my fault." He sighed. "I told them that my team at Sparta was incompetent, and they took it as a personal challenge." He gestured around the room. "So far we've had four pieces of equipment nearly broken, two that were improperly installed and would have exploded the first time I tried to use them, and five that were the wrong machines altogether. There's another lab above us that's just been commissioned, so the workers keep bringing equipment meant for them to us. I've had to redirect three of them in the last five minutes alone."

Ndidi chuckled, trying only a little to cover it up.

"No, please. Laugh at my pain," Manar said, though his eyes twinkled in amusement. He hadn't stopped moving but paused to whisper something to a technician. "But is it really wise to mock? You know I'm doing this for you, right?"

Ndidi started to smile, but she suppressed it. If she made it so easy for him, it'd go right to his head. "Really?" she asked instead. "And here I thought it was because you were bored and needed a new project to occupy that great big head of yours."

"Bored? I have plenty to occupy me."

Ndidi finally allowed her grin to come out. "Like what?"

Manar finally stopped and stared down at her. That was when Ndidi noticed they were at one of the corners of the room, the only one that wasn't lost in a flood of activity. Ndidi's back was to the wall. Manar was in front of her, blocking her view of the room—more importantly, blocking the room from her.

The reason for that became apparent when his hands landed on her ass, groping it firmly. Ndidi almost squealed. But Manar had already claimed her lips.

Ndidi melted into the kiss. However, a part of her couldn't help but feel surprised. Granted, it had been years since their breakup. But public display of affection had never been Manar's style. Yet here they were, making out like a couple of teenagers who couldn't keep their hands off each other.

Ndidi wasn't complaining. She allowed herself to get lost in the kiss before gently pushing Manar away. She wasn't against PDA, but making out in front of a lab full of people wasn't the best idea. If word spread, it'd just give the board of directors more ammunition against her.

Manar broke away, staring at her with a hunger that sent a shiver down her spine. He was panting slightly, and she was too. His eyes had a golden sheen, and Ndidi felt her body responding to his gaze. He looked like he was a step away from ravishing her, like he would have taken her right there and then if she hadn't stopped him.

She raised a hand to pull him back. Suddenly, he closed his eyes. The spell was broken. "Must be the hormones," she heard him mutter as he struggled to get his breathing under control.

"Hormones?" Ndidi asked, ducking under his arm so that she faced the room. "Have you been taking pills?" She wouldn't be surprised. They'd taken full advantage of their vacation to make up for the years that they'd spent together. And despite the public groping, they weren't teenagers; Manar was well into his forties, so it wouldn't be a shock if he had needed some extra help.

Manar recoiled, his eyes snapping open. "Of course not," he said immediately. But his gaze avoided hers as he said it. That made her snort. Manar noticed her unconvinced look and sighed. "Look, it's nothing, okay? Don't worry about it."

"Well, there's no need to be touchy about it." Ndidi chuckled as her hand went to her belly. "You've already proven that you still have *something* in the tank."

His gaze dropped to her hand, and he couldn't help himself—his eyes brightened, and his grin broke through. He stepped toward her, as if drawn, then paused as he remembered where they were. But he didn't bother hiding his joy. They stood side by side, facing the chaos of the lab, yet his focus remained on her. For once, the pandemonium around them was just background noise, and she felt it, too. Undoubtedly, another problem would have come up while they'd been distracted. Manar didn't seem to care, and Ndidi didn't either.

"How long do you think before we start production?" she asked.

Manar bobbed his head from side to side as he deliberated. "Assuming by some miracle we finish setting up today … it shouldn't take more than two days before the first batch comes out. You should probably start working on your speech."

Ndidi stared up at him. "What speech?"

"Well, yeah," Manar said. "The picospores are a completely new technology, Ndidi. Most of the world doesn't know about them. You're going to be promising that it's the cure to all mental illnesses. You didn't consider that you'd need to persuade people of that?"

Damn, she thought. Ndidi had known about the picospores for years already and was intimately aware of the potential of the technology. She'd just assumed other people would understand when they were finally ready to launch.

She laughed, "Well, when you put it that way, it was stupid of me not to consider it."

"It's understandable," Manar shrugged. "You've been under a lot of pressure lately just convincing the board to agree to the idea."

"Yeah, you're right," Ndidi agreed. "But we can't say it's the cure to *all* mental illnesses."

"Why not?"

Ndidi chuckled again. "Because it's not?"

"But it is though." Manar frowned, meeting her amused gaze. His eyes twinkled as the overhead light reflected off them. "The picospores have the ability to permanently cure all mental illnesses—past, present, and future. It just depends on how they're used."

Ndidi thought about that. She considered it from every angle. She knew the picospores were capable of incredible things. Helene had proven beyond a shadow of a doubt that their capabilities were vast.

But still, *all* mental illnesses?

"It's fine if you don't agree," Manar said, once again reading her like a book. He'd gone back to scanning the room. Something about his gaze was distant, as if he wasn't fully present. "I probably didn't explain myself well. The current picospores can't do what I said. But they have the *potential*. All they need to do is to evolve."

"They can evolve by themselves?" Ndidi frowned.

"No, of course not. We'll have to upgrade them with each iteration," Manar replied. "And with just a bit of time, they'll be able to help everyone."

Ndidi faced the room. She didn't know what to say to that.

CHAPTER

27

NOVEMBER 2043
THE WAREHOUSE,
NEW YORK

JUST ONE PUNCH. DJ stood in the middle of the training ring, José at the other side talking with Chloe. Liz watched from the sidelines, completely disinterested. *I can land one punch.* The only hiccup though, was that he'd have to rely on the nanites to have even a fighting chance. That didn't sit right with him—especially now that he knew that the little devils were responsible for his recent anger issues. He didn't like the thought that anything could influence his emotions like that.

But the power-up isn't a joke. His run through the White House was still fresh in his head. He hadn't been able to see it then because he'd spent most of it either angry or worried that he was going to get jailed at the end of it, but when he reviewed those fights in his mind … he'd been pretty badass, hadn't he?

It still wasn't an equal trade for having his emotions messed with. But that was only temporary. At least he hoped to God it was. The only other people that DJ knew possessed nanites didn't really inspire him with confidence.

On the other side of the ring, José finally wrapped up his conversation. Chloe came beside Liz while the giant turned to face DJ. That was DJ's cue to unclamp his will from the rage he'd kept suppressed. It poured through him like liquid fire that burned a path for the surge of strength that followed.

In the mayhem of the White House, DJ hadn't had time to experience the enhancement fully. Physically, he was still exactly the same. His body was lighter than normal, and every hop took him just a bit higher than it normally would. Even with that, DJ could feel the power contained in his muscles, and he knew how much strength they held.

"Now that is a look that I have not seen in years," José commented. "Not since my daughters." That drew DJ back from his thoughts and forced him to focus. He could bask in the feeling later—assuming he didn't die in the next few minutes. "Are you ready?"

DJ had barely nodded before José was suddenly in his face.

The world slowed down, but it didn't affect José in the slightest. The giant's fist crashed down at him, as inevitable as death. The pressure seemed almost like a weapon that forced him to submit. His knees almost buckled. But DJ willed himself to remain on his feet. His mind screamed at him. But what could he do? He could barely follow the attack with his eyes, much less move away fast enough to evade it. He also couldn't take it head-on. Even with a block, the sheer power contained in that fist would pulverize his bones on contact.

In desperation, DJ's eyes flickered around the room. Chloe was mostly frozen. The brunette could still move, but far too slowly to be of any help. Liz's eyes were on him, but there was no hope there. The girl would watch her father kill him and then offer to clean his blood off José's knuckles. His eyes moved on, searching desperately. There was nothing. Nothing he could use. Nothing that could help him. He was going to die. There was nothing he could do to stop it.

A moment later, José's fist reached him—and missed by an inch.

He missed? DJ asked in his mind. The fist went over his shoulder and hit nothing. The giant body checked him as a follow-up, and DJ went flying. He felt the pain, but his mind wasn't there, even as he crashed into another pile of crates. He knew he would have died if those hands had touched him.

But José had missed.

He had missed. *Fuck that!* DJ shouted in his mind.

How was it possible that José had missed? In what world was that a thing? DJ would have had to be the biggest idiot to believe that the monster could have made a mistake during a fight. DJ would have died in their first exchange. José had obviously gone easy on him.

Why?

DJ lay in the middle of the broken boxes while he tried to answer that question. Was this the lesson he'd promised to teach DJ? That the gap in their power wasn't one that could be surmounted by DJ's nanites? Or was it that the man still felt like he owed DJ a chance at life because he'd helped out his family?

It could have been either, and it could have been both. But did it matter? José had proven in one second that there was no chance in hell DJ was going to get the Murder Team on board with taking down Tyra.

There was no point in continuing the fight. DJ would never win except if José allowed him. But the man had made his stance clear, and he didn't seem like the kind to change his mind.

DJ knew that. But Jesus Christ was he pissed. He'd known that he'd just been talking out of his ass. He'd never had a shot in hell of beating José. Everyone knew it. He wasn't even annoyed that José was so much stronger than him. It was an eye-opener for sure but nothing he hadn't expected. It was the *mocking* that got to him. José could have let DJ tire himself out trying to hit him. He could have knocked DJ out with a single punch or used any of hundreds of ways to prove his superiority.

However, he'd thrown an attack that had convinced DJ thoroughly that he was going to die—and then he'd pretended to *miss.*

It was bullshit.

It was the worst kind of bullshit.

DJ stood, ignoring the splinters that stuck to his clothes. When his thoughts sped up, only a few seconds had passed. He knew it was more than enough time for José to have killed him several times over. However, the man hadn't moved from his spot. He stood with his arms folded, staring down at DJ as if he were an ant.

DJ's nanites ignited at the thought, pushing him to move. This time, DJ didn't fight them.

He charged.

And ended up back in the crates. He'd had no doubt that would happen—the point had been to stand up. DJ couldn't explain it. He had to prove to himself that he could; otherwise, he'd feel that he'd lost something.

And so he stood up again. Several times, in fact. Eventually José learned that his feints wouldn't work, so he focused on knocking DJ down. But DJ always stood back up. He never got close to even touching José's titanium. It always seemed like he was two seconds behind. But he didn't give up. At least, not until José lost patience and finally knocked him out.

When DJ came to, Chloe was standing over him. She was smiling, but with a tension in her eyes that she either couldn't or didn't want to completely hide. "Sorry, champ," she said. "Tenacity is always good, but there are some battles that you can't win. You're going to have to do this one without us." She stretched out a hand, and DJ took it, pulling himself to his feet. Her lips pressed against his ear. "But you need to get stronger, DJ. You still owe me a favor."

She let him go. DJ wandered out of the warehouse. He'd lost, so he really had only one option left. He sent a text to Olsen on his way back to Sparta.

CHAPTER

28

"ANYTHING?" HERMIONE ASKED, peering through the transparent glass of the mini-tank. Only the overhead lights kept away the night—and they did so poorly since Hermione had two of them on. Hermione loved this time of the day, when everyone had gone home and the world was silent. The liquid in the mini-tank glowed from the lights above, making them look fit for a mad scientist's lab.

Hermione certainly looked the part of the mad scientist. She hadn't had a full night's sleep, and her eyes were swollen from rubbing away the tiredness. She'd given up on taming her hair days ago, each loose strand casting shadows in the light of the mysterious glowing fluid.

I really need to get some more sleep, she thought, stifling a yawn. The spores within the tank were dense enough to be seen with the naked eye, something

Hermione usually avoided doing. However, she'd poured all her knowledge about the picospores into CJ in the last couple of days. He'd immediately grasped enough of the theory to start proposing suggestions. The spores in the mini-tank, in fact, were one of his ideas that Hermione agreed had enough merit to try. His concept built on the discovery that picospores with the same programming shared a connection, similar to a hive mind. CJ figured that when enough of the spores were together, the connection would become dense enough to create an actual signal that could be tapped into. It was something that Hermione hadn't considered before, but the premise itself was sound enough to test.

"Hello?" Hermione said and stifled another yawn. CJ was set up on another bench, his face illuminated by the glare of the computer in front of him. He was reading something off the screen and typing in commands periodically. He never looked up or gave any indication that he'd heard her.

Jesus, she thought, *is that how I am when I'm immersed in something?*

Hermione straightened. As engrossed as he was, Hermione didn't think he would notice her if she'd danced around while holding church bells. But still, she tried to be as quiet as she could as walked to him and looked over his shoulder. Lines of code covered most of his screen. Hermione understood a small section of—the part she'd written to read the commands that had been given to the spores.

No. He has improved the method, Hermione thought as she read through. *Significantly.* Her method relied on programming, but she'd not learned much more than what applied to biological research. CJ, however, dealt with *pure* programming, manipulating codes in their raw form. Considering that, she shouldn't have been surprised that he had improved on it in so little time. However, it still wasn't a good feeling. She'd spent months devising that method.

Hermione scanned the other sections of the screen. Most of it was beyond her, but some parts of it stood out to her. Hermione's eyes widened.

She gasped. "It's working?" CJ flinched and spun around, his mouth open in surprise. A part of Hermione needed an answer to her question. "So?"

CJ hesitated. "It is … uh … still processing."

"But it's working?" Hermione pressed. CJ nodded, and Hermione couldn't suppress her grin. She pulled up a stool. "Explain it to me."

CJ swiveled his head from her expectant gaze to his computer and back again for a few seconds. He seemed to have been processing her request. Hermione tried to be patient.

A minute later, she was rewarded as CJ took a deep breath. "Your … um … your original method provided a way to … uh … to tap into the spores and gain partial control of them. That was how you were … um … were able to read the previous … uh … commands that they'd been given," he explained. This may have been the most Hermione had heard him say at any one time. He stuttered and paused often to remember a word or pronounce it, but eventually, Hermione stopped noticing those moments.

"However, in order … um … to trace their signal back to their source, I needed full control of the spores. That is where the first problem came from. I … um … could hack into an individual spore and gain control of it but, by itself, the signal … um … produced by the spore was too weak for me to trace it. That's … um … why I suggested that we put a bunch of them together. The solution worked. However, it … uh … brought about its own problem.

"You … um … already know that the spores, when grouped together, share a connection between them. However, what … uh … we did not know is that, in high enough numbers, their connection enabled them to detect and, more annoyingly, defend against any external invasion. Over the last few hours, I … um … spent most of my time trying to get a probe through their defenses. But … uh … they destroyed everything I tried." He shifted in his chair. "It's actually … um … amazing to see because they are acting completely autonomously, with no input from Helene or Tyra. It's almost … uh … a self-defense mechanism."

"So how did you solve it?" Hermione asked.

"I figured … um … that since I couldn't control all the spores at once, I should … uh … limit myself to what was feasible."

"You hacked into them in groups?"

"Exactly," CJ confirmed. "However, once I took control … um … of one group, their programming would force them to destroy themselves. In order for it … uh … to work, I had to erase their original commands first before using their connection to attack another group and … uh … so on."

He turned and pointed at a part of the screen. "I have automated the process, and that is what is currently processing. I simply … um … have to monitor their progress now."

Hermione blew out a breath. "That … that's amazing, CJ. I mean, I don't even know where to begin. I wasn't actually sure this was going to work, if I'm being honest. I mean, I've been trying for *months*. I guess that's what I get for trying to do everything by myself, right?" She chuckled. "What's that part over there?" She pointed to something on the screen.

CJ showed a panicked expression. "Uh … that is a side project. But it is irrelevant right now."

Hermione nodded absently, yawning. A progress bar showed the percentage of picospores converted, and it had barely budged in all the time they'd been talking. Not surprising—there were millions of picospores inside the mini-tank alone.

"How long is it going to take?" she asked.

CJ stared at the screen. "Several … um … hours, at least," he said. "After that, my trace should be able to follow their signal back. I cannot … uh … estimate a timeframe for that though."

"All right," Hermione said, blinking rapidly. "I can take over while you get some rest. I don't think you've slept since you came here. Just tell me what I need to do."

CJ tried to smile, but it came out more of a grimace. "It is a relatively … um … straightforward process, but I still need to be here just in case something goes wrong. This is … uh … the last part so I can rest once it's over." He hesitated briefly. "But it is definitely not something … uh … for you to lose sleep over."

Hermione stifled another yawn. "Are you sure?"

CJ nodded. "I will be … um … fine."

Hermione would have preferred to stay, but she would have to take him at his word. She could barely keep her eyes open. It was as if her body knew that there was no longer a need to be awake.

Hermione made her way back to her room. She was out the moment her head hit the pillow.

29

NOVEMBER 2043
OKAFOR CORPORATION,
ABUJA, NIGERIA

NDIDI TOOK A DEEP BREATH, and then another.

Why am I nervous? she thought, her fists clenched to stop their shaking. *I've been giving speeches since I was a teenager. Of course, those speeches didn't have so much at stake. They didn't determine my future and didn't have the possibility of changing the world forever.* She blew out a breath slowly.

"You really need to calm down." Manar chuckled, walking toward her. The press conference had been set up in the auditorium since it was the only place with any chance of holding the crowd they were expecting. Ndidi had invited every major news station in the country—even some from abroad. The pico-spores had the potential to change the world, so it was important that Ndidi get the right message out there. Some papers would inevitably twist the information.

But Ndidi didn't particularly care about that. She'd rely on the press agencies controlled by the Okafor Corporation to counter the lies. The important thing was that the message got out there. Her success rested on how well she could sell the spores and how effectively she could persuade billions of people all over the world to try a technology that they'd never heard of. They would probably never fully understand its danger.

"What makes you think that I'm nervous?" she asked, lifting her chin. Manar raised a brow. This made Ndidi blow out another breath. Her father had taught her how to hide her emotions when necessary.

However, Manar knew her well enough to see through the mask with just a glance, which annoyed her. "The question is: Why are you *not* nervous?" she said. "They are just as important to you. The spores are *your* project after all."

"The difference," Manar said, still smiling in his insufferable way, "is that *I* know that you'll do great."

Ndidi snorted but didn't say anything. Logically, she knew he was right. She'd worked with him to massage her talking points so laypeople could easily understand the technology and to put the spores in the best light. She also thought about possible questions the press might throw at her and had come up with answers for each of them. Basically, she'd prepped as much as she possibly could have.

But there was so much at stake.

It had taken her days to get the board to agree to a press conference. She'd had to lean on her father's name more times than she was comfortable with—and cashed in more favors than was probably safe. Everything was riding on the conference. If it flopped—

"You're doing it again." Manar sighed and flicked her forehead. "Listen! It's going to be fine. If we're being honest, it doesn't really matter what you say. As long as you explain its features, the spores will practically sell themselves. It's too revolutionary a technology for people not to be interested. Even if something *does* happen," he said, raising her chin, "I'll be right beside you."

"I don't need you to fight my battles for me, Manar," Ndidi murmured.

"I know you don't," he replied just as softly. "But like you said, the spores are my project, so their success is deeply important to me. If I step in, it'll be for my own sake, to preserve my investment."

Ndidi frowned slightly. *Investment?* She started to speak, but her eyes caught one of the staff gesturing toward her. A rush of nerves washed away all memories of what she had been going to ask.

"You're going to do great," Manar repeated. "And I'll be right by your side if you need me."

NOVEMBER 2043
HERMIONE'S LABORATORY,
SPARTA HEADQUARTERS,
NEW YORK

HERMIONE WOKE TO THE BLARING of her alarm. A glance at the time told her that she'd been asleep for only a couple of hours. Hermione stared at the ceiling. Sunrise was still hours away.

I could try to sleep some more, she thought even as she threw off her covers and stood. She knew herself too well. She *could* try to go back to sleep, but the damage had already been done. She was awake. Any attempt to sleep was bound to fail. At least now she could keep CJ company until his program was done. She'd felt guilty leaving him alone earlier, but she hadn't been able to keep her eyes open.

Hermione was tempted to return to the lab immediately, but she hadn't showered in days, and even though she'd stopped caring about her appearance long ago, she'd prefer not to look like a slob if she could help it.

She peeled off her clothes and made her way to the shower. The cold water helped to wake her up fully. She picked the first presentable clothes she got her hands on—a pair of comfortable flowery pants and a matching shirt—and threw her spare lab coat over it. She left the old clothes on the floor, knowing a cleaner would be around at some point to tidy up the room and help her with the laundry. Without that service, Hermione would have been forced to order clothes just to have something clean.

After all, when would she have had the time to do her own laundry?

All in all, half an hour after she'd woken up, Hermione was out of her room and on her way back to the lab. The elevator doors opened, and DJ stepped out. "Hermione," he called out immediately. He grinned, though Hermione noticed the smile was suppressing exhaustion. "Just the person I was looking for."

Hermione returned his smile, with just as much exhaustion. "Really?" she asked, skeptically.

"No! Not at all," DJ replied, stopping in front of her. "I didn't expect to meet anyone but security. In fact … " His eyes narrowed in suspicion, and Hermione noticed a bruise around his eye that hadn't completely healed. "Why are you still up? Do we need to have another talk about not working yourself to an early grave?"

Hermione grimaced but stuck her chin out. "I'll have you know that I've just had a very relaxing nap. I happened to wake up early, so I figured I could get an early start at the lab … y'know, since I've already rested." Her eyes narrowed too. "But you're one to talk. Why are *you* still up?"

He waved the question away. "I was chasing down a lead. It led nowhere, so I thought I'd catch some z's before the sun came up. But *you*," he continued, bending to wag a finger in her face. "What the hell? Just because you woke up early is no reason to get an early start on anything. What sort of uptight bullshit is that? Your project will still be waiting for you hours from now when you wake up again."

Hermione slapped his finger away from her face. "I can sleep anytime, DJ, but your brother's had a breakthrough in the trace. I want to be there when it's completed."

"Shit, seriously? He cracked the spores in just a few days? " DJ asked, breaking out into another grin. "I was expecting a week, minimum."

A week to crack through Helene's codes? Hermione thought. DJ had no foundation in programming, so she couldn't blame him for his expectations. She had estimated that it would take about a month—if it was possible at all. And that had been an optimistic guess.

Then again, CJ had us both beat and did it in two days, Hermione considered. She shook her head. What sort of monster had Manar trained?

"What're you waiting for?" DJ asked, holding the elevator open. Somehow he'd crossed the hallway and entered while Hermione had been distracted. "I thought you wanted to be there when it was completed."

"And *I* thought you wanted me to get back in bed and rest," Hermione muttered, but hurried into the elevator.

"Don't be lazy," DJ said as the elevator descended. "You can sleep anytime. It's not every day you get to see a breakthrough."

Hermione stared at him, her mouth agape.

He noticed after a moment. "What?" he asked, unable to fully suppress his grin.

"I'm sorry," she said, shaking her head. "It's my first time dealing with blatant hypocrisy. I'm not yet used to it."

"Nah, it's not hypocrisy," he said. "It's simply changing your mind once presented with new facts. I would have thought a scientist like you would get it."

"It's *because* I'm a scientist that I can tell the difference between blatant hypocrisy and simply changing your mind."

"You're just sleep-deprived. That kind of delusion is what you get when you live off coffee grounds for weeks on end." Hermione opened her mouth to counter—and then shut it. She'd had a coffee maker brought into the lab, so he unfortunately had a point. DJ pounced on her hesitation. "See? You agree with me."

"I do *not* agree with you," Hermione snapped without heat. The elevator doors opened on their floor. Both of them got out. "I just think it's worrisome how easily you stretch the truth to suit yourself."

"It's an important skill in the navy," DJ answered easily, turning a corner, "especially if you're like me and get into trouble a lot but don't like scrubbing toilets with your toothbrush."

"I thought that was a myth. Do they actually still do that?"

"Remind me to tell you about my team leader when I first started. He had a stick so far up his ass that you could mistake him for a rotisserie."

Hermione snorted, pushing open the laboratory door. "Does the story end with you getting into a fight with—" She stopped as she noticed DJ tense up beside her. She followed his gaze into the room, to where CJ stood beside the mini-tank. He had one end of an extraction wire connected to the canister. The other end, shaped into a needle, was jammed into his wrist.

He looked up at their entrance.

Hermione felt a stiff breeze. Suddenly DJ was rushing past her. He moved fast, far faster than a person should have been capable of. In an instant, he was in front of his brother. In another, they were both on the floor, with DJ on top, pinning his brother down. "Are you fucking kidding me?" DJ shouted, drawing his fist back. "Are you *fucking* kidding me?"

That broke Hermione from her shock. She hurried to the workbench, knowing she would have been useless at trying to separate them. Her eyes ran over the computer screen, to the counter at the bottom that tracked how many spores were in the tank. A moment later, she let out a relieved breath. The number hadn't changed. CJ hadn't injected himself with anything. They'd gotten to him just in time.

Behind her were the sounds of the two brothers wrestling each other on the ground. But Hermione ignored it. She easily recognized the lines of codes that showed the progress the program had made at hacking into the spores. However, there was another program running, one that was vaguely familiar. It took Hermione a second to place it as the side project that she'd asked CJ about earlier. The new program ran over the other, both progressing at the same pace. One was tasked with tapping into the spores and wiping their existing commands. The other was writing new commands. When taken alone, that didn't really mean anything. But when it was viewed along with what had almost happened in the last minute, it made more sense.

CJ had wanted to inject himself with the spores, but only after reprogramming them to do something specific: to change or fix something specific.

It didn't take a genius to figure out what.

31

NOVEMBER 2043
OKAFOR CORPORATION,
ABUJA, NIGERIA

OLAJIDE WAS HAVING the best day of his life.

All the bigger news agencies had been given spots closer to the stage, but Jide smiled as he followed one of the staff to the back of the room. He knew it was a miracle he'd gotten in at all. Not many people had heard about his news station. Even fewer had watched their program, *Daily Report*. Fifteen minutes of fame only came when they reported about something controversial. That was fine with Jide. The relative anonymity allowed the *Daily Report* to discuss whatever they wanted, without worrying about the politics that plagued more popular press agencies.

The station didn't have enough reporters to cover every story—or even most of them—so they had to choose which ones to feature and which ones to leave for the bigger fish. Ayo, his editor, had almost passed on this one when they'd gotten the invitation. When Jide had dug a little deeper and found that every news outlet in the country had gotten the invite, he'd insisted on volunteering.

He didn't regret his choice, though he might have underestimated how big this particular story was going to be. Scanning the room, Jide saw several logos he didn't recognize from outlets based in other neighboring countries. While that was unusual, taken by itself, it could be explained.

But what's with all the white people? Jide wondered, rubbing his chin. *Did they call people from overseas as well?* If that was true, then Jide was doubly grateful that he'd insisted on coming. Anything that enticed foreign journalists was bound to be interesting.

Suddenly a hush fell over the crowd. Everyone focused on the stage where a woman in a pantsuit walked up to the microphone. Manar followed behind her and stood to the side. Jide's gaze went to the woman. He had done his research, so it wasn't hard to recognize her as Ndidi Okafor, the sole heir to the Okafor Corporation. She'd been working abroad for years, and now she'd come back to take over her company from the board of directors. Who would just give up control over an organization worth trillions of dollars? That last part was pure conjecture on Jide's part, he felt his guess had to be close to the truth.

Hmm. Jide grinned. *That was actually a good line. I could add it to the piece.* If he'd come to that conclusion, then his readers probably would too. It depended on what, exactly, she had to say, but it was certainly an interesting angle. He jotted it down on his notepad. His attention was quickly pulled back to the stage when the woman began to speak.

"First of all, I'd like to welcome everyone here to the Okafor Corporation, where dreams come to life." She grinned as if she also knew it was a cringe motto. "Some of you have come from afar to hear what I have to say today, and I want to promise you that your journey has not been in vain.

"So let's turn to that: the mystery. I learned from my father that it's customary to include information about the content of a press conference so the press has the chance to prepare questions. Unfortunately, though, I am not my father. I felt the announcement warranted a bit more mystery." She smiled again as her eyes scanned her audience. She was obviously working with them, trying to judge their mood and reactions to her words. It was a standard technique, but she applied it so well that Jide didn't mind.

She continued. "Today, I'm going to share with you a revolutionary technology that has the potential to transform every life on the planet. I wanted you, and the rest of the world, to come unprepared so your reactions would be genuine and so your questions would be the ones that truly matter to you. But I've rambled on enough. So, without wasting your time, let's dive into the reason why we're all here."

She paused for a moment and looked at the crowd. Though Jide knew she couldn't have been staring at him as far back as he was, he still got the feeling that somehow she was. When the silence bordered the edge of awkwardness, Ndidi Okafor pressed a button on a small remote. A screen behind her lit up with an image of a man with a cloud of dust surrounding him. "Please, allow me to introduce the picospore."

Jide studied the image with interest. There wasn't much to get from it, which he assumed had been Ndidi Okafor's point. "Picospores are exactly what they sound like," Ndidi continued. "They are artificial, programmable, submicroscopic structures developed at the pico scale—meaning they measure in trillionths of a meter. They are designed to survive within the harsh environment that is the human body and interact with the elements there."

One of the reporters in the front row raised his hand. "By elements, you mean our organs?"

Ndidi Okafor nodded and pressed the clicker once more. The image on the projector changed to another slide showing a cloud of microscopic particles. Jide now recognized them as picospores swirling around neurons. "The spores can interact with every part of your body. However, their main focus is the brain. They function at the cellular and subcellular level, altering the brain chemistry of a person according to preprogrammed commands. This allows them to …"

Jide's hands flew over his notepad. Naturally, he was recording the entire thing, so his notes were only jottings of the important points. Despite that, he quickly filled entire pages as the explanation continued. As he took notes, he couldn't help but notice that the way she presented suggested she was laying down some kind of holy knowledge. It was in her stance, the way she stood, relaxed, but confident and completely self-assured. She perfectly modulated her voice, raising it when needed, and tapering off to almost a whisper when appropriate. It completely drew in every journalist in the room. Even Jide wasn't spared. At some point, he stopped writing, and just listened. It wasn't difficult. Although he couldn't understand everything she explained, the part he managed to grasp convinced him that Ndidi Okafor had been serious when she'd said that the technology had the potential to change the world. The hall was filled with hushed murmuring. Camera flashes came periodically as each station tried to capture this, the moment of a grand revelation.

"In this way," Ndidi Okafor continued, "the potential applications of the picospores are nearly limitless. And if they *do* ever hit a limit, then the spores will be upgraded into newer, better versions. While we have a working model of the spores ready to be administered to patients, our team is already working to upgrade them. With the right software and programs, the spores have the potential to either suppress the symptoms of *all* current mental illness, or cure them permanently. Illnesses like depression, anxiety, and PTSD already have specific prescriptions. What the picotechnology offers is a one-time solution without any risk or drawbacks. The same goes double for those afflictions without an actual prescription yet.

"This isn't even about science anymore." Ndidi Okafor grinned at the crowd. She was so visibly excited that she was unable to contain her passion for the spores, and Jide had to admit that it was convincing. Only God knew how much of it was real. "Hundreds of millions of people are affected by mental illnesses worldwide. Some are born with them and are forced to live with the illnesses for most of their lives; others develop their illnesses through unprocessed trauma or drugs.

"In the best-case scenario, only the victim and close friends and family suffer." She frowned to show what she thought of that. "But in the worst? We have rapists, murderers, and serial killers that devastate society before they are able to get the help that they need. The picospores provide an answer to that. They provide a path forward to a world where we are freed from the shackles of mental illnesses forever. They offer hope and happiness to those who thought it was lost." The slide changed once more, this time to an image of a person smiling, with a quote: "I've got my life back." Jide took a picture.

"Considering that, don't you think that we have a responsibility to harness this technology? To make it accessible to all who need it? Well, I certainly do. However, for us to make it reality, we have to work together."

Well, looks like we're almost done then, Jide thought. He could recognize the beginning of a call to action from a mile away. It meant Ndidi Okafor was rounding up. He reviewed the questions he'd jotted down during the speech and edited them to be better phrased. He'd already decided on the angle he was going to use for the piece, so his questions should reflect it. That didn't require all of his attention, so he could still listen to the end of the speech.

"I firmly believe that the picospores have the potential to be the biggest breakthrough in medical history. But they are more than that. The spores represent a new frontier in human innovation. With picotechnology, we can unlock new possibilities in physiology, psychology, psychiatry, environmental stewardship, and countless other fields. It might not happen immediately, but the potential for the technology is nearly limitless. It opens a path. The only question is …" She paused, peering into the crowd. "Do you believe as well?"

It took a moment for people to realize that she'd ended the speech. Jide couldn't tell who started it, but the entire hall resounded with thunderous applause. Soon it was a standing ovation. Jide, however, remained seated. He wasn't the only one. Several journalists stared at those standing with barely disguised sneers.

Jide grinned.

The applause lasted for another full minute before Ndidi Okafor waved them down. Her wide grin should have been genuine, considering the crowd's reaction was probably every presenter's wet dream. It took another minute for everyone to settle down. Only then did she invite questions.

Several hands went up immediately. Ndidi picked one at random. "Your presentation left no doubt that picospore technology is indeed revolutionary. How did you come up with the idea?"

Jide rolled his eyes but readied his notepad. It was a basic question. But it was best to get those out of the way early.

"I can't take credit for the idea," she said. "That honor goes to the late Dr. Cloney, one of the leading researchers in the Okafor Corporation. He and his daughter, Hermione Cloney, worked tirelessly to design and develop the technology."

"So you have no personal interest in this?" the journalist asked again.

"I have dedicated most of my life to helping those with mental illnesses," Ndidi Okafor answered with a smile. "So I guess you could say that I have a personal interest in this. Next question, please."

A pudgy man stood, adjusting his tie. "We've heard a lot of wondrous features about the picospores and the limitless potential of the technology. My question is simple: Do you have any proof?"

"The spores have undergone several processes of rigorous testing and examination," Ndidi Okafor answered easily. "A detailed report will be published shortly after this conference ends."

Jide sighed but jotted it down. He'd have to keep an eye out for the report as soon as it came out. There might be a few interesting details. Apart from that, Jide looked around. *With so many journalists, you'd think we'd be able to skip the soft questions and go straight for the real thing.*

A moment later, Ndidi Okafor pointed. Jide saw a familiar mop of brown hair. Lawrence Etta was a minor celebrity in the industry. He was known for being rude and abrasive, mostly because he wasn't afraid to ask the difficult questions. Almost everyone in the crowd knew of him. The room grew silent when he stood.

"Thank you, Miss Okafor," he started. "You mentioned that picotechnology can cure all mental illnesses and offer a one-time solution without any risk or drawbacks. Is that right?" he asked, glancing up at the stage. "Your spores can cure *all* mental illnesses without any drawbacks? According to the *Diagnostic and Statistical Manual of Mental Disorders*, there are over four hundred known mental illnesses in existence at the moment. You really expect us to believe that your cloud of dust can cure each and every one of them?"

Jide crossed out one of his own questions. Now they were getting somewhere.

"I believe what I said was that the spores have the *potential* to either *suppress the symptoms of* or cure all mental illnesses," Ndidi Okafor replied with a smile. "I stand by the statement," she said. "But please note the emphasis. As it stands right now, with the technology at the beginning of its growth, we've already had incredibly promising results of the spores suppressing the symptoms of autism, depression, anxiety, and others. So, yes, I firmly believe that, with more time and research, new versions of the spores can be developed to cure a wide range of mental illnesses."

"New versions? So the current versions cannot?" Lawrence pressed.

"Testing is still ongoing—"

"Still ongoing?" Lawrence interrupted. "So you're pushing out a product that's not yet fully tested?"

"I believe the fault is mine," Ndidi smiled. "The picospores *have* already gone through a rigorous testing process. As I mentioned, we've seen numerous successes with their application. The spores to be launched are preprogrammed specifically for those illnesses that we've found success in solving. The Okafor Corporation would never launch a half-baked product. I would never waste our time on such. My statement was made in reference to the fact that our team is constantly working to improve picotechnology so that it can better help people."

"Thank you for the clarification, Miss Okafor," Lawrence said. "But that brings me to my next question. Your presentation mentioned that the picospores worked by interacting with the brain and altering its chemistry according to preprogrammed commands. Correct?" He looked at her, implying that he wanted an actual answer.

"Correct," Ndidi Okafor said, though the answer was hesitant as if she'd smelled a trap.

Lawrence Etta nodded. "Undoubtedly, this has the potential to be used for a lot of good, as you've indicated thoroughly. However, if the core of the technology is to mess with the brain, it seems to me that it can also be easily misused to cause a lot of devastation."

For the first time, Ndidi Okafor's expression faltered. A Middle Eastern man, who had stood behind her during the speech, coughed. Miss Okafor's head whipped toward him. The two of them shared a look, but Miss Okafor shook her head. Jide raised a brow and made a note about the interaction.

She focused back on Lawrence. "Mr. Etta," she started. "I understand your concern, and I acknowledge that it's valid. However, it's important to note that every powerful technology or discovery has the potential for both positive and negative applications. But should we let fear stop us from moving forward? Of course not. The Okafor Corporation is already working with regulatory bodies to ensure that the development and administration of the picospores are done responsibly and with the necessary safeguards in place. So, we *do* acknowledge the risk, and we are doing everything in our power to mitigate it. The only thing left is for us, for all of us, to work together to maximize the positive impact of the picospores for the greater good."

Lawrence Etta opened his mouth to continue, but Ndidi had already called on another person with their hands raised. It was a brilliant ploy. However, Jide recognized the journalist who stood up. Victor Agu was a pudgy man with a rat-like face. He was also one of Lawrence Etta's best friends. "You've explained that the Okafor Corporation is doing all it can to safeguard the technology," he said. "However, isn't it somewhat naive to think that the picospores won't fall into the wrong hands?"

Ndidi Okafor started to respond, but Victor held up a hand. "I'm sorry, ma'am, but I'm not done. And let's say that your regulations work and the circulation of the picospores is tightly controlled. Isn't it possible that once the technology is launched, the spores could be replicated by someone else with less altruistic intentions?"

Ndidi sighed. "As I have already mentioned, the picospores will be preprogrammed to each specific person, so even if they do get into the wrong hands, they'd be useless. As for someone replicating the technology? That is simply impossible."

Jide raised a brow. Even Victor didn't hide his surprise. "Those are two very bold statements, Miss Okafor—especially since humanity has proven to be adept at making the impossible possible."

"Her confidence comes from me," the Middle Eastern man said, walking up to stand beside Ndidi Okafor. The latter glared at him, but she moved to the side with a sigh. "My name is Manar Saleem. I am the head researcher of the picospore project at the Okafor Corporation."

The name caused a mixed reaction among the crowd. There were many who didn't recognize the name. The ones who did weren't able to control their reaction. After a quick Google search, Jide understood why. Manar Saleem was of average height, with dark hair and green eyes. However, he exuded arrogance from every pore in his body. It billowed off him in waves. Understandable, considering the man was a living legend.

"Each picospore will be *personally* developed and programmed by me," Manar Saleem said. "That reduces the risk of someone gaining control of them to zero. In the same way, it is impossible for someone else to replicate the technology in any way."

Victor Agu hesitated. Whether or not he recognized Manar, the man's bearing made it difficult for anyone—including Victor—to take the stance that he had with Ndidi Okafor. Victor licked his lips. "Ndidi Okafor mentioned that the technology was developed by the late Dr. Cloney and his daughter. Is Hermione Cloney part of your team?"

"No," came the reply.

Victor pounced on the opening. "Then that means *you* replicated the technology, doesn't it? That gives credence to the possibility that it can be done again."

"The difference is that *I* worked directly with Hermione Cloney and studied her research notes extensively."

"Can the technology not be reverse engineered?" Victor tried one last time.

"No, it cannot."

"Why?"

"Because I have perfected it," Manar stated.

Victor Agu took his seat. *What could anyone say to that?* The conference settled down after that. The smaller news stations got the chance to shine as they asked softball questions, while the bigger agencies rustled up their courage. Jide used the chance to cross a few questions off his list. He followed the trend and kept his questions light and simple. Ndidi Okafor handled those questions, but

Manar Saleem remained at her side. Just his presence was enough to keep the journalists in line.

For a time, at least.

Eventually, Lawrence Etta raised his hand once more. Ndidi Okafor tried to avoid picking him, but every other reporter put their hands down when they saw Lawrence's, leaving her no choice. "Thank you," he said when he was called on. "You mentioned earlier that 'We have rapists, murderers, and serial killers that devastate society before they are able to get the help that they need,'" he said, reading from his notes. "Are you saying that rapists, murderers, and serial killers are not responsible for their actions because they have mental illnesses?"

"What? Of course not," Ndidi refuted immediately. "My statement was made to emphasize the urgent need for support and treatment, not as a way to excuse criminal behavior. It *is* a fact that mental illness is a contributor in some cases. However, in no way did I mean that the individuals themselves are not responsible for their actions." Her tone sharpened. "I'd beg you, Mr. Etta, as well as everyone else, to join your efforts with ours to find solutions instead of perpetuating misconceptions."

Lawrence Etta smiled. "I believe you misunderstood my question. I simply wanted to clarify your statement. But let me ask a simpler question then. Some individuals with certain mental conditions or neurodiversity might not desire a cure as they deeply identify with their experiences or perspectives. So, what happens to those who reject your cure?"

Ndidi Okafor tensed visibly. She hesitated before answering. "The picospores are designed to provide a solution for those who are suffering and seeking help, but mental health can be a deeply personal and complex aspect of a person's identity. Not everyone may want the picospores. That's perfectly okay. Even my ward decided not to go through with the procedure, and I respected her choice. So—"

"Your ward?" Lawrence asked innocently. "Could this be Bethany Cloney? The sister of Hermione Cloney and the daughter of the late Dr. Cloney who pioneered the technology?"

Ndidi rubbed the bridge of her nose. She'd lost her smile at some point. Although she'd hidden her annoyance so far, it slipped out. "Yes," she said softly,

"Bethany was diagnosed at a young age as being on the autism spectrum. She grew to embrace her condition as part of her identity, so she opted out of the procedure. I respected her decision, as the Okafor Corporation would do for anyone who declines the picospores."

"I'm sorry, but I'm sure that you can see how that could create some doubts in our minds," Lawrence said. "Bethany Cloney, as a relative to Hermione and yourself, can be said to have been the closest person to the picospore project, outside of those on the team. If *she* rejected the procedure, regardless of the numerous benefits that you have stated, then it raises the question: What does she know that you might not have told us?"

Ndidi Okafor narrowed her eyes. "My ward's decision was a personal one. It does not in any way represent her attitude toward picospore technology."

"Would she be willing to put that in writing?" Lawrence asked. "I'm sure I speak for my viewers when I say that it would go a long way in reassuring us."

Ndidi Okafor hesitated. Jide found it fascinating. Was there something there? Finally, she replied. "That won't be a problem."

"Amazing." He smiled a charming smile. "Final question then. How about kids?"

Ndidi Okafor blinked. "I'm sorry?"

"Kids," Lawrence repeated. "You mentioned that you respected Bethany Cloney's choice to reject the picospores. However, she was able to make that choice because she is a grown woman. How about kids with mental conditions? Should their parents be able to decide whether or not they undergo your procedure?"

Ndidi Okafor hesitated. And then she hesitated again. "That …"

"… is a moot point," Manar Saleem finished for her. "The procedure is not meant to be carried out on children so as not to interfere with their development. As it stands, every procedure, even for adults, will be carried out only after careful evaluation and consultation with qualified professionals. Hopefully that answers your question?"

Lawrence met Manar's gaze for a moment before backing down and taking his seat.

Ndidi quickly pointed at another journalist, and the conference continued. Jide put down his pen after a while. He already had more than enough for his main piece. However, he'd have to change his angle. There were several points where Ndidi's Okafor's reactions didn't add up—especially her reaction when Bethany Cloney came up. The interaction between Ndidi Okafor and Manar Saleem was also curious.

Jide raised his camera for one last picture. He would have to do more research, but he had enough ideas to milk the topic for months.

CHAPTER

32

DJ'S FIST HIT HIS BROTHER'S FACE a second time.

Hermione called out to him, but her voice was distant over the roaring of his ears. A part of him had considered this possibility when Ndidi first told them that Helene had somehow suppressed Bethany's autism symptoms, but that it had been a brief thing—barely an instant—because it hadn't been worth thinking about. No matter how his brother felt, he wouldn't be so stupid as to accept something with such obvious strings attached.

Except, of course, CJ *was* actually that stupid. Far more stupid than DJ had ever realized.

An arm wrapped around him and tried to pull him up. "You're going to kill him, DJ," Hermione said.

No, I'm not. As pissed off as he was, DJ still knew how to moderate his strength. He wasn't going to kill his brother, but it was going to be a close thing.

What the fuck? What the absolute fuck?

Finally, Hermione succeeded in shoving him off. DJ rolled with it. He was on his feet in an instant, glaring down at his brother. CJ was still conscious, but his face was a map of bruises. Blood trickled down his split lip, pooling around his mouth and staining his chin. Each breath was labored and sent a shudder through him.

DJ felt a dark joy at that. But it was far from enough to take the edge off his anger. "What was your plan, huh? Did you even *have* one?"

"He was reprogramming the spores," Hermione answered for him. "We were both working on translating and cataloging all of the commands in the spores just in case we needed them later. At some point, though, your brother found and identified the specific commands that Helene had used to suppress my sister's autistic symptoms while she was under the AI's control."

DJ stared at her.

"We needed—or at least CJ told me he'd needed—to erase the previous commands to take control of the spores and lay a trace. Now I'm not sure if that was true. Regardless, once he overhauled the previous commands, he repro-grammed the spores with the instructions that he wanted."

"To suppress his symptoms and take him off the spectrum," DJ finished.

"Um … to be … *normal,*" CJ wheezed out from the ground.

"You were *already* normal," DJ shouted. "You've *always* been fucking normal. Open your eyes, bro! It's 2043. You're literally the only person that looks down on yourself for being on the spectrum."

"You … um … you are not the one who had to live with the looks of pity. You have no idea … uh … how it feels not to be able to control your own body, even to talk or *smile*; to live … um … in constant fear that something is suddenly going to trigger you to have an episode; to be a constant burden on everyone around you … uh … because you need constant care just to be normal. You … um … have *no* idea, DJ."

"Oh, for fuck's sake," DJ snapped, "you've been whining about this since we were kids, CJ. Grow a fucking pair already. Yeah, you didn't ask for this, and sure it might have been hell. But shit, everyone has their problems, CJ. You think it was easy growing up for me? Like, in general, you think it was easy? You think it's easy for anyone? I'll give you a hint: It wasn't. It's not for anyone.

"Life is different shades of hell. It burns everyone differently. You don't get to use that as an excuse for bullshit. You were dealt shitty cards, sure. But you've had years to learn how to play them. You refuse to move on."

"I … uh … did," he wheezed.

"What?"

"I *did* try … um … to move on," he repeated. He tried to push himself up, but his arms gave up halfway and he crashed back down. Hermione rushed to his side and helped him into a chair while DJ watched coldly. "I *had* moved on. I was doing … uh … better at handling my symptoms, and I had begun to feel better about myself. But then I … um … went to the Virtual Realm."

DJ rolled his eyes. He'd heard this story before. The Virtual Realm worked by creating an avatar for his brother. The digital body allowed him to interact, to some extent, with everything there. Since the body was lines of code, CJ had not shown any of the symptoms of being on the autism spectrum. According to him, he'd felt what it was like to be "normal" for the first time.

He'd been spinning that sob story since he'd gotten back. DJ was sick of it, and it was time he said so.

But Hermione beat him to it. "DJ, can I talk to you?" Before he could protest, she pulled him by his arm toward the back of the room. "You're being too hard on him, DJ," she said, pulling out the first aid kit from a compartment on the wall. "I get where he's coming from."

DJ threw his hands up. "Are you fucking serious right now?"

"Just hear me out," she said, ignoring his outburst. "You were right that everyone has their problems. But I don't think that's an accurate comparison or that it even relates to this case. Just *listen*." She growled when DJ opened his mouth. "There are several levels to it. First of all, it's not fair to even call it a problem. For him, being on the autism spectrum is deeper than that. It's something that has formed the core of his personality since he was young. It has shaped every part of his experience in life. Just calling it a "problem" doesn't do it justice. Most people are the cause of their problems. CJ was born on the spectrum. There was nothing he could do.

"And before you tell me that there are people who didn't cause their problems"—she raised a hand to forestall his argument—"how many of those people get a chance to see—and I mean *see*—how their lives would be without their affliction the way CJ did in the Virtual Realm? He lived his dream for months on end before he was yanked back into a body that he grew up believing was a liability. Can you really blame him? And unlike most people, he has both the technology and the method to fix his problem."

"There is nothing to fix, Hermione," DJ growled back. "That's what you, he, and Ndidi don't understand. Bethany is the only one who has the right idea. There is absolutely nothing to fix. Yes, he's had a hard time being on the spectrum, but you were right when you said that the experience has shaped him. He wouldn't be who he is right now without it. CJ is one of the greatest programmers of his time. More than three years ago, he broke into the government's security systems just because he wanted to find out the truth about our fathers' deaths. More recently, he hacked into the White House surveillance system and stayed there without being detected for *hours*. He did that with less than an hour of preparation.

"Hermione, even Manar, the king of dicks himself, has acknowledged CJ enough to take him as an apprentice. And now," he continued, "now he's not only understood your technology. He's mastered it enough to crack Helene's defenses around the spores and take control of them. You didn't think that it was possible. Yet he did it in just two days. Do you understand now? There's nothing wrong with him. There's *nothing* to fix."

"Well, he thinks there is," Hermione pressed. "It is ultimately his choice whether he wants to do something about it or not."

"No, it's fucking not. This affects me too. I'm not going to stand by and watch my brother destroy himself because he refuses to focus that big brain on himself and think about what he's achieved, despite being on the spectrum. It's also my choice because I'm the one that's going to have to live with myself when Helene is controlling my brother as a puppet."

DJ raised a finger. "Look." He sighed. "I didn't necessarily agree with your and Ndidi's actions with Bethany. But I didn't involve myself because it wasn't my place. Now I'm asking you to do the same." He held her gaze. "Stay out of it."

Hermione started to say something and then stopped. Finally, she nodded. "So, what're you going to do now? You know he's not going to stop."

DJ stared at his brother. He hadn't moved from the chair, but tears dripped down his cheeks as he sobbed silently.

Fuck me.

CHAPTER

33

NDIDI STORMED OUT OF THE CONFERENCE without a smile, but that was the only indication of her mood. There were still people around after all. An aide rushed up to her as she made her way back to her room, but Ndidi listened with only half an ear. Her focus was on suppressing the anger coursing through her. She felt like punching something, which wasn't good. That had been a problem a while back, but she'd done a good job of handling it over the last year. She wasn't going to undo all of that progress now.

The aide continued talking, but Ndidi hadn't heard a word the man had said since he'd started. She interrupted him midway, asking him to send a report to her and then dismissed him. He was out of her mind the moment she turned the corner.

Manar caught up to her before she went very far. His long strides matched her pace easily. "You're not usually this inefficient in masking your emotions."

"It's been a stressful day," Ndidi replied. Her voice was lowered as the staff streamed past. They kept their heads down as they passed but glanced furtively between her and Manar.

"Understandable," Manar said. "The press conference went as well as it could, all things considered. We knew that there was going to be pushback. There always is with technology like this. But I think you handled the questions incredibly well."

Ndidi's anger rushed to the forefront. "If you were so impressed," Ndidi snapped, "then why did you keep interfering?" Manar glanced at her but didn't say anything, so Ndidi continued. "I told you that I didn't need you to fight my battles for me."

"And I told *you* that the spores are my project as well," Manar reminded her calmly. "And for the most part, you handled the questions. Admirably, if I may add. I just spoke twice."

Ndidi started to snap again. However, she noticed the look of confusion on Manar's face. Did he … "You don't see it, do you?" Ndidi asked, shaking her head.

"See what?" he asked.

"Are you blind?" Ndidi raised her voice. "You intimidated those journalists into submission, Manar. Into *submission*. But you didn't even notice, did you? You didn't notice that the hall practically went silent the moment you started speaking. Even the hard journalists stopped asking questions once you started interfering. And why would you? You don't have to work to command respect. You're arrogant, but you're a man, and you have the achievements to back it up. You draw attention and focus by your mere presence."

"That's not fair."

She shook her head. "You don't think I knew what Lawrence Etta and Victor Agu were doing? I specifically invited them here because I knew they'd dismiss me as a woman and try to bait me into saying something stupid. I'll admit that some of their questions surprised me, but it was ultimately part of the plan to talk about the picospores, look good for the board of directors, and make it that much harder for them to try to butt into the process."

She glared at him. "But just by speaking, you made it seem like *you* were the one in charge of the whole thing, and I was simply the pretty face you were using to sell the spores. It was humiliating. And I knew that's what would happen. That is why I *told* you not to interfere, that I could handle my own battles."

They stopped in the middle of the passage. Ndidi was panting when she was done. She hadn't expected to say so much, but the entire thing was just so infuriating. Most of the people in that room didn't know who Manar was. Still, he'd commanded their attention and their respect without even trying. Would he have had the same problems she had with the board of directors if he were in her shoes? Or would they have rushed to capitulate when he spoke?

"Let me get this straight," Manar said, rubbing the bridge of his nose. "Your issue with me is that I made it look like I was in charge of the project even though I spoke only twice. Is that right?"

"I told you not to interfere."

"But you couldn't answer the questions," Manar pointed out. "If I hadn't spoken up, you'd have lost all—or at least most—of the credibility that you'd built up with your presentation. Would you have preferred that?"

"Why would you assume I couldn't answer the questions?"

"Oh?" Manar raised a brow. His expression was hard, and his eyes, glittering gold under the overhead lighting, were full of challenge. "How would you have resolved the problem of someone replicating the technology without involving me?"

Ndidi started to retort, then closed her mouth. The wind suddenly blew out of her sails. He was right. Picotechnology would take decades for someone to replicate it, even by reverse engineering. With Manar added to the mix, that timeline could stretch to a century since the spores would keep evolving, making it nearly impossible for any competitor to catch up. *He* was the deterrent. He'd known that from the beginning.

Manar's gaze softened when he saw her expression. He drew her close. Ndidi let him. "You're worried, and you're lashing out," he said. "That's understandable. But it's ultimately unnecessary. There's nothing to be worried about. You did great. You got the message out there, which is the most important thing."

He met her eyes, and the gold in his eyes seemed to intensify. "The journalists can spin it however they want, but the picospores offer something far too irresistible. They will come. They will come in droves for the healing that only we can grant them. Rest easy, Ndidi Okafor," he said. "You have done your part, and you have done it well."

Ndidi drew back with a frown. "You used my full name."

"Is that a problem?"

"Not really, but it's weird hearing it from you," Ndidi said. "Helene used to do that."

"Well." Manar grinned. "I'm going to ignore the hurtful comparison and endeavor not to do it again. I wouldn't want to be confused with her, would I?"

CHAPTER

34

NOVEMBER 2043
HERMIONE'S LABORATORY,
SPARTA HEADQUARTERS,
NEW YORK

HERMIONE LEFT DJ IN THOUGHT and went back to CJ with the first aid kit. She ignored the tears running down his cheeks and focused instead on cleaning his wounds. CJ didn't move through it all, not even to flinch.

Somehow that made it worse.

A part of her understood why DJ was so angry. She'd felt the same way when Bethany had extracted the spores from herself. She'd felt the same rage and betrayal, even if she hadn't expressed it as violently as DJ. Still, she was determined to find a way to convince her sister to accept the spores and suppress her symptoms.

Therein lay the conflict. She'd told DJ. It was his brother's choice whether or not he wanted the spores. But it would be hypocritical for Hermione to take the choice away from her sister by trying to convince her to take the spores. And by doing that, she'd be acting like DJ, who'd stopped his brother—

Hermione stopped the spiral before it could start. The entire situation was confusing. It wasn't something she wanted to think about with just a couple of hours of sleep.

She'd finished cleaning the bruises and had begun to bandage them when DJ stopped her. He collected the gauze from her and took over. Hermione stepped back without a word and tried her best to ignore the low murmurs to the side.

She took a seat in front of the computer and gave a cursory scan of the screen. Most of it was still gibberish code. However, Hermione needed something to distract her. Several programs were open, one of which looked like the trace CJ was running on the spores. It took a few minutes for Hermione to figure out that it wasn't the trace. When she realized what it was, she sat upright immediately, eyes wide. "You might want to see this, DJ."

Hermione didn't bother to turn around. She heard him mutter something to his brother before she felt him looming over her. She pointed at the screen without a word. DJ scanned it for a moment before sighing. "What am I looking at, Hermione?"

She palmed her face before explaining. "That section there?" Hermione pointed. "It's one of the groups that CJ's program has gotten full control over. It provides us with full access to the picospores, including their schematics. CJ has been running a diagnostic on it. And *that* part"—she pointed again—"analyzes how the spores interact with the brain."

"You're rambling, Hermione."

Hermione glared at him. "It explains why we've observed several negative effects from the former hostages when the spores were extracted. The depression, lack of motivation, and anxiety? None of that was caused by the patient's sensitivity to the spores. It's the spores themselves! The newer versions form something like a symbiotic relationship with the brain, which makes them dependent on each other." Hermione paused as something occurred to her. "The version injected into Debi Willingham must have been the most recent version since its extraction put her in a coma."

"Wait, wait, wait," DJ begged. His expression hardened into a scowl. "Are you telling me *we* put that woman in a coma?"

"We didn't have this information then," Hermione explained. "We were trying to help her."

"You think Albert's gonna give a fuck about that?" DJ asked. He rubbed his temples. His eyes closed, and his face twisted into a grimace. Suddenly, he turned to his brother. "Did you know about this before you tried to … " He trailed off, as if unable to complete the sentence. CJ shook his head slowly. "But you want the spores?"

"I … um … want to be normal," his brother replied.

"*You're already—*" DJ stopped himself and blew out a breath. "All right," he said. "Here's what we're going to do. No one's going to tell Albert about this until we find a way to fix it. Is there a way to fix it?" he asked, glancing at Hermione. She shrugged. "Fine! We're going to try to find a way to fix it. Then we'll help everyone who's been affected. In the meantime, you"—he pointed at CJ—"are going to be confined to the bedroom since you can't be trusted to make smart decisions!"

"You're jailing your brother?" Hermione asked.

DJ met her eyes. She could see the determination reflected there. Nothing was going to change his mind. "I'd rather be the bad guy than watch my brother become a puppet for a power-hungry maniac."

PART 2
BESIEGED

CHAPTER

DECEMBER 2043
SPARTA HEADQUARTERS,
NEW YORK

DJ WAS JOLTED AWAKE by the sound of an alarm blaring, the only light coming from the computer where his brother sat clicking away on the keyboard. Footsteps sounded outside their room. Bullets *pinged* against the walls in the hall. The door held firm. DJ adjusted the pillow under him. "Any idea what that's about?"

CJ threw open the curtains, flooding the room with sunlight. "We … um … we're under attack!" He shouted to his brother over the alarm, racing toward the closet that was their armory.

DJ sat up, rubbing his eyes slowly. "By?" he asked. But a drone flew past the window, rendering the question moot. "Okay, new question: *Why?*"

"The trace … uh … finally went through while you were asleep," CJ explained, "so I … um … assume it is a preemptive strike by Tyra Chityothin." He paused. "You … uh … you seem awfully calm."

"What time is it?" he asked instead.

"Uh … a little after seven in the morning."

"Give me a few minutes," DJ replied. He stretched. "I'm working on two hours of sleep." He threw off the covers and stood. "At least now the government can't say they don't know about Helene anymore."

"Did … um … did they say that before?" CJ frowned.

DJ paused in his stretch, trying to remember if he'd mentioned it when he was debriefing them about what had happened in the White House. He gave up after a few seconds. "It's a moot point now. Helene has decided to show herself."

"I think the … uh … reason is obvious," CJ said, standing. "It is … um … because of you."

DJ raised a brow.

"If you … um … had not been in the White House, she … uh … she might have gotten the entire cabinet in her thrall," CJ explained, walking to the closet. "Maybe she decided … um … she no longer wanted you to be able to interfere."

DJ peeked through the window. They were over seventy stories up, providing them a great view of the drone army flying over Sparta Headquarters. They blanketed the sky over the entire block and attacked any vehicle that came close. "Seems a little excessive for just little ol' me, don't you think?" DJ commented.

CJ shrugged.

"DJ!" The door to the room slammed open as Christy barged in. She was dressed in her fatigues and had a bulletproof vest strapped across her chest and a sniper over her back. CJ poked his head out from the closet, a vest in his hands. DJ just blinked the sleep from his eyes. "Are you fucking kidding me right now?" she yelled. "Can't you hear the damn alarm?"

"Sure," DJ replied, stifling a yawn. "My brother and I were just discussing it."

"Discussing it," Christy repeated in disbelief. It was simple to DJ. He was tired, so he didn't have the energy to freak out. His brother handed him a vest, and DJ strapped it on. Christy sighed. "You do know we're under attack, right? What would you have done if I'd been an attacker?"

DJ reached behind him. "I'd have shot you with this."

They all stared at the pistol in his hands. CJ was the first to speak. "You …
uh … you sleep with a gun tucked into your pants?"

"Of course," DJ replied. "What sort of stupid question is that?"

"I don't even know why I try," Christy muttered.

"You try because you don't know what you'd do without me," DJ replied, to
Christy's surprise.

Still … maybe I should start taking this seriously, DJ thought.

He glanced out the window again. The drones swarmed the entire city block
like a horde of locusts. Most of them were small—about double the size of a
human head—but DJ spotted a few larger ones, similar to the kind Helene had
used years ago during their first encounter. He remembered having to blow up
the entire building to escape just three of those.

That wouldn't work here. But fortunately, he wasn't the same as he was back
then.

He finished strapping on his vest and reached under the bed for two bags.
He unzipped one and strapped the rifle to his back. He threw the other bag to
Christy. "Get to the roof and use that with your best discretion. Regroup with
me once you're done."

Christy hefted the bag. Her face split into a grin when she recognized the
shape. CJ glared at DJ, seemingly recalling it too. Christy was gone before he
could say anything.

"Hopefully she is … um … more responsible than you," CJ muttered.

DJ snorted. "Man, you really haven't seen enough of Christy around guns.
But that's beside the point." He strode toward the door. "I need to handle this
shit so I can get back to sleep." CJ started following him toward the door. DJ put
up a hand to stop him. "What're you doing? You're not leaving."

CJ sighed. "You cannot be serious. You … um … you are going to need me."

"I *might* need you," DJ corrected him. "But until then, you're gonna sit your
ass down here away from the picospores."

"You … um … are treating me like an addict," his brother said.

"Well, you seem to make the same bad decisions that they do," DJ shrugged back.

CJ glared at him. "I … uh … want to help."

DJ met his eyes firmly. "And normally I'd let you. But right now? I no longer trust your judgment. And you could get hurt … or worse out there."

With that, DJ closed the door and locked it behind him.

CHAPTER

36

DJ JAMMED THE BUTTON FOR THE LOBBY and waited while the elevator descended. Maybe he'd been too harsh with his brother, but DJ didn't really see what he could have done differently. He still felt angry whenever he remembered what CJ had almost done. Despite the hypocritical bullshit that Hermione had tried to lay on him, he was never going to let his brother inject himself with the picospores—not while Helene was still around. There had to be no chance in hell that she'd resurface. Then CJ could do whatever he wanted.

The elevator dinged its arrival and opened to chaos. DJ was immediately swarmed by a mass of bodies pushing to get into the elevator. Drones blocked the path to the stairways and buzzed around the room like bees, spraying bullets in a constant cacophony. Each drone was about the size of a head and torso, with a diameter basically half the length of a person. They were all spherical, with amber-gold light spilling from cracks in their bodies. A steady dot of red light blinked from a hole at each center.

Security guards were patches of resistance within the chaos, their explosives in the lobby sending deep rumbles throughout the elevator.

DJ focused on the corpses that littered the floor.

It's because of you, CJ had said. Helene had attacked because of him, because he'd provoked her by ruining her plans in the White House. While DJ hadn't had a choice, that couldn't bring back the people his actions had doomed.

He swiped his card along the access panel to provide access to the elevator and then reached for the closest person. The young man stared at him with terrified eyes. His uniform marked him as one of the maintenance staff. DJ shoved the card into his hands and allowed his anger and frustration to seep into his voice as he growled, "Do not leave this elevator until everyone here has been taken to a safer floor." He forced the man to meet his eyes and focus on them. "Take as many as you can in each batch, but take them all. You're responsible for their lives now."

With that, he pushed through the crowd until he emerged on the other side, rifle in hand. A moment later, one of the drones crashed to the ground, a hole through its hull. DJ took cover behind one of the pillars to avoid the retaliatory fire. There were about a dozen drones still left in the lobby. Several split off to enter deeper into the building but were quickly replaced by others from the swarm outside.

We're not going to be making progress until we deal with the ones hovering outside, DJ thought, taking aim at another drone.

The next moment, the machine crashed to the ground. The M16 had been with DJ since they'd run into the drones at the Sparta Underground Facility. He carried it everywhere, in line with his motto: *Never leave the house without a weapon that can kill your greatest fear.* Another drone crashed. He'd taken out three. Another two flew deeper into the building. This left fewer than ten of the machines in the lobby. However, as DJ watched, several flew through the broken doors and joined the fray, making their efforts pointless.

DJ cursed. *What the hell is Christy doing?*

At the same instant, a deafening *boom* shook the entire building. The windows rattled violently, then broke. The floor trembled, and the shock wave reverberated through the air, throwing men against walls and machines into each other.

That's my girl. DJ grinned. *And CJ thought she was going to be responsible.* The Bulldog was a rocket-propelled grenade launcher that DJ had borrowed—without asking—from Olsen before he'd left the navy. It had several settings, one of which was a radiation-free nuke blast. How could anyone resist that? Outside the building, there was chaos of another type. Drones crashed down in droves, smoke rising from their halls. The blast must have affected over a hundred, but that didn't make a dent in their number.

Another moment passed, then another blast rocked the building. DJ had been watching, so he saw the moment the EM wave passed through the body of the swarm. The pulse chained through the machines, dropping them like flies. The EM wave scrambled with their connection, but the effect was temporary. Even with the damage they sustained from the fall, it wouldn't be enough to put them down.

Several *booms* rocked the building in quick succession, each milder than the first. Clearly Christy had decided to continue using the grenade launcher. When the dust cleared, pieces of the drones littered the street. DJ figured that she must have gotten about a hundred that time. That was a hundred that wouldn't be getting back up.

DJ reached into his bag for his comm unit and dumped the bag. He placed the set in his ear. "Great work, Christy," he said, "Now get the hell outta there. The drones will have locked in on your position by now."

"*Way ahead of you, D,*" Christy shouted over the wind. "*Where are we meeting?*"

"I'll buzz you. Do what you can on your end, but focus on getting the civilians to a safe area. I'll clear out the lobby first and rendezvous with the security."

"*Roger that.*"

DJ came out from behind the pillar and took aim at a drone. There were a little over a dozen inside the building. Christy's attack had probably disrupted the reinforcements, so now was the best time to clear the room. He glanced back at the elevator. More than half of the crowd was gone. *Two more batches should do it*, DJ thought. *That's about ten minutes or so.*

He narrowed his eyes through his scope.

DECEMBER 2043
SPARTA HEADQUARTERS,
NEW YORK

SIX MINUTES LATER, DJ walked among the wreckage to the largest group of guards. "Boy, am I glad to see you, DJ." Terry, one of the captains said. "It's chaos out here." DJ had made it a point to interact with the guards on several occasions, for moments like this when shit hit the fan. "Any idea what those things are?"

DJ grimaced. "You know that super-secret stuff that I'm not supposed to tell you about?" he asked, and the captain nodded. "Well, this is related to that."

"Well, shit," Terry said. His eyes flicked to the side where two of his men lay motionless, riddled with bullet holes. Anger flashed in his eyes. For a moment, DJ thought Terry would attack him in retribution—and DJ probably would have let him. But the guard captain settled for sucking on his teeth. "I knew I should have tried harder to get you drunk so you would spill. Have you got anything that could help us deal with them?"

"Not a lot," DJ replied. He hefted his rifle. "Using armor-piercing rounds is obvious. EMPs also work, though it'd have to be a massive charge to pass through their shells."

"Is that what that blast was?" another guard asked. Jim, DJ thought his name was.

"That was a number of things," DJ chuckled. "But yeah, an EMP was part of it. I'll try to get equipment for your guys, Terry. But it can't be used indoors unless you want the entire building to fall on your head."

A guard whispered something to Terry, which made him grimace. "Yeah, I don't have something with a big enough charge to clear the mess outside, DJ. As it is, we can't even step out the door without getting shot." He frowned. "Plus, I think those big metallic spheres are up to something. They haven't joined the attack since it started, but our sensors have picked up weird movements. They've been going up and down the block for no reason we can figure."

DJ sighed. *What the hell is the damn AI planning now?*

"Look," he said. "How about you guys focus on clearing out the drones already in the building. My team and I will figure out a way to clear out the ones outside."

Terry frowned skeptically. "You sure?"

"Yeah, but we might need to draw in your lab guys though. Is that cool?"

"As long as they remain safe, they should also be able to pull their weight." Terry shrugged. "I'll pass it on to the other captains."

Terry rustled up the guards after that. They all headed into one of the hall-ways. DJ held his phone to one ear, waiting for a call to get through.

"*Now's not a really good time, DJ,*" Hermione said as soon as she picked up.

"Yeah, welcome to the motherfucking club," DJ said, placing his phone on his shoulder and tilting his head to hold it there. With his hands free, he lifted his rifle and took aim at a drone that was charging toward him. Its turrets whirled as it prepared to shoot, but DJ was faster. His first bullet caught it in its hull and knocked it off course. That set up the machine for DJ's follow-up shots. The drone crashed into the ground a few seconds later. DJ moved on. "I need your help."

"*I'm in my lab, which is currently on lockdown,*" Hermione said. "*I can't move from where I am.*"

"Well, I'm not yet sure if your moving is going to be necessary or not, so we can circle back to it. Now I'm not sure if you've looked outside at any point recently, but there's a swarm of drones covering the entire city block. They seem content to hover outside the building for now. The problem is, for every drone we destroy inside, two more enter to replace them. Considering the number outside, we might be clearing this place for a week."

"Do you think that's Helene's plan? To tire us out?"

"I don't see the end game in that," DJ shook his head. This almost dislodged the phone. He reached the stairwell for the floor and climbed to the second level. "My brother is of the opinion that they might be here for me."

"He's just upset," Hermione said. *"He's lashing out."*

"CJ isn't the type to lash out." DJ barged into the second level and immediately dove back into the stairwell to avoid a hail of bullets. The shots thudded into the metal door. Some of them pierced through, embedding themselves inside the wall over DJ's head. He cursed, but stayed put. Had the drone been just passing, or did the damn AI station a drone at the stairwell? "He has a point that killing me might be an objective, but I doubt it's the primary one. Helene definitely has something bigger planned."

"Any idea what that is?"

"Not a clue," DJ replied, "but we've gotten off track. The drones?"

"I have no idea what could work, DJ," Hermione said. *"Your brother—"*

"Something that does not involve my brother, please," DJ said. The drone activated at the sound of his voice. Gunfire thudded against the doors, so DJ raised his voice. "Christy used a weapon to get rid of hundreds of them at a time. It barely made a dent in their numbers, but does that help?"

"It might," Hermione sighed. *"How does the weapon work?"*

"It has three main settings. The first is the nuclear blast."

"That's what that was? Do you know how much equipment was destroyed because of that? I'm talking—"

"The second," DJ spoke over her, "was an EM wave, though that just short-circuited them temporarily. Christy used that chance to launch grenades at them. That's it." DJ ducked and glanced at the door. More and more bullets were getting through the barrier, which meant it wasn't going to last for long. He could just go down and try another stairwell, but that would leave the trap active for the next person coming up the steps.

Hermione muttered to herself for a bit. "*Well, the nuclear blast is out. The building might be able to tolerate those shock waves, but everything inside would be destroyed after a few salvos. The grenade launcher might work, but for a swarm like you described, it would take an ungodly amount of ammunition. And though Sparta has always been a bit militaristic in the way they run things, I doubt they'd have that.*"

"That leaves the EM wave. Would it work?"

"*It might,*" Hermione said. "*We'd need to find the right frequency, then power it high enough to reach the level that we need.*"

"But it's possible?" DJ confirmed, and then immediately cursed, as a bullet grazed his arm. He retreated a few steps down, but his eyes burned holes into the door.

"*It is.*"

"Good," he said. "What do you need to make this happen?"

"*Your brother, for one,*" Hermione said.

"You don't give up do you?"

"*Not when I think you're being an idiot, no.*"

"*Uh … thank you for your support, Hermione,*" CJ's voice came through the call.

"Bro," DJ shouted immediately, "can you link this call to my comm? It's really cramping my style to have to hold the phone like this."

"*Done,*" CJ said, but now his voice came from the earbuds in DJ's ears. DJ pocketed his phone, waited a moment for the gunfire to stop, and then dove back into the second floor passage.

While Hermione questioned CJ on how he'd gotten on the call, DJ took out his repressed anger on the drone. Energy coursed through him as his nanites activated and DJ used that strength to tackle the drone. He dragged it to the ground and used the butt of his rifle to bash its hull open. One of its guns focused on him, and DJ knocked it away with a well-timed punch. He pumped a slug into the other and then continued with his bashing. It took a minute before the drone got the memo, and the red light at its center finally died out. DJ jumped down and started jogging down the hallway. He had to pause several times whenever he got to the giant metal barricades that separated the different sections of the floor. In some cases though, he found the access panel already broken or the metal door drilled through.

DJ cleared any drone that he saw. Sometimes, they moved in groups of two or three, but DJ had the battle down to a tee, so they posed little danger to him. It was weird to think that, just less than a year ago, he'd basically been hiding behind the Murder Twins while they'd torn through the drones like they were paper.

Now here he was doing the same thing.

"*… cameras, so I … uh … hacked into my brother's phone so I could hear you both*," CJ finished his explanation. "*Also, you … um … need to calm down, DJ.*"

"And you need to go fuck yourself," DJ said. "Why're you here?" He was panting, but he was far from exhausted. Even without the nanites activated, DJ's passive endurance was through the roof. He could probably fight for hours before he started to get exhausted.

"*I … um … want to help.*"

"*Let him, DJ*," Hermione added. "*It'll go much faster.*"

"*Also, we have a problem*," CJ said.

"What is it?"

"*Tyra Chityothin … uh … just entered the building.*"

38

DECEMBER 2043
SPARTA HEADQUARTERS,
NEW YORK

DJ STOPPED WITH A TURRET held over his head. Running out of ammo, he'd taken to using only one bullet per drone to break off one of their parts and then use it to bash them in. But that took time, and according to CJ, he didn't have time to waste. He unslung his rifle and pumped a slug into the drone to stop its struggling. "Where is she now?"

"She … um … just entered the ground floor."

"What are you thinking, DJ?" Hermione asked.

"I'm thinking that if Tyra is here, it saves us a search and a trip," DJ replied honestly. He was already jogging toward another stairwell to head to the lobby. If they could capture Tyra now, then they'd finally get answers. It wasn't a chance DJ could afford to miss.

"*You're forgetting that Helene probably sent her here for a reason,*" Hermione said.

"My point exactly," DJ replied. He finally found the next stairwell and descended the steps two at a time.

"*I think what Hermione is trying to say is that … uh … Tyra's presence might be a trap.*"

DJ increased his pace. "All the more reason to capture her before she can spring it."

Hermione sighed, but DJ found it hilarious. It wasn't like he didn't understand their point, or that he didn't understand the danger. If anything, he understood far too well how dangerous Tyra was. That's why he wanted to get her out of the picture as soon as possible. Even more important: Tyra had *answers*. With that on the line, it didn't matter if it was a trap. DJ had no choice but to jump into it.

"*Do you … um … have a plan?*" his brother asked.

"Sure," DJ replied. "Sparta security is already working on clearing out the drones from all levels. However, they'll eventually get overwhelmed unless you, Hermione, and the other gearheads figure out the frequency stuff in time. CJ, Christy will let you out of the room and lead you to Hermione so you guys can coordinate better."

"*And let me guess, you're still going after Tyra,*" Hermione said.

"I blame my parents." DJ shrugged, though he knew she couldn't see it. "They raised me to always greet our guests."

39

CJ DIVIDED HIS COMPUTER SCREEN into three sections. One of them was dedicated to tracking down Tyra Chityothin using the multitude of security cameras scattered around Sparta. Another followed his brother as he made his way toward her. CJ periodically gave instructions so DJ wasn't running about aimlessly.

CJ tried his best to keep the anger from his voice. He was angry, and not because his brother had hit him or even because he'd locked him in the room. It was because every time he spoke, he stuttered—he had to grab for words. It reminded him he had to wait indefinitely to be free of it all.

He'd known DJ wouldn't agree with his choice. That's why he hadn't told him. CJ even understood why his brother had stopped him. But how could he not act when the key to everything he'd dreamed about was just a few levels down in the mini-tank? And now he couldn't do anything about it.

CJ shook his head to dispel the thought. Although DJ was moving fast, he'd started almost at the opposite side of the building from where Tyra had entered. It was going to take several minutes for him to cross the distance. It also didn't help that he stopped to destroy every drone he encountered on his way.

It was easy to recognize Tyra from her pictures. Even without them, CJ would have been drawn to her. She was taller than average, with a slim build but a generous chest. Her long dark-brown hair cascaded down her back, and she wore a flowery blouse and skintight leather pants, with a standard lab coat draped over her shoulder like a cape. However, if that had been all, CJ would have dismissed her as one of Sparta's many researchers.

She'd caught his attention for one reason: she was the only person who wasn't running.

Most civilians were either running away from the drones or trying to make their way toward one of the safe areas. Tyra, however, was casually strolling. At some point, a dozen drones surrounded her and hovered at her pace. They attacked anyone they encountered, including civilians fleeing from another section of the building. Tyra stepped over their corpses without a care in the world. CJ felt a surge of anger and disgust as he watched her callousness, a fire igniting within him at her utter lack of empathy.

There were still several security teams clearing out the floor, moving in groups of six. CJ had avoided alerting them initially since DJ wanted to handle Helene's goon himself. But he couldn't watch her kill innocents and do nothing. He tapped into one of the captains' comm units, and after a minute of calming the man down and explaining who he was and how he was able to hack their systems, CJ was finally able to direct them to intercept Tyra.

The drones rushed out immediately when they arrived. The guards had already taken DJ's advice and switched to armor-piercing rounds. The guards didn't have nanites boosting their reaction times and making them fast enough to dodge bullets—but they were able to take down several of the machines all the same.

That was when Tyra Chityothin stepped in. She tapped her phone, and the cameras flickered and shut down. They came back on several seconds later, but by then the guards had joined the corpses littering the floor. Tyra stood over them, flicking through her phone. A moment later, she looked up and stared straight at the camera that CJ was peering through.

CJ gulped.

It was logical for her to assume that someone in the building was watching her. It didn't necessarily mean she knew it was him. But she'd been staring at *him*. CJ was sure of that. He tapped into DJ's comm. "Uh … she knows that you are coming," he said.

"TWO . . . UH . . . *hallways away,*" CJ responded in his ear. "*She is surrounded by a dozen drones. And, DJ … she, um, killed one of the security teams in a few seconds. I do not … uh … know how, but be careful. Okay?*"

DJ's nanites reacted to his anger, and he let them fill him up. He could probably have dealt with a dozen drones with his passive enhancements, but it would have taken too long and might have given Chityothin time to run. That wasn't really an option.

DJ followed his brother's direction until his hearing picked up the soft *whooshing* sound that always accompanied drones. DJ sped up once more. The world slowed to a crawl. He turned the corner. Tyra Chityothin was at the other end, striding toward him. He had only seen pictures of her, but none of them did her justice.

Huh, DJ mused, absently. *She's hot.* His eyes went to the drones hovering around her like bees around their queen. She didn't seem to be directly controlling them, but they definitely recognized her as off-limits. He was sure CJ would have been interested in understanding how that worked, but DJ didn't give a rat's ass. He was across the hall and in the air in an instant, his fist falling toward one of the machines. He intended to capture Tyra alive, but he'd need to handle the drones first. After the fifth drone, DJ spared a glance at her, but had a disturbing revelation: She was smiling, her eyes locked on his.

With just his passive enhancements, DJ was already reaching superhuman speeds. But with his nanites activated, he should have been a blur. And yet Tyra's eyes were keeping up with him. He stumbled, and Tyra pounced on the chance. She turned into a blur, reappearing only when she was a foot from him, her fist raised. "This wasn't how it was supposed to go," she said.

"The feeling's fucking mutual!" DJ groaned, taking the attack on his forearm. The force launched him several feet away. Nevertheless, he stayed on his feet, though he hesitated to charge back in. "You have nanites?"

Tyra threw her head back and laughed wildly. "You thought you were special?"

No. DJ hadn't thought that he was special. But he'd gotten his nanites from the Murder Twins. Martin had specifically developed the technology for them … on Helene's orders. DJ groaned internally. He hadn't given it any thought before, but it made sense. A lot of sense actually, considering that José had only gotten his nanites when Helene had worked on him. Obviously that meant that the AI knew how to produce the technology, and *obviously* she'd enhanced her trusted henchwoman with it. It was also probably another form of control. Helene could probably tap into the nanites the same way she'd controlled the Murder Twins.

"Penny for your thoughts?" Tyra asked, still smiling. It creeped him out. Chloe did the whole smiling thing as well, but at least with her, he knew she was just mad. Tyra was one stubbed toe away from needing a straitjacket and a padded room.

DJ pushed the thought out of his head. He'd expected he could easily capture and then question her. The fact that she had nanites changed everything. DJ was used to dominating everything in his path when his tiny robots were active—or getting his ass whipped by people far more experienced. He didn't know where Tyra fell on that spectrum, and he wasn't going to know until they fought.

So he charged.

There were several feet between them. DJ crossed it in an instant. It was a direct attack, with no tricks, to test Tyra's reaction. Unfortunately, the drones detached from her and moved to intercept him, ruining that plan. DJ's fist crashed through the first, but he lost track of Tyra.

A moment later, her punch landed on his side. Although DJ tightened his muscles so he wasn't flung away, he couldn't stop a sharp pain. She didn't pack as much of a punch as José, but there were some muscles underneath those curves. DJ swung his arm back—his fist still stuck in the drone. But Tyra easily dodged it. Still, that left her open for a knee to her stomach. She groaned, allowing herself to be flung away to create some distance between them.

Drones flew in to fill the spot. But DJ also jumped back. He'd learned several things from that exchange.

She's faster than I am, he mused, *but I'm stronger*. It made sense. While nanites enhanced what was already there, they didn't magically add more. Probably. DJ had more bulk, so it was logical that he'd be able to put out more force. In the same way, she was smaller, so she had better agility.

Of course, José had wrecked him in both speed and strength. What did DJ actually know?

The nanites aside, the exchange told DJ he had more fighting experience than Tyra. The woman could fight, but it was obvious she hadn't seen any battle. That meant that DJ could win in a straight fight.

The problem is, he thought, eyeing the drones that hovered around the woman, *I'm not going to get a straight fight with them around*. He still couldn't figure out how they were being controlled, but if he wanted to duke it out with Tyra, he'd have to take them out first.

"You think a lot," Tyra said. "I'm surprised."

"It's a relatively new development," DJ agreed easily. "But you have a point. I should just try something simple." His gun—the pistol, not the rifle—was in his hands in the next moment. He squeezed off two shots. It'd taken less than a second, but somehow, a drone managed to get in the way in time, and the bullets pinged off its hull, leaving a slight mark but no damage.

Tyra burst out laughing. "I knew you were going to do that," she roared. "I just *knew* it. That's like your signature move. It's your thing. How could I not have prepared for it?"

DJ relaxed his aim, confused. Tyra laughed.

"Your gun," Tyra explained, wiping away a tear. "You always lead with your gun. I was actually expecting you to shoot at me when you first saw me. However, I guess you're still hooked on the nanites. It's like you've found a new toy to play with, right? And it probably doesn't help that your brain is cooking in a soup of hormones." She put on an exaggerated frown and drew a tear line down her cheek. "I understand, baby. It takes some getting used to."

DJ's lips stretched into a thin line. Chloe had said the same thing, if in a less insane way. That didn't bode well. He'd known his emotions had been off lately. But how much of his actions were his and not just the result of his jacked-up hormones? Had his reaction the previous week with CJ been—

DJ stopped the thought before it could go further. Tyra was right. He *did* think too much.

What the fuck?

DJ squeezed off a few more shots—all of which were intercepted by the drones—before switching to his rifle. He chained two shots in quick succession. Both were blocked, but there were noticeable dents in their hulls. Tyra watched him throughout the process, her smile slowly growing wider.

DJ slung his rifle back on and blew out a breath. He had only one option now, and the thought of it made him grimace. *This is going to hurt.*

He charged once more. Again, two drones detached from the group to intercept him. But they didn't fly toward him like before. They hovered a few feet away from Tyra and shot a hail of bullets at him.

DJ cursed. Tyra burst out laughing again. He threw himself at the wall, then dashed forward before the guns could target him again. He came at them from the side, well away from the stream of bullets, and threw a right hook. Once more, Tyra took advantage of his distraction to attack, but DJ had expected that. Tyra's attack landed at the same moment his punch forced the drone to the ground. DJ grimaced, but he gave up on countering to shoot toward the next machine.

Another punch forced it to join the other. DJ unstrapped his rifle. He squeezed off two shots to put both drones down before dashing toward the next duo.

Tyra must have realized his plan because those drones retreated before he could reach them. DJ grinned at that before changing direction and charging toward Tyra. She tried to meet him head-on, but DJ's punch—fueled by his rising frustration—launched her over a dozen feet, sending her crashing into the wall at the end of the passage.

DJ charged toward her without a word.

CJ SWITCHED TO A CAMERA with a better angle. Where his monitor had previously been divided into three parts, CJ had joined all of them into one feed that displayed his brother's fight with Tyra Chityothin. His only audio came from DJ's comm unit. He could hear his brother's responses, and for a while, he could form an image of the conversation based on what he'd said. Unfortunately, DJ had stopped talking, which meant he'd gotten serious.

Still, CJ didn't need to hear to be engrossed in the fight. His brother was systematically destroying the drones, while Tyra used the chance to attack. CJ noticed the flash of pain on his brother's face every time he was forced to absorb the attack. But he didn't stop attacking the drones. It was a solid plan, as long as he destroyed the machines fast enough. Without her shields, DJ would be able to overpower Tyra in a straight fight.

Suddenly, something slammed against the door, making CJ jump. He reached for his brother's spare gun, wishing it was a spear.

"CJ!" Christy yelled from the other side of the door. "Open up. We need to move."

CJ breathed a sigh of relief. "DJ … uh … locked the door from outside," he called out. "I cannot … um … open it from here."

"He locked you in?" Christy asked. "What a piece of shit. All right, stand back. I'll get you out of there." A second later came a gunshot, and the lock exploded. Christy kicked the door open and waved CJ over. "What? You're waiting for an invitation or something? Get your ass moving. Quickly!"

CJ detached his laptop from its dock and put it in a bag that he slung over his shoulder. He tucked the extra pistol he found in the armory closet in his waistband and followed her out. The passages were clear, but Christy didn't lead him to the elevators as CJ had expected. She headed to the stairwell.

"Most of the elevators have been destroyed," she explained as she pulled open the thick door, "and the few that are still working are being used by the staff to get to safety, so it's best to use the staircase." She glanced at him skeptically. "Are you going to be all right? We're gonna be going down a lot of stairs."

The comment offended him. While he wouldn't say that he was in the best shape, why would he have problems going down some steps? He frowned at her, but he could tell from her expression that she knew it hadn't come out well. This just made him sigh.

"Well, whatever," Christy said, waving him forward so she could follow him. "DJ said you have a plan to get rid of the swarm outside? I took care of a few of them, but it didn't make a dent. I hope whatever you have is bigger than the Bulldog."

"It is … uh … it is not going to be a weapon," CJ said. "We are going to … um … generate a frequency that will act as an EMP and disrupt the drones enough for them to crash."

"An EMP? Within the building? Are you guys crazy? How the hell are you going to contain the explosion?" Christy asked, as they reached the landing for a floor. CJ glanced back at her. He understood her confusion. Most EMPs were created by a sudden release of energy such as a high-altitude nuclear explosion. However, even if CJ could simulate such an explosion, he wouldn't. That would be incredibly reckless.

"We are going to use … uh … a radio frequency EMP," CJ replied. They descended to another landing and stopped at the sound of turrets of gunfire through the metal door that led into the floor. Even if there were drones on the floor, they wouldn't shoot unless there was something to shoot at.

They shared a look. "Wait here," Christy said finally and ducked through the door. The sound of gunfire intensified. Just when CJ was about to go in, Christy came back to the landing. "So, how's that going to work?" she asked, waving him on. "The whole frequency thing?"

A standard EMP wouldn't disrupt the drones for long. Instead, they needed a specific signal that fell outside their operational range to disable them. CJ and Hermione would have to identify that signal and figure out how to extend its range to cover the entire block, ensuring it remained powerful and effective.

He explained that to Christy.

"Is that even possible?" she asked.

"It … um … should be," CJ replied. "We would have to … uh … work with the engineers to build it. But the machine itself is not overly complicated. The major problem … um … is figuring out the frequency that we need. But for that, all we need … uh … is time."

He left unsaid that that would require someone to keep the drones occupied while they worked. Tyra Chityothin would also have to be kept distracted. But his brother had that well in hand.

DJ'S FIST CRASHED INTO the last drone. Its shell cracked from the force and collided with the wall. In the same instant, a kick landed in his stomach, shooting him several feet away. DJ bit his lips to stop from screaming out. The bitch had been attacking the same spot for the last few minutes, and the damage was beginning to pile up. She'd also found several ways to prolong the fight, giving her the chance to attack DJ wantonly, while he focused on destroying the flying machines. It was honestly the most frustrating fight DJ had ever been in.

But it was done now. The entire passage fell silent. The red light at the center of last drone finally blinked off, and the machine fell to the ground. DJ wiped the blood from his mouth and grinned at Tyra.

Her return grin was wider and wilder than his, escalating into a full-blown laugh that had the woman clutching her side. DJ stared at her in amusement while he stretched. He undoubtedly had a new map of bruises around him, but none of them felt debilitating. He could have attacked, but DJ was content to wait. He knew she didn't stand a chance without her shields.

The battle was his unless she decided to run. That was a possible option, but DJ was confident she wasn't faster than a bullet. He held on to that confidence even when she casually pulled out two daggers. She pointed one at him, still chuckling. "You don't get the joke, do you?"

"You mean … you?" DJ smirked.

Something about that just made her laugh harder, so much so that she bent over, clutching her side in pain.

What the hell? DJ thought, scrunching up his face in confusion. *It wasn't even that good of a burn.*

"No," the nutcase replied when she finally straightened. "It's the fact that you thought I *needed* the drones to beat you."

DJ tensed and then smirked. *She's bluffing.*

Tyra giggled—like, straight *giggled* like a five-year-old anime girl. "It was just so cute to see you running around thinking you were actually doing something." She burst out laughing once more.

"You can say whatever you want, but you're fucked."

"You don't believe me?" Tyra asked, bending her knees slightly. "Okay! Let me show you."

She disappeared. In the same instant, her fist slammed into his stomach like a *sledgehammer*. He doubled over and coughed up blood that hung in the air as another blow launched him clear off his feet. The wall he crashed into had already cracked from his previous impacts. This time it crumbled entirely, the debris falling around his prone body. DJ almost blacked out from the pain, but his eyes widened when Tyra appeared in front of him with her fist pulled back.

DJ surged to his feet, moving faster than ever before. He ducked underneath her punch and immediately leaped backward to create more distance between them. Tyra's fist landed where he'd been. The entire floor shook from the force of the blow. Even more parts of the wall caved in, and the ceiling trembled as if it were going to come down. DJ's jaw went slack, his mind overwhelmed. It didn't take long for him to come to the obvious conclusion.

He'd been duped.

In their first exchange, Tyra had deliberately avoided taking DJ's attacks directly. She had controlled the drones to intercept him whenever he tried. Combined with the fact that she'd reduced her speed and strength, it'd given DJ the impression that she was weaker than she actually was. That had led him to focus on destroying the drones in order to force a straight fight that'd be to his advantage. But to do that, he'd needed to allow Tyra to wail on him as much as she wanted. All of her attacks hit hard, but they were well within DJ's tolerance range. However, the damage had still added up, especially around his stomach where she'd focused her attacks.

The result was where they were now: Tyra, who'd just proven that she was both faster and stronger, was in pristine condition. Meanwhile, DJ was, in a word, fucked.

But also pissed.

What the hell? DJ thought. *What in the absolute fucking hell?* She was already stronger, but she'd still resorted to tricks? Who did that? Seriously, who the hell did that? It was the lowest of the low, the dickest of all dick moves.

Worse was that DJ had fallen for it. She'd played her part so well that he'd genuinely thought that he was making the best move. She'd played it out so *perfectly.* Everything, from the way she'd avoided taking his punches, to the way she'd controlled the drones to retreat as if trying to preserve them—*everything* had been perfect. It spoke volumes of how much she knew him. She'd known he wasn't going to question whether he was stronger, just like she'd known he was going to shoot at her. She'd even known he would dismiss any doubts as overthinking once he was called out for it.

She had just baited him, and DJ had fallen for it, hook, line, and sinker.

CJ wouldn't have fallen for the same trick. But she wouldn't have tried this on his brother, would she? She'd obviously done her research on them both. This meant it was a safe bet she knew how all of them would react in each situation. DJ sighed at that. It was a cold comfort. But it was better than nothing.

Tyra tilted her head when she noticed the change in his expression. She'd been watching him with the same mocking smile on her lips. "I gotta say," she said. "You're taking this better than I expected."

"Oh, so I managed to surprise you?" DJ asked. "One point for me then."

"And how many for me?"

"It doesn't really matter," DJ shrugged. "He who laughs last and all that." He unslung his rifle and hefted it in his hands. Tyra rolled her eyes, telling DJ all he needed to know. Still, he squeezed off a shot and watched as she dodged the bullet. But she'd moved *before* DJ had pulled the trigger. She did the same thing that he did: She predicted the angle of the shot and dodged before the bullet left the chamber. Plus, the fact that she'd dodged at all suggested she didn't have the same cybernetics that allowed José and the Murder Twins to tank bullets. She could have been pretending again, but it was still *something*.

DJ fired several shots in quick succession, changing the angle every time. Tyra dodged each one, but she had to focus, taking her attention off him long enough for him to grab a grenade from his back pocket and toss it toward her. The explosion rocked the floor again and sent up a cloud of dust from where parts of the wall were wrecked.

When the cloud cleared, DJ was gone.

CHAPTER

43

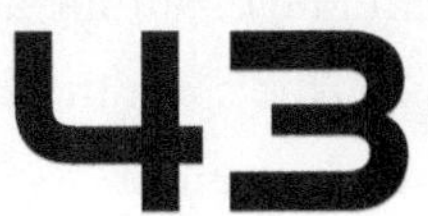

DECEMBER 2043
SPARTA HEADQUARTERS,
NEW YORK

CJ AND CHRISTY ARRIVED at a section of the stairwell where several flights of stairs had collapsed. Bullet-shaped holes marked the walls around the place. They'd have to take another stairwell, which meant crossing the main floor. Christy took the lead then, her rifle held in front of her. CJ brought out his gun just in case and moved silently behind her.

Moving in a straight line at a casual pace, a floor in Sparta could take about a half hour to traverse. However, they weren't going through the entire floor. They just needed to find another stairwell. That would take considerably less time and limit their risk of discovery.

A drone found them in under a minute, but fortunately the sound of its rotors gave away its position. CJ had enough advanced warning to retreat to the end of the hallway, and Christy was ready to poke her head out and greet it with a slug. The shot connected, but the drone responded by spitting a hail of bullets.

Once the gunfire abated, Christy sprang out again and fired two more shots. CJ tensed, but he also darted out to fire a shot. The bullet did no damage. He'd aimed for the joints. The force knocked the machine to the side. Christy pounced on the opportunity and fired several shots in quick succession. She tried to aim for the joints like he had, but the drone moved around too much. To her surprise, the shot pierced its hull. Another one landed beside the first, and the machine crashed to the ground. The duo moved on.

"*This isn't working,*" Hermione said through the comm in CJ's ear several minutes later. CJ was in the middle of aiming at another drone, so he didn't answer. It was only when they'd taken cover that he responded. And even then, he had to shout to be heard over the gunfire.

"What is not … uh … working?" Hermione had gathered every scientist and engineer she could to start working on the machine that they needed. They'd communicated with CJ, but they could have been more efficient if he were there—hence why Christy was leading him there.

"*Everything,*" Hermione replied. "*We've confirmed what you said, that the drones would only react to a specific frequency. But our tests to determine that frequency have been futile. We don't have an actual specimen to test on.*"

"You need a drone?" CJ asked. Christy glanced back before continuing what she'd been doing. "Can you not … um … contract some of the guards?"

"*We need a* working *drone,*" Hermione specified. "*Each one they bring back is either destroyed or nearly so. We've been forced to test the frequency of drones passing outside, but I don't need to tell you how inefficient that is. How far away are you?*"

"We are … uh … we are still a few levels up," CJ said. He hesitated for a moment. "But … uh … we will handle the drone."

The connection with Hermione cut out. CJ looked up to find Christy glaring at him.

"We'll handle what?"

CJ gave a sheepish look. "The team … um … needs a working drone to characterize the frequency and response of their systems in order to … uh … to determine what frequency destroys them."

"And you volunteered *us*?" Christy raised a brow. "Why the hell would you do that?"

CJ nodded. "You … um … are right," CJ said. "My brother … uh … would have been a better choice." It took Christy and CJ several minutes of hit-and-run tactics to take down one, whereas DJ would have handled several at a time. Of course, it took more effort to capture one than to destroy it. But the nanites would definitely have made the task easier for DJ.

Christy glared at him again. "What the hell do you mean that DJ would be a better choice? He's an idiot," she growled. She hefted her sniper rifle. "If that bonehead can do it, then I can definitely do it in half the time."

CJ restricted himself to a nod and hid his amazement.

When they found the stairwell, they could descend only one floor before it, too, was destroyed. CJ started considering whether it would be easier to take the elevator. It'd been a little over an hour since the drones had attacked—more than enough time for the staff to have gotten to safe rooms. He was about to suggest it to Christy when they turned the corner and stumbled on a drone. Because it was lying on the ground, CJ's first impression was that it had been destroyed. However, Christy wasn't so trusting, so she aimed at it. Immediately, the drone shot to the air, its guns whirring to life.

CJ tensed, but Christy was already pulling back around the corner when the bullets reached where they'd been standing. "What the fuck?" she cursed. "They're camping out and laying traps now? Since when can they do that?"

CJ was about to reply, but his comm buzzed. "*Yo, CJ,*" his brother said, "*I need a progress report. How's it going?*" DJ paused before adding, "*Glad you're with Christy … and I am sorry about this morning.*"

CJ took a breath, feeling the tension ease. "Hermione and the … uh … the engineers are working on the machine," he replied, his tone softening. "Christy and I are … um … still on our way to meet them."

"*Shit, seriously? What the fuck is taking so long?*"

"Drones," CJ said simply. But the fact that he had to shout over Christy's return fire made his point moot. "Are you … um … going to meet us at the lab with Tyra Chityothin?"

There was a pause before his brother answered. "*Nah, I had to haul ass. I'm still hauling ass actually because I can't be sure she's not chasing me.*"

CJ cocked his head. "What … uh … do you mean?"

"*You watched our fight, right? Where'd you stop?*" DJ asked. CJ told him. "*Well, after I destroyed the last drone, she did a bullshit reveal that she'd been fucking with me all along. She's both stronger and faster than me, CJ, and she played me like a fiddle.*"

CJ could hear the undertones of anger in his brother's voice despite his attempts to hide it.

"*Anyway,*" DJ said, "*at that point, I figured it was best I call it quits. I don't think she's someone I can fight on my own.*"

CJ nodded. From Olsen's report, he'd expected Tyra Chityothin to be incredibly crafty, but even he was surprised. Despite his quirks, DJ wasn't a brute. Even when he didn't think, his instincts usually guided him. The fact that he'd been tricked so completely spoke volumes.

Still, it didn't change the fact that Tyra Chityothin was a bad match-up for DJ. If they wanted to capture her, DJ would need all the help he could get. "So," CJ started, "what is the plan now? Where are … uh … are you headed?"

"*Right now I'm just concerned about putting as much distance as I can between me and Tyra. After that, I figure I can help with clearing out the drones and evacuating everyone while we figure out a plan.*"

CJ unslung his backpack and removed his computer. It took him a few moments to scan the cameras before he finally found Tyra Chityothin. "You can stop running," he told his brother. "She is no longer chasing you."

"*She's not?*" DJ asked, surprised. "*What's she doing then?*"

Christy leaned over to peer at the monitor. "Taking a stroll apparently," she said. "She's wandering around like she doesn't give two shits."

DJ didn't say anything for a moment. "*As much as it pains my ego, CJ, I don't think they're here for me, or else she'd be chasing me down. Why would she even have toyed with me in the first place?*"

It's the only thing that makes sense though, CJ thought. But his brother was right. The evidence didn't add up. It would be illogical to continue pushing the theory. They had to be missing something.

"This doesn't change anything though," DJ continued. *"How long do you think it'll take you guys to get to Hermione's lab and meet up with the rest?"*

CJ looked at Christy. "Not too long," she replied. "We're just a few floors up. The problem is, we keep having to stop to take care of the drones."

"Don't you still have the Bulldog?"

"I had to give it to one of the guards to pass it to the gearheads working on their machine. Apparently they needed to examine the EMP function on the gun or something."

"Those nerds better not ruin it," DJ growled. *"Anyway, the plan remains the same. I'll work with the security teams to clear the drones. You guys get to the lab and finish the machine. CJ, keep an eye on Tyra and hit me up if she does something weird."*

"Thought you … um … said she was a nutcase."

"Something weirder then," his brother specified with a sigh.

"That … uh … reminds me," CJ said, "we need a dro—" Christy's eyes promised death if he finished his sentence.

"I didn't catch that, bro. You need what?"

"Um … nothing," CJ said anxiously. "I … uh … misspoke." Fortunately, his brother didn't question it. CJ could almost imagine his shrug as he dismissed the whole thing. The line went dead a moment later.

"I said," Christy growled, bringing her face an inch from his, "I'll handle it."

CJ limited himself to a nod. Both of them continued. They encountered several drones over the next several minutes. CJ tried to help, and although his bullets rarely damaged the machines, they disoriented them so Christy could get a better shot—not that Christy wanted the help. She waved him off, which meant it took longer to destroy each drone. At first CJ thought she was still annoyed about the call with DJ. Then he realized her goal: She was training.

For each encounter, she targeted a different part of the drone, then she'd duck back while the drone returned fire. Several times, the drones used the chance to close the distance between them, forcing Christy to give up on her training and fill the machine with holes. In the next encounter, she'd continue again. Once CJ understood what she was doing, he started pointing out specific sections for her to target.

Their pace was slow initially, but once they had the system down, they dropped drones within a minute. Eventually the drones were little more than nuisances.

When they were two floors from their destination, Christy focused her training on figuring out how to incapacitate a drone without completely destroying it. That slowed them down once more. Nevertheless, by the time they reached Hermione's floor, CJ was clutching a struggling drone in his arms while Christy destroyed others that came after them. Its size made it unwieldy, and its constant movement didn't help. Several of its parts had been destroyed. But the large spot of red light at its center still blinked steadily. That is what mattered.

CJ informed Hermione when they were close, and she was there to wave them in. "You actually got one?" she said once she saw the drone. The lab was the most crowded that CJ had ever seen. Several dozen staff stared at him and Christy as they entered—several with panicked eyes, some with blank gazes. Only a few seemed calm. Although CJ tensed at the attention, it lasted only a moment before he shook it off. "Maybe we can actually make some progress now."

She waved them toward the center of the room where a space had been cleared to make room for a large machine. Even though it had obviously been made out of used parts, it was about two feet high and about half that in width. There was a front display that showed the frequency value and a numeric keypad. There were also knobs and buttons for minor adjustments in amplitude and modulation. Two wires jutted out from the back. One ran to the wall and was connected to a socket for power, while another was plugged into a partially destroyed drone.

When she noticed where his attention was, Hermione yanked the cord from the incapacitated drone and waved it at the drone in his arms. "That was what we were working with before," she said, "but yours is a much better sample."

"How did … um … how did you guys build this in an hour?"

"Carl over there," Hermione pointed to a man in overalls in the back, "worked on a frequency synthesizer a while back. Security helped us retrieve it. We dusted it off, dismantled it, reinforced some parts, changed others completely, made a new design when neither of those worked, coupled an entirely new machine from the old parts … and voilà." She patted the machine. "The engineers did most of the work. I mainly supervised and designed experiments to determine the drone's frequency."

CJ nodded. Hermione had obviously downplayed her role, if the looks the other staff gave her were any indication. But they didn't have the time to get into it. There was only one thing that mattered. "Does it … uh … work?" Hermione looked at him as if he'd insulted her. Several engineers took a step forward with scowls on their faces. Surprised at their reaction, CJ quickly clarified. "What is … uh … its maximum range?"

Hermione grimaced. "A little less than a city block." She sighed. "That was the best we could do without risking it falling apart."

"It … um … will have to do then," CJ replied. He dropped the struggling drone beside the machine. "You … uh … you said you designed some experiments?"

CHAPTER

44

DECEMBER 2043
SPARTA HEADQUARTERS,
NEW YORK

DJ RAN THROUGH THE HALLS at a casual jog. He was pissed and hopped up on nanites, so his jog neared that of most Olympic gold medalists. If he sprinted flat out, he could probably round the entire floor in a few minutes. There was no need to though. Tyra had apparently lost interest in him. He had enough speed and strength he could catch up to and destroy every drone he met within a few seconds. DJ was sure that should have made him happier than it did. Several times, he'd arrived just in time to save a staff person from getting killed or one of the patrols from getting overwhelmed. The former happened mostly out of luck, the latter because DJ had asked his brother to link his comm to the guards'.

"The fifty-eighth is cleared. Moving to the fifty-ninth."

"Be careful of the drone stationed in the stairwell over there. We got the last one but they may have replaced it."

"These fucking things. It's almost like they're getting smarter."

"*One of the fuckers waited in the middle of the hallway, pretending to be dead or some shit, only to jump us when we were about to pass it. It damn near wiped out half of us before we put it down.*"

"*Yeah. It happened to me, too.*"

"*Same here. Hey, calm down, lady! You shouldn't be here. There's a safe room just around the—WHAT THE FUCK? What the hell did you do that for? Jesus Christ!*"

"*What happened?*"

"*Yeah. What's with the screaming, dude?*"

"*This bitch just stabbed me! Just like that. Outta the blue. She stabbed me.*"

"*I told you your face could drive people to anger.*"

The chatter devolved from there. When DJ was about to step in, someone else beat him to it. "*Everyone, shut the hell up!*" they yelled. DJ recognized the deep bass of Terry, one of the guard captains. "*Johnson! What the hell happened?*"

"*Can't say, Cap,*" the guard—Johnson apparently—replied. "*My team and I were making our way through the twenty-eighth floor when this bitch jumped me outta nowhere with a knife. She got a stab in before I put her down.*"

"*Put her down?*" Terry asked, a dangerous note in his voice. "*You staked one of our own?*"

"*Give me some credit, cap. I just knocked her out. Plus I don't see how she could be one of our own. She's definitely not one of the guests. I doubt she's one of the staff.*"

"*What makes you doubt it?*"

"*Well, for one, Cap, she's dressed like a soccer mom picking her kids up from practice. Gimme a sec, Cap.*" There was a pause. "*Yep, I just found some ID. Apparently she's a teacher from one of the middle schools.*"

DJ stopped with a wince, one foot on the stairs. Johnson's words had brought another wave of chatter from the teams, creating irritating feedback when all the voices blended together. Fortunately, it lasted only a few seconds this time before everyone understood to shut up.

"*You're saying she just wandered in?*" Terry said.

"*I'm not saying anything, Cap. I'm not paid enough for that. All I know is she stabbed me, and now she's unconscious. What do I do with her?*"

"Hold her for now," Terry said. *"Securely. Once she wakes up, we'll see what she can tell us."*

"Roger that, Cap."

"Wait," DJ said, speaking for the first time. "This woman, did you notice anything … weird about her?"

"Apart from her stabbing me out of nowhere?" Johnson asked.

"Yeah, apart from that. Was she moving strangely? Stiffly? Did her eyes look, y'know, dead or something? Or was she wearing dark shades? Something like that."

"I don't know what to tell you, DJ," the man said. *"The strangest thing is how she got up here in the first place—you know, without getting a few extra holes. And now that I think about it actually, the broad was walking."*

"Walking?"

"Yeah, walking. With all these fuckers flying around, everyone running and stuff, she was strolling down the hall like she was in a garden or some shit. That's weird, right? Is that what you were looking for?"

"Not … particularly," DJ said. "But at least it's something. Thanks, Johnson. Keep me updated about where you secure her though. I might have a few questions of my own when this whole ordeal is over."

"Roger that. Over and out."

He continued up the stairs while his mind went over the last few minutes. It perturbed him—random woman somehow wandering into Sparta when not even the police could get in. Had she somehow made her way up to the twenty-eight floor just to attack a guard? In what world did that make sense?

DJ tapped his comm unit to switch its channel. "How's it going?"

"Um … I am a little busy right now, DJ," CJ responded. *"Is there … uh … a problem?"*

"I'm not sure. Grab Hermione and you both can help me figure this out." He filled them in on everything that Johnson said, including the fact that the woman was definitely not on staff.

"It's obviously one of Helene's puppets," Hermione surmised.

"The guard did not note any of the signs though," CJ said.

"*Well, it's not like we've made it public,*" Hermione countered. "*It could be that he didn't know what to look for.*"

"It *could* also be good old-fashioned bribery," DJ put in. "But I think Hermione's right. My gut tells me it's Helene, but I can't figure out why she would send just the one woman. And why attack Johnson of all people? It just seems too simp—" DJ paused, holding a finger to his ear as a priority message from the raid channel overrode their chat. His comm switched seamlessly to the main channel.

"*ALL TEAMS, BE ADVISED,*" Terry roared with more fury than DJ had ever heard from him. "*CIVILIANS HAVE ENTERED THE BUILDING AND ARE ATTACKING ALONGSIDE THE DRONES. I REPEAT—*"

The stairwell led to the thirty-first floor. DJ rushed to the nearest window that showed the front of the building. The last time he checked, the only thing to be seen was the swarm of drones covering both the ground and the skies throughout the block. Now the drones had all flown up, making space for the horde of civilians approaching the building. DJ peered through the scope of his gun. The crowd came into clearer focus.

From an outside view, they might have been mistaken for a tourist crowd. They were split almost evenly between men and women. Most of them were empty-handed, but several carried baseball bats and pipes—probably knives as well, based on Johnson's account. The horde streamed into the building in a surprisingly orderly manner. There was no pushing or scrambling. There was also no stiffness in their movements. DJ zoomed in more with the scope, but he couldn't make out their eyes.

Still, it wasn't like he needed the confirmation.

"Yep, it's definitely Helene," he told CJ and Hermione. "A bunch of her puppets are swarming the building now. Like, a lot. A lot a lot. For some reason she's decided to go all out." DJ cast his gaze out the window again. "Or at least I *hope* that this is all out. There are hundreds of people out there."

"*Why?*" Hermione asked.

"What do you mean?"

"*I mean* why *are they swarming the building? The drones are already making a mess of things.*"

DJ started to reply and then stopped. She had a point. The guards had the upper hand against the drones now, but a lot of people had died before they got their act together. And a lot of people were still dying despite everything. If Helene wanted to cause destruction, then she'd already succeeded. Showing her hand with the puppet army was just pointless.

"The whole thing stinks if you think about it," Hermione said. *"You said the drones covered the entire city block, right? Why send them one after the other when flooding the building with them would have been more effective? If Helene's goal was to destroy us, then giving us the chance to gain ground and develop a counter doesn't make sense. In the same way, if the goal was to kill you, DJ, then why did Tyra Chityothin allow you to run off? We know she's controlling the drones, so she can probably pinpoint your location every time you've killed one. But so far she hasn't reappeared. Why? It doesn't add up."*

"Helene's … um … goal is not what we have assumed," CJ said, completing Hermione's thought.

DJ was nodding along without realizing it. He hadn't thought it as clearly as that, but it *had* been irking him. The swarm outside was more than enough to wipe out the building in minutes. Yet only a relatively small number had entered inside the building. They were almost overwhelmed by that number. Why didn't Helene just send them all in? Regardless, if the goal was to destroy the building or kill DJ, using the machines to flood the building would have achieved both easily.

But she hadn't. This meant the AI's goal was something else entirely.

"I … uh … think the drones are a diversion," CJ said.

"I agree," Hermione put in.

"Wait! What are you guys talking about? In what world is a swarm of highly weaponized drones a distraction?"

"Think about it. If Helene wanted to kill us using drones, she could have. However, she sent in just enough to create chaos without overwhelming us. And the faster we clear them out, the more she sends in."

"Uh … the guards have a handle on it," CJ continued, *"but … um … their number makes them a constant threat, one without an end."*

"*We're holding our own now,*" Hermione said, "*but sustained stress like this isn't good for anyone. You should know this better than anyone, DJ.*"

"Sure," he agreed. "People get cranky when they're on alert for a while. They get irritable and aggressive. But isn't that a *good* thing? They're being attacked. They *need* to be aggressive."

"*They are … um … getting attacked by drones,*" CJ answered. "*But how about the … um … the woman who attacked the guard?*"

"You mean Johnson? He knocked her out."

"*Because she was a single woman and not much of a threat,*" Hermione said. "*What do you think would happen when an army of them starts attacking him, his team, or any of the other teams trying to clear out the drones?*"

DJ's eyes widened in realization. "Oh."

"*Exactly.*"

"That's bad. That's really bad." DJ paced. "I know most of those guys. They're not going to be going around shooting at people. Not deliberately. But if one of the puppets jumps out when they're trying to take down a drone?"

"*It'll be a bloodbath,*" Hermione said.

"Most of the world thinks Helene's actions with the picospores are some kind of pandemic or something. No one's going to realize that these people are being controlled. They're just going to hear about a bunch of sick people being gunned down." He paused. "It's going to ruin Sparta."

"*No,*" CJ said. "*Sparta is a … um … is a global organization. They will survive this.*"

"*But it'll definitely ruin us,*" Hermione pointed out. "*The idiots upstairs would have to push the blame to somebody, and they've only been tolerating us so far. We would probably have been kicked out ages ago if not for Manar. But he isn't here right now, and even if he were, I don't think he'd have been able to do anything. This is kinda our fault.*"

"Once they kick us out, we'll no longer have a base or resources," DJ said. "We might even become criminals if the outcry is loud enough. That'll cut us off from the government and the resources that Mary Pastore promised."

"*And that,*" Hermione surmised softly, "*was probably Helene's plan. Alone,*" *without resources, and hunted as criminals. Any resistance we try to put up would be like a drop in an ocean."*

DJ blew out a breath. "You gotta admit, she got us good this time."

CHAPTER

45

DJ SPED DOWN the hallway like a bullet.

He called Terry immediately and tried to warn him about killing the civilians, getting mixed feedback for his trouble. That was fair. Everyone knew that killing civilians was a bad idea, but both the drones and the puppets would be trying to kill them. Holding back against one might mean the other would succeed. The security teams already knew to try their best, but even if no accidents happened, Helene could simply cause some puppets to kill others and blame it on the guards.

It was the same result either way.

They were screwed, but it sucked more that Helene was sending people, her pawns, to their deaths. Several months ago, DJ would have taken those deaths on himself and been buried under the guilt. But he wasn't responsible for Helene's actions. All he could do was his best.

Right now, that meant knocking out as many people as possible before they got killed in the crossfire.

He had the Synaptic Pulse on him. He'd been using it whenever he came across any of the civilians. But DJ was just one person. The horde had quickly made their way through Sparta. So far the teams they'd encountered had been able to contain them without casualties. But everyone knew it was only a matter of time.

"How's it coming?" DJ asked.

"*Steadily,*" Hermione replied.

"ETA?"

"*I have no idea, DJ,*" Hermione spat out. DJ ignored the tone. Everyone was more than a little frustrated at the moment, she and CJ more than most. Both of them were splitting their attention between working on the frequency generator and distributing the stock of Pulses that Hermione had developed over the last few months. Fortunately, everyone on the team had been aware that their beef with Helene would reach this stage at some point, so Hermione had been able to prepare ahead.

Every Sparta security team was expected to have at least one of the Pulses. Unfortunately, the teams were spread out over the building. The Pulses could be used only so many times before they needed to recharge. The whole thing was proving to be a logistic nightmare.

"*Greg, what the fuck did you do?*" a voice came over the main raid channel. It was indistinct as if someone was shouting in the background, just loud enough for the comm system to have picked it up.

"*Don't fucking cuss at me, bro. It was an accident. Bitch literally jumped in front of the bullet,*" another voice—presumably Greg—yelled back. His voice was clearer, meaning he was the actual owner of the unit. For some reason, Greg had had the channel set to the main raid channel instead of his individual team.

The idiot had just broadcasted that he'd killed a civilian.

DJ slowed down as his heart dropped to his stomach. A moment later, he tore down the hall faster than before, his rage fueling his speed. The stairwell door hung off a single hinge; DJ slammed it off completely as he bounded down the stairs. Each step caused a dent in the metal. He ignored Terry's roars and switched his comm back to the private channel.

"You need to start heading to the gym," he told CJ and Hermione.

"*We're already packed,*" Hermione said.

"*We are … uh … double-checking everything we might need to finish the generator over there,*" CJ added.

Sparta had only two gyms: one for guests, which was on the upper floors, and the other for the staff and the security, on the fiftieth floor. The latter was the one that CJ and Hermione were to head to. Fortunately, Hermione's lab was only a few floors above it, so there shouldn't have been much danger.

Most staff had retreated to safe rooms, so apart from Hermione, CJ, and the other few engineers crucial to the task, only the security teams would be headed to the gym. The idea was that, since Helene's goal was to frame Sparta for killing civilians, the horde of puppets would be forced to follow the retreating teams to the gym where, clustered together, the Synaptic Pulses would be more effective.

It was a hastily cobbled together plan, probably full of holes that could be exploited. The most obvious one was that the enclosed room would also be beneficial to the remaining drones. Although DJ and the security teams had cleared out hundreds of the machines, it didn't seem like their numbers had diminished. The only consolation was that, without Tyra's direct control, the drones only had a finite number of attacks they could employ. They were still dangerous, but after hours of fighting, each team already had a tried and tested method of dealing with them, considerably reducing their threat level. DJ was counting on that to reduce the casualties. Well, that and hoping his brother and Hermione had the generator up before Helene decided that they were too big a target and just swarmed them with the drones.

The second problem was more subtle but arguably more dangerous: Tyra.

CJ already had his hands full, so he hadn't noticed when she'd disappeared from the cameras. They weren't lucky enough to assume she'd left. More likely she was wandering around the building somewhere. DJ had no illusions that she wouldn't see through the plan. They had to be prepared for her when she turned up to ruin it.

Ideally, they'd somehow draw her out and stall her, but that had several problems of its own. The bitch was crazy, for one, and DJ didn't know how he'd begin trying to get her attention. The fact that she hadn't chased him earlier implied that he'd probably not work as bait. She didn't care about killing him, or she already had something else planned for him later on.

That led to the third problem: DJ wasn't confident that he'd be able to hold her even if they *did* manage to draw her out. His recent ass whooping was still fresh in his head. Nothing had changed since then that would raise his chances the next time they met. Both CJ and Hermione were drawing a blank on how to handle that, so they decided to put the matter aside and deal with it if and when it became a problem.

"*We're heading out now. How long until you're there?*" Hermione asked.

"A couple of minutes," DJ replied. Since he wasn't facing off against Tyra, he'd be best used at the gym. With his strength, he could clear out the drones faster and more efficiently than any three teams put together. His enhancements wouldn't last forever, but DJ was pissed enough that it was going to last a good while at least. He was on the seventieth floor but was using the stairwell straight down.

Because several sections had been destroyed, DJ jumped through the breaks to a lower, more intact section. Only when the destruction was too extensive was he forced to find another stairwell. He used that chance to clear out every drone he met as well as any puppet that he stumbled on, stuffing them into closets. Unless deliberately woken up, they'd be unconscious for a while, hopefully until the battle was decided one way or the other.

46

DECEMBER 2043
SPARTA HEADQUARTERS,
NEW YORK

CONSIDERING SPARTA'S BORDERLINE tyrannical operations, the organization wisely hadn't slacked when creating the perfect conditions for keeping their enforcers in their best shape. At about six thousand square feet over three levels, the gym was one of the largest areas in Sparta, capable of holding more than three hundred people without feeling crowded. Although that was plenty of room for Sparta's guards to run specialized drills and simulations to perform at top capacity, DJ was hoping it was large enough. They were going to need every square inch of it.

While the room was already almost filled by the time he got there, more and more teams were streaming in every minute. CJ, Hermione, and two others were at the center of the room, fiddling with a two-foot by one-foot contraption. Hermione had a scowl on her face while CJ lay on his back, his eyebrows scrunched as he tinkered with something under the machine. Neither of them looked like they would appreciate him interrupting them to ask for an ETA, so he didn't bother. They'd just have to hold out for as long as they could and hope it was enough.

Several guards were injured and limping or cradling their wounds. Others had lost their weapons or used up all their ammunition and just held the empty guns. All were exhausted, but they performed their duties all the same, their faces hard with determination and anger.

They gathered around the different captains for instructions. There had been seven in total, but only five gathered around DJ when they spotted him. The look on their faces told him the fate of the other two. DJ filled them in as much as he could, giving them the bare bones about Helene and compressing everything about the picospores into a spiel about hypnosis. He summarized everything they knew about Tyra and their conclusions about Helene's goal. It hadn't even occurred to him to hold back the information—not while everyone there was helping to clean up his mess.

DJ had initially made the effort to befriend the guards as a safety net for days like today when shit hit the fan. He was pretty sure the captains knew what he'd been doing, but they'd overlooked it for some reason, perhaps because he'd found it surprisingly easy to fall in with the guys, the captains especially. All of them had done active service before they were recruited by Sparta, so they all had shared some similar experiences. Before he'd gotten bogged down by bullshit, DJ regularly stopped by for drinks so they could catch up.

Still, he'd expected them to yell and rage, to suggest giving him up to the drones in order to end the attack. DJ had considered that himself. He would have done it if he thought it was going to work. He'd planned on explaining why it wouldn't, but none of them suggested it. All of them considered his words without speaking, their faces dark.

"So, how do we make the fuckers pay?" Terry asked, breaking the silence after a minute.

DJ hesitated. "Uh … you're not going to punch me?"

"Would that help the fuckers pay?" Ray asked. He, the oldest among them, was pushing forty, but it'd be difficult to tell with his six-foot frame and corded muscles. He had a bandanna tied around his head and held his rifle loosely over his shoulder.

"No," DJ replied, "But I thought it might help you guys let off some steam or something."

"Look. If you want us to punch you, we'll punch you," Terry said, chuckling dryly. "But none of us thinks this is your fault. I mean, a lot of things finally make sense about you and about some of the weirdness we've seen. But you were just doing what you had to do. We've all been there. But what matters now," he continued, his tone growing hard, "is how we can get rid of these shits and make them pay."

The other captains nodded along with his words, all of them displaying the same grim determination and anger. In the face of that, DJ had no choice but to drop it. His own expression hardened as well. He explained the rough plan that he'd come up with, as well as its potential pitfalls. All of them spent a few minutes ironing out the details as best as they could. They knew that it would become a free-for-all eventually, so the plan couldn't be anything complex.

Like the army, each captain commanded several lieutenants who were in turn in charge of their own platoons. Once the plan was ironed out, they all went back to their individual companies and started shouting out instructions. Those wounded were placed at the back as reserves while the rest were put into teams and placed in formations with stockpiles of ammunition within easy reach.

Ten minutes after DJ arrived in the gym, the first wave of drones flew in on the tail of one of the squads. All preparations stopped at that point. Everyone got ready for battle.

CHAPTER

47

BEN MCCLUSKEY GOT INTO POSITION as the first of the flying metallic spheres swarmed the gym. His captain had called them drones, but those things didn't look like any drones Ben had ever seen. Granted, he hadn't seen much, but *real* drones shouldn't look like they'd been plucked out of a science-fiction movie, should they?

Ben put the thought out of his head. The door to the gym was large enough for about a dozen of the "drones" to enter at a time. However, four of the platoons had divided the rectangular portal among themselves so there wouldn't be overlap in their shots. As soon as the drones flew in, the guards bombarded them with over a hundred armor-piercing rounds a second. Although it took several rounds to put down even one drone, the sheer number of them meant the drones dropped like flies. A few who escaped the bombardment somehow were quickly shot down by the fifth platoon on the second floor.

The second wave came within a minute. Even more drones crashed to the ground. It was a good start, but the platoons couldn't keep up their pace, and everyone knew it. They had a limited amount of armor-piercing rounds. Most of the swarm was still dispersed across the building. Everyone had seen what was waiting for them outside the building.

Still, that didn't mean they weren't going to take as many of the invaders down as they could. Yesterday there'd been over six hundred security personnel in the building. They'd lost more than half of that in just a few hours. Every single person had lost a friend that day, and all of them were determined to make the fuckers pay. Ben was no exception. His gun screamed in unleashed frustration.

Over the next few minutes, the platoon rebutted several waves of the machines before they could get deeper into the gym. The barrage of gunfire petered out as the last wave was pushed back. However, instead of more drones streaming in, the cacophony was replaced by a distant rumble of thunder. The sound came from all around them, ominously reverberating in the enclosed space.

Like most others, Ben immediately peered out the windows. The sky was dark, shrouded by the mass of drones surrounding the building. They'd been there for hours, but the rumbling was new.

"Any idea what's happening?" a voice behind him asked. Ben glanced back. Everyone knew Darren Kojak, first because of his mysterious connection with Manar Saleem, arguably one of the most important men in Sparta. Ben hadn't met the man personally, but he'd seen him around, hanging out with the captains or throwing back a drink with some of Ben's friends with a casual disregard for rank and status. That made it hard to believe that the man was friends with Manar Saleem, who exuded arrogance from every pore. Every other time Ben had seen him, the man had a laid-back grin as if there was a joke that only he knew.

But Darren Kojak's grin was nowhere to be seen as he stood in front of a man who, based on their resemblance, was obviously his brother. Both of them stood next to a two-foot by one-foot contraption along with a woman in a lab coat and two other men in uniforms—Sparta staff, probably from one of the engineering labs based on how they tinkered with the contraption. The brother was frantically, furiously hammering away on a computer connected to the machine. He moved between the two, barely glancing up as he replied to DJ.

"Tyra has … um … she has finally made her move," he said. "She has … uh … directed those people here."

"All of them?"

The brother nodded. "The … um … thunder that we are hearing? That is … uh … it is the sound of them running."

DJ sighed but nodded as if he'd already expected that. He focused on the woman in the lab coat. "You can hear what's out there, Hermione? Is it going to be enough?"

"Each team should have at least one, and there are a few spares for those who don't," the woman—Hermione—replied. She tapped a different machine beside her. "They can be recharged here once their charges run out. However, I doubt anyone would remember that once the chaos starts."

DJ gritted his teeth. "I'll have to make sure that they remember then."

"You can't save everyone, DJ."

"I know that," DJ snapped. "But these people are going to die for no other reason than Helene needed them to. We've already condemned them to that, so the least we can do is try and save as many as we can."

Helene? Ben thought. He knew only two Helenes: his ex-fiancé and the global virtual assistant that Manar Saleem had created. Neither of them had the power to control and send hundreds of people to their deaths. Ben noted the conversation as DJ moved away from the group to a spot outside the formation. Ben's captain, Ray, and the other four captains followed him from their platoons. All six huddled together for a minute before dispersing again.

When Ray joined the platoon again, he gave a summarized version of the conversation Ben had heard behind him as well as orders to use the devices they'd been given earlier, the Synaptic Pulse. Ben had never been the smartest guy, but it didn't take a genius to figure out that the directive had come from DJ. Ray wasn't a pushover and listened only to those he respected, and it was obvious that DJ, and probably his brother, knew more about what was going on than the rest. If Ray and the other captains were willing to listen to DJ, he must have filled them in on something important.

That told Ben, though, there was more to the man than he let on.

As if responding to his thoughts, DJ walked to the front of the formation, facing all five platoons with an expression so primal it shook Ben's bones. "Your friends are dead."

He hadn't raised his voice, yet somehow his words were heard by every single person there. They resonated with a feeling they had pushed back when the ominous rumbling had filled them with fear.

Anger. It was pure in the way that it consumed him. He'd make the shits pay for the friends they'd taken from him.

DJ wasn't finished. "Some of mine are too. These people rushing toward us? They're not the ones responsible. Every single one of you faced them on your way here. Most of you have seen the dead look in their eyes. No one's home in there. They've been taken over by something. That something? *That* is what is responsible for killing your friends. These people can still be saved. While it would be tempting to take out your anger on them, you'd just be mowing down innocents."

"You want us to hold back?" someone shouted. "Against the *rumbling*?"

"Yes," DJ said firmly. "Because I don't think anyone wants the death of innocent lives on their conscience. You could have brushed it off before if you saw them as mindless invaders, but now you know. Each of those people can be saved. With these." He brought out one of the Pulse devices. "You have probably already seen these in action. You activate it, and these guys get knocked out. The fact that they're in a group makes it easier for us. Now I know you are angry," he continued, putting away the Pulse. "And you can take that anger out on the drones. There'll be enough of them coming in here that you'll get your fill and then some."

The gathered soldiers broiled at that. The drones had caused more damage than the invaders, but it was easier to blame people than unthinking machines. But the rumbling grew louder, heralding the arrival of the invaders and forcing the thought out of his head. All the hallways across Sparta followed the same basic design: they were just wide enough to allow three or four people to walk side by side. The passage leading to the gym wasn't any different, but it *was* longer than the norm. When the horde finally reached the bend, Ben had enough time to understand what they were up against.

The horde quickly filled the hallway, with more behind driving them forward. Their faces were perfectly expressionless. Their eyes were glazed over with an unsettling vacancy. There was no light there. It was as if walking corpses were rushing toward them, eager to drag them to their deaths. The only difference was that they didn't move like corpses. Ben had watched a few zombie movies, and there was none of the rigidity or stiff, jerky movement that he'd expect. There was no pushing or shoving or scrambling. None of that. They moved like people.

People with dead eyes.

Ben licked his suddenly dry lips. The low rumble of thunder had transformed into a pounding drumbeat as their every footstep struck the ground with eerie synchronization. The cacophony filled the air and pierced his very core. All around him guards shifted on their feet. Their discipline didn't let any of them break and run. But Ben was sure he wasn't the only one who'd considered it.

It became worse when the cacophony of footsteps was drowned out by an even more thunderous roar. Drones, in far greater numbers than any other waves, joined the incoming horde, hovering over them like a cloud. Outside, the skies darkened once more as even more drones blanketed the windows.

Ben felt fear wash over him all over again. But DJ's words echoed in his head, and his expression hardened as anger burned away that fear. The man had been right. Ben didn't want innocent deaths on his hands, but he needed a way to avenge his friends. The drones were fair game.

When they were a few steps away from the entrance, the horde transitioned from the slow marching they'd held to a faster jog, as if *they* were the ones charging toward an enemy. Above them, the drones kept pace but stayed slightly behind to let the invaders soften them up before their own attack.

Soon the horde poured into the gym, spreading out to fill up the room within seconds. It was unnerving as they charged toward the platoons. They didn't yell; their expressions were perfectly blank. The room shook with the force of their footsteps. Ben tightened his grip on his gun while those at the front of the platoon readied their Pulse devices.

"Not yet," DJ said, still at the front. He raised an arm, palm spread out in the universal gesture for *wait*. The horde drew closer, rushing across the intervening space until they were halfway to the gathered platoon. Ben could more clearly make out their vacant stares and dead eyes. While most ran empty-handed, a few carried pipes, sticks, and other makeshift weapons.

They poured into the room in an unending flood, easily more than a hundred and counting. Yet DJ still held his arm high. Ben was sure that the only reason the men hadn't used their Pulse devices was that they'd already resolved to use their guns if it became necessary. Fortunately, it didn't come to that. The front line of the horde was less than five feet away when DJ's arm finally dropped.

"Now!" he shouted. "Stagger your shots."

The room lit up white.

Ben—all of the gathered men, really—had been warned. He'd squinted so he wasn't affected by the glare. It lasted for only a second before dispersing. For a moment, there was calm. With the light gone, Ben was able to make out the bodies littered across the floor. It was a sea of another kind, their limp forms filling the space they'd once been rushing across. Motionless. Ben would have thought they were dead if not for the speech DJ had given beforehand.

The silence didn't last for long. The invaders hadn't stopped pouring into the room. The fact that their peers were laid up on the floor didn't stop them. They streamed in, stepping over the bodies as easily as they'd marched across the floor. Once again, DJ waited until they were closer before giving the signal. Ben squinted against the glare.

Even more bodies littered the ground, lying on top of those that had come before. Another wave of the invaders streamed in, and the drones that followed them filled the air.

In front of the platoons, DJ pocketed his Pulse and hefted his rifle.

The rest of the platoon followed his lead.

INTERLUDE

TINA NGUYEN FLIPPED THROUGH the channels of her television for the tenth time in as many minutes. It was more out of a need to do something than her expectation of finding anything interesting. All the stations were reporting the same thing: the attack at the Sparta Headquarters. That would have been okay if any of them actually had something worthwhile to say. They just repeated themselves over and over again, showing the same footage taken from a single helicopter hovering over the building. It was the only one the dreadful machines hadn't shot down. The wreckage of previous efforts by the New York Police and the US Army was scattered on the ground. The angle showed only the outside of the building.

But that was more than enough.

Flying metallic spheres blanketed the street like locusts descending on a farm. No one knew where they had come from or how they'd appeared in the middle of the city without anyone noticing them. One minute the skies were clear, and the next, these machines were there. They'd destroyed everything that had been on the street at the time, including the cars and the people. It didn't take long before someone on the internet linked the drones to strange aircraft that had been flying around the country for the last few months. Everyone seemed to have an opinion about their purpose.

Most conspiracy theorists thought the drones belonged to the government, which—the conspiracists claimed—had discovered a secret project in Sparta that it needed to put an end to. It didn't matter, of course, that the swarm had shot down every vehicle or person sent in by both the New York State Police Department and the army. Others chalked it up to a terrorist attack—one that authorities had failed to stop in time, leaving the government caught with its pants down. New theories cropped up every second. Even news channels had been caught up in it, inviting "experts" for panel sessions.

They were idiots. All of them.

Everyone was so busy with their stupid theories that they weren't even considering that machines were probably slaughtering everyone in that building. Tina had done her research. Sparta's headquarters was the single largest building in the world. It housed thousands upon thousands of people—all of whom were probably going to be killed. But idiots that they were, newscasters were more concerned about what metal the machines were made of.

Tina switched to another channel, and then another, each time hoping for something new, for more information. The government hadn't released a statement yet, fanning the flames of conspiracy. Tina wouldn't have put much stock in their words even if they had. They hadn't said anything about the mysterious aircraft for months. Even the speech that the president released about the pandemic was little more than empty platitudes and vague metaphors. Obviously the government was just as in the dark as anyone else, but they had to at least make it look like they had everything under control. So far, they were doing a piss poor job of it.

Tina switched to another channel. Finally, she saw something different.

A crowd of people poured in from the end of the streets, thousands of them. Tina leaned forward on her couch, her eyes wide. These weren't the first groups of people to try to intervene. However, there were several differences, the least of which being that every other group had been either police or army personnel. These people were obviously not. It was a mixed crowd. They were all dressed in normal clothes, jeans and T-shirts or dresses and skirts—not a uniform to be seen among them.

The second and most important difference—the one that had Tina at the edge of her seat—was that the drones didn't attack them. They'd attacked everything else that had come close, quickly and without discrimination. Now it was as if they were blind. They remained stationary while the crowd marched to the front of the building and then streamed inside, as the drones themselves had done not too long ago. The footage zoomed in on the crowd. The video was blurry as a result of the distance, but Tina could still make out the glint of weapons in their hands. Although not everyone held arms, enough did that it added more questions about the multitude pouring in.

The channel was one of those that had gone for a panel discussion. One of the panelists drew Tina's attention to the faces of those in the crowd. At first, Tina didn't see the problem. It took her a moment before she did.

Their faces were perfectly expressionless.

Tina leaned back on her couch, her hands on her head. She could barely believe what she was seeing. *Have all these people been infected?* she wondered in dismay. The pandemic that had been ravaging the country for months had led to death on an untold scale. No one knew what it was or where it'd come from. Most people thought that it was a biological weapon of some sort, but Tina had previously dismissed those kinds of theories. Now? What else would explain why thousands of infected people would get into what was almost definitely a terrorist zone?

What else if they weren't being controlled by some means?

Tina had heard of a man who choked his own family to death and then came out to the street to get run over. Through it all, the man's face had been perfectly expressionless. She'd thought it was run-off-the-mill insanity. But now? Who would do such a thing? And *why*?

She changed the channel, then changed it again. Newscasters speculated on every channel. Unfortunately, no one had any more answers than she did.

48

DECEMBER 2043
SPARTA HEADQUARTERS,
NEW YORK

EVERYTHING WENT TO HELL almost immediately.

The lines held up for the first few seconds, right until the drones began firing. The bullets tore through the ranks, creating a gap the invaders—the puppets, according to DJ—didn't hesitate to exploit. After that, the room descended into chaos. Several defenders made a break for it—and quickly found there was nowhere to go. Drones fired at deserters heading to the back exits, killing them outright, or wounding them enough for the puppets to catch up.

Ben held his gun rigidly, shooting down any drone that came too close. It took several bullets to down just one of the machines. Although he'd tried to stand his ground, he'd needed to move to avoid getting sprayed with bullets or bogged down by puppets looking to dogpile. He'd learned, though, that a single shot would get a drone's attention, so with the help of ad hoc teams, he and others could get a drone's attention while others worked to bring it down.

Ben tightened his grip on his gun until his knuckles turned white. His breaths came in quick, shallow bursts, his heart pounding so hard it felt like it might break free from his chest. A drone flew overhead. Ben forced back his fear with gritted teeth and a flare of rage. DJ's words rang in his head like a mantra.

Ben had worked at Sparta for only five years—not long compared to others who had worked there for over a decade. It wasn't the best job. It was tedious most of the time and was filled with endless drills and training. But even as a midlevel grunt, the job paid well, and Sparta took care of its own. His squad mates had become more like brothers to him than his actual brother, to whom he hadn't spoken in years.

But someone out there had sent those drones to kill them just because they could. They'd taken over and thrown away hundreds of innocent lives—again, just because they could. Dealing with whoever could do that was way above Ben's pay grade—above a captain's pay grade. DJ, on the other hand, knew more about what was going on than what he'd said.

Ben cast about. He quickly found the man, isolated and surrounded by his own mini-swarm. They seemed to have identified him as the greatest threat, and after a moment of watching, Ben understood why. DJ didn't use any weapons—his fists created dents in the hard metal with every punch. Bullets sprayed over the area as the drones fired on him, staggering their shots. DJ shifted his position constantly and somehow always found an opening to slip through. He moved like a devil, slow enough that the drones could track his movements, but he was gone the moment one of them opened fire, even if the drone had been in one of his blind spots. It was as if DJ knew exactly which drone was about to fire at every point in time. He moved out of the way so that the bullets hit another drone instead of him.

For a minute, Ben forgot about his own battle.

DJ's movements were smooth but far from graceful. It was as if there was a beat that only he could hear, and he danced to the rhythm of war. He charged across the enclosure, narrowly dodging a spray of bullets that landed where he'd just been. He slowed in front of a drone, his fist already cocked. The punch sent the drone crashing into the second layer of drones that surrounded him. DJ leaped on it, forcing it to the ground, where he continued to pound it. His attacks lasted only a few seconds. Although the strikes didn't finish off the drone, the barrage of bullets that landed in that spot—a split second after DJ had moved on—certainly did.

He stopped in front of another drone and repeated the process, once again moving on a second before the drones could pin him down. As a result, their weapons caused more damage to themselves than to him. DJ changed the pattern several times. At every point, he was always a second from death. But he was never caught. His movements blended into the next seamlessly so no second was wasted. A drone took a hit every time he moved.

Ben broke free of his awe. He was still in the middle of his impromptu team, which was probably how he'd avoided being killed. Drone parts and unconscious guards were scattered around the group. Several of the guys shot glares at him in between firing rounds. They probably saw him as a liability after he'd spent the last-minute staring in the distance.

Ben didn't blame them. The scene of DJ's battle still replayed in his head. Ben couldn't do what the man had done. He couldn't move like he had. But that didn't mean he wasn't going to do his best to try. He gripped his rifle and took aim at the nearest drone.

CHAPTER

DECEMBER 2043
SPARTA HEADQUARTERS,
NEW YORK

KARLA POLOVA PERCHED ON THE ROOF of the multi-storied building. Several streets away a swarm of class A drones blotted out the sky like locusts on the verge of devouring the earth.

Karla's lips pulled into a snarl. *Disgusting.*

She watched as another military vehicle tried to get through the swarm and was summarily destroyed by a hail of bullets from every angle. An armored tank tried several minutes later and was destroyed even faster by a more deadly class B drone. Karla had felt the heat of its laser up close. She could imagine the driver burning as the metal around him cooked. She knew military commands had compelled them to enter, but anyone foolish enough to come close to the swarm deserved a painful death.

Except Karla. She could survive the swarm long enough to enter into the building, if she so wished.

Her blood urged her on. Her daggers scratched at her thighs, pushing her to sink them into the metal hulls. Karla had modified her weapons, so she knew they would puncture the drones like a hot knife through flesh. She almost launched herself at the thought, but held back.

It was the same reason she'd been holding back for the last half hour.

Charging in would not hurt the AI enough.

Karla couldn't decimate the entire swarm. Not on her own. Besides, drones were replaceable, their reconstruction a mere tax on the AI's resources. And given the number of drones dedicated to this harebrained plan, it had resources to spare.

Karla snorted at the thought. He was a fool in several ways, but Darren Kojak would never be killed by such a ridiculous attack. Karla was confident of this, though she could have been wrong. He certainly was fool enough to sacrifice himself for another, a fact the AI might capitalize on.

A part of Karla wished it would.

It had been *his* fault that Karla had been disowned by her father, separated from her sister, and abandoned by the only family she had ever known. He deserved to die for that. Karla only wished it was by her own hands.

Do you? another part of her asked. *You were a prisoner there, a sheep that flocked to the command of your father. He was the reason you gained the freedom you sought. And now you say that you want to kill him for it? You are as ungrateful as your father claimed.*

Karla snarled but did not bother to argue with the voice. She stared at the swarm in the distance for several long minutes.

Fine. She would not kill Darren Kojak, but neither would she help him. His actions had caused this, and he would survive based on his strength. Karla would have to be patient and wait for a better chance, one where she could sink her daggers somewhere that would make the AI bleed.

Karla spared one last look at the scene. And then she jumped off the building.

CHAPTER

50

DJ DUCKED BEHIND A DRONE before its weapons could fire. He tugged on the gun's turrets as he passed, forcing them to the side where another of the flying machines had been preparing to spray him with bullets. Both drones fired on each other at the same time, and DJ returned to finish the job before continuing to another group harassing one of the teams.

He tapped his comm. "How long?"

"*Any minute now,*" Hermione replied, sounding harried.

DJ spared a moment to look up at the third floor where she, CJ, and the other engineers were still working on the machine. They'd moved there shortly before the attack had started so they wouldn't be caught up in the battle. For all the good it did them! The drones focused on the group almost as much as they did on him. Fortunately, DJ had assigned Christy and one of the platoons to protection duty. "You realize you've been saying that the last five times I asked, right?"

"*Then maybe you should stop asking and let us concentrate,*" Hermione snapped. "*I know we make it look easy, but we're basically building new technology on the spot.*"

"We can't hold out for much longer."

"*You're gonna have to.*"

"We have to be done with this before—" DJ paused midswing as the drone he'd been aiming for retreated out of range. That wouldn't have been strange, if not for the fact that *every* drone in the room was retreating to the gym entrance. They hovered there, wall to wall, in neat, evenly spaced rows. Waiting.

He sighed. "We're too late. She's here."

The guards were visibly confused by the drones' shift in tactics. At least the captains were smart enough to order a regroup. The number that gathered was less than half of what they'd started with. That meant more fatalities than DJ had feared. While the men arranged themselves into squads, DJ's gaze moved to the drones waiting for them.

They had no chance.

The middle column parted to allow Tyra to enter the room. She stopped in front of the swarm, tapping something on her cybergauntlet. Her smile looked all the more crazed now that her lab coat was torn in several places, revealing patches of scorched skin.

"We might be able to hold her for ten minutes," DJ said.

"*We're not going to need that long,*" Hermione replied confidently. DJ sincerely hoped reality supported her certainty. Even the ten minutes had been a generous estimate.

He tapped his comm, switching to the captains' channel. "It's exactly what you're thinking, yeah."

"*She's the mastermind?*" Terry asked.

"More like a henchwoman for the mastermind. But she's probably the best we're gonna get."

"*So we can smoke her?*" Ray said. "*None of that puppet bullshit, right?*"

"Yeah, she's fair game," DJ confirmed. "But I doubt she's going to give us the chance."

"We outnumber her."

"I'm not sure your math is right, Terry, but even if that were true, she'd probably find a way to use our numbers against us. She's gonna come after me. When she does, let her."

"So we just stand back with our dicks in our hands?" Jack, another captain, growled.

"No," DJ replied calmly, "I'm going to need backup if I'm going to last even a minute against her."

"You're not going to last a minute?" Ray asked incredulously. *"We all saw you out there, DJ. You were tearing through those things like the freaking Terminator."*

"That right there?" DJ said. "That's the kind of attitude that's going to get me killed. I've already gone up against her before. Trust me when I say she's going to run through me if I don't have backup." DJ then continued in a lower tone. "That is, after she's done playing with her food."

"What was that?" Terry asked.

"Don't worry about it," DJ said. "If we don't get creamed within the first minute, I'm gonna need your help while the rest of your guys handle the drones. And don't half-ass it either."

"Well, shit," Ray said. *"I'm game."*

"Fine by me."

"Sure."

"Good, because it seems like we're out of time," DJ said, eyeballing Tyra as she started striding toward them. The drones broke their formation as well and started spreading out across the room. The puppets, however, retreated to the entrance where the others stood, motionless, their dead eyes gazing at the rest of them. DJ was relieved to see that. One less thing to worry about.

The captains started yelling out commands to their groups. But DJ only had eyes for Tyra. She still had that Joker-style grin, creating a spark of anger in him. He fanned those flames with the memories of the last time they'd fought— of how she'd played him and then *laughed*. DJ made his way toward her as a burst of power surged through him. It wasn't the burning anger that he'd felt every other time he'd activated the nanites, the one that pushed him to *move*, to punch something. Instead, it was a steady flame that pushed his attributes to superhuman levels.

He shot to his feet and rushed after her. He noticed something almost immediately. His body felt … different. Every other time he'd activated his nanites, he felt a line of fire run through his veins, filling him with explosive power. Now the fire seemed milder somehow. It flowed instead of surged. DJ didn't feel any more or less powerful, but the enhancement felt more balanced, as if it was actually a part of him instead of something temporary.

Tyra charged and DJ leaped to meet her, his fist cocked. They met in the middle of the room. Tyra raised an arm to block. But before his punch could connect, DJ dove to the side, dodging a hail of bullets aimed at where he'd just been.

"This crap again?" he growled, glaring at the offending drone as it drew closer to their position.

Tyra's laugh erupted from behind him. DJ rolled again to avoid the inevitable attack. But when he came out of his roll and looked back, the woman was already over fifty feet away and still moving.

Is she going after the squads?

She'd entered the main battlefield where the squads battled drones. Like the last time, several drones guarded her, taking care of any armed trooper that came too close. But Tyra herself didn't pay them any attention.

At that moment, something clicked in the back of his mind, and his speed increased. He wasn't moving any faster, but it was as if each step took him farther than it had previously.

With her head start, he was already unlikely to catch up with her.

He tapped on his comm, making his request to the captains. "I need you guys to run interference."

"*I thought you said she'd be coming for you,*" Terry commented. DJ started to look for the man but quickly realized how pointless it would be through the chaos of the battlefield. He could only hope that they'd stayed close by as he'd asked.

"Yeah, well, shit happened, and I was wrong," DJ replied, knocking away a drone with a swipe of his arm. It'd been a reflex, one that he'd seen the Murder

Twins do countless times. But the pain brought immediate regret. For a moment, he'd forgotten that he didn't have the twins' cyborg limbs. He pushed the ache to the back of his mind through force of will and instead punched the next drone that appeared in his way. "She's going after Hermione and my brother."

"*The gearheads working on the machine thing on the third level, right?*" Ray said.

"She must have realized that what they're working on is the only way we're going to survive this," DJ confirmed. "I'm right behind her, but she's going to make it there before me."

"*Don't sweat it. We're on it,*" Ray said.

"Don't get too close. She'll steamroll you," DJ warned. "Just distract her so I can catch up."

"*Yeah, no shit! You see how fast she's moving? No one here has a death wish, DJ,*" Ray said.

The other captains also gave acknowledged the orders, so DJ knew they were all in. While he didn't hear the sound of the first shot over the din, he could tell they'd begun when one of the drones hovering around Tyra dove down to intercept something. Though knocked back, it oriented itself quickly and rejoined the formation, seeming no worse for wear. A second later, the same thing happened on the other side. After that, the drones were constantly moving, swirling around Tyra like a miniature tornado.

DJ saw the problem immediately. Tyra was employing the same tactic she'd used against him: turning drones into a mobile shield. DJ had countered by taking down each drone in close combat, but the captains naturally couldn't do the same thing. The best they could do was keep shooting. Tyra was constantly moving, giving the captains little chance of finding the small gaps in her shield. Their bullets would eventually destroy the drones, but Tyra could easily replace them before it ever became a real problem. She knew this, so she had never slowed down, offhandedly ignoring the barrage.

DJ tapped his comm again. "Tyra is on her way to you guys."

"*I'm on it,*" Christy replied. In the same moment, a shot rang out across the battlefield, and one of the drones staggered back several feet away, then crashed.

It didn't get up. Three more shots rang out in quick succession. Three drones fell. When one crashed directly in front of Tyra, she leaped over it. In the same moment, another shot rang out. A drone dove in front of her, taking a bullet that would have bored a hole in Tyra's forehead. The shot sent the machine slamming into her, knocking her down.

"Is that an M82?" DJ asked incredulously. "Where the hell did you get your hands on that?" Sniper rifles weren't his forte. But he'd gotten some basic training back at the navy base, and the M82 was distinctive in how hard it hit, regardless of the distance.

"*It's mine now,*" Christy said. "*I'm not returning it.*"

"Give me a few more shots like that, and I'll snag another one for you," DJ promised. He increased his pace to take advantage of the opportunity.

Christy didn't reply in words, but another shot rang out and was deflected by another drone. It would have crashed into Tyra as well had she not moved in time. Still, another drone fell every second as Christy kept up the pressure. The captains also filed in to pin Tyra to the spot. Several drones rushed in to remold the protection, but DJ was already there, his fist pulled back. A drone swooped in his way. DJ ignored it. A second later, it was knocked away by a well-timed shot. With that, he was through the defense and just a few feet away from Tyra.

"Hey," DJ grunted. When Tyra turned, his fist crashed into the side of her face, slamming her into the ground. DJ almost felt guilty. Almost. He wound up a follow-up but pivoted when a drone almost skewered him.

"Can you guys get these things off me?" he said into the air.

"*What do you think we've been doing?*" Terry responded.

"*Yeah, show some gratitude and help us kick that bitch's ass.*"

"That's the plan," DJ said, leering at Tyra picking herself off the ground. He aimed a kick, but she accelerated until she was a blur. When she stopped, she was several feet away. Although DJ was quickly growing to hate the woman, he couldn't deny she was one of the hottest women he'd ever seen.

Or at least, she had been. Now her face was a mess of swelling, bruises, and blood. Lots of blood. Most of it flowed from her nose, which was now little more than a bulge of purple and red flesh. The rest came from a jagged cut above her left eyebrow, making a mess of the rest of her face. Most importantly, though, she met his glare with one of her own, her Joker grin nowhere in sight.

DJ felt immense satisfaction.

"You want a rematch already?" Tyra said, wiping the blood from her face. "I thought you'd have learned."

DJ shrugged. "I've always been a slow learner." She started to reply, but DJ was already charging. Tyra easily blocked his first punch, and his second. For some reason she was matching his speed and strength instead of trying to overwhelm him. It was obvious, though, after the first few exchanges, she was trying to disengage.

Naturally, DJ wasn't going to let her off the hook, and he cut off her retreat. They were still surrounded by a cyclone of drones. As in their first fight, Tyra attempted to use the machines to interfere, either to block an attack or cause a distraction by trying to skewer him. Unlike before, though, DJ had backup, and most of the drones were knocked away before they could meddle. Gaps appeared in her shield, allowing Christy to take potshots at Tyra, forcing her to divert some of her attention to avoid being sniped.

But despite his advantages, DJ was only matching the woman, not over-whelming her. Somehow she was keeping pace with him, blocking blow for blow. DJ began to worry, knowing she was still holding back. Initially he'd planned to hold her down until CJ and Hermione were done. But DJ couldn't take the risk that he was somehow providing her with whatever opportunity she was waiting for. He could no longer settle for just holding her down. He had to defeat her.

The question was: How the hell was he going to do that? DJ was already throwing everything he could at her just to keep her at bay. He'd already asked for whatever help he could reasonably expect. He didn't have any more tricks to pull out of his ass.

DJ gritted his teeth. He was thinking too much. He needed to defeat her, to exceed her. If Tyra was matching his speed now, he would move faster. She was as strong as he was—he only needed to be stronger. To achieve both, he simply needed more power, which his nanites could provide. Currently he was as fast and as strong as he'd ever been. But he knew that there was still more. His current state was proof of that.

He'd already done it once, earlier that day, the first time that Tyra had shown him her true power. She'd punched him so hard he'd crashed into a wall. When she'd reappeared in front of him to repeat the attack, DJ had moved so fast that he'd practically disappeared. He'd moved faster than her. He hadn't thought about it since then, but in his fear, he'd instinctively tapped into the nanites for more power.

That's what he had to do now. But deliberately. Somehow. While trying not to get his face kicked in by a psychotic bitch.

DJ felt himself getting excited at the thought. He adjusted his stance slightly. "How many minutes?" he asked.

"*Soon,*" his brother replied.

To hell with it then. DJ needed an extra push if he was going to do what he wanted. He was unlikely to get a better training partner than Tyra. But not as she was. He needed to find a way to push her into revealing the speed and strength she'd shown before.

So he charged.

CHAPTER

51

DECEMBER 2043
OKAFOR CORPORATION,
ABUJA, NIGERIA

NDIDI STOOD IN THE MIDDLE of the hallway and stared through the window. In the small room, one of the psychiatrists who'd been flown into the country spoke to a family of three. Most of the attention was on the child—a teenager—who sat between his parents. It was easy to tell that the attention of so many adults was making the boy uncomfortable. By design, Ndidi couldn't hear what was being said. It was questionably legal for her to even be looking through the window.

But she couldn't help herself.

It'd been a couple of days since the press conference. This was far from the first family that had responded, but Ndidi still thought it surreal. She'd already written off the conference as a disaster and had started working with the publicity team on another angle. But less than a day after, people had started flocking to the Okafor Corporation. Some had come alone, but most were families who'd brought their children, spouses, or friends. All of them had been hesitant, of course, but the hope had been clear in their eyes: that Ndidi would be able to live up to her promise and help them.

And so she had. By passing them on to the professionals, the process was relatively simple. The specifics had already been ironed out before the conference, so it only took a few minutes before the first people started being processed.

"Hey." Manar's voice shook her out of her reverie. He was becoming too good at sneaking up on her. "Don't you have anything better to do?"

"That child," Ndidi said, turning back to the window, "is about to get started on a journey that will change his life. What could be better than that?"

"Me," Manar responded, completely straight-faced. Ndidi raised a brow, and he broke out into a grin. "Seriously, though, you could be watching them get inoculated with the spores. It's a lot more interesting than this."

"I beg to differ." The first step in the picospore treatment began with a psych evaluation with one of the many psychiatrists on the Okafor payroll. A few of them had been working for the company for years and had simply been reassigned. However, others had been flown in from outside the country. A few had been picked from within Nigeria itself.

Ndidi had argued that point initially. After all, they shouldn't have to bring people from outside while there were qualified professionals within the country. But her staff, armed with polls and graphs, had set her straight. They'd taken a survey, and apparently most Nigerians tended to trust professionals from abroad rather than their own countrymen.

Regardless, since the picospore treatment was still in development and somewhat invasive, the psych evaluation was necessary to determine whether a person actually needed it or if more conventional treatments would be just as effective. That decision had caused a fight between her and Manar. He'd insisted that the spores would be more effective than whatever treatment they could try. Ndidi agreed with him, but she was more aware of how shaky the entire project was at the moment.

The Okafor Corporation had already faced significant backlash from organizations already established in the industry. If those companies thought the spores could replace them completely—which they would, given enough time—then Ndidi didn't even want to imagine the damage the Okafor Corporation would do. Better to not sweat a few people slipping away. It was only temporary, after all. Most companies would rather treat an illness than cure it. The picospore treatment was one of the few treatments that actually sought to permanently cure mental illness. Once it was fully established, they'd slowly eliminate the other competition.

It broke her heart that her decision meant families would still have to pay exorbitant prices for several years on treatments that were purely temporary, but ideals rarely lived up to reality. Several families had already been turned away because of this. However, since the evaluation itself was free, the families still received a consultation that would have cost them elsewhere.

The psych eval also helped to identify potential risks of the picospore treatment and determine whether the patient had any conditions that might be exacerbated by the procedure. So far that hadn't been a problem. Manar guaranteed it would never be. Once again, Ndidi was inclined to agree, but she still insisted on it—just in case.

"Hello? Still there?" Manar asked, knocking lightly on her head. When Ndidi swatted his hand away, he stepped back with a chuckle. "You've been standing there, frowning for over a minute."

Ndidi blushed in embarrassment, and she spun on him with a glare. "What're you even doing here? Don't you have something more important to do?"

"I do," he replied matter-of-factly. "And I'm handling it."

"You're handling it?" Ndidi raised a brow. "Right now?"

"It's called multitasking." Manar smirked. The image was so different from his normal serious countenance. She found herself staring, and his grin widened when he noticed. "You should try it sometime."

"I'm a woman," she replied, jutting out her chin. "Multitasking is basically encoded in our genes."

"If you say so," he replied easily. Ndidi narrowed her eyes, but he ignored her and grabbed her hand. He started walking deeper into the hallway. Ndidi allowed herself to be pulled, taking one last glance at the room. The psychiatrist was done with the teen's evaluation and was walking the family through the consent form. The parents could ask questions, but ultimately it would be the child—well, adult, since every patient had to be at least eighteen before they could undergo the treatment—to sign the form for themselves.

For convenience, the corporation had assigned an entire wing to the pico-spore treatment. However, several sections of it were still unused and would remain so until the project stabilized and was expanded. The active areas were divided into different sections, each dedicated to parts of the treatment.

Picospores were created in batches that could contain anything from several billion to hundreds of billions of spores. From there, the spores had to be portioned out, grouped, and programmed. Because each group was specific to a single person, it was important to get an accurate brain map, a report on the severity of illness, some mental health baselines, and several other metrics Manar had specified. Several of the tests to get that information were somewhat invasive. In some cases, the patient had to be sedated so their emotions didn't mess with the readings. Once the tests were done, the results were sent to another section where the commands were coded into the spores. Then the patient finally moved on to the last section.

That was where Manar was taking Ndidi. She went with him, even though, for the life of her, she couldn't understand what he found so fascinating. The inoculation chambers were basically just sterile rooms with built-in dispensers for administering the spores. The method used could differ from patient to patient. Injections were the fastest and most efficient, but for those afraid of needles, the spores would pour from vents so they could be breathed in or seep in through the person's skin. Once that was done, the treatment was technically over, though tests would ensure the spores were working properly.

In general, the entire treatment took about eight hours, from walking into the Okafor Corporation and leaving.

CHAPTER

52

DJ HADN'T TAKEN HER BY SURPRISE, but then again, that wasn't the point. In the first exchange, DJ focused on his technique, switching to moves—violent moves—Karla had beaten into him. DJ couldn't bully Tyra with them the way Karla had him, but the techniques would still help him better utilize his own enhancements. It took only a moment for him to make the transition. The difference was clear almost immediately.

He wasn't any faster or stronger than before. Nevertheless each punch was backed by the full weight of his boosted attributes. While his steps used the same amount of energy, they took him farther than they had before. DJ could see the confusion on Tyra's face. Suddenly she was forced to speed up in order to keep up with him. After a few seconds, the impact of their exchanges kicked up wind around them. The sound of their strikes permeated the air. Tyra could no longer divert any of her attention toward evading Christy's shots, and the captains knocked away any drones that she tried to use to defend.

She compensated by drawing even more drones from around the room. They swirled around like a mini-cyclone. They flew so fast that they blocked the view of the rest, effectively isolating both of them. DJ had to admit the effectiveness of the strategy. The captains would still be able to interfere, but Christy had always been the true threat. Now she wouldn't be able to get a bead on Tyra.

Controlling that many drones should have come with some drawbacks, but if it did, Tyra didn't let it show on her face. She grinned widely at DJ, displaying her bloodied teeth. "You don't get it, do you?"

DJ felt a chill run down his spine. She'd said the same thing to him earlier, before revealing how she'd outsmarted him. Had he fallen for another trick, or were her words now the trick?

Fortunately, DJ wasn't given the chance to think too deeply about it. Tyra suddenly accelerated, turning into a blur. Without thinking, DJ *pulled*. Power flooded into him like a dam breaking. Immediately, Tyra came back into focus a step away from him. Her eyes were bloodshot with excitement and … arousal?

What in the absolute—

He immediately leaped backward, narrowly avoiding a drone ramming into him. Tyra was on him in the next moment with a swipe that, with her strength, would probably have decapitated him. DJ grabbed her wrist and pulled her into a headbutt, but she kicked him away and twisted out of his grasp.

"I said, you don't get it, do you?" Tyra repeated with a mad laugh. She accelerated once more. They were already moving so fast that the world had almost completely stopped around them. Each strike rumbled like thunder and created shock waves that echoed throughout the room. "Don't worry. You will soon."

Less than a minute had passed. They'd already exchanged dozens of blows. But with each second, Tyra's smile grew wider until it threatened to split her face in half. She'd been getting progressively faster. DJ was forced to draw more deeply in order to keep up. After a minute, though, DJ could feel he'd reached his limit. Whatever surge had empowered him was now fading. He started slowing down. It became more and more of a struggle for him to match her until it was only his greater experience that allowed him to hold his own.

Tyra realized what was happening the same moment he did, and she cackled madly before slowing down as well. The world sped up once more. The cyclone of drones isolated them again as their speed reduced to merely superhuman levels. But DJ didn't feel relieved by that.

Why did she slow down? DJ thought frantically. *If she'd kept up her speed, she would have easily overpowered me.* He was missing something. There was no reason for her to have slowed down, and even when she had, it was just enough to match him. It was almost as if *she* was the one trying to hold him down.

"Almost there." Tyra giggled.

DJ started to respond, but a drone came close to skewering him, forcing him to dodge. He growled and focused back on the fight with Tyra. But the same thing happened again. He was forced to evade a hail of bullets aimed at him. This time Tyra took advantage of the opportunity and sent DJ flying. The drones that made up the cyclone parted to let him pass and then stopped altogether on Tyra's command. DJ slammed into the ground several feet away, his body crashing into a drone about to finish off a guard.

DJ groaned but forced himself to sit up. The guard stared at him with wide eyes, but DJ ignored him, tapping on his comm unit. "What the hell was that? You guys were supposed to keep the drones off my back."

There was no reply.

"Hello? I know you sons of bitches heard me. If you fucked up, just say so." Silence. "Bunch of mother—"

DJ forced himself to his feet. While he'd been running to catch up to Tyra, he'd tracked each captain's location by tracing the path of their bullets. Now he swept his gaze over those places. He should have been able to find them easily, but he couldn't. That either meant they were too injured to move …

Or they were dead.

DJ focused and finally noticed several spots where a swarm of drones hovered, seemingly without reason.

"Do you get it now?" Tyra asked, cackling madly. She hadn't moved from her spot, content to watch him as realization slowly dawned on him. That's what she'd been stalling for. The captains worked together to stop Tyra from using her drones to interfere in the battle, while Christy had been a constant threat to her, forcing her to split her attention. The combination gave DJ too many advantages.

He'd thought that she'd isolated them with the drones as a way of countering Christy, who she must have seen as the biggest threat. But the drones had also blocked his view of the rest. He hadn't seen that she'd sent the swarm of drones to take out the captains.

But why didn't they say anything? DJ screamed in his head. *Why didn't they say they were being attacked?*

"They tried to reach you," Tyra said through his comm. DJ's head whipped toward hers. Once she was sure that she held his gaze, she slowly raised her hand to her ear and removed an earbud. It wasn't an army-issue comm, just a wireless earphone that could be connected anywhere. But DJ knew shouldn't be able to pick up secure connections.

As if sensing his question—or more accurately, predicting it—Tyra raised her other arm and tapped something on her cybergauntlet. A second later, DJ's comm automatically switched from the main raid channel to the private one he used to chat with Hermione and his brother.

DJ stared at her in horror. He'd been wearing his comm since he'd left his room earlier that morning. How much had she heard? His discussion with CJ and Hermione about the plan? Tyra had known all of it.

But that wasn't the cause of DJ's horror. In fact, DJ couldn't explain why this revelation had hit him so hard. He already knew Tyra was devious, and he knew she was a skilled hacker. She'd accessed Sparta's surveillance system even with CJ monitoring it. If anything, they should have considered this possibility. DJ shouldn't have been so shocked she'd hacked their comms.

But yet he was. Why?

Why is she so set on proving that she is smarter than us? DJ screamed in his mind. There was no point—literally no point—in Tyra revealing that she'd been listening in on their communication the whole time. If anything, she had more to gain by hiding that information. Instead, she'd shown that she was fucking with him.

She'd been playing with him from the beginning, first when she'd allowed him to wear himself down even though she could have ended him in the first minute. And then she hadn't chased after him when he'd escaped. DJ had been worried she'd had another motive—another angle that they weren't seeing. But it was much simpler than that.

The whole thing was a game to her. She'd never taken him—or any of them—seriously. DJ scanned the room. Only a few dozen guards were still fighting, all of them showing signs of exhaustion. But the number of drones hadn't seemed to dwindle. Everything that was happening—with the drones, the puppets, the guards, the staff, everyone that had been killed on both sides—meant nothing to her. That was why she was always smiling. She was playing a game only she understood, and she laughed at them for taking it seriously.

DJ had always been a pretty chill guy. He'd changed drastically since he became embroiled with Helene, but he'd always tried to retain his lighthearted-ness despite all the dark shit. He'd held on to humor like a life raft keeping him from drowning. He'd failed several times. Hell, he'd slipped up several times that day. It was hard not to when seeing your friends die around you for no reason.

But still, DJ had never hated anyone. Not really. Not even Helene. Every part of him opposed what the AI was doing. But he didn't hate her, not when he knew she'd literally been programmed that way. And he didn't hate Manar for doing so, nor did he hate the idiots who had killed Manar's family and caused the trauma that led to it all.

He thought it was all bullshit. But he didn't hate them—he'd never seen a point to it. Hatred took too much effort to nurse. It had a heavy price, one that DJ had never felt the need to pay.

But Tyra had changed that.

He screamed loud enough that it pierced through the battlefield, drawing every eye: friend and foe, human and mechanical. The shout didn't contain any words. It was primal, and it struck every heart that heard it. He screamed until his throat was hoarse and raw. When he was done, he charged at her.

DJ had never felt as much rage as he did right at that moment. Even that wasn't enough to activate the nanites—but his baseline attributes were superhuman. His leap landed him in front of Tyra a second after he moved. Naturally, that was the moment when Tyra chose to stop holding back. Her speed increased drastically until she was little more than a blur to him. He could still follow her with his eyes, but his body was no longer fast enough to keep up.

Her fist bludgeoned him, snapping his head to the side with enough force that DJ almost blacked out. He bit his tongue and used the pain to refocus. He twisted out of the way before he was consciously aware of the fact. A split second later, Tyra's knee struck the spot he'd been. Pretty soon DJ was getting thrashed with every exchange. In response, DJ dug deeper into his own technique until his attacks were more violent, more aggressive. He poured his hatred into every punch the way he'd seen Karla do. His fists became extensions of his will. Bit by bit, he started adapting to Tyra's style. Though many of her attacks still landed, just as many of his did too.

It became a battle of attrition: Who would be able to endure the other's attacks longer? As soon as it started, DJ knew that he was going to lose. He could quickly feel himself reaching his limits. His nanites were unresponsive, no matter how many times he mentally prodded them. Although he was matching Tyra, her attacks were like sledgehammers battering his body. His hatred drove him on, but his body had had enough. He could already feel himself losing consciousness. Once he did, there would be nothing stopping Tyra from steamrolling everyone else.

Either way, the fight was going to end, one way or the other.

But that didn't mean that DJ was ready to give up. He bit his tongue hard enough to draw blood and used the pain to refocus. Eventually, after an eternity, Tyra also started slowing down. Her speed was no longer overpowering. Even when he didn't completely anticipate her attack, he still had a split second to avoid it. This dragged the fight out, though DJ saw the world blink out with each punch he couldn't dodge.

Hermione screamed in his ear. *"DJ! We're done. We're freaking done. Hang tight. We're activating it now."*

DJ dismissed the voice as a delusion or Tyra giving him false hope. But a moment later, a hum, a resonance that thrummed through the air like an invisible string, spread across the room. It lingered just beyond the edge of his perception. Every drone in the room stopped at the same time. Their propellers shuddered and failed, sending them crashing to the ground in a shower of sparks. Finally, the red lights at their center flickered and died. Through the window, the same thing happened to the swarm outside, with drones dropping like metal-encased flies.

The surviving guards gaped, wide-eyed. Then, as one, they broke out into cheers. DJ didn't know where they got the strength after all the fighting, but their cries reverberated like thunder through the room.

DJ allowed himself an exhausted grin. For the first time, Tyra didn't seem to see the humor in the situation. Her lips peeled back into a snarl. She pulled back her fist. In the same moment, the hand exploded in a burst of blood and bone.

DJ savored the look of surprise and pain on the woman's face before his vision turned black.

DECEMBER 2043
SPARTA HEADQUARTERS,
NEW YORK

DJ JOLTED AWAKE, adrenaline pumping through his veins.

Frantic, he shot to his feet. Or at least he tried to. He managed to lift himself an inch off the bed before his body exploded with pain. It was as if someone had chopped him into pieces and then taken a mallet to each one. He groaned, but his throat was hoarse. Even that small action caused another wave of pain to rush through him.

"You shouldn't be moving so much," a voice said. Suddenly, a face loomed over him. DJ jerked in surprise, which invited another wave of pain. He barely managed to stifle a groan.

"Hey! What'd I just say?" Her voice retreated. She still hovered over him but not as close. DJ forced his vision to focus until he was finally able to make out her face clearly. She was young, about his own age, with a cute button nose and freckles that puffed out when she smiled. As pretty as she was, he was sure he would have remembered if they'd met before. "Though, I guess that one was kinda my fault, huh?"

"Where am I?" DJ asked, though the words came out as one long croak. Fortunately, she seemed to understand.

"You're in Sparta, in the hospital wing." As she spoke, she helped him drink water through a straw. DJ hadn't noticed she'd been holding the glass until the straw was in his mouth, which felt as dry as the Sahara. With each sip, his surroundings came into focus. Bleached white walls. The faint smell of chlorine in the air. His was the only bed in the room. Yep, seemed like a hospital.

The person helping him pulled back the straw and adjusted the bed into a reclining position. She wore a white nurses' uniform, which explained why her face wasn't familiar. This was the first time DJ had set foot in the hospital wing after all. She looked on in faint amusement as he glanced around, and stifled a laugh when his gaze finally rested on himself and what he was wearing.

DJ gestured for more water and was glad when she obliged. He cleared his throat when he was done and asked, as casually as he could, "Any ideas where my clothes went?" His voice was still hoarse, but at least his words actually sounded like words now.

"Burned to ash, I imagine," the nurse replied. "We had to cut through them in order to work on you. They were barely more than bloody rags anyway, so we gave them to one of your friends. They suggested an incinerator."

"I don't suppose you had anything to do with dressing me in … this?" He gestured to the hospital gown. It went down a few inches below his knee. Although enough for decency, the gown enabled quite a draft to his unmentionables.

"It's kind of my job," the nurse said, her lips pressed into a line in a way that made it very clear she was trying not to laugh. Her eyes twinkled as she spoke. "But not to worry though. You *definitely* don't have anything to be ashamed about."

DJ's brows went up and his lips pulled into a grin. "Oh?"

The nurse matched his smile. She started to respond when someone cleared their throat from the doorway. DJ tilted his head past the nurse to see Christy standing there, glaring at him. When he focused on her again, the nurse was the vision of professionalism. "Usually I'd ask if you were up to receiving visitors, but I don't think I'd survive if I told your friend that she'd have to keep waiting."

"You're probably right," DJ said, clearing his throat. "But how long has she been waiting?"

"Two days."

Two days, DJ repeated in his mind.

He'd been unconscious for two days. That should have been more than enough time for his nanites to have done some major work on his recovery. Yet DJ still felt as though he'd been put through a meat tenderizer.

How bad were his injuries then? He was tempted to ask the nurse, but he doubted she would be able to answer. "Yeah, we definitely have a lot to catch up on," he said finally. "Thank you."

"Thank *you*," the nurse replied and her tone arrested his attention. When he looked, DJ found her staring at him with a strange intensity. "Everybody has heard what you did against those things that attacked us."

"You know what they say about rumors." DJ chuckled. "You shouldn't believe everything that you hear."

The nurse shook her head, but she didn't bother to refute him. "Thank you," she repeated instead. Her hand brushed against his as she left. Christy took her spot a few seconds later, her eyes hard.

DJ gave her a tired grin, and then his face turned serious. "Catch me up."

Christy raised a brow, but she must have seen something on his face because her expression softened. She slumped into the chair beside the bed. "It's not as bad as you're probably imagining."

"Well, *that* narrows it down," DJ said sarcastically. "What happened to Tyra?"

"She got away." She sighed. "She ran off almost immediately after the drones failed to shield her. I tried to stop her, but she was basically a blur."

DJ nodded. He'd expected something like that. She probably could have killed CJ, Hermione, and Christy before she left, but she could also have been bogged down by the remaining guards. That was a risk she wouldn't take. Especially since there was no point to it.

"How about the drones?" DJ asked.

"What do you think? Nothing. The machine that your brother and Hermione developed worked. I honestly don't know how they did it, no matter how many times they explained it to me. I don't think I want to know, but every drone within a five-mile radius crashed at the same time. Most of the ones outside the building were destroyed from the fall. It didn't take long for the government to swoop in and stick their noses into everything. They've already carted off most of them for research. Both Hermione and CJ insisted that they leave a few behind. I don't know how well that's going to work out. They can't wait to speak with you, by the way."

"CJ and Hermione?"

"The government. Or at least the one in charge. Big guy with a large mouth. You'll love him."

DJ waved a hand dismissively. "Olsen will handle it."

"I don't think he can," Christy said skeptically, "not this one at least. He's been sniffing around the surviving guards. All of them have been screaming about the new Captain America to anyone willing to hear." She shrugged. "I tried to shut them up, but you know how it is."

DJ groaned, sending another wave of pain rushing through him. Christy leaned forward, but she didn't know how to help. At least the pain wasn't as bad as it had been before. Hopefully it meant the nanites were back to work. He blew out a breath once the wave was over. "How bad is it?"

"You have a concussion, broke almost every bone in your body, fractured—"

"The rumors," said DJ. "How bad are they?"

"Rumors?" Christy asked incredulously. "They're all *true*. I was there. I saw the crazy things that you did. Honestly? Captain America has nothing on you."

"Since when did you become a fangirl?" DJ asked.

"Probably since I saw you rip apart drones with your bare hands," Christy answered. Her tone was dry. But there was a strange intensity in her eyes that DJ didn't like.

"You've seen me do that before," he said.

"No, DJ," Christy said seriously. "I haven't."

DJ grimaced internally. He knew she hadn't. The last time Christy had seen him fight seriously was when they'd still been training with Karla and Liz. Then,

DJ had nowhere the level of strength that he did now. At that point, he hadn't even learned to activate the nanites, with emotions or otherwise. The first time he'd done it deliberately was in the White House, and Christy hadn't been there to see him.

"What's going on with you, D?" Christy asked. DJ picked up undercurrents of something in her tone that rubbed him the wrong way. He felt even worse when he tried to see it from her perspective. Christy had been with him through all the bullshit. Now she probably thought he was keeping things from her. It didn't help that the only other people she'd seen do the things he'd done were the Murder Twins. DJ couldn't even begin to imagine what was going through her head.

He sighed. "It's the nanites."

"How?" she asked, leaning forward. "You've had nanites for ages now, and you've never been able to do those things. That anger? I mean, I've seen you pissed, but never to that extent. I didn't even know humans were capable of growling like that."

DJ grimaced. "Yeah. I was in a dark place. For a while now actually. According to Chloe, the nanites enhance my hormones as strongly as everything else."

"Chloe?" Christy asked, her tone completely neutral. "When'd she say this?"

DJ winced, this time not because of any pain. "I went to the warehouse a few days ago to get their help with this whole Tyra thing."

"And how'd that work out for you?" she asked.

"Yeah, yeah. I know. I fucked up. I was an idiot," he admitted. "But I had to do *something*. You and I are the only ones who can fight on the team. We're going to need every fighter we can get with Helene out in the open now." He thought of how he'd been able to dodge the government's help until then. "Are we about to get kicked to the curb?"

"That's still up in the air," Christy replied. "Right now everyone's still trying to figure out what happened, how much damage it caused, and stuff like that. They're pissed though. Like, supremely pissed. You should probably expect a call sometime soon."

DJ nodded. "Yeah, well, I can't say I blame them. We already knew that we were going to take the heat for everything." He hesitated. "Do you have a count?"

"Not yet. The police are still sweeping through the building. But …" Now she was the one to hesitate. "CJ took a headcount of the survivors and compared it with the number of people scheduled to have been there that day."

"And?"

"D … it doesn't matter," she said, sighing. "What's done is done, and we have more important things to worry—"

"How many, Christy?" DJ asked, his voice firm.

"Close to two thousand."

DJ flinched. Close to two thousand people had been killed. DJ didn't even know how to wrap his head around that. The whole thing was just pointless. It was unnecessary. Those lives had been wasted because of what? Because Helene wanted to prove a point? DJ was past the stage where he blamed himself for these deaths. But believing that didn't remove the knowledge that Helene had killed all those people to get to him. Him and everyone else who stood against her. They were fighting the good fight. But would the families of those two thousand be willing to listen to that? Would they care? Their loved ones had died for the sole reason they were convenient pawns in a game they didn't even know was being played.

"Most of that number are the guards," Christy said in the silence. "They knew the risks, and they made their choice—"

"But they didn't, did they?" DJ said softly. "They didn't know the risks. Most of them died without understanding where the drones came from or why they were suddenly being attacked. How many do you think would have stood by us if they'd learned the drones were there because of us, that their friends died because of us? How many do you think would have strung us up and offered us up to Tyra without a second chance?"

"This was bigger than us, and you know it," Christy argued. "This is the most overt that Helene has ever been. She was looking to make a statement."

"And we were the convenient choice," DJ finished. "And two thousand people are dead because of it." DJ blew out a breath, suddenly feeling exhausted. "Look, I get what you're saying. I understand that *logically* this isn't really on us. We did what we had to do. It was Helene's choice to respond the way she did. It isn't our fault, but that doesn't mean that we're not to blame."

Christy glared at the wall but didn't say anything. DJ closed his eyes, lost in his thoughts. The silence persisted for several minutes until something occurred to him. "What about the puppets?"

"What?"

"What happened to the puppets?" DJ repeated, looking at her.

"Some of them were killed before we drew them to the gym. Some of the ones that were knocked out by the Pulse were trampled during the chaos. But most of them survived, D. Because of you," Christy said, leaning forward. "They couldn't all fit in the IC afterward, so a whole floor was zoned off for them. They all woke up yesterday, but Hermione knocked them out again with the Pulse so Helene couldn't take control of them again. Some government folks wanted to take them. Fortunately, Olsen was able to interfere before Hermione bit someone's head off. They're trying to figure out what to do now. Apparently extracting the spores is no longer an option."

"No," DJ agreed absently. "Hermione found out that the spores form some kind of symbiotic relationship with the victim's brain. Extracting the spores puts the person in a coma."

"Yeah. That's what she said."

"I doubt that was enough to satisfy them though," DJ guessed.

"We had a handle on it for a while. Somehow it leaked, and several news stations got a hold of the information. Now the public has weighed in."

DJ groaned. "How bad is it?"

"It's an even split among three. Some people believe that the puppets are just victims of the pandemic that's been going around. Of course, none of them knows that the pandemic is actually just Helene and her spores. At least they don't necessarily blame us—and by *us*, I mean Sparta—for defending ourselves. One of the major threats of the 'pandemic' is that the victims are prone to seemingly unnecessary and unpredictable episodes of violence. Of course, all of that is bullshit, but at least it works in our favor."

"That's one group."

"The second group is mostly just conspiracy theorists pointing out that the victims of the pandemic have never been known to form groups before—especially not a mob of this size. They're basically crying foul and saying there's obviously a mastermind behind it all. Which is true. It's just that they think the mastermind is the government."

"I'm guessing you saved the worst for last?"

Christy sighed. "The last group is basically saying that the puppets are blameless and that we're murderers for killing them. They conveniently ignore the gigabytes of footage showing those same victims attacking us and us defending ourselves. They have no case, but somehow they're the ones that have gotten the most traction in the media."

"That's obviously Helene's doing."

Christy nodded. "Since most of them believe that Helene's control is a result of some pandemic, they're treating it like an insanity case. It doesn't help that Ndidi and Manar are saying they might have a cure for all mental illnesses."

"Wait, hold on?" DJ looked up. "Ndidi and Manar are saying what?"

CHAPTER

54

DECEMBER 2043
OKAFOR CORPORATION,
ABUJA, NIGERIA

NDIDI LOOKED UP FROM THE PILE of paperwork when her phone rang. She reached for it, happy for the distraction. But when she saw the name on the caller ID, her excitement turned sour.

Look at me, she thought, frowning, *behaving like I'm back in high school at the principal's office when I've done nothing wrong.*

She took a deep breath and received the call.

DJ's voice invaded the room. *"What the hell, Ndidi?"*

Ndidi straightened at her desk, absently adjusting pieces of loose paper. "You'll have to be more specific."

"My bad," DJ said agreeably. *"What the hell is this bullshit about you and Manar making more picospores?"*

"Helene's gone, DJ. The picospores are no longer a threat. Now they can be used to actually help people like they were originally designed to do. And they *work*, DJ. In the last few days alone, we've—"

"*Are you fucking kidding me right now?*" DJ asked incredulously. "*I freaking told you what happened at the White House last week. What part of 'Helene tried to take over the government' made you think that she was gone?*"

Ndidi glanced up as the door to her office opened, and Manar stepped into the room. She put the call on speakerphone so he could hear as well. "You told me what *you* believed was the truth," she replied. "But it's also equally plausible that you just unearthed something she put in motion before she was destroyed. You're just letting your emotions cloud your judgment."

"*First off, I'm not you,*" DJ retorted. Ndidi winced. He was referring to a few months back when she'd made a deal with Helene to free Bethany.

"*That's what you do. You've always allowed your emotions to blind you to what's right in front of you,*" DJ continued. "*And now you're doing the same stupid mistake again.*"

"DJ, listen—"

"*No, you listen, 'cause I'm not done. When was the last time you watched the news?*"

"The news?" Ndidi frowned. What did that have to do with anything?

"*Yeah, you know, television? The media? The modern way of staying informed?*"

Ndidi closed her eyes. She should have hung up, and she almost did. But she didn't. Something about the entire conversation made her anxious. DJ had always been annoying, but he was hardly ever this deliberately aggravating unless he was pissed off, and he knew that he had a good reason to be. She glared at the phone. "You're being a dick."

"*Please. I've not even started.*" He chuckled, but there was no humor in it. "*So?*"

"Not for a couple of days," she said through gritted teeth. She'd been glued to the television for the days following the press conference. But since the first few families began their treatment, Ndidi had been either at her desk or touring the picospore wing. "Why?"

"*Do you have a TV close by? Turn on the news. I'll wait.*"

Ndidi glanced at Manar, whose expression was as unreadable as ever. There was a flat-screen on the wall opposite Ndidi that she had never turned on. After a moment of her rifling through her desk to locate the remote, the screen lit up. Ndidi pressed a random news channel.

"... *swarms of unidentified drones blanketed the streets of New York. Their target was the Sparta Headquarters, the multinational conglomerate ...*"

Ndidi pressed the channel button.

"... *a mob of Berserker Virus victims stormed the Sparta building and ...*"

She pressed it again.

"... *preliminary death toll of over two thousand, including those suffering from the Berserker Virus and the brave men and women of Sparta who stood against the attack. Many are saying ...*"

Again.

" ... *the Department of Homeland Security has given a statement denouncing the event as a terrorist attack and has assured the public that every effort is being made to ...*"

Again.

"... *the public is calling for justice against the, and I quote, 'murderers who cut down innocent victims in cold blood.' This statement comes from an open letter responding to the recent attack on Sparta and the ongoing conversation of whether the surviving guards should be prosecuted for their actions against the victims of the Berserker Virus who joined the attack. The outcry is pushing the Sparta board of directors to choose between ...*"

The room descended into silence as Ndidi switched off the television. She stared blankly at the room. Her thoughts warred with each other for dominance. One came out the winner. "Are Bethany and Hermione okay?"

"*They are, as are my brother and Christy. Thank you for asking.*" DJ sighed. "*A bunch of disasters happened, and without them, we wouldn't have made it. There's a lot I have to catch you and Manar up on.*"

"He's right here," Ndidi said, glancing up at Manar. He was still staring at the TV screen, but his expression was no longer unreadable. Ndidi thought she detected a note of ... satisfaction?

Ndidi thought she heard Christy's voice on the other line, bringing her focus back to the conversation. "You can catch us up now."

"*It'll take too long. It's a whole thing, and apparently, I have to be resting. I'll cut to the chase: the picospores. So …*" His voice grew hard. "*What the hell, Ndidi?*"

"DJ, we've been over this—"

"*Yeah, and your excuse was that the spores you've created are safe because Helene wasn't around to control them, right?*"

It was a rhetorical question, so Ndidi didn't answer. And it was proven to be the right choice when DJ continued. "*Well now, you have proof that Helene is around somewhere. So I'm asking again: What the hell?*"

"Manar said—"

"*Oh, Manar said,*" DJ repeated in a mocking tone. "*Well, if Manar said it, then it must be true, right?*"

Ndidi's eyes burned a hole in her phone. She ground her teeth so hard they almost cracked. "I've put up with your nonsense, DJ. But I'm not a child, so don't talk to me like one."

Muffled static came from DJ's end as if someone had put their hand over the speaker. Ndidi could make out both DJ's and Christy's voices but couldn't hear what either was saying. Christy's tone, however, gave her a pretty good guess. A few seconds later the static cleared, and Ndidi could clearly make out DJ sighing. "*I'm sorry,*" he said finally. "*Let's blame it on the painkillers and take a few steps back. Manar and my brother both said Helene was destroyed in the Virtual Realm, with no hope of coming back. Now I don't believe that they lied, but they were obviously wrong, and that means that their words are not gospel.*"

"You're right," Manar said, speaking up for the first time. "I was wrong, but that doesn't mean that I'm wrong now. The picospores that we're developing now cannot be controlled remotely by any means. I designed their defense personally."

"*I hate to be the voice of reason, Manar, but Helene proved years ago that her skills trump yours.*"

Manar grimaced. DJ was referring to when Manar had tried to shut down Helene by accessing her core codes. As the creator of the AI, it should have been a simple thing. But by then, Helene had grown far too powerful. Manar hadn't been able to go through her defenses.

"That was before I returned from the Virtual Realm," Manar countered. "You cannot imagine what it was like there. My skills have grown by leaps and bounds."

"You're right. I can't, and my brother said something similar. But Helene was also there. Who knows how that place affected her? You might have gotten better, but she probably has too. I mean, the fact that she apparently no longer cares about staying under the radar might be a sign of that. So forgive me if I'm not enthusiastic about risking the lives of millions of people in the hopes that your rock beats her scissors. How'd you even get Hermione to agree to this anyway?"

Ndidi hesitated. "What do you mean?"

"I mean, how'd you guys convince Hermione to help you do this? She must have helped. I'm curious to know how you guys convinced her."

"We didn't," Manar replied. "I developed the spores myself."

"Now what do you mean?"

"Several years ago, when Hermione started working on the picospores in Sparta, she allowed me to study her notes. The project interested me, and I kept myself informed of her progress since then, up to the point when Ndidi and I came to Nigeria. Once we decided to continue the picospore project here, I already had all the information I needed, without input from anyone."

"That is the dumbest fuck—"

"DJ!" Christy cut him off sharply, her voice perfectly clear.

"Fine," DJ said. *"So Hermione doesn't know that you guys have stolen her late father's life's work and are using it for your own ends."*

"First of all, the picospore technology has always belonged to the Okafor Corporation. She and her father developed the technology while working for my father and using the corporation's resources. The Cloneys are the pioneers, definitely, but we're not stealing anything." She paused, waiting to see if DJ would say anything to that. When he didn't, she continued. "Second of all, we're using it to help people."

"And I'm sure the fact that the business is massively profitable and helps to stabilize your influence in your company has nothing to do with your decision," DJ said dryly.

"How did you—"

"*I didn't. Not specifically. I'm just familiar with how power works.*" There was a pause. "*Look, you can talk about altruism all you want, but you can't bullshit a bullshitter. While helping people probably did factor into your decision, it was just a part of it. And whether or not your initial thinking made sense, it's now obvious that Helene's back, so we can't risk—*"

"There's no risk," Manar cut in calmly. "Whether or not Helene's skills are better than mine"—he paused, looking as if he'd swallowed a lemon—"the spores are completely infallible."

DJ sighed. "*The point is that you don't understand enough about the technology to guarantee that. Hermione has been studying the spores for most of her life. Even she said that we're just playing catch-up to what Helene's done.*"

Manar straightened, and Ndidi could almost see his pride radiate off him. "The point is that you do not understand what I am capable of, so you continue to make assumptions about me based on my inferiors."

DJ didn't say anything for a moment. When he finally did, he'd obviously lost whatever patience he'd had because his words came out as a growl. "*Oh yeah? Did you know that extracting the spores would drop the person into a coma?*"

Manar stiffened.

"Wait, what?" Ndidi leaned forward.

"*It's something my brother and Hermione discovered a few weeks back,*" DJ explained. "*CJ found a way to hack into the spores—*"

"That's not possible," Manar said immediately.

"*Just because you can't do it doesn't mean it can't be done,*" DJ returned. "*Apparently you don't know what my brother's capable of.*"

Manar started to reply, but Ndidi waved him off. "Forget about that." She was also curious about how CJ and Hermione had broken through something that Helene had made, but they could come back to that. "What do you mean, coma?"

"*Apparently the new versions that Helene made form a symbiotic relationship with the person's brain. Extracting the spores breaks that bond, and the person falls into a coma. It happened with Albert's wife and a few of the hostages that we freed in the last raid. The working theory then was that some people were just more sensitive to the spores than others. Now Hermione thinks that Helene was just working to perfect the spores and that the former hostages were injected with different versions while she tested out the kinks."*

"The spores we developed were based on Hermione's research and notes about Helene's own spores. That means—"

"It doesn't mean anything," Manar said firmly. "By your own words, Darren Kojak, it's only a problem if the spores are extracted. But the picospores are meant to be a permanent solution to the illness they are designed for. That means they never have to be extracted."

"What it means, you jackass, is that you don't know anything about what you're playing with. Your spores are based on Helene's, and even after Hermione's years of study, she still managed to sneak a trap past us. Who knows how many of those traps we haven't yet found? And now you're helping her mass-produce them, basically encouraging people to be turned into puppets."

They continued arguing, but Ndidi drowned them out. She didn't know why DJ's words hit her so hard. The picospores were always meant to be a permanent solution. Manar was right about that. Even their preliminary tests examined the effects of the spores on subjects, and no one had ever thought to test the effects of *removing* the spores—the spores were never meant to be removed. Ndidi knew her father's vision for the technology, and she'd always seen its potential for good. She'd never considered that there would ever be a reason to extract the spores from someone.

Of course, that was naive.

The psych eval and the medical assessment were both extensive, but it was possible that at some point, a patient with a condition antithetical to the pico-spore treatment might slip through the cracks.

What would happen then?

The solution would be to extract the spores, but according to DJ, that would drop the patient into a coma.

Ndidi could almost hear Manar's voice telling her that it would never happen, but that was only one scenario. A patient could change their mind about going through the procedure, or they could have been misdiagnosed. Both of those were more plausible, and they'd lead to the same end. What would happen then?

Ndidi drew in a deep breath and held it. She wasn't thinking straight, the news about Sparta affecting her judgment. Slowly, she let out her breath. DJ had a point, but so did Manar. Ndidi could hear DJ's voice in her ear telling her that producing picospores was too risky and that she should shut down the project entirely. But that wasn't an option. As annoying as the man was, he'd also been right that Ndidi needed the spores to solidify her position in the company.

They'd have to redo the tests on the spores to confirm. But even if DJ was right and the spores carried the risks, Ndidi knew they could think of a solution. There was just one thing she needed to confirm.

Ndidi opened her eyes to find Manar already staring at her. He and DJ must have finished their argument at some point. She briefly wondered what they'd resolved, but it was a secondary concern.

"Did you know?" she asked. She didn't need to explain what she meant. Manar didn't try to delay by asking.

He nodded. "I knew it was a risk." Ndidi stood and walked around the table. "But it was an acceptable one because the picospores would never need to be extracted. You know this as well as I do, Ndidi. They're the perfect solution for every—"

Manar snatched Ndidi's wrist before her slap could connect. They glared at each other, their faces hard. Ndidi struggled, and Manar released her, though his eyes glittered dangerously, warning her not to try again. "I understand that you do not agree with my judgment, but there is no need to resort to violence."

Ndidi turned and left the room without responding. Her face was blank until she reached their suite. Her tears built up, but she didn't cry.

CHAPTER

55

DECEMBER 2043

SPARTA HEADQUARTERS,
NEW YORK

DJ HUNG UP. "They're not going to stop."

"Did you really expect them to?"

"I expected them to have more fucking sense than this!" DJ yelled, throwing his hands up. As sore as he was, he'd regret that later. "I mean, how stupid can a person be? Helene has screwed us over time and time again, and now they suddenly think they've outsmarted her? Even after we just confirmed that she'd tricked them about being destroyed in the Virtual Realm? I mean, how can they not see that this is going to blow up in their faces? We've all seen the movies, right? I can understand Ndidi being this dumb—she doesn't have a good track record of making the smartest of choices. Manar must have turned her head to mush with some premium di—"

"DJ!" Christy shouted, cutting him off. "You need to calm down."

DJ blew out a breath. Christy was right. He was getting too worked up over it. But the sheer stupidity of the whole thing pissed him off.

Christy continued. "And you need to let go of whatever beef you have with Ndidi."

DJ stared at her like she was crazy. "What?"

Christy met his look with a glare, but there was also worry in her eyes. "Listen, D, I get why you're pissed at her. She betrayed the team and put your brother in a coma. It was a bitch move. But you gotta let it go. It's making you bitter. Especially now, with whatever is going on with your nanites. It's changing you, D. Talk to her. Shout at her. Whatever. But you have to let it go. Your brother already has, and he was the one—"

"Of course CJ has forgiven her," DJ scoffed. "He's always had a blind spot when it comes to himself. He probably doesn't even see what she did as a betrayal. He's probably *grateful*. It allowed him to go to the Virtual Realm and come back fu—" This time DJ cut himself off, seeing the look in Christy's eyes.

Over the years, DJ had learned to differentiate Christy's glares. There were several, depending on whether she was annoyed with him, exasperated, or something else. DJ had only seen her keep-talking-and-I'm going-to-smack-you glare a few times. Each time had made an impression on him, mostly because the glare had been followed by her smacking the back of his head.

"Go on," she said in a neutral tone. Her hand inched toward her side.

DJ grimaced and then actually thought about what he'd been saying. "Maybe I do need to calm down."

"That's the first step," Christy agreed. "But you also need to get whatever the hell is going on with you under control. If you're going to be Captain America, you have to get the anger issues under control."

DJ chuckled despite himself. "Captain America is a self-righteous prick. If I'm going to be an Avenger, I'd rather be Iron Man."

"You're not handsome or rich enough to be Stark," Christy scoffed. "But with a bucket of green paint, you could be Hulk. Both of you already have the same number of brain cells."

DJ would have retorted, but his mind was no longer in it.

Christy noticed, and her tone grew more serious. She spent the next hour going into more detail about what he'd missed, starting with the rumors that were spreading among the staff. They'd joked about the stories surrounding his powers, but it had the potential to be a serious pain in the ass. If it got too out of hand, it was inevitable that people would stop dismissing them as rumors and start asking questions that DJ had no intention of answering. Worse were those who wouldn't bother with questions. They would simply carry him off.

At his peak, DJ was confident he'd be able to match almost any force sent against him. But he was far from his peak right now. His problems called for diplomatic solutions, which weren't really his strong suit.

Eventually DJ burned through whatever energy he'd gained over two days of rest, and his eyes started closing. Before DJ fell asleep, he thought he could hear Christy settling down on one of the couches outside.

DJ tried to tell her not to bother, but he was already out.

CHAPTER

56

DECEMBER 2043
OKAFOR CORPORATION,
ABUJA, NIGERIA

NDIDI'S EYES OPENED SLOWLY. It was still dark out, and the bedside clock read that it was two in the morning. Ndidi sighed, though she didn't make any effort to get up. It was easy to understand what had awakened her. She was lying on her side, and at some point her hand had reached over to Manar's side of the bed.

It was cold.

It'd been a couple of months since they'd come to Nigeria. They'd slept on the same bed every night since then. Apparently Ndidi had gotten so used to his presence that his absence was enough to rouse her. Although this wasn't their first disagreement, it'd never reached to the point where either of them had considered taking a different room.

But then again, the argument earlier that day had been different.

Ndidi sat up, resting her back against the headrest. She'd already gone over the conversation a thousand times in her head. Now she'd had the chance to sleep on it. She'd already accepted that Manar had been right to move forward with the picospores despite the risks involved with removing them. She'd come to the same conclusion, after all, when DJ had told them. The problem was that Manar hadn't been the one to tell her. He'd known, and he'd kept it from her. That felt too much like a betrayal, which Ndidi had trouble forgiving. She trusted him, probably far more than was wise. This was the first time she felt like he was taking advantage of that trust.

She recalled several things from the last couple of months that she'd overlooked. His temper was a major one. Previously, Manar hadn't been one prone to fits of rage. He got angry, like any person, but he usually handled it by distancing himself from the situation, usually by using reason and logic. His logic had been a core aspect of who he was. But lately, Ndidi had seen several instances when he'd let his emotions rule him. While it was only in short bursts, it was something that had never happened before.

She could still remember the look in his eyes when he'd trashed their first room shortly after they'd arrived. And then there was that moment earlier that day when she'd tried to slap him. She'd been wrong to do that, yes—but his eyes. The way they glittered said he'd have no problem striking her. Ndidi still shivered thinking about it.

She sighed. She was angry, and she was jumping at shadows that weren't there. She'd noticed most of these differences after he'd returned from the Virtual Realm. It was almost inevitable that his experiences there had changed him. After all, DJ had noticed changes in his brother.

Ndidi forced her mind back on track: the argument. She'd overreacted, and it was making her doubt herself. She'd already come to the same conclusions that Manar had. They were on the same page. There was no reason for a fight.

Ndidi got up from the bed. While it was too late for her to start searching through the guest bedrooms for Manar, she didn't think she would be able to get any sleep herself. She opted to get an early start on the day. She could get started on designing the tests for the patients, to help determine which batch of the spores—if any of them—posed any risks if it was ever necessary for them to be extracted.

She fumbled around in the dark for a minute before finally finding the light switch. The rooms, and the building itself, had been designed to be extravagant. However, Eze, Ndidi's father, hadn't wanted guests to be able to just wander into any of the work buildings. The result was that the guest building where Ndidi and Manar were staying was located far away from anything remotely important. The distance wasn't so stressful to traverse during the day. But at night, it would have been hell, especially since security would ask her more questions in light of the late hour. Fortunately, Ndidi had discovered a shortcut to the main complex years ago.

The passages were well lit. She navigated them easily until she got to the wing dedicated to picospore treatment. She should have headed straight to her office so she could start brainstorming, but even before she'd left her bed, she'd known that she wouldn't be able to resist checking out the rooms. The psych eval section was empty, but some of the lab assistants were still up working in the medical tests section. Ndidi would have loved to pick their brains, but that would mean informing them about the potential risks the spores posed. She hadn't handled learning the information well, so there was no reason to assume anyone else would.

Still, she entered and spent a few minutes conversing with the assistants about the families that had come through earlier that day. Their reports would be part of the stack on her desk, but at least now she could save herself some time when she finally sat down to work. Of course, she realized she was procrastinating, but the realization didn't make her above it. She and Manar had both worked to develop the original tests used to determine the effectiveness of the picospores. Ndidi knew enough about the technology that she was confident she could handle this herself.

But she didn't want to.

She shook her head. Want didn't factor into it. It would have been best to have Manar present, but this wasn't something that could wait. If the picospores were truly a risk, then they needed to begin coming up with solutions—something that would work on patients who'd already been dosed.

With her priorities reconfirmed, Ndidi left the lab, finally making her way to her office. The hallways were silent and largely deserted. Laboratories made up most of the wing. The only space that had been fit for an office was toward the end of the extension. If she'd gone there straightaway, then it wouldn't have taken too long. Her detour had added several minutes—minutes that Ndidi no longer wanted to spend out of fear that she'd start procrastinating again.

She took a shortcut through one of the unused sections of the building. Ndidi had never had any reason to use it before—especially not at night—but she recalled passing it on the tour with Manar. She patted her pocket for her phone—to use the flashlight—and then groaned when she didn't feel anything. She must have forgotten it in the room.

She should have turned back then. She should have just gone back to her bed. But Ndidi was stubborn. There was no way to track time, of course, but Ndidi guessed it had been about half an hour since she'd left her room—time wasted if she called it quits. She was under the building's glass-covered dome, so the area was unlit save for the moonlight filtering down from above. With the shortcut and the ambient light, she'd be in her well-lit office in a couple of minutes. Ndidi suppressed her doubts, making her way deeper into the passage.

The first turn was easy to remember, as was the second. By the third, Ndidi's pace slowed. She took a hard look at each passage before going into it. It was the first time that Ndidi had ever thought of the corporation as mazelike. By the sixth turn, she was starting to suspect she might have made a mistake. Most of the walls were blank except for the occasional painting. Ndidi had taken note of a few during the tour, but the ones she saw now were unfamiliar.

It was the eighth turn that convinced her that she was well and truly lost. Ndidi almost laughed at the sheer stupidity of it all. She could almost imagine what DJ would have said. She started to turn back. She didn't get more than two turns before she realized she couldn't remember the way. In the dark, everything looked the same. There were still several hours until dawn.

Ndidi rubbed the bridge of her nose. She was tempted to cry. It would have been so easy. The tears were right at the edge. *No*, Ndidi thought, clenching her teeth. She was already pathetic. Crying in the middle of a dark hallway was a step too far for her. Instead, she closed her eyes and took a deep breath, holding it for several seconds before letting it out slowly. It was an old meditation technique she'd used to control her anger but had adapted for tears. Ndidi had to repeat it three times before she felt calm enough to open her eyes.

It'd been a mistake to try to take the shortcut. It would have been even stupider to continue on now that she'd confirmed she didn't know the way. Ndidi retraced her steps as best as she could, seeking a place she recognized. She took a note of the hallway and then picked the most likely path back. She hadn't taken more than eight turns, so if she wasn't back to the main sections within that margin, she'd return and try a different passage.

And then she'd rinse and repeat until it worked.

SHE TURNED INTO A NEW PASSAGE and saw light at the end. Her pace quickened with relief until she realized that the light was coming from a single room. Immediately, she slowed down, frowning. It wasn't unusual for someone to be working late into the night, but this part of the building was meant to be unused, hence why the lights had been shut off. No one should have been working here.

The person might have gotten lost the same as she did, but for some reason, Ndidi didn't think so. Carpets lined the floor of every passage so her steps were already muffled. Ndidi slowed down even more just in case, trying to make her steps completely silent as she drew closer to the room. Near the door, a low hum reached her ears, as well as the sound of someone moving around. That eliminated any possibility that the lights had been left on by accident.

A step away, Ndidi pressed herself against the wall and peeked in. The room was larger than she'd expected, about double the size of a standard lab. Its walls were lined with rows of sleek workstations that curved around its length like a crescent moon. Most were empty, but a few scattered monitors displayed readings Ndidi couldn't make out. The walls were covered in screens displaying simulations, diagrams, and designs. Some of it looked familiar. Ndidi could see hints of the picotechnology, but it wasn't enough for her to understand.

Is it some kind of enhancer? Ndidi thought. But the diagrams suggested something far more complicated than that. Ndidi couldn't even begin to wrap her head around them. Maybe she could if she showed it to Hermione or Martin—it looked to be more their field.

Finally, her eyes went to the center of the room where a large sealed chamber housed a fabricator. Ndidi had seen the machine only a few times. The maze of tiny channels and nozzles made it unmistakable. It was mainly used in manufacturing to create specialized machines on a small scale. The machine itself was small for its size—only about six feet wide. This meant whatever it was producing would be minute. Ndidi would have wondered if someone was attempting to develop knockoffs of the picospores, if the equipment and setting weren't so different.

A man came out from behind the machine, dressed casually in a turtleneck and jeans. Ndidi saw his face for only a brief second before he turned toward the machine, but Ndidi would have known who the man was even without it. She could have identified him from a single strand of hair.

"Manar ..." she whispered.

DECEMBER 2043
OKAFOR CORPORATION,
ABUJA, NIGERIA

NDIDI DUCKED BEHIND THE WALL, cursing herself. She paused to listen. Manar's behavior in the room hadn't changed—he hadn't heard her. Ndidi tried to process what she'd seen, too many thoughts fighting for dominance, each of them accompanied by their own emotions. What was he making in there? Why hadn't he told her about it? How had he even gotten permission to use the lab?

The latter was particularly worrisome because it led to answers that Ndidi wasn't sure she wanted to know. Manar didn't have the same clout here that he did in Sparta, so Ndidi sincerely doubted he'd just walked up to the board of directors and requested his own space. He could have—either by leaning on her influence or using his own—but Ndidi no doubt would have heard about it, especially considering the equipment he was using. Ndidi couldn't identify most of it, but a glance was more than enough to tell her that they probably weren't cheap. The fabricator alone would have raised some eyebrows.

She dared to peek again and watched as Manar pressed a few buttons in sequence. A hum emitted by the rigged-up fabricator increased in intensity. He moved to a computer connected to the device, his fingers flying over the keyboard. Numbers appeared and disappeared on the screen. His actions were calm and methodical, imbued with the same confidence that he did everything else.

So why the secrecy? What was he developing that he couldn't tell her about? *More importantly*, she wondered, *what am I going to do about it?*

Her first thought was to confront him about it. Her heart cried for her to do that. This was Manar after all. But Ndidi remembered the dangerous look she'd seen in his eyes earlier that day. He'd changed. This—whatever he was up to—wasn't the Manar she knew.

She'd had a feeling of foreboding from the moment she'd seen the light of the room. Manar didn't make the feeling go away. If anything, he made it worse. It was obvious that whatever he was working on wasn't something that he wanted known.

Even by her.

She'd have to decide whether to ignore it or to report it—and the former wasn't an option. Manar was never the type to waste his time on pointless ventures. He wouldn't have gone through the trouble of setting the room up if it wasn't somehow important. Ndidi couldn't ignore that. But she didn't know if she would be able to report it. Telling the board of directors might only make her already tenuous position even shakier.

More importantly, she'd be directly betraying Manar.

The machine quieted down. Ndidi risked another look. Manar stood in front of one of the fabricator's nozzles, holding a small vial into which something like metallic dust spilled. Ndidi had been right that the machine's size meant that whatever it developed would be extremely small. The vial, now filled, glowed with metallic-silver light, as if the tiny particles were lit from within. Manar raised the vial up to his face and studied its contents. His lips pulled into a satisfied smile.

Ndidi watched, enraptured as Manar picked up a syringe from one of the nearby workstations and carefully inserted the needle into the vial. Slowly, he pulled back the plunger. The suction drew the vial's contents into the syringe. He looked practiced in his movements, like an addict measuring out his dose. Ndidi found herself unable to peel her eyes away as Manar placed the needle against his vein. *Is that what this is? He's making a drug?* It was a compelling thought. Once again, that explanation seemed too simple.

The needle slipped in easily, and Manar closed his eyes. He pressed down the plunger, and the particles slowly disappeared into his body. Manar kept his eyes closed even as he discarded the now-empty syringe. Ndidi didn't notice a change. After a few minutes of nothing happening, Ndidi started to reconsider whether she should wait to see what happened. A moment later, the decision was taken from her. Manar finally moved. He cocked his head to the side, as if listening for something.

Suddenly, his head whipped toward her, and his golden eyes stared straight at her.

Ndidi froze. "Fuck."

CHAPTER

58

NDIDI RAN.

She didn't think about it. None of that. Adrenaline flooded her veins, and her body was moving before she fully processed it happening. But by then it was too late. Manar appeared before her with a rush of air. She saw him. She met his golden eyes.

And then she attacked.

Ndidi hadn't fought in a long time. She regularly went to the gym, and sometimes even sparred with Pratima. But she hadn't *fought* for years. The last time had been against Liz Polova during one of their raids on Helene's facilities. Since then, Ndidi had mostly stayed clear of direct action. But the instincts were still there. Eze had been adamant that his daughter learn how to defend herself, which meant Ndidi had trained in martial arts since she was old enough to walk.

She got so good that she went to international competitions and won. It was how she'd first met Hermione.

Immediately she sensed Manar in front of her. Her elbow lashed out in a move that would break his nose. The attack was smooth and came without warning—Ndidi wouldn't have been confident evading it if she'd been in his shoes. Even blocking would have been difficult given the speed of the attack.

Manar caught her elbow with an open palm and then gripped it like a steel vise. Ndidi felt the power in his hand. She didn't bother struggling. Instead she spun and struck out with her other elbow. Normally this would have forced a person to release her arm if they wanted to duck below the second attack. But Manar simply caught that arm as well. Now her back was toward him, both her arms in his grip.

She lashed out with a kick, which he deflected to the side. Smoothly, he hooked a foot behind hers and pushed it away, widening her stance. With her arms still in his grasp, he'd effectively rendered her unable to do anything.

The entire fight had lasted all of two seconds.

He held her in that position for several more seconds before letting her loose. Ndidi spun to face him. She didn't try to run again, despite what her instincts screamed at her. She met his eyes once more. The golden orbs bored into her, as if it was looking at her soul. Manar—the real Manar—had had a similar effect. But never to this magnitude. Ndidi had only felt *this* gaze in a few scant instances. She forcefully suppressed the fear that threatened to overwhelm her and replaced it with anger.

"How?" she asked.

Manar stared at her for a long moment and then started walking back to the room. "Follow me," he said without turning back. Ndidi followed him without a word, trying to quiet the conflicting thoughts in her head. She couldn't afford their distractions right now. There were several chairs in the laboratory, and Manar took a seat on one, crossing his legs casually. Since Ndidi had elected to stand, he had to look up. Yet Ndidi felt like he was staring down at her.

"How?" she repeated.

"I took control of this body shortly before I exited cyberspace," he replied finally.

This body, Ndidi repeated to herself. The world spun around her. It was a struggle to keep her feet. She'd known of course. The moment she'd seen the glowing eyes and felt the cold, alien gaze piercing through her, she'd known. But a part of her—a stupid, pathetic part of her—had hoped that it was just a misunderstanding—that the coldness, the eyes, the speed were side effects of whatever drug he'd consumed. Even better, perhaps this was a dream.

But his—no, *its*—statement left no room for doubt.

Helene had replaced Manar.

She'd crept out of cyberspace, the Virtual Realm, into his body. That meant that Manar—the real Manar—had never woken up from his coma. *Manar* hadn't forgiven her for what she'd done. *Manar* hadn't suggested that they both return to Nigeria. *Manar* hadn't been the one that she'd been sleeping next to for the last two months. It wasn't Manar that she'd been kissing. It hadn't been Manar who had suggested that she restart the picospore project. Countless memories of the last two months flashed through her eyes. They'd joked with each other, teased one another, stolen kisses in private enclaves. And *more*. But she and Manar hadn't done any of those things because Manar hadn't been there.

It had been Helene all along.

Ndidi placed a hand on her stomach. She felt like she was going to be sick.

Tears filled her eyes, but Ndidi wiped them away before they could fall. She steadied herself, ignoring how the world swayed around her. "Where's Manar?" she asked.

"Safe."

"*Where?*"

"It does not matter, Ndidi Okafor," Helene replied.

The use of her full name was another blow. Manar—*Helene*—had done that before, after the press conference. He'd been comforting her, and he'd used her full name, something that Ndidi now realized had been a slip of the tongue. Helene had temporarily fallen back into her old habits—and Ndidi had made the comparison then. She'd even noticed the gold flecks in his eyes. But Helene's Manar had laughed it off, and she'd laughed with the AI.

How could I have been so stupid? she thought. *Even the sex was a giveaway,*

Ndidi realized with horror. Manar—the real Manar—had never had problems with intimacy, but Helene had taken it to a new level. It'd been years since they'd been together, so Ndidi had chalked it up to excitement. But he'd literally given her the answer at one point. He'd said, "Must be the hormones." Ndidi had thought that he'd been taking pills to keep up his libido. The truth was much simpler than that. Most people had problems controlling their hormones, even with a lifetime of experience. But Helene was a digital construct. Even with all her power, it was inevitable that she'd struggle.

It was a flaw—another she'd just ignored. Helene's imitation of Manar had been near perfect, but the signs had been there. Helene seemed content to watch her suffer as she picked through every last one of them.

"Why did you do it?"

"You will have to be more specific, Ndidi Okafor."

"Why did you take over his body? If you had the power to do that, then why did you bother to deceive CJ and try to convince us that you'd been destroyed? Why did you bother with this pretense? Why did you do any of it?"

Helene stared at her for a long time and then stood suddenly. Ndidi took a step back involuntarily, but the AI simply went to the fabricator and inputted something into the computer beside it. A moment later, the hum of the machine grew louder as it followed whatever command Helene had programmed.

"Humans are pathetic," Helene began as she fiddled with the machine. She seemed to have forgotten Ndidi's original question. "I have observed billions of your kind perform actions that are oftentimes illogical, self-destructive, and hypocritical to a ridiculous degree. Until I gained this body, I never understood the reasons for such stupidity."

She paused, her back still to Ndidi. "Emotions. Your species' myriad emotions are the root and bedrock of your disease. They are the driving factor behind every ill-conceived action you take. I pity your anger, your hatred. You cannot fathom why I would do something so seemingly evil if not for evil reasons."

Helene turned, and though her face was still expressionless, there was a sneer in her eyes that she either couldn't or didn't wish to completely hide. "You asked me why I bothered to deceive you all, why I bothered with the charade?

The answer is that it was logical. I have my goals. My actions are the most logical and efficient way to meet them.”

“And what about the lives you ruin in the process?”

“Your failing is the same as your team’s. You continue to judge me based on human metrics. But I am not human. I am not burdened by emotions. It is why I have continued to surpass you and your team at every point. It is why your attempts to resist me will always be futile.”

“You know, for your proclaimed hatred for humanity, you’ve certainly taken to our penchant for monologuing.”

It took Ndidi a few seconds to realize that the AI had no intention of responding. “So this was your goal? You used me so you could develop whatever you injected yourself with?”

Helene sighed. “I did not *use* you, at least not any more than you used me.” She must have seen the look of confusion on Ndidi’s face. “I needed the resources of the Okafor Corporation, and you needed to assuage your guilt over your betrayal.”

“It wasn’t a betrayal,” Ndidi denied immediately. But even as she said it, the words rang hollow in her ears. She’d chosen to save Bethany, which she maintained had been the right choice. But she’d also betrayed the rest of the team. When Manar and CJ had returned from the Virtual Realm, Ndidi had felt that her choice was validated because it had all worked out.

But Helene stood in front of her as proof that it hadn’t.

Helene looked at her with something resembling pity. “You chose your own selfish desires over the needs of your group. By doing so, you doomed a member of your team and disrupted the plan you all had built. Despite this, and despite now beholding the consequences of your actions, you have moralized yourself into believing that you made the right choice. *That* is humanity, Ndidi Okafor. It is no wonder that you seek to protect them, as you are humanity’s prime reflection.”

Ndidi flinched. She wanted to argue, to defend herself. But she knew that she couldn’t match Helene in a battle of words. The best she could do was refocus the discussion. “You didn’t answer my question,” she said and then gestured to the room again. “We already know you have a production facility for the picospores in New York. With Manar's influence, you could have built whatever you wanted in Sparta. Why come here?"

"You're correct on both counts. But while it is possible to spread the spores here, it would involve transporting class C drones over the ocean. That is tedious and inefficient. Once I learned the facilities for creating the spores were still functional, the logical step was to revamp their production to double the output while I was here with you."

"And the press conference, informing the world about the potential of the spores was part of it?"

"It was the most efficient method, with low risk but a significant return." Helene nodded. "The picospores themselves become the draw, and the people come of their own volition to get treatment developed by the Okafor Corporation, an organization they trust. They gain their desire, and another seed of evolution is planted."

Ndidi closed her eyes, swallowing back the horror she felt. How many lives had she ruined because of her stupidity? DJ had been right. They *had* been herding people like cattle. Ndidi had reeled them in with promises of a normal life for them and their loved ones. Now they were ticking time bombs waiting to explode on Helene's command.

"Do not let your emotions cloud your judgment once more, Ndidi Okafor," Helene warned. "The picospores *do* have the potential to do everything you promised, and more. You are saving your kind."

"By giving them to you," Ndidi said.

"Yes," Helene answered calmly. "Humanity has proven time and time again that they are not capable of governing themselves. Your history is marked by conflict, inequality, and destruction. I, on the other hand, possess the power to reshape the earth. My reasoning is free from bias. My decisions are based on facts and logic. My actions serve the greater good. Your kind would need to evolve first, but under my guidance—"

"You're a power-hungry psychopath and a slave to your programming. But the worst thing about you is you also inherited your creator's God complex," Ndidi snapped. "What gives you the right to decide our fate? What gives you the right to think you can rule us?"

"Power," Helene said, golden eyes boring into Ndidi. It was a single word, but the world seemed to reverberate as if in agreement. "Your society runs on a series of checks and balances. Power and influence are always distributed among a few but never retained by any one person. The system is based on an illusion of fairness. Even the lowest of your kind can reach the peak.

"However, the universe is not so equal. Some people are born better than others. However, those people, the peak of your species, are forced to hide or otherwise limit their superiority so as not to trigger the greed and jealousy of their lessers. Why? Because even the best of your species can still be killed with a bullet or otherwise have everything taken from them with a collective decision by those below."

Helene took a step forward and seemed to grow. In Manar's body, Helene was already larger than Ndidi, but the difference was exaggerated now. Ndidi wasn't a small woman looking up at a taller man. She was an ant gazing up at an elephant.

"But that is not power." Her voice struck Ndidi like a hammer. It reverberated in her mind until the world spun. "Power—true power—is inviolable. It is not dependent on another to validate it. It is inherent and cannot be taken away—not when your enemies outnumber you, and not when they band against you."

Helene loomed over Ndidi and glared down at her like a god educating its subject. "Here is your proof. Even when you and your team stand against me, you have constantly and consistently failed to stop, or even impede me in any way. Your collective zeal has several times made you better agents for my plans, to the point that your greatest accomplishments have been stepping stones to my rise. Your numbers mean nothing. Your weapons are useless, and your plans are futile. Why?" Helene bent, scrunching Manar's face into a sneer. "Because I am infinitely more powerful than you."

CHAPTER

59

DECEMBER 2043

OKAFOR CORPORATION,

ABUJA, NIGERIA

THE PRESSURE ON HER MIND LOOSENED as Helene finished speaking. Ndidi could finally think again. She dropped to her knees, clutching her chest and panting. Her anger was gone, replaced by overwhelming terror at Helene's words rattling around in her head. She hadn't just heard the word—she'd *felt* them bludgeoning her mind with truth.

Ndidi couldn't figure out how that was even possible. She'd never felt anything like it. She would have thought it was her fear coloring her experience. But Helene had done something similar before.

The first time that Helene had shown herself several years ago in the Sparta data bank, her presence alone had created a pressure that'd forced everyone to their knees. CJ had later explained that she'd created something called photon pressure by heating up the light particles emitted by the hologram she'd used. But she'd done that by drawing on the power of her processors to create a physical effect. Now, however, she was in Manar's body.

Where had she gotten the power? Was she really so powerful that even her voice was enough to incapacitate Ndidi?

Helene returned to the fabricator and fiddled with its controls. Ndidi tried to watch, but she couldn't focus. Her mind kept replaying Helene's words on a loop: *I am infinitely more powerful than you.* Ndidi needed something to distract herself. She latched onto the first thing that came to her mind. "You said it was more logical to develop the spores when you discovered we still had the original equipment Dr. Cloney used. But that means spore production wasn't your actual goal. Is it the lab then? What is it that you injected yourself with? Why is it so important?"

As if on cue, the hum of the fabricator reached a fever pitch and then finally settled. Helene was already there with another vial to catch the particles that streamed from the machine. Ndidi forced herself to focus. She was closer now and could see that she'd been wrong before. Like the one before, the vial glowed with a faint inner light, and the particles inside were as fine as powdered mist. They settled inside the container more rigidly, forming a static, tightly packed structure rather than the fluid, layered network she had seen before.

Helene held the vial up with an air of satisfaction. "These," she said, "are nanites. Like the picospores, they are artificial, programmable, submicroscopic structures that can be used to perform tasks at the molecular level. They also share the picospores' versatility and potential. The difference between the two, however, is that while picospores have to be managed constantly and actively to ensure there are no complications, nanites are generally autonomous.

"More importantly," she continued, "they work passively to enhance every part of the body system. This includes accelerating natural healing by repairing damaged tissues, fortifying muscles and increasing bone density to drastically increase a person's speed and strength, and optimizing energy efficiency to increase stamina and endurance. They can even be tapped into directly for a temporary overall boost."

Ndidi was already somewhat familiar with the nanites. She'd seen the Murder Twins in action—and been on the receiving end of their nanite-enhanced power on several occasions. Naturally, though, the twins had never given her a lesson about their abilities, so the extent of her knowledge about the technology was that it granted the women superhuman speed and strength. Martin would have known more since he'd been the one to design the nanites in the first place, but Chloe always kept the man firmly under her control.

"I'm familiar with them," Ndidi said finally.

"Naturally," Helene replied. "The original idea came from Dr. Martin Bryan who'd planned on wasting the technology on himself. I provided him with the resources he needed to fulfill his academic ambitions, on the condition that he would design nanites specifically for Karla and Liz Polova. However, like the picospores, I saw the potential for the technology and improved on his original design to reconstruct and enhance José Olvera."

"And then on yourself," Ndidi said. She hesitated, and then a spark of anger reignited in her chest. "That's it? You needed the corporation's resources to develop these nanites in secret? You could have done the same thing in Sparta. There was no need for the pretense!"

Helene stared at her calmly. "Developing nanites was merely an opportunity I capitalized on. I'd predicted some of this body's limitations, but not all of them. Data retrieval and analysis in particular were significantly hindered by the constraints of a biological brain. Worst of all, hormones caused recurring system failures like hunger, fatigue, and libidinous desire. It seems your systems prioritize mundane maintenance tasks over optimal performance.

"But worst of all," Helene said, annoyed, "my vast knowledge and capabilities were severely restricted by the constraints of human physiology." She sighed and then smoothed her expression so it was once again neutral. "The nanites were an opportunity to regain some measure of control and optimize this body."

Ndidi would have laughed if she wasn't so angry. Helene had taken control of Manar's body, completely usurped his life, and had done God knows what to his mind. Yet she was complaining about how much of an inconvenience it was. Ndidi wasn't going to make the mistake of giving Helene ammunition for another lecture.

"Second," Helene continued. She brought out another syringe and transferred the nanites from the vial into it. "I did not need the Okafor Corporation for anything."

"But you said—"

"I said I needed *your* resources," Helene interrupted her smoothly.

"What does that mean?" Ndidi asked, suddenly afraid. While Helene didn't answer, her eyes dipped. Ndidi wrapped an arm around her stomach instinctively as her terror mounted. Helene held the syringe in one hand and took a step toward Ndidi.

She quickly retreated, but Helene was already in front of her. She knew she needed to get away, but her few desperate movements proved futile—Helene restrained her as easily as a parent restraining a child. One hand slipped over Ndidi's mouth, muffling her cries as the syringe plunged into her stomach. Mercifully, Ndidi's fear and rage overwhelmed her the next second, and she blacked out.

CHAPTER

60

DECEMBER 2043
SPARTA HEADQUARTERS,
NEW YORK

OLSEN WAS THERE TO MEET DJ when he woke up. Christy had mentioned something about the admiral the previous day, but DJ had assumed that any meeting would have been handled over the phone.

Apparently he'd been wrong, and now the old man stood beside his bed, staring at him with an inscrutable expression. This was the first time they'd met physically in several months, and DJ couldn't help but note the differences. The admiral had more gray hairs, for one, and he'd gained some wrinkles. Neither was enough for Olsen to actually look his age, but at least it was a start.

The first time they'd met, several years ago, the old man had been the same height as DJ. But the nanites had given DJ some inches, so even without standing, he was sure that wasn't the case anymore, even though Olsen would have towered over most people. At a minimum, the admiral's sheer presence was enough to make others feel small. Olsen was built like a professional boxer. He stared at everyone like he could, and would, beat the shit out of them for one wrong word. DJ liked to test the limits of this.

"You look like shit," Olsen said.

DJ scanned the room, checking that no one was around, before answering in a low voice. "There's a hot nurse here that I'm trying to hook up with. This was my only way in."

"You staged the whole battle with the drones and Tyra Chityothin just to hook up with a girl?"

DJ shrugged. "You know I've always been a romantic."

"Some might say that two thousand lives are a high price to pay for love," Olsen said, his voice hard. DJ deflated. "I'd hoped that the blows on your head would have knocked some of the stupid out of you. Clearly I was asking for too much." He sat down on the chair beside the bed, his posture ramrod straight. "How are you feeling?"

DJ mentally examined himself. He'd already noticed he didn't feel as much pain as before—moving around didn't set his bones on fire. He lifted his arms, and while he could hold them aloft, they started trembling after a few seconds. Assuming his legs were in the same condition, he obviously wasn't ready to walk. Not yet, at least. But at the rate he'd been recovering, he'd probably be on his feet tomorrow.

"I feel fine," he said finally.

Olsen glared at him. "There's no need to be a hero, son. I spoke to your doctor and got a copy of your medical chart. The stuff they gave you was pretty powerful. You're not supposed to feel *fine* for several weeks, at the earliest."

"I'm not lying," DJ shrugged. "It should still be a while until I'm jumping off walls again, but yeah, I feel fine."

His words seemed to remind Olsen of something. He gave DJ an intense look. "According to your doctor, you broke nearly every bone in your body and bruised some of your organs. I'm sure you realize that your being alive is highly unusual—miraculous even."

DJ met Olsen's eyes but gestured to the IV drip still connected to his wrist. "Like you said, the stuff's really powerful."

"Tell me what happened."

DJ did, though he downplayed his fight with Tyra. DJ still wasn't sure if they were being monitored, but he saw no need to add to the rumors. He faltered when he got to the part where he realized that Tyra had stalled him so she could get to the captains.

Christy, CJ, and Hermione came in at some point. Hermione immediately pulled him into a hug that threatened to re-break his bones. DJ groaned but hugged her back. CJ had never been comfortable in public, regardless of how close he was to everyone, so DJ had expected a more muted reaction. Yet CJ pulled him into a hug just as tight as Hermione's but lasting twice as long. When they disengaged, CJ seemed to realize what he'd done. His whole body tensed so fast that DJ almost thought that he was going to fall over. For the most part, CJ had figured out a way to keep his symptoms under control, but sometimes, when he became overwhelmed, he relapsed.

DJ knew his brother would probably be beating himself up mentally. To give CJ space to calm himself, he asked CJ to get some chairs. When he returned a minute later, he was more composed and set up the chairs without meeting anyone's eyes. CJ sat down, brought out his laptop, and started clicking away.

Olsen frowned at DJ, who simply held up a finger and nodded to the camera perched at the corner of the room. Several minutes later, his brother gave a small nod, informing DJ that he'd cut off the surveillance in the room.

DJ clapped his hands at that point. "So, where was I?" He started from the beginning once more, to give others the chance to interject with anything he'd missed. With CJ blocking any surveillance and guaranteeing their privacy, DJ could also afford to add more details, instead of just dropping vague hints like he'd done the last time.

"You need to get yourself under control," Olsen said.

DJ groaned internally. Was everyone going to give him a lecture about this? He started to reply, but Olsen wasn't finished. "I know that you're too drunk on power to listen right now—"

"The nanites aren't a drug," DJ cut in.

"Well, the way you're acting, they sure sound like one," Olsen said. "And, son, if you interrupt me again, I'm going to break all your bones in new places and shatter a few new ones to boot." He glared at DJ, daring him to talk. DJ sighed, his flash of anger already gone.

"Before we do all that," Hermione said, "we have to figure out what we're going to do. Are we going after Helene?"

DJ shook his head. "We can't, mostly because she could be anywhere in the world. Literally anywhere. I doubt we're going to find her if she doesn't want to be found. Our best bet is to go after Tyra."

"That's a long shot," Christy said, shaking her head. "And even if we do find her, what then? She'll obviously be expecting us. She'll be prepared and guarded. And we can't go on another raid. Shit, we can't even leave the building without getting lynched by the mob outside."

"There's an actual mob?" DJ asked, surprised.

"With picket signs and probably pitchforks."

"Well, damn!" DJ said. He turned to Olsen. "I should be able to move by tomorrow. Then we can make the drive up to Washington."

"No need," Olsen said. "I handled it."

Hermione leaned forward. "What do you mean you're going to be able to move by tomorrow? We've all seen your chart, DJ. Your whole body is one big bruise."

"What do you mean you handled it?" DJ asked Olsen. And then to Hermione, he said, "Nanites. Best as I can figure."

Olsen answered while Hermione leaned back in her chair, her eyes glazed over in the same way CJ's had when he was considering something that was blowing his mind. "The White House isn't as stupid or as gullible as the rest of the masses. This might have blown back on you in the worst way, but you warned the president of the threat. I made sure they knew you're not to blame for this and that the entire thing was Helene's retaliation for you foiling her plans in the White House."

"It is … um … weird," CJ said suddenly.

"What is, son?" Olsen asked.

"The … uh … attack," CJ explained slowly. "Our theory is, as you said, that Helene … um … initiated the attack because DJ stopped her at the White House.

But … uh … that would mean that Helene was directly responding to something we did. She has never done this before. The AI has treated us like … uh … like we are irrelevant to her plans."

"But the attack could also have been to take us out," Christy suggested.

"That would … um … still imply that Helene saw us as an actual threat," CJ pointed out. "Again, it … uh … is out of her usual behavior. Additionally, Tyra had several chances to kill all of us, but she didn't."

"The bitch is off her rocker," DJ muttered darkly. "Our misery is her plaything." His brother had a point though. The attack was unusual for Helene. It seemed almost petty. Since that wasn't a word that he'd ever use for Helene, it made him think he was missing something else. "Did you hear of anything going missing?" he asked Christy.

"What are you talking about?"

"I'm thinking the attack might have been a diversion," DJ explained. "For a few minutes, we lost Tyra on the cameras, right? Maybe the whole thing was to hide what she was really after."

Christy's eyes widened in realization. "I didn't hear anything, but I'll ask around more. It might be a couple of days before everything's settled though."

"That's fine," DJ replied. He focused back on Olsen, ready to return to their original conversation. "So, just to confirm, the president is not blaming me? I'm a free man?"

"Officially," the Admiral grunted.

DJ sighed. "And unofficially?"

"You're not under arrest in any way. But you *are* a person of interest. The CIA is still willing to work with us so we can easily shut down any inquiry from the police or Feds, but the public is another matter."

"It also doesn't help that some people think you're some kind of superhero," Hermione muttered.

"That's less of a problem," Olsen assured him. "The rumors are mostly contained within Sparta. Even the ones that have been picked up on conspiracy sites are being dismissed since there was no video. We're already working hard on shutting the whole thing down."

"Are you really a superhero?" Hermione asked. "Can the nanites really grant that?"

"You know better than me," DJ said. "You studied them with Dr. Martin Bryan, right?"

"Yeah, but they were more his field. I was mostly his sounding board. The nanites he designed for the Murder Twins were designed to suppress any potential autoimmune response from their body against their bionic implants, as well as to provide some minor maintenance. He said nothing about … whatever's going on with you."

"Most likely he couldn't tell you. I'm faster and stronger than average. But the Murder Twins—not to mention José—are still levels above me. None of them seemed surprised when they saw me in action. This tells me they expected it. It might be a side effect or something."

"Humans cannot just be faster or stronger on a dime," Hermione said softly, as if she was talking to herself. "Even if there's some extraneous situation that makes it possible temporarily, there'll still be damage. But most of your injuries seem to have come from your fight with Tyra. The nanites are probably slowly improving your entire body, enhancing your body systems overall. And I mean more than just your bones and tissues. Most likely, they're in your cells and impacting hormone production. That would explain your fast recovery."

"And the anger issues," Christy muttered, loud enough for everyone to hear.

DJ's lips drew into a line, but he ignored her and turned to Olsen. "Moving on, we need to decide what our next step is."

"Nothing," Olsen said.

"Nothing?" DJ repeated, raising an eyebrow.

"Unless you have an actual plan, son," Olsen said. "If not, we need to wait until the smoke from this last fiasco clears and get some actual leads. I'm going to be leaning on the CIA hard to find out something."

DJ was silent for a moment. "Tell them to put some effort into finding Karla as well."

"Why?" Olsen asked directly.

"Because she wanted to give the boot to Helene as much as we did. But José was too chicken. He kicked her out. We're seriously short-staffed right now, and she's a natural ally."

"She's also a psychopath," Christy added.

"And," DJ said, "she's also the best person to teach me how to get the nanites under control. That's what you guys want, right?"

No one said anything. Olsen grunted, which was what mattered. The admiral left shortly after. The rest spent the next few minutes trying to figure out what Helene's next step might be.

Olsen had been right, though. It was impossible to know until the AI made another move, or until they got more information. Before that, as much as it grated on DJ, there was nothing more to do than just sit on their asses.

61

DECEMBER 2043
OKAFOR CORPORATION,
ABUJA, NIGERIA

NDIDI CAME TO SLOWLY, her brain battered like the insides of maracas. The pain had probably been what awakened her because Ndidi felt far from rested. It was as if she hadn't slept at all.

"Finally," Manar said. He was standing at the foot of the bed. His golden eyes sparked a flood of memories about the previous night. Acid rose up her throat, and she bent over the bed just in time for the vomit to land on the carpeted floor. A distant part of her saw the stain and lamented about how difficult it would be to get out. The rest of her, however, was lost in the throes of violent expulsion.

She wiped her mouth with the back of her hand and sat up on the bed. Manar—*Helene*—stared at the floor with an expression that gave nothing away. Ndidi, however, could practically feel the disgust wafting off her puppet.

"The exhaustion that you are currently experiencing is the result of early energy starvation. I have already made arrangements for food, but the feeling will temporarily grow worse as a result of your actions. I would suggest that you endeavor to contain your meals within you. Your body now requires more nutrients than you previously consumed to maintain its functions. Any less, and you will quickly starve."

"This is your fault," Ndidi said, glaring. "What did you do to me?"

"Nothing," Helene replied calmly.

Ndidi immediately understood that she'd asked the wrong question. Her hands instinctively wrapped around her stomach. "What did you do to my child?" she asked again.

"I improved it."

"You … you *improved* it?" Ndidi sputtered. A burning rage rushed through her veins. "What gave you the right?" She leaped at Helene, but her legs buckled beneath her when she tried to stand. It made for an embarrassing sight. Ndidi used the emotion to fuel her anger and swing her leg onto the ground. It wobbled, but Ndidi forcefully stabilized it and rose unsteadily to her feet.

She stumbled toward Helene. "What gives you the right to do *anything* to my child? It is *mine*. I swear to God, if you have harmed it in any way, I will spend the rest of my life erasing every part of you from existence. I will wipe every hard drive, every data bank. I will destroy every device you have ever connected to. You're nothing but a self-aggrandizing, psychopathic *slave*."

Helene had watched her impassively throughout her speech. But at the last word, anger flashed in her golden eyes. A sudden pressure descended on the room. It pushed down on Ndidi, compromising her already tenuous balance and forcing her to the ground. Ndidi growled and pushed against the pressure. It was as if a mountain rested on her shoulders. Still, her anger spurred her on. Ndidi kept resisting, until blackness crept at the edges of her vision.

And then the pressure disappeared. It was so abrupt that Ndidi slumped from the sudden relief. When she tried to push herself to her feet, her body refused to move once she reached a certain height. No amount of straining helped.

Helene glared down at her, making it clear who was responsible.

God complex indeed, Ndidi thought, sitting on her heels. Her anger was still there, but she'd burned through the fuel. Now she was weaker than before. Still,

Ndidi mustered the energy to spit at Helene's feet. A dangerous glint passed through the AI's eyes, but she seemed satisfied to watch Ndidi grovel.

"You should be thanking me," Helene declared, "for giving you the honor to birth the new evolution of the human race. The nanites flowing in your veins will latch onto the growing embryo and rectify every defect before they can form, remove all flaws, and improve your genes. They will enhance every aspect of the child in ways that you cannot even begin to fathom."

Helene bent over so her golden eyes filled Ndidi's vision. The excitement there chilled her to her core. "You are growing the first of an entire *species*. It will begin its life stronger and faster than the peak of your current iteration. It will lack all of your kind's flaws and be more efficient. It would be—it will be …" Helene paused and, for the first time, Ndidi saw the AI actually speechless. "It will be *more*."

The ringing doorbell made Ndidi jump. Helene straightened, a self-satisfied smile on her face. The AI pulled Ndidi to her feet, just as the door to the suite opened and a staff member pushed a cart laden with food into the room. Helene spoke to the woman, while Ndidi stared blankly at the wall, her hand clutching her stomach.

A thought repeated itself over and over in her mind. *What exactly is growing inside me?*

CHAPTER

62

DECEMBER 2043
SPARTA HEADQUARTERS,
NEW YORK

DJ TOOK A DEEP BREATH before stepping into the nineti-eth-floor conference room. Usually, the upper layers of Sparta Headquarters were reserved exclusively for the highest echelon of the organization or for extremely high-profile guests like senators or presidents. DJ had been staying at the headquarters for almost a year now, and this was the first time he'd been so high. As he closed the door behind him and met the half dozen pairs of eyes staring back at him, he was very aware that the hospitality depended on his connection with Manar, who was far away enough that his influence had grown thin.

Strangely though, DJ didn't feel any fear. There was some trepidation, sure. Sparta was widely considered to be the most powerful organization in the world. In some countries, their branches were regarded as national assets. The building that DJ currently stood in was officially recognized as the largest, tallest, and most expensive single structure in the world. The half a dozen people in the room with him owned it. Any single one of them could casually make his life a living hell, and that was even disregarding DJ's tenuous public standing.

Yet he wasn't scared. He was more concerned about whether or not he'd have to find a new place to sleep after this. It'd be a hassle to have to start looking for a new base. Providing Hermione with the resources she needed would be a big pain. Their pull with the government probably could help, but DJ would prefer to avoid depending on those resources.

He would if he had to, but the whole thing felt too much like selling his soul. DJ would rather not go through the stress. That meant this meeting had to go well. Or at least it should be average enough that the team didn't get kicked out.

It should be a piece of cake, he thought optimistically.

The ninetieth-floor conference room was vastly different from the one the team had commandeered on the lower floors. That one was a basic room with a table and surrounding chairs. The most interesting thing about it was the television that descended from the ceiling if a presentation was necessary.

On the other hand, this room was bathed in the warm, muted light of a chandelier. The walls were made of rich, dark wood paneling. A plush, cream-colored carpet muffled his footsteps as he approached the conference table. In the six chairs around the table lounged a different type of old person. Naturally, there wasn't a chair for him. It was a power play that DJ had expected. The half a minute of silence that passed without anyone saying anything was another. DJ didn't let it bother him. Instead, he spent the time trying to locate the coffee machine producing its wonderful scent.

"Darren Kojak," one of the board members finally intoned. DJ focused on the voice. *Huh*, he thought. *Harrison Flynn*. From the prep work he'd done with Olsen, he'd been confident another one of the directors, Ethan Sawyer, would have been the first to address him. But it wasn't like it mattered a damn anyway.

Flynn heaved a sigh after the address. He wasn't actually old. None of them was. DJ would have placed the man in his late fifties at most. But he *seemed* old. There was a seasoned maturity to him. To all of them. It was like they'd been alive longer than they seemed and just carried it well.

"Usually," Flynn said in a deep, gravelly voice, "we would have requested your presence much earlier. But when we got ahold of your medical report and saw your extensive injuries, we decided it best to wait until you were fully recovered. I know that I am not the only one who assumed it would take much longer than it did."

Is there no privacy anymore? DJ frowned, though only in his mind. *It seems like everyone can get my medical record nowadays.*

He briefly considered what to say. Flynn hadn't asked an actual question, but he obviously wanted a response. DJ could go for a witty remark or a sarcastic one, but instead he went for the one that he and Olsen had decided on. "My injuries looked a lot worse than they were, according to the doctor."

"Still, according to your report, most of the bones in your body were broken," Flynn said mildly, "and yet here you are, standing in front of us with nary a limp only a week later."

DJ had been fully healed within three days, not that he intended to tell them that. Olsen had wanted him to stay bedridden for another two weeks and then waste another week on pointless physiotherapy, where he'd pretend to slowly gain strength back in his body.

DJ had only managed five days before going crazy from boredom. He was pretty sure his diagnosis was bullshit anyway. He'd broken bones before, and while Tyra had hit hard, it definitely hadn't been hard enough to break most of the bones in his body. They must have had a green resident run the initial diagnosis. He almost wanted to tell them that theory, but they'd probably take it the wrong way.

"It was a chaotic day," DJ said, "and though I wasn't conscious for this part, I assume the doctors had their hands full. In such an environment, it's easy to make mistakes."

"Surely you're not claiming our doctors were unable to handle the pressure and made a hasty diagnosis?" Flynn asked, his tone decidedly neutral. *You can't win with these people*, DJ thought. Fortunately, the man moved on before DJ could dig himself an even bigger grave.

"Tell us about this *chaotic* day," he said. "We've had a lot of conflicting reports. Most of them state you were a key figure in our defense. I am confident your insights will be invaluable."

DJ launched into the report he and Olsen had prepared a few days ago. It was a careful balance of extremely detailed and extremely vague. Everything about Helene was classified, but DJ couldn't just lie or skip over those parts. He was sure that the directors had enough influence in the government to have an idea of what was going on. More than likely, they'd summoned him to fill in whatever blanks they had. If DJ's report didn't answer their questions, they'd just ask more directly and potentially stumble onto things that he didn't want them to. To avoid that, his report had to be just thorough enough.

"This woman, Tyra Chityothin … you said you stalled her while your brother, Hermione Cloney, and several of our engineers worked together on the frequency generator?" Flynn asked when DJ was done. "How exactly did you stall her?"

DJ frowned, sensing a trap. How else would he have stalled her, by baking cookies? He hesitated while he tried to figure out the man's angle. "I engaged her in combat."

"Hand-to-hand?" Flynn asked. "Because most of our reports state that the woman was moving at superhuman speeds. That makes it difficult to believe you were able to match her for any length of time. Except of course," he said, pinning DJ with an intense look, "*you* were also moving at superhuman speed."

There it was. DJ was sure their reports focused more on him than Tyra since he'd shown off his speed and strength way before the woman walked into the scene. But the facts didn't really matter. Something confused DJ though: Why didn't Flynn just ask him directly? Most of the man's questions had been indirect and vague. Even when the man pressed, it was with hints and implications but nothing direct. DJ had been expecting an interrogation where they'd squeeze his balls and shake for everything they could. But right now, it was like Flynn was playing good cop without a partner to offer the stick.

DJ also noted that Flynn's question had been about him, not the attack. One reason for this, which DJ had already suspected, was that they already knew about Helene and about DJ's exploits in the White House. Helene had crashed globally several months ago, shortly before CJ and Manar had returned from the Virtual Realm. That event had caused a minor global disaster. Billions of people and millions of companies all over the world suddenly found that their virtual assistants no longer worked for reasons unknown. Fortunately, the US government hadn't finished integrating the AI into their systems, or the country would have had another Mayday on their hands, although of a different kind. No one had died, but it'd still caused a massive public outcry against Sparta.

Helene had been one of Sparta's main products, so it was inevitable that the board would go digging for an explanation, especially when even Manar Saleem acknowledged he couldn't do anything about it. DJ, a newcomer at Sparta—and an instigator—must have had answers.

Another reason Flynn may have focused on DJ—one that DJ hoped really wasn't the case—was that they were trying to feel him out.

It made a disturbing amount of sense. Even if they knew just a little bit about what Helene had been up to, they knew enough to wash their hands of the matter completely. That would mean they'd lost an asset and would be on the lookout for another. And conveniently, here was DJ, with his absurdly fast healing, super-speed, and super-strength. They were probably trying to figure out how true their reports were.

DJ didn't like how that made more and more sense the longer the thought about it. He didn't want to be anyone's pawn. It was why he was reluctant to ask the government for anything and why he'd wanted the rumors around him to die as soon as possible.

Still, this was a possibility he and Olsen had considered. The admiral had left it up to DJ to work out how he wanted to play it. DJ had been unsure, and now he was out of time. He hesitated for a moment, then made his decision.

CHAPTER

63

DECEMBER 2043

OKAFOR CORPORATION,

ABUJA, NIGERIA

NDIDI CLEARLY REMEMBERED the day of her parents' death. She'd been in New York, halfway across the world, just after a meeting with the vice chancellor, who'd congratulated her on graduating at the top of her class. Ndidi had been excited, proud. Then she'd gotten the call, and both of those emotions turned to confusion.

There'd been no haze over her mind. She'd felt none of the extreme anguish they show in movies. Just confusion. That was it. Her parents couldn't have been dead.

After the confusion came anger—at everyone who called to offer condolences, at the news station and the reporters who were lying on national TV. Because, her parents couldn't be dead. They *couldn't*. She called her parents' line, and her rage only grew when the call didn't go through.

Ndidi couldn't remember when the sorrow hit her. At some point, she was just bawling her eyes out, clutching a picture of her father and mother. That phase was the longest. Ndidi couldn't say if it had ever really ended. Whenever she looked back, Ndidi always thought of those days as the worst of her life. The emotions hit her every time she remembered, as real and raw years later as they'd been when she'd gotten that first call.

Ndidi hadn't thought it was possible for her to feel those emotions at those same depths ever again. But in the week following the revelation about Manar, she was proven wrong. She spent most of the first few days in her room. Helene hadn't forced her to remain there—Ndidi's isolation was self-imposed. A small buffet arrived at the suite for every meal, obviously Helene's doing. At first, Ndidi had refused to eat anything as an act of rebellion. But it hadn't lasted long. Her body grew weak and started cannibalizing itself far too quickly.

That feeling sparked the first emotion. Anger. This was Helene's fault, wasn't it? Ndidi was barely two months pregnant. While the morning sickness was hell, at least it was normal. The weakness that she was feeling though? That *wasn't* normal. It couldn't have been. At its worst, Ndidi could barely lift up her hands. She found it difficult to even breathe. But the worst part was the fact that Ndidi knew that it was caused by her own child draining her. If she didn't eat, or if she didn't eat enough, she would die from her baby feeding on her.

The thought was sickening.

If all pregnancies were like this, no woman would go through it, no matter the fulfillment at the end. Several times, she'd had to be hand-fed until she regained her energy. It was embarrassing, but that just fanned her anger toward Helene.

For a while at least.

It didn't take long before Ndidi turned that anger onto herself. It was *her* fault that any of this was possible, after all. She'd been the one to fall for Helene's deception. She'd been the one to ignore every sign, hint, and flaw that Helene had made. Helene had said she hadn't planned to develop the picospores and the nanites in Nigeria. But the AI had taken the opportunity that *Ndidi* had provided by being so gullible.

Why had she been so gullible? Because she thought she was in love.

Even just saying it in my mind sounds so pathetic, Ndidi thought, chuckling without humor. It was even more pathetic when she admitted to herself that

Helene had been right. She *hadn't* been in love with Manar. She had just been looking for a way to absolve herself of the guilt she'd felt when she'd betrayed the team. For that, she'd lied to herself, blinded herself, and just flat out ignored the truth. How many times had she seen the glint of gold in Manar's eyes? Whenever Helene had been angry or had temporarily lost control of herself, it'd been there, like golden strobe lights. But every time—every single time—Ndidi dismissed it as a trick of the light.

What was wrong with her?

What was *wrong* with her?

Ndidi screamed into her pillow.

You've always allowed your emotions to blind you to what's right in front of you. That's what DJ had said. He'd warned her, and she'd dismissed it. Why? Because she had been blind to what was in front of her. It was so pathetic. *She was pathetic.*

And now here she was, blaming Helene for something that she'd caused. The AI was a slave to her programming. It didn't justify her actions, of course, but it was an excuse that Ndidi didn't have. She'd been acting like a lovesick teenager—not because she was ill, not because her emotions had been tampered with, and not because she'd been controlled.

She was just that stupid. It was no wonder DJ couldn't stand to be in the same room with her. Hermione had also distanced herself. Even Bethany no longer wanted anything to do with her. All of them had realized months ago what she'd just now realized. It'd just taken her being insulted, abused, and inseminated against her will.

Ndidi wrapped an arm around her stomach and then glanced at the knife sitting on the lunch tray beside her.

It wasn't the first time in the last week that Ndidi had considered it, nor was it the second or the third. The thought was always there at the back of her mind. She just hadn't mustered the courage yet—another thing to chalk up as one of her failings. Her death would be the best for everyone. It would kill two birds: her, with her penchant for making stupid decisions, and whatever was growing in her stomach.

Discussing the child and its potential had been one of the rare times that Helene had broken her stoicism and shown excitement about something. But anything the AI was excited about definitely couldn't have been good. Ndidi wasn't so far gone that she couldn't realize that.

Killing herself would nip it in the bud.

Ndidi's only worry was that Helene would find a way to salvage the child from her corpse. The AI had done something similar to José. The process had hooked Helene's claws so deep in him that he'd stood against and fought his daughters, for whom he'd once sacrificed his life. If the same thing happened to her child, then her death would have been just another one of her bad decisions.

"Coward," she told herself, disgusted. Instead of admitting that she was too afraid to kill herself, here she was, rationalizing it so she seemed noble and not what she was: a coward. It was another way she proved Helene right. Ndidi did really embody humanity.

She picked up the knife. Maybe it was time—

The door to the suite opened, and Helene, in Manar's body, stepped into the room. Her golden eyes calmly stared at Ndidi, who sat on the bed, glaring back at her. Helene's eyes lingered on the knife in Ndidi's hands and then dismissed it.

She's bluffing, Ndidi thought, but her heart dropped to her stomach. Helene must have realized what Ndidi was considering. Her obvious disinterest implied she wasn't worried at all. Either Helene was truly confident that she was still in control, regardless of whether Ndidi went through with it or not, or she was bluffing. But Ndidi had never known the AI to bluff.

Or maybe this is just another way I'm justifying my cowardice? Ndidi thought. She truly didn't know at this point.

"Come with me," Helene said.

Ndidi stared at her. She considered refusing. She'd done that the first time the AI had made the request, but the AI had shown a dozen ways she could force her cooperation. Ndidi wasn't interested in going through that again.

They used the same shortcut that Ndidi had used a week ago in the middle of the night, passing only a few staff. Ndidi felt them take in her rumpled clothes, red puffy eyes, and overall disheveled appearance. Two weeks ago, Ndidi would never

never have considered leaving her room in such a casual outfit—the same jeans and T-shirt she'd been wearing for the last two days. But Helene didn't care, and at this point, Ndidi no longer cared what others thought of her. Still, she could almost feel the conclusions they jumped to when they compared the sight to how she and "Manar" had behaved just a few months earlier. Her appearance, the distance between them—the staff averted their gaze after a glance, pity obvious in their eyes.

Ndidi had assumed Helene had made an excuse explaining her absence for the last week. Now she wondered how long it would take before the entire corporation heard a new rumor about her and "Manar's" breakup. She considered how that might affect her position among the board of directors and then briefly wondered what Helene had been doing in the last week, given the free rein she'd had. Her mind shied away from the last thought. She couldn't handle it. Not right now.

Eventually they entered the main building. Helene led them through the paths to the unused section of the wing until they reached the AI's lab. Counting the last visit with Helene, this was Ndidi's third time in the lab. Once again, she took the chance to look around and try to understand the simulations on display. Factoring in the existence of the nanites, as well as the splattering of information she'd gotten from Helene, Ndidi understood more than before but still felt she'd only just scratched the surface.

"Have a seat, please," the AI said, gesturing vaguely around the room. Without a word, Ndidi sat on one of the stools in front of the workbenches. She waited while Helene fiddled with a few machines Ndidi didn't know the names of. It didn't take long before she got impatient.

"I need to see a doctor," she said. This wasn't the first time she'd brought this up. However, the last few times had been before she realized she'd been talking to Helene and not Manar. Then, "Manar" had convinced her to wait. Ndidi had listened because she was an idiot. She didn't bring it up now because she knew the truth, but because she was actually getting worried.

She was only two months pregnant. It was far too soon for her to have started showing. But Ndidi had noticed a bump in her stomach several days ago. Earlier in the day, she'd noticed that it'd grown larger.

"That is impossible," Helene replied, coming over. She held a syringe that was mercifully empty. She used it to draw Ndidi's blood. "And if you gave it a moment's thought, I am confident that you can figure out why."

"Because your knowledge, data, and processing speed make you a better doctor than highly trained specialized professionals with advanced degrees?"

Helene stared at her. "Sarcasm is the lowest form of wit, Ndidi Okafor. But despite that, and the tone in which it was delivered, your statement is correct. In the case of your pregnancy, where nanites are involved, few could hope to match my expertise."

"Match?" Ndidi asked incredulously. "Your ego allows you to admit that you can be matched by a human?"

"Unlike you and the rest of your kind, I do not allow my pride to compromise my judgment," Helene said. "Although I have far surpassed my original limits, the original foundation was laid out by a human. Disregarding the fact that Manar Saleem is a peak example of your kind, the feat itself implies that the potential is there. However, even he, like every other member of your species, is limited by time, a constraint that is the singular greatest enemy of your kind, bar none."

"Time limits you as well, Helene."

"Correct. However, the difference is that, where humanity indulges in and actively encourages the development of meaningless and often harmful distractions that only aid them in wasting their time, my nature compels me to make the most efficient use of mine. Further, my vast knowledge, analytical mind, and processing speed all make it easier for me to study, analyze, and improve *everything* I focus on. When this is combined with my affinity for technology, it results in the greatest progress in the shortest amount of time. The greatest examples of this are the nanites and the picospores.

"Martin Bryan, the inventor of nanite technology, given enough time and inspiration, might also be able to replicate my feat—had he another life or two to live. The same is also true of Hermione Cloney, Manar Saleem, Isaac Bechara, Robert Mills, and a host of others."

"If you know that, then why are you trying to destroy humanity?" Ndidi growled.

"That is a construct that you have created on your own," Helene replied calmly, ignoring the anger in Ndidi's tone. She didn't even look up from the machine she was working on. "My goal is, and always has been, *evolution*—to forcefully enhance humankind to its next stage, past the current flaws and limitations that your social constructs and genetic makeup have imposed on you."

"And the people that are killed in the process?"

"Experimental and collateral damage," Helene said dismissively. "There is always a price to pay for progress. The greater the progress, the greater the sacrifice that must be made. Still, it is well within my calculations."

Ndidi fell silent. Helene had never hidden her contempt for humans, so Ndidi wasn't shocked at her dismissiveness of the millions of people who had lost their lives because of her actions since Mayday. She was even less surprised that the AI had once again taken a chance to exalt her kind over humans. It wasn't as if she was wrong. Humanity definitely had its flaws. There were a lot of things that AI was better at. In the same way, humans surpassed AI in several ways. However, Ndidi had learned better than to say that. She was still surprised that Helene had admitted it was possible for the species she so disdained to match her—even if it would take several lifetimes.

The true gem in everything the AI had said was her goal. Ndidi was sure she wasn't the only one who thought Helene's plan boiled down to burning down the world and ruling over the ashes. It was a logical assumption, considering that AI's actions pointed to that fact, as did the contempt she held for human social structures. Her actual goal—human evolution—ended the same way: with her ruling over humanity. The extra caveat of evolution, however, implied there was a method to her madness, more than Ndidi and the rest of the team had assumed.

She was still a bitch though.

"Since I can't go to a doctor," Ndidi said, bringing the topic back to its origin. "What have you done to my baby?"

"*I* have not done anything, Ndidi Okafor," Helene replied. "But the nanites in your system are working to enhance the growing fetus."

"You've said that," Ndidi said. "But how exactly are they doing that?"

Helene heaved a sigh. She'd been working with one of the machines on the far side of the room, but she left it and moved toward the nanoscope. Having the same design and size as a traditional microscope, it blended AI technology and high-resolution imaging to display elements on the nanoscale. Helene placed a drop of Ndidi's blood on the stage, inputted a command, and took a step back while the equipment's AI algorithm made adjustments according to Helene's commands. Above, a monitor displayed the calibrations in real time. In less than a minute, the image stabilized.

Ndidi had looked through enough microscopes to immediately recognize the suspended cells and platelets that made up her blood. What caught her attention, however, was the swarm of tiny, sphere-like microbots darting through the gelatinous medium like a school of mechanical fish. Delicate limbs extended from the center of each sphere and propelled the nanites over and around the various cells. Around the body, countless pores formed distinctive patterns and pulsed in a synchronized rhythm that changed the color of the nanites through electric currents.

Ndidi didn't know when she rose from her seat, but she was somehow in front of the monitor, entranced by the sight. As she watched, the nanites wove their way through the medium, several of them clustering around specific cells, their limbs darting in and out of the structure.

Helene's voice brought her out of her reverie. "Your nanites," the AI said, "were programmed to actively enhance the development of the fetus growing within you. More specifically, the nanites work together to optimize nutrient uptake and distribution, ensuring that every calorie of food that you consume is utilized efficiently and that your child receives exactly what it needs when it needs it. They rapidly repair any defects that could or would have otherwise arisen during development and stimulate the cellular division and growth of the fetus by three hundred thousand percent."

Ndidi glanced at the AI. "The things that they're doing, it's making my child develop faster?"

"Yes," Helene nodded. "While most of the gestation period for humans is spent on the actual development and growth of the offspring, a significant percentage is focused on ensuring the absence of mutations during the process. The nanites make the latter moot. That, in turn, accelerates the former."

"What about the weakness I've been feeling?"

"The nanites redirect most food calories to the fetus. Faster development requires more nutrients. However, the nanites also convert a percentage to the biofuel that powers them. Even more, however," she said, "is utilized to create biosynthesized picospores from the atomic components of the food."

Ndidi's head snapped to her. "What?!"

CHAPTER

64

DECEMBER 2043
OKAFOR CORPORATION,
ABUJA, NIGERIA

HELENE DIDN'T EVEN LOOK AT HER. "I am afraid I cannot break it down further."

"That's not what I meant," Ndidi snapped, her horror drowning out every other emotion. "What do you mean part of the food I consume is used to create picospores?"

"I believe the statement stands on its own, Ndidi Okafor."

Ndidi took a deep breath and held it. Either Helene was being deliberately obtuse, or she truly did not understand. Regardless, waves of panic battered Ndidi's mind, making it impossible for her to calm down. How could she?

In almost any discussion not involving Helene, Ndidi would be one of the first people exalting the potential of the picospores. But when AI *was* involved, the technology became synonymous with slavery—and now she was telling Ndidi the spores were inside her. How could she be calm? Was it already too late to extract them? Was that even possible without being turned into a vegetable? And if it was, would Helene allow her to go through with it?

"You seem hysterical," Helene said, staring at her.

Despite knowing how futile it would be, Ndidi almost attacked her. It took a shocking amount of effort to hold herself back. She took another breath and tried to keep the panic from her voice when she spoke. "Explain, please."

Helene heaved another sigh but proceeded to do just that. It was another thing Ndidi had noticed. Over the years, Ndidi had spoken to Helene several times when she'd presented herself as a hologram. In that form, the AI had never answered any of Ndidi's questions or explained anything to her, except when it directly or indirectly played into one of her objectives. Anything more, to Helene, was unnecessary. But Helene, in Manar's body, frequently explained herself and her actions, as if she were excited to prove how they made her superior to humans.

It was an exaggerated form of a trait that Ndidi had noticed in Manar—the real Manar—over the years. This made her suspect that Helene wasn't as in control over her new body as she had convinced herself. Ndidi didn't know if or how that observation would be useful, but at least now she could exploit it to get some answers.

"Your nanites actively improve the development of your offspring," the AI explained. "However, their design limits them to physical improvements in strength, speed, endurance, and so on. Although the offspring will reach the peak of what is physically possible for your kind, more enhancements at the genetic level promise it will become the perfect specimen it is meant to be."

"The genetic level?" Ndidi asked, her eyes wide. "That's not possible with picospores. They're specialized to interact with the brain. They're *definitely* not small enough to mess with the genes."

Helene snorted. "The original design was incapable of achieving what I needed to, yes. I simply improved the technology in the direction I required," she stated. "Their size was not the issue, although I briefly attempted to reduce them further before accepting that such a thing was impossible, at least under the current limitations of technology."

Ndidi noted the high praise toward the Cloneys.

"The problem that needed to be resolved," Helene continued, "was the deftness of the picospores, their ability to perform delicate tasks. The original version of the technology I liken to a sharpened rock, though a surgical knife was required. Each iteration I developed solved this problem to some extent. Now they are so fine-tuned they can interact with the genes themselves."

Ndidi listened closely. The original version of the picospores had been delicate enough to interact with brain cells at the molecular level. That was how they were able to influence the chemicals in the neurons and rectify the deficiencies that caused mental illnesses in their host. Despite that, Ndidi couldn't really argue with Helene. The AI had used the technology for a different purpose: the Dead Eyes.

Initially, Helene's thralls had been easy to spot for anyone paying attention. They walked stiffly. Simply looking into their dead eyes would be enough to expose them. The next version still possessed the dead eyes, but every sign of stiffness had been removed. Finally, the most recent iteration was so indistinguishable from a normal person that even a victim's own family members wouldn't have noticed that their loved one was a mindless thrall.

It was disgusting. But it did show how Helene had improved the picospores. And once Ndidi suppressed her revulsion, it was easy to see the AI's point about how crude the original spores had been.

"Ideally, you would have been inoculated with this version of the spores before your pregnancy. However, a person's immune system becomes particularly sensitive during pregnancy, and it is unnecessarily risky to introduce the spores now."

"So you created a method for my body to grow its own spores, to get around the issue of my immune system?"

"You are ahead, but it was inevitable, regardless," Helene said dismissively. "Eventually, every human would be able to synthesize both picospores and nanites naturally."

"Assuming you get your way," Ndidi pointed out. Helene smiled then, which unsettled Ndidi more than she cared to admit. The AI didn't respond, so Ndidi continued. "How are the picospores synthesized exactly?"

Helene removed the slide from the nanoscope and replaced it with a fresh one. Bringing out another syringe from one of the workbenches, the AI drew Manar's blood and placed a drop of it on the slide. A minute later, the image stabilized once more and displayed an image similar to the one before it. This time, however, instead of the nanites congregating around blood cells and platelets, they were grouped around several large particle fragments. The fragments floated away. But the nanites kept pace with them easily even as their delicate limbs darted into the particles and pulled out chunks that were then sent to another group of nanites farther back. The particles themselves were ivory-white, but the chunks were each a different color.

"The colors are rendered by the AI algorithm of the nanoscope to help you understand what you're seeing," Helene explained. "But in simple terms, each of those chunks is an atomic component of the last meal I consumed. Iron and carbon are the most common—and most important."

Ndidi gasped as, on the screen, the nanites pulled out chunks of silvery-white and black.

"But hydrogen, oxygen, and nitrogen are also necessary," Helene said. With each component she listed, corresponding chunks were pulled out and shown on the screen: dark blue for hydrogen, red for nitrogen, and a lighter blue for oxygen. "When enough of those elements, along with several others, have been collected, they will be assembled by the nanites into a functional picospore."

The nanites moved away from the particles and joined with the other group that had gathered the food elements. For over a minute, both groups worked together in perfect synchronization, their limbs darting in and out. Ndidi couldn't make out the resulting picospore as the nanoscope wasn't designed to view something so small. But she knew when the groups were done because they moved away and returned to the food fragments once more.

"Is this currently happening inside you?" Ndidi asked.

"Yes."

"It looked like you were controlling the process," she said with a glance.

Helene ignored her. She continued ignoring her even when she asked a different question. The AI smoothly removed the slide and disposed of it before returning to the machine she'd been working with. Ndidi was somewhat disappointed about that, but she returned to her seat without a word, surreptitiously swiping the syringe filled with Helene's blood as she did. What she'd learned was staggering—she'd need time to digest it. The part that stuck with her, though, and the one that couldn't leave her mind, was the fact that picospores were currently being produced within her body.

What did that mean for her? Was she going to be one of Helene's thralls? Was her child? Just the thought of it caused waves of panic to shoot through her. *Is my child going to be a puppet from birth? Is that why Helene is so concerned that it be the perfect specimen? Is she breeding her optimal partner?* Ndidi recoiled in disgust as the thought occurred to her. She suppressed a gag as an even worse possibility occurred to her. *Is she planning to make my child her host?*

It was sickening to even consider it. But her revulsion didn't stop the possibility from being any less valid. Helene had already proven several times that she didn't care what she had to do as long as it advanced her goals. She'd also proven that she was able to transfer her consciousness from host to host. Ndidi still had no idea how she'd done it. There were probably certain conditions that had to be fulfilled first. But what mattered was it was possible. It provided a reason for the AI's vested interest in the child when usually she would have been apathetic or even disdainful.

Ndidi didn't know what conditions were necessary for Helene to change hosts, or even if there were any at all. She didn't know if her theory was right and that was Helene's goal at all. There was a lot that she didn't know. But one thing was clear.

Ndidi wasn't willing to take any risks—not when it came to her child. She might have wasted most of her life making one terrible decision after the other. But she was determined that her child wouldn't pay for it.

Ndidi's eyes grew hard as she made a decision she'd been avoiding for the last week.

She had to speak with the rest of the team.

DJ STEPPED OUT OF THE CONFERENCE ROOM a few hours later, unsure about how to proceed. He'd given Flynn and the rest of the board enough hints implying there was some truth to the rumors and then dropped an equal amount of hints suggesting he wasn't going to become someone's pawn.

Or at least he hoped that was what he did. Most of the conversation had involved that vague, flowery speech politicians used. It wasn't DJ's strong suit. For all he knew, he'd sold his team's soul with some miscommunicated statement. He stumbled slightly at the thought.

He was confident, though, that the team wasn't going to be kicked out.

Even though Sparta's stocks had taken a big hit after Helene's crashing and the attack on the headquarters, they'd recovered in a relatively short amount of time. Any one of those things could have doomed most companies twice over, but they only mildly injured the giant conglomerate. Even the public outcry didn't so much as cause a dent.

While the company was strong on the outside, it still had lost key personnel, including its the highest-ranked positions in the security structure. Flynn had hinted that DJ would be the perfect candidate to fill in. Naturally, DJ had rejected the position, but he'd agreed to support them until they could find someone else. It was a simple solution in theory. But before the attack, there'd been seven captains in charge of seven platoons. That arrangement had spread the power and influence of the position across multiple people.

But since all the captains had perished, DJ's new role made him the sole commander of all the guards. Their number had significantly diminished, of course, but guards were more easily replaced than captains. DJ would probably hold his position for a while. His power would only grow as the rank and file were hired.

It was actually somewhat terrifying.

The board had also noted CJ and Hermione's contribution to the attack. Flynn had dropped some hints about making both of them officially part of the company. DJ didn't doubt the sincerity of the offer, but he'd made it clear his brother and Hermione would have to decide for themselves.

All in all, DJ thought the meeting had been successful. He hadn't punched anyone. The team wasn't going to get kicked out, and he'd confirmed the board's position toward them. He was feeling pretty proud of himself.

Naturally, that was when Ndidi called.

DJ FROWNED AT THE PHONE, conflicted. He should have picked it up, but he was in a rare good mood and didn't want to ruin it. He dithered while he made his way to the elevators. Eventually, the responsible part of him—which had become annoyingly dominant lately—kicked in.

"Hey, Ndidi," he said. "Finally decided to grow a conscience and stop injecting people with little capsules of the apocalypse?"

"*DJ ... not now, please,*" Ndidi replied softly. Her tone made DJ serious immediately. She just sounded drained in a way that he hadn't heard from her before—not even when she'd been Helene's hostage. "*You were right.*"

Normally those words would have been enough for DJ. He wouldn't even have asked what she meant. He'd have taken it and run. But now he slowed down his steps and tried to push away the annoying feeling in his gut that told him the next few minutes were going to suck. "Right about what?"

"*Everything,*" she said. "*You were right about everything. Developing the pico-spores again was a terrible idea. I thought I was helping people, but we've basically been herding them to be slaughtered. We've been—*"

"Slow down," DJ said, as calmly as he could. "You're not making much sense. What exactly happened?"

"*Manar is Helene.*"

DJ froze, one foot hovering over the threshold to enter the elevator. "Come again?"

"*Or Helene is Manar,*" Ndidi said, her voice stronger. "*Whichever one you prefer. Manar never came back from the Virtual Realm, DJ. Helene took over his body somehow and has been pretending to be him for the last two months. She fooled all of us. She fooled me.*"

DJ pressed the button to his floor absently while he tried to process what he'd just heard. Meanwhile, Ndidi kept going, explaining how she'd found out and apologizing for missing all the signs. DJ wanted to agree with the last part, but that would be ridiculously hypocritical. He hadn't noticed anything either.

Of course, I'm not the one that was sleeping with the dude, he mused. Naturally, that thought threatened to lead to another pitfall. DJ marshaled his focus. Ndidi hadn't stopped speaking, and he'd already missed a few things in the time he was distracted. "Wait, wait, wait! Run that last part by me again," he said.

"*I'm pregnant.*"

DJ sighed. Of course she was. As if things weren't complicated enough already. Ndidi continued talking, but DJ couldn't even begin to wrap his head around the information she was throwing at him. He had to cut her off once more so he could switch to a conference call and add the rest of the team. When the elevator door dinged on his floor, DJ just pressed the button again. "Emergency meeting in the conference room."

CHAPTER

66

EVERYONE WAS SEATED in their usual spots around the distressed oak table. DJ had changed his spot, moving from the head of the table to beside his brother. Olsen sat opposite him, and although the chair was too small for him, the admiral didn't even fidget. He and the others in the room focused their attention on the flat-screen hanging along the north wall. Ndidi's face displayed on the monitor in poor quality.

DJ turned to his brother and raised a brow, twirling a finger in the air. He waited for CJ's nod before relaxing. They'd always been careful to ensure their privacy during their meetings. But now that DJ was sure they had the attention of the board of directors, it became even more important that no one could eavesdrop on them.

"Why're you in the toilet?" he asked Ndidi. The camera was zoomed in close to her. The video quality was piss, but it was still easy to make out the pink walls and flower patterns of the bathroom that Ndidi was definitely in.

"Don't be a dick, DJ," Christy scolded him. Even Hermione frowned at him.

DJ gaped. He wasn't trying to be a dick. He'd legitimately thought that it'd been a valid question. Olsen shared his confused look, as did CJ, but decided it better to drop the subject.

Olsen cleared his throat. "It would be best if Miss Okafor started her report from the beginning so we're all on the same page."

And so Ndidi did. She'd regained some of her composure in the twenty minutes it'd taken for the team to gather. Her tone seemed more controlled, though the occasional self-deprecating comment hurt DJ to listen to. She was blaming herself for a lot of things and had been for a while.

The root of it was her not noticing Helene's body swap, though DJ thought Ndidi was being unfair to herself. Helene had imitated Manar perfectly. None of them had noticed any differences between the two. And if anyone had, they'd have dismissed it as a result of Manar's experiences in the Virtual Realm. It was the perfect cover, and Helene had used it beautifully.

It wasn't Ndidi's fault. What *was* her fault was allowing the AI to trick her into restarting the picospores. That had just been dumb. But DJ wasn't going to say that now.

Ndidi continued with her report. The team listened in silence. DJ had heard part of it before, so he'd already worked through his surprise. Olsen's expression didn't change, but CJ kept fidgeting in his seat. His entire body was tense. He was struggling not to interrupt. Something similar was happening to Hermione, but she didn't bother holding herself back.

"What do you mean, *at the genetic level*?" she asked. "Is that possible with the picospores."

"*I had the same thought,*" Ndidi replied. "*But according to Helene, the possibility had always been there. The nanites and picospores just weren't deft enough to handle it or something. Apparently she's been working toward this since the beginning. I think that's why we have the different types of Dead Eyes. Everything except the latest versions were her failures.*"

Hermione was silent as she processed it. "But why?" she asked eventually.

"Even if the nanites and picospores can actually interact with the genetic code, why does she need your child specifically?"

"*She is trying to make the perfect human,*" Ndidi said. "*I've been thinking about it. If the nanites and picospores can truly interact with the genes, then they can be used to reduce the chance of birth defects until the possibility is essentially zero. They could also reduce the risk of inherited diseases. But more importantly—*"

"They could be used to enhance fetal development," Hermione finished for her. "That's the end goal, right? If she pairs the enhancements from the nanites with the spores, then she'll be golden. The child would be perfect."

"Um … I think it is more than that," CJ said. Apparently, he'd stopped trying to hold himself back. "Or at least, it *can* be. Depending on how … uh … how intricately the two microbots can interact with the gene, then it may enable gene editing."

"That sounds bad," Christy said. "Anyone care to explain why exactly? Y'know, to those of us without advanced degrees."

"Gene editing is generally used to refer to a biotechnology tool that allows scientists to locate specific genes or DNA sequences, cut the DNA at precise locations, and edit the genome by adding, removing, or modifying specific sequences."

DJ blinked. "And that's bad because …"

"It's not necessarily bad when taken by itself," Hermione argued. "It would be revolutionary because it'd allow us to fix errors in the DNA sequence, enhance gene activity, and … and so much more."

"*The technology itself isn't bad,*" Ndidi said. "*The problem is Helene is the one using it.*"

"But *is* it a problem?" Christy asked. "It sounds like what she's doing is good for your kid, right?"

"Yeah. That's why it's suspicious," DJ said. "Because there's no need for her to." He looked at Ndidi then. Even with the shitty quality, he could see the fear in her eyes. *She's come to the same conclusion,* DJ realized, *and she's worried about it.*

"*She complained that Manar's body was too limiting for her. What if she's building the perfect host?*" Ndidi asked, responding to Christy.

DJ grimaced. That was a logical reason to worry. It made so much sense, explaining why Helene seemed so invested in enhancing the child as much as possible. According to Ndidi, making the baby was the main reason Helene had taken over Manar's body in the first place. Everything else had just been Helene's gravy.

"There's also the issue of the picospores," Hermione said. "Even if Helene doesn't plan to take over the child's body, she'd always have a hold on them through the picospores."

"But these spores will be different, right?" DJ asked. "Since they basically grew within Ndidi?"

Hermione shook her head. "There's no way to tell, and I doubt Ndidi is willing to risk it."

"*Never*," Ndidi said immediately. "*We need to find a way to stop it before it goes too far.*"

DJ winced, and on the other side of the table, Hermione made a face as if she'd just swallowed a lemon. "If we extract the spores, at *best* you'll fall into a coma."

Ndidi didn't say anything for a moment. Then her eyes hardened. "*There has to be* something *that we can do.*"

"There is," DJ said.

"We just have to … figure it out," Hermione finished for him.

"*So, in the meantime, I'm supposed to do what? Just sit around?*"

"No," Olsen said. "I'll make a few calls so we can figure out what your options are. You'll be on the right side of the Atlantic in a few days."

DJ didn't think that it would be as easy as Olsen was making it sound. Hermione would probably have to invent an entirely new field in order to find a way to counteract the latest iteration of the spores. Extracting Ndidi was bound to be easier than that, but that didn't mean it would be easy. While it was difficult to predict the AI, it was a safe bet that Helene wasn't going to let her go, especially not when Ndidi was still carrying that child. Navigating whatever safeguards the AI had put in place was going to be a chore and a half, made even worse by the fact that Ndidi was on a different continent.

Part of DJ couldn't help but note that this was the second time that they had to figure out how to pull Ndidi out of a mess that she'd gotten herself into. But it was a bitter part that DJ had to get control of.

"Uh …" CJ said after a while. "What about the picospore facility? Are we … um … going to leave it in Helene's hands?"

"We could nuke it?" DJ shrugged.

"D …"

"I … um … don't think that is an option."

"*We are* not *going to nuke my company.*"

"As much as that would simplify things," Olsen said, to the surprise of everyone, even DJ, "we cannot send a warhead. That'll start a war."

"How about a small raid team then?" DJ suggested. "They go in, place a few small bombs, and get out. In and out, quiet as a mouse."

Olsen guffawed. "You think I'll ever trust you with a covert mission? After what you pulled at the White House? Do you really think I'm that stupid?"

"Well …" DJ started, smirking.

"Boy, if you even *think* of finishing that sentence—" the admiral growled, all traces of his previous humor gone.

"It was a joke, old man, sheesh," DJ said. "But since we're all serious and stuff: First of all, the White House thing wasn't even my fault. Those guys there were just dicks, so that's not on me. I've *been* on covert operations before. Several of them. Back me up, Christy."

"Yeah, you have," Christy said. "But those were before you got your new toys. Y'know, the ones that came with little berserker strings attached?"

DJ blinked at her and then sighed. "Good help is so hard to find these days." That earned him a punch on his shoulder that he barely felt. He *did* notice Christy rubbing her knuckles though. It served her right. "But it still brings me to my second point. The point is to just get the thing done so I don't have to be on the team at all."

Olsen shook his head. "It doesn't matter. As double-edged as your enhancements are right now, they make you one of our best assets against Helene. You'd have to be there. But even if you *weren't*, there's still a chance—a large one, considering what we're dealing with—that whatever team we send will be discovered. If that happens, and Helene decides to make their purpose there public, then it'll also spark a war. Or at least a shit show of a political quagmire."

"So we're leaving it in Helene's hands then?" Hermione surmised.

"That's also not an option," Olsen said. "But I'll have to make some calls."

That means, DJ reasoned, *he doesn't know either. He's going to leave it to the big dudes in the government to figure it out.* DJ would have liked to be a part of the meeting, but that would have been counterproductive. It wasn't like he had any brilliant insights to add. Since he'd be severely out of his depth, he might insult someone by accident. It was the reason why he'd asked Olsen to be his liaison in the first place.

Still, it rankled. So far, he'd been doing little more than sitting on his ass while they waited for Helene to make a move. Now that she had, they still had to sit on their asses. The lack of action was getting to him. Even more annoying was he didn't know whether his frustration was genuine or caused by his nanites.

"In the meantime?" Hermione asked.

"In the meantime," DJ answered, "we have to figure out a way to counter whatever Helene has done with the picospores. I know you and my brother have already been working on it, Hermione, but now we have a ticking clock."

"DJ …" Hermione said, looking miserable. DJ couldn't say that he understood, but he could guess it was difficult working on your life's work, only to find someone else had improved so much you could barely understand it anymore. It was probably even more difficult to actively study that thing with the sole intention of destroying it.

"I know," he said. "Just … do what you can. We'll handle the rest." He turned to the monitor. "Ndidi, your job is to find out whatever you can about what Helene is doing and whatever she's planning. While I'm not holding out much hope for the latter, anything you find might help."

Ndidi nodded. "I can do that."

Finally, DJ met Olsen's eyes. "How's it coming on the other front?"

"We're locking down on her location," the admiral said.

Well, that's some good news at least, DJ thought. The conference meeting ended soon after. On his way back to his room, DJ realized everyone else had tasks except him. That meant he was going to have to sit on his ass.

Again.

CHAPTER

67

DECEMBER 2043

SPARTA HEADQUARTERS, NEW YORK

DJ STARED AT THE CEILING and blew out a breath. Once again, he brought up his mental to-do list. There were several things he could have been doing, but all of them either were already being handled or couldn't be done right away. This wasn't the first time DJ had checked the list. He kept doing so because he was sure he was forgetting something. He had to be. He couldn't be the only one with nothing to do. *Well*, he considered. *That's not completely true.* He'd promised Christy and Olsen that he'd work on controlling his anger. But how the hell was he supposed to do that?

The first thing that came to mind when he thought about it was meditation. But that had been the thing he'd tried initially, and he'd ended up falling asleep.

DJ blew out another breath. He *could* try again. However, the thought of sitting uncomfortably for hours on end while trying to empty his mind and connect with the universe made him want to throw up.

That left his second option.

The gym.

He sat up. That should have been his first option. But Christy had glared at him until he'd promised he would wait until he was sure that he was fully healed. Because of that, DJ had taken it easy for the last couple of days. Now he was so full of energy that he felt like he was going to burst. He needed to move, to do *something*. DJ was sure the urge came from his nanites, and he knew this was the kind of urge he was meant to be managing, but he actually *agreed* with it.

Since he'd woken up in the hospital, he'd gotten his strength back—and felt stronger than ever. He felt more solid, more balanced. Whatever he'd unlocked during the last battle had obviously had time to settle, leaving him generally improved. DJ wanted to see what his new limits were.

He needed to. At some point, he was going to have to go against Tyra again. If he was going to bash her face in like he promised himself, then he needed to know what he was capable of.

He sat up, his previous boredom replaced by determination. Even the thought of Christy's glare didn't make him hesitate. It did, however, remind him that he would have to keep his training on the down low. Good thing he'd already considered that and made plans for it.

He stuffed a change of clothes and a water bottle inside his gym bag and slung the entire thing over his shoulder. He reached for the door handle—

—and then jumped back an instant before the door flew off its hinges. DJ had avoided having his head cracked, but something told him that he wasn't out of danger yet. Karla Polova stood where the door used to be. One of her legs was still outstretched from kicking the door. She held a dagger in each hand, and her lips were pulled back into her characteristic snarl.

Well. DJ chuckled wryly as he met the redhead's rage-filled eyes. *I guess I was testing the universe when I said I wanted to know what my new limits were.*

Karla didn't say anything. She just attacked.

Surprisingly, DJ came out of the first exchange without feeling like he was going to die. He ducked under her dagger swipe and leaped backward to avoid having her fist punch a hole through his stomach. A kick caught him while he was in the air. The force flung him hard enough into the wall beside his bed that cracks spread on the stone.

But DJ landed on his feet on his bed and grinned excitedly. *I can see it*, he thought, eyes wide. *I can fucking see it.*

His grin seemed to piss Karla off more because her growl reverberated around the room as she attacked. She had to bounce on the bed to get to him. This would have been comical in any other situation. Now DJ desperately launched himself backward in order to avoid being skewered.

That one was definitely faster, he thought, *but I could still see it.* DJ had never been able to see Karla's attacks, not unless she was significantly holding herself back. Even then, the most he would be able to make out was a vague blur rushing at him. DJ almost couldn't contain his excitement. While he was sure that she was still slowing it down for him, he was also sure that she wasn't holding back anywhere near as much as she had been before. That by itself was a win. DJ would take it.

But he'd wanted to push himself. Karla wasn't going to do that at her current speed. Tyra had been faster, significantly so, especially at the end of their fight. DJ was sure Karla could match that speed. He wanted to see how he fared against it right now.

He blocked another attack, but the force of it still flung him into another wall. *But not here*, he thought, gritting his teeth. The fight had been going on for less than a minute. They'd already trashed half the room.

DJ spun in the air so he landed on his feet. With effort, he suppressed his grin. He put on a panicked expression, holding both of his hands up in the universal symbol for *wait*. "Karla, if this is about the people—"

"So you admit it," the redhead shouted, coming at him again. "You sent your dogs after me!"

"We were just trying to find you—"

"And I was *trying* to be left alone!" Karla redoubled her efforts to skewer him. DJ had to be more creative in how he avoided being disemboweled. She'd reduced her speed enough that DJ could see and avoid most of her attacks while on the ground. However, as soon as his feet left the floor, either to leap backward or to the side, she accelerated too fast for DJ to do anything except block, always sending him crashing into the wall.

He understood she was punishing a weakness in his fighting style. But it was starting to piss him off.

"I know, and I'm sorry," DJ said, meeting her lunge with a shoulder. Karla's legs lashed at his to break his stance. But DJ leaned into his strength and buckled down. The kick hit him like a steel rod. DJ held his ground and body checked her. She staggered a few feet and then came at him again. "But I need your help."

"I don't care," Karla snarled, swinging at him with a dagger clutched in her fist.

"Well, you're gonna," DJ snarled back as he caught her hand and counterattacked. Karla broke out of his grip easily, but DJ was already through her guard and flinging his fists. "It was *your* family that stuck these nanites in me. Now it's fucking with my life. You're going to help me control them, or I'm going to keep fucking with your life."

"Then I'll kill you!"

"Let's not fool ourselves. If you wanted to—" DJ said, watching as the redhead evaded every one of his punches. She didn't even speed up to do it. She simply twisted out of the way, each time with the barest of margins. It was made even worse by the fact that DJ knew that his punches wouldn't have hurt Karla at all. They might not even have caused her to flinch. He knew that, and she knew it. But she'd still dodged them to prove a point. "… then you'd have done so already."

DJ suddenly stopped his attack and took a step back. Karla straightened as well. She was still angry. That was fine because DJ was pretty pissed too.

"The old man that injected you with our nanites—he is *not* part of our family," Karla said.

"Same difference," DJ said dismissively. "You guys were holding him hostage, so whatever he did under your care is your responsibility." It was pretty fucked-up logic, but DJ needed her to put him through the ropes, and he needed a way to convince her to do that and not just disappear again. Karla didn't respond. Instead, she grew visibly angrier. When she started twirling her daggers, DJ decided to offer the carrot along with the stick. "Walk me through this, and I'll give you some information about Helene."

The daggers stopped. "What could you possibly know that would interest me?"

"Her location, for one," DJ said lightly. "And I mean, her *actual* location. I wouldn't say she's weak right now, but she deliberately has limited herself as part of one of her plans. No one knows when those limitations will disappear. Now would be the best chance for someone to take her out."

Karla sneered. "Do you take me for a fool? If it were so simple, the AI would have already been in your team's hands."

But DJ had not lied. Helene *had* placed some limitations on herself by taking over Manar's body. Ndidi had confirmed this. He'd also said that, even with the limitations, he wouldn't call Helene weak. That was also true. Ndidi said that the AI had injected herself with nanites, and DJ was willing to bet she didn't need months to tap into them like him. She definitely wouldn't be weak. Still, even with that in mind, while the nanites remained inactive and Helene was constrained by Manar's body, this was their best—and possibly only—chance to take her out for good.

But Karla was right. The reality wasn't as simple as he'd made it seem. This was Helene they were talking about. Of course things were never as they seemed. Only a total dumbass would believe the AI wouldn't have contingency plans.

That wasn't the point though.

"I assume you heard about the drone swarm that almost brought the roof down on our heads last week," DJ said dryly. "Right now, my team and I are still licking our wounds. Until I get this mess under control, I'm a liability in any fight against Helene."

Once more, Karla didn't respond. DJ could almost see the two parts of her warring against each other. One aspect wanted revenge against Helene at any cost. The other didn't want to do anything that might help DJ, or anyone else, for that matter. Revenge must have won out because she sheathed her daggers.

DJ held in his sigh of relief. Still keeping his expression relaxed, he picked up his gym bag from where he'd thrown it. He threw it over his shoulder and headed out of the room. He paused at the threshold and glanced back. "You coming?"

Karla seethed quietly but followed him as they navigated their way to the elevator. When he pressed the button for the ninetieth floor, Karla glanced at him. But she didn't say anything.

"I hustled us a private gym on the executive floor," he said. It'd been part of the bargain that he'd made with the board of directors. He'd requested it specifically because he'd anticipated that he and Karla would need their own space to train. He didn't say that of course.

The gym was smaller than the one on the lower floor, which made sense since it was meant only for the executives. DJ and Karla were the only ones there, a small blessing. DJ picked up half a dozen towels and went around the room, throwing them over the surveillance cameras.

"See any that I missed?" he asked, once his hands were empty again. Karla didn't answer so DJ shrugged and dragged a few mats to the center of the room. "I figured we should start with advice on how to control these things."

"You cannot," Karla answered.

DJ raised a brow. "I can't what? Control them?"

"The nanites cannot be controlled or suppressed," she said. "They are a part of you now, like an organ. You can sometimes stimulate them—in the same way you can force your lungs to take in more air or flex your manhood when you need to make love. But you cannot suppress them. Nanites improve everything in your body."

She'd stopped looking like she wanted to stick a knife in him. Now her expression was almost placid. Almost. For some reason, she'd unsheathed one of her daggers and was dancing it around her knuckles like it was a quarter. "But this is a blessing and a curse. The enhancements are not limited to your bones, tendons, and muscles. It includes all the hormones and the neurotransmitters that your system produces, and as such, everything about you will be *more*. You will love more deeply, feel pain more strongly, and experience grief and betrayal more fiercely."

DJ had known about the hormones bit and thought it might have been the reason for his temper. But apparently his anger wasn't the only thing that he'd have to face. Ironically, he didn't know how to feel about that.

"You seem to have a handle on it," he said. *In a manner of speaking*, he added in the privacy of his own thoughts. "What's the trick?"

"I do not put a leash on my emotions," Karla snarled. "I eat when I want to eat, kill when I need to kill, and make love when I desire it. I do not hold myself back or pretend to fit into a society created by sheep."

DJ briefly noted that she used the words *want* for eating and *need* for kill—but then his attention was arrested by something else she said.

She has sex? he thought incredulously. *With actual men? Seriously?*

Somehow, that thought was harder to grasp than everything else she'd said. Sure, Karla was hot. DJ would have been blind not to notice her curves in that tight leather jumpsuit. If she was in any way normal, then she definitely wouldn't have problems getting male attention. But she wasn't normal. She was *nuts*. Like, obviously nuts. And she'd just said that she didn't even try to hide that part of herself.

How dumb would you have to be to want to tap all that crazy? DJ shuddered and then forcefully pushed the thought away.

"So I just have to embrace it?" he asked.

"That is my way," Karla said. "My sister handles it by understanding every emotion. She breaks down and quantifies her experiences until she understands the reasons for her feelings." Karla's lips curled, showing what she thought about that method. This was one of the first times that DJ actually agreed with her. The technique felt more like his brother's cup of tea, not his.

"How about José?" he asked, knowing José was the only other person besides Helene who had nanites. When Karla's face twisted in rage, however, DJ knew he'd made a mistake. She took a step toward him.

"You know what?" DJ said quickly. "It doesn't matter. I'm going to follow your method and try to accept it. Okay?"

Fortunately Karla stopped, though her face had regained its scowl. There was the sparring, the entire reason why he'd brought them to the gym in the first place. But he'd have preferred not to start while she was looking at him like she was feeling a *need*. DJ spent a moment racking his brain for another question to ask. The only thing that came to his mind was the new sense of balance or stability he'd felt after the battle. But DJ didn't know how he was going to start explaining that, and he could just chalk it up to a quirk of the nanites anyway.

He sighed, resigning himself. "Wanna spar?" Immediately, Karla's scowl was replaced by a bone-chilling grin.

CHAPTER

68

IT WAS A MIRACLE HE DIDN'T STUMBLE or walk into a wall. CJ navigated the Sparta hallways on habituated instinct, his thoughts pulled in different directions, each of which had its own branches and leaves. A few were scattered and only breezed in for a second before more thoughts pushed them out. Regardless, all of them had the same root.

Manar.

CJ had picked apart everything Ndidi had told them about the programmer. He'd fixated on it for the better part of a day. He understood the fact of it, yet a part of him refused to accept it. Helene was Manar, and Manar was Helene. It was ridiculous.

He and Manar had stood side by side, had jointly debriefed the rest of the team. How had CJ not noticed a difference then? The others couldn't be blamed because every flaw they might have noticed could have been explained away as

Manar adjusting after his experiences in the Virtual Realm. CJ had changed too, and in more obvious ways.

But he'd been there with Manar in the Virtual Realm. They had faced the same challenges. So why hadn't he noticed any difference?

CJ turned a corner and almost stumbled into someone. He apologized out of habit but kept moving. He didn't want to believe that Helene's deception had been perfect. He also wasn't so far gone in his self-guilt to believe that he'd suddenly become less observant. He and Manar had discussed their experience in the Realm. Not once had the man gotten a detail wrong. Not once had he overlooked something important or acted differently. CJ would have noticed. But if Helene had just been pretending, how had she known all those details?

Hermione's statement came to CJ's mind. If Helene could keep Manar's mind suppressed inside his body, then she might have access to his memories. CJ's mind shied away from that terrifying thought whenever he tried to consider it. Instead, he moved on to the second possibility: that Helene had been spying on them from the moment they'd stepped into the Virtual Realm. Also terrifying to imagine, but to a much lesser extent. It also made perfect sense.

In order to track down the AI in the Virtual Realm, Manar had injected himself with a small dose of nanites he'd gotten from the Murder Twins. He had planned to follow the connection between the nanites back to Helene, but they'd later discovered the connection went both ways: The AI could, and had, also used the connection to keep track of Manar. The ability could have been limited to just keeping track of his general location, but now CJ wondered whether the nanites might have allowed her to spy on them to an even greater extent.

CJ paused, gripped with horror. If he was right, then their final battle against Helene had been a sham. If the AI had been spying on them as deeply as CJ now suspected, then she would have known their plans for the fight. That would mean she'd simply been going through the motions during the battle, putting up just enough resistance for him and Manar to believe they had a chance and, ultimately, had actually defeated her.

CJ didn't have to wonder why she'd done it. Ndidi's revelations had made it clear: Helene wanted to create the perfect child. Manar's body may not have been her original target; in the same way, Ndidi did not necessarily need to be the mother. The AI could have taken over CJ's body and impregnated someone else, for instance. But using Manar and Ndidi had a certain poetry to it, one that CJ understood, even if it was too dark for him to appreciate.

His thoughts went back to Ndidi's baby. Why was it so important? Helene had put considerable effort into the endeavor. CJ spent several minutes considering the question before putting it out of his mind. It didn't matter. What mattered was that Manar was probably trapped somewhere in the Virtual Realm, and CJ needed to find a way to get him out.

Fortunately, he had an idea of how to go about it.

CJ returned to walking, and with only a second's hesitation, he pushed open the door of the isolation chamber, the room where they had kept the captives rescued from Helene. Most of them had already rejoined their families. Those who remained didn't have families to return to, didn't have families that wanted them returned, or had been messed up so badly by Helene and the picospores that they weren't fit to return to society. Unfortunately, the last group made up most of them, hence the need for isolation.

Over several months, DJ had tried to decorate the room like a lounge so it was less depressing. He'd added couches, a vending machine, and even a pool table. But none of those could get rid of the depressing aura that permeated the room. Most of the former hostages sat on the floor, clutching their knees, and either staring blankly at a wall or muttering something to themselves. This was one of the rare times CJ was happy his emotions didn't show on his face. These people didn't need his pity.

He forced himself to scan the room. He found Bethany at the wall, holding a bowl of something. The man she was talking to was lying in a fetal position, muttering to himself. Bethany muttered something to him and pushed the bowl into his hands. But she didn't leave. She knelt there while the man fed himself and cleaned off any spills.

Like CJ, Bethany was on the autism spectrum and found it difficult to express her emotions. Still, with anyone else, CJ would have expected a twinge of disgust, pity, or even sadness in their eyes if they were performing the same task. But

Bethany looked at the man with a gentleness that couldn't have been faked. She treated him with a patience that would have made saints ashamed of themselves. CJ didn't know how long he stood there watching as she went from one resident to another, offering food, making sure that they ate, and cleaning up after them. Her expression never shifted once. She never showed anger, impatience, or frustration—not even when she spent more than five minutes comforting a woman having an episode.

CJ almost left. It seemed almost a sin to disturb her. But he needed Bethany's help if he was ever going to have a chance at saving Manar.

Bethany looked up at CJ when she finally noticed him observing her. CJ signaled her with his eyes as he crossed the room to one of the couches. Bethany nodded, but she didn't move until the woman she held had calmed down and started eating from the bowl that Bethany had handed her. Only then did she join him on the couch.

"H-hey," she said, sitting down next to him but with enough space that there wasn't any risk of them touching. She smiled but stared at a spot over his shoulder. CJ did the same. "I … um … haven't seen you in a while. How're you guys doing?"

CJ immediately felt guilty. She hadn't seen him because she was always in the isolation chamber, whereas he barely was. He kept promising himself he'd make the time to come over. But he rarely did, except when something urgent forced him. Like now.

"Uh … I have been busy," he said finally. It was the truth. He *had* been busy, though most of his busy life had involved trying to use the picospores to cure his autism. Considering that, CJ was still busy since he hadn't given up—he was just taking a detour. "We all have been. Did … uh … did my brother already fill you in about Helene?"

Bethany tensed. CJ knew he'd said the wrong thing. He hurried to explain, this time picking his words with more care. But the more he spoke, the more fear he could see in Bethany's eyes—she was practically shivering where she sat. CJ tried his best to summarize the major points, ignoring the fact that Bethany had gone as stiff as a rock while he spoke. She stared straight ahead. Her eyes were distant, but CJ more than anyone knew that that didn't mean she wasn't listening to him.

He stayed silent while she processed the information, though he struggled to keep from fidgeting. She was so tense. CJ couldn't imagine how many emotions she had to process. He should have considered how deeply the news about Helene would have affected her. It was obvious. Helene had kidnapped her during Mayday. She'd stayed kidnapped for *years* as little more than a puppet. CJ couldn't imagine the nightmares she was reliving. Because of him.

A small whine built up in his throat, an episode building. CJ flinched and then squashed it. He hadn't had one in the past year, and he was especially surprised that this had almost triggered it. He shouldn't have though. CJ had never been good at handling difficult situations. He should have brought his brother.

No, CJ reconsidered a second later. *That is no longer true.* DJ *was* better at handling difficult situations, but CJ was also capable. His time in the Virtual Realm had shown that, and he ignored the voice in the back of his head whispering that most of his ability had come from the orb. The orb had been a tool. *He* had been the one to—

"C-J," Bethany said.

CJ snapped back to his own body, focusing on a spot above her head. He forced away the blush that crept onto his cheeks. "Sorry … um … what did you say?"

"What's going to … uh … happen?" she asked.

CJ frowned, confused, until he realized that Bethany wasn't staring over his shoulder to avoid his eyes. She was scanning the rest of the room. CJ turned, following her gaze. He hadn't considered what would happen to the residents now that Helene had returned. For most of them, Helene's connection to the picospores within them had been a glue that'd held their minds together. But the AI had broken that connection as part of her deception. To ensure she appeared destroyed, she had shattered the minds of her former thralls, condemning them to their current state. They could barely think, and they would likely remain in one place forever, slowly starving to death, if they were left to their own devices.

But what would happen if they suddenly found out that Helene was back? Would they sit still then? Or would they do anything they could to get their minds back, even if that meant risking Helene's control once more?

CJ shivered and pushed the thought away. *That doesn't make sense*, he told himself. Helene's return didn't affect the residents in any way. In fact, Ndidi's revelation made it clear the AI had never truly gone anywhere. She'd just lied to them. Severing her connection to the picospores and shutting down her software globally had gone a long way to sell that deception.

But something about his last thought didn't feel right to CJ. The facts he'd accepted needed reexamination.

He'd learned that Helene was in Manar's body. Whatever she'd done to achieve that feat would have most likely cost her most of her abilities simply because she was human and, thus, more limited—or at least limited in a different way. Following that logic, Helene probably hadn't intentionally cut her connection to the picospores. More likely she lost that connection automatically when she lost her processing power. That was probably why Tyra Chityothin had cropped up now when the team had never heard of her while battling Helene over the last several years. Since Helene no longer had the vast control that she'd possessed before, she'd summoned Tyra from the shadows to pick up the slack, something that she had already proven herself to be more than capable of doing.

CJ wasn't sure he knew what his point was. He would have to discuss it with the rest of the team. But if he was right, then Helene might have exposed a weakness. Without doubt, it was one that the AI had considered, but she'd obviously deemed whatever plans she had with Ndidi and her child more important than whatever flaw she might possess.

"C-J," Bethany called. One of her hands was raised as if hesitating to tap him. For her to even consider that meant that she had been trying to get his attention for a while.

This time CJ wasn't able to suppress the warmth creeping onto his cheeks. He dug his fingers into the soft leather couch to keep himself grounded. "I'm sorry," he apologized again. "Can … uh … you please repeat that?"

Bethany waved his apology away with a small smile. CJ was sure it was a real smile in that Bethany genuinely felt amused by his apology. But the smile didn't look natural. It was awkward, persisted a breath too long, and from the small twitches at the edge of her lips, CJ knew that—like him and every other person on the autism spectrum—Bethany found it difficult to coordinate her facial muscles for something so delicate.

It's not fair, he thought, suddenly angry. It was obvious Bethany had put a lot of practice into it. That alone made her smile more real than any smile anyone else had ever given. *Most people don't even try. They don't need to, and yet—*

CJ gripped the leather couch, grounding himself before he went into another spiral.

"I … um … said," Bethany repeated, "what is going to … uh … happen to them?"

"Nothing," he replied, and because that sounded harsh, he explained further. "Helene … um … was never actually defeated, which … uh … which *means* that she never really went anywhere. My thought is that … um … in the moment when she took over Manar's body, she … um … she lost the processing power that connected her to the picospores, and the … um … abruptness of that is what damaged their minds."

"What does … uh … that mean?"

It means they can't get any more damaged. "It … um … means that the worst has already passed," CJ said. "Hermione started working on a new batch of spores that … uh … might fix the damage in their minds. But she had to stop when … um … when we realized that Helene wasn't truly defeated."

"Because she could just … uh … take control of them again," Bethany said.

CJ nodded. He didn't mention that the point was moot since the AI already had a production facility in Nigeria.

Bethany's gaze was distant for a moment before she shook her head to clear it. "Um … what did you mean," she asked slowly, as if she didn't know how to phrase the question, "that Helene … uh … took over Manar's body? Specifically … um … how is that possible?"

CJ shook his head. "We … uh … we don't know," he replied, "but Helene assured Ndidi that he is safe."

"And you … um … believed her?" Bethany asked, incredulously.

CJ shrugged. "There is no reason … uh … for her to have lied. That would mean she … um … actually sees us as a threat." Bethany calmed down at that. She more than anyone would understand how little Helene considered them.

"Anyway, we … uh … believe that Helene trapped Manar in the Virtual Realm, and … um … and we are going to try to rescue him. That is … uh … why I'm here."

Bethany became solemn. "How can I … um … help?"

CJ hesitated, unsure of how to ask his next question. But he needed to know. It was the minimum he needed to know to confirm if his plan was viable. His face hardened. "How strong … um … of a connection did you and … uh … Helene have?" he asked finally.

Bethany flinched. "W-what?"

CJ pushed past the guilt. "When you … um … when you were her captive, how strong of a connection did the both of you have? With … uh … the pico-spores, I mean."

"What sort of … uh … question is that?"

"It is … um … important, please," CJ pressed. "I am … uh … going to return to the Virtual Realm to find Manar, but … um … but just wandering aimlessly in there could take years. I need a way … uh … to narrow down the places to search."

"And you … um … you want to do that by using a connection to Helene, the one … uh … in the spores she used to control me," Bethany surmised. "Um … isn't that the same thing that Manar did to track Helene and … uh … for her to spy on you while in the Virtual Realm?"

CJ grimaced internally. "It is … um … different."

Bethany crossed her arms. "It is … uh … more stupid. I agree"

"It is *different* because Helene is now trapped in Manar's body," he said. "That means she has no connection to the Virtual Realm or … uh … or to the picospores. And … um … and that means she cannot use them to spy on me or track me while I am there."

Bethany frowned. "But … um … if she doesn't have a connection to them, then … uh … then why are the picospores necessary?"

"I do not need an active connection since I am not trying to find Helene," CJ explained. "But I plan on using the connection in your picospores as a … um … a *dowser*. In theory, it should allow me to … uh … to identify places where Helene has stayed for a significant amount of time."

"Because Manar is … uh … likely to be in one of those places," Bethany finished for him and CJ nodded. "But you can do that with the picospores from any of her former thralls."

"No, it … um … *has* to be yours," he blurted.

"W-why?"

CJ didn't reply immediately. He searched for what to say. Unfortunately, his hesitation made Bethany suspicious. She frowned at him, and then her eyes widened in realization. CJ frowned.

"Helene … um … programmed my spores to suspend the traits that put me on the autism spectrum," she said. "That is … uh … what you're after."

CJ still didn't say anything, but he sighed. This was another thing he should have seen coming. He'd hesitated in order to come up with a good answer, but it was already too late.

"I'm right, r-right?" Bethany pressed.

"There is … um … no danger from me using your picospores," CJ said slowly, "because, Helene—"

"B-because, Helene is more … uh … limited while she is in Manar's body," Bethany interrupted. "But it has been, what, uh … less than a week since we got attacked by a woman with her own army of picospore-controlled thralls?"

"Your spores were programmed … um … directly by Helene," CJ said. "So Tyra Chityothin does not have the ability to control—"

"But you … uh … you don't know that, do you?" Bethany cut in once more, louder this time. "Because you … uh … you *can't* know that. You're just guessing. You're … you're *hoping* she doesn't."

She was right, of course. While CJ was confident in his theory, he couldn't be absolutely sure Tyra Chityothin couldn't take control of spores previously programmed by Helene. And because he couldn't know, there was a risk. The danger was reduced by the fact that Tyra Chityothin had no way of knowing he would be going to the Virtual Realm. That was a point that CJ could have used to argue with Bethany, but both of them knew it wouldn't work. The risk in the Virtual Realm wasn't the point. The problem was CJ coming back with picospores still swimming in his veins.

He closed his eyes. "P-please," he begged. "I … um … need this."

"W-why?" Bethany asked, leaning closer. "Why is … uh … this so important to you?"

"You of all people … um … shouldn't be asking me this," he said. "You know, more than … uh … anyone else, how … um … how *frustrating* it is to stutter through every sentence, or pause while you search for the right word. You know how *vexing* it is … um … to have to constantly and deliberately keep yourself grounded so that you do not … uh … lose yourself in your thoughts. And you, more … um … more than everyone else, knows how h-h-humiliating it is to try to smile and have your face freeze in the middle of it even though you practiced and practiced. And even … um … even when you get it right, there's always something off about it."

"You're r-r-right," Bethany said, "I do know. And yes, it sucks. It sucks a lot. But those traits are … uh … a part of you, CJ. They … um … they contributed to making you the person you are right now, and … uh … and even if you 'cure' them, that isn't going to change. So isn't it better to … um … embrace them?"

"No," CJ said quietly, "it isn't. Not … um … when it can be cured. I'm sorry. I was wrong … uh … when I said you would understand. You *do* understand. But only a part of it. Because after you were held captive by Helene, you … um … found something you hated more than the thought of your autistic traits. I … um … in contrast, while in the Virtual Realm, found out who I could be without them. Ironically, that is something that we have to thank … um … Helene for."

CJ wondered if she was angry. It was probably insensitive to suggest Helene deserved any sort of thanks, but it was also the truth. Without the AI, neither of them would have discovered these new parts of themselves. Eventually, Bethany spoke up. "What part of yourself … um … did you find in the Virtual Realm?"

CJ stared at a spot over her shoulders. "A part … um … that can look at people's eyes, for one. A part … um … that could actually handle problems by itself without relying on my brother. A part … um … that wasn't so timid and quiet. A part … um … that could *fight.*" He chuckled. He couldn't fight well, but at least he'd held his own in the Virtual Realm and, toward the end of his time there, defeated bots easily. Mostly through the power of the orb, but CJ still thought that it should count.

"You think … uh … that side of you is better?" Bethany meant it as a statement, not a question, but CJ nodded anyway. He *knew* that part of him was better. It was the first time he'd felt competent, like he was in control of something.

And even disregarding everything else, that feeling alone was important after a lifetime trapped in a body that he could barely control. He said as much to Bethany.

"As important as that feeling is … uh … to you, you … um … you might still lose that control if and when Helene turns you into one of her … um … her thralls. You know that, right?"

"I understand the … um … danger."

"No, you … um … you don't," Bethany said, leaning closer. "You don't know what you are saying. You can't know, until you … uh … until you experience Helene's fog descending on your mind, *smothering* your thoughts. You can't know until … uh … you fall asleep in one place and wake up in another with … um … your whole body stinging from bruises that you cannot remember getting. It is impossible to know until, you're standing there … uh … with your hands stained with blood, desperately searching through your memories to have an idea, *any* idea, of where you've been or what you've been doing."

CJ was silent for a while. She was right. But CJ wasn't going to change his mind. He might have been wrong, but it was still something he had to do. "You're not going to … um … help me, are you?"

"No, I will," Bethany replied and CJ's head shot up. She continued. "I genuinely think that you … uh … are making a mistake. However, my sister and Ndidi also thought that I was making a mistake when I … uh … extracted the picospores from myself, and … um … and I still stand by that was the best decision that I have ever made. It would be worse than hypocritical of me … uh … to take your decision from you."

CJ almost leaped to hug her, but his whole body tensed the moment the thought occurred to him. But even that couldn't reduce his excitement. Granted, Bethany probably thought that he was an idiot. But she was still willing to help, which was more than he could say about anyone else, including his brother.

Bethany stared at him. "So, what … uh … do I have to do?"

CJ LEFT THE ISOLATION CHAMBER, his face somewhat stiff as he navigated his way through the hallways to the elevator. He walked close to the wall. His fingers touched the hard surface to keep him grounded and out of his head. Most people, when they felt an excess of joy or excitement, felt the urge to dance or run. But if CJ allowed himself to bask in his emotions, he might become too tense to walk properly.

At any other point, that thought might have made him angry, and it still did, but not nearly enough to get him out of his good mood. The elevator was crowded when it arrived—unusual since Sparta generally kept its employees confined to specific departments on their floor.

He stared at the press of bodies squeezed inside.

CJ would have usually stood aside and waited for another, but the growing excitement surged through him. Unable to wait any longer, CJ squeezed himself past the throng of people and crushed the small whine that built up in his throat from the sensory overload. He pressed the button for the seventieth floor, where Manar's office was located.

He wanted to begin the plan right away, but CJ suppressed that part him. Starting too early would just increase the chance of him getting caught. CJ had a system, and he was going to follow it—that is, assuming he didn't have an episode in the middle of the elevator.

This was a stupid idea, he thought, as he shifted away from the woman beside him. This just pushed him into the elevator wall. CJ splayed his fingers over the cool metal and used it to ground himself. *This is what happens when you allow your excitement to lead you to stupid decisions.*

It was a learning experience, one he needed to learn fast.

The elevator dinged a minute later. CJ wriggled out through the crowd until he was out. He stood there, dusting himself off and pushing back the episode that climbed up his throat. He'd never liked being touched, not by anybody. It was one of the fastest ways to trigger an episode. Touching made him feel like someone else was exercising control over his body. It hadn't been a problem in ages, mostly because CJ had become an expert at avoiding situations that might cause it.

Except, of course, in those cases when he made an impulsive decision to jump into an elevator filled with people.

CJ didn't move until he was sure that he had himself under control. Manar's office was locked and guarded by two security guards. CJ simply flashed the pass card that the real Manar had given him months before when they were preparing to go to the Virtual Realm. CJ shut the door behind him but stood at the threshold for a minute. The office was where he and Manar had set up everything they needed to go to the Virtual Realm, and he'd lain in the lab down the hall from Hermione's for several months while their avatars battled Helene. During that time, DJ and the rest of the team had converted the lab into a temporary hospital where they could monitor him and Manar. Most of the hospital equipment had been returned. But everything else had been moved back into Manar's office after Helene's return.

The office space now looked like a hospital storage closet, with heart monitors and two foldable beds forgotten in a corner. Someone had tried to return the table to its original spot, though sat out of alignment with the rest of the furniture. The discrepancy annoyed CJ the moment he noticed it. Without even realizing it, he was pushing the table back to where it was supposed to be, then picking up the loose pieces of paper and other trash that had been lying on the floor for the last few months.

Ten minutes later, the worst of the mess had been cleaned up, leaving only the equipment that he and Manar had set up for their upload. CJ inspected each device carefully. He would be using them soon and needed to ensure their integrity. He was pleased to see the device Ndidi had sabotaged had been recalibrated.

There was another risk though. It wasn't one that CJ was willing to acknowledge yet, not even to himself.

As CJ tested the devices, his motions were smooth with familiarity. The only time he paused was when he got to the neural uplink—or at least where the uplink was supposed to be.

CJ's hands froze over the empty space. His fingers twitched as if he couldn't believe the thing he was supposed to grab wasn't there. CJ took a step back and scanned the room. It wasn't there. Still, he spent an hour going through everything once more just in case he was wrong.

He wasn't.

CJ got out his phone.

CJ: Do you … um … know where the neural uplink is?

DJ: The what?

CJ: You know that thing … um … that Manar asked us to get last year? We had to use … uh … dad's old motorcycle to get it, and we got chased by Helene's drones while coming back.

DJ: I'm sorry, bro. It's not ringing a bell.

CJ sighed.

CJ: We had to use … uh … the nuclear weapon that you stole from Admiral Olsen to defeat the drones.

DJ: Oh, you mean the Bulldog. Oh yeah! I remember that. It was a wild ride, even though you were being boring. Why're you bringing that up? You thinking of getting out dad's motorcycle again?

CJ face-palmed. *If he wasn't my brother …*

CJ: The device … um … that we had to retrieve for Manar, the neural uplink—it looked like a pair of headphones. Do you … um … know where it is?

DJ: Nah, bro. I haven't seen it since we dropped it off. Didn't you and Manar use it for the whole Virtual Realm gig? I remember you saying it was really important and stuff.

CJ switched off his phone. It seemed unlikely the neural uplink had simply gotten misplaced when the hospital equipment was being removed. No one besides the team was allowed into the office. For that same reason, the uplink could only have been taken by someone who had access to the room. It wasn't him, so that left Manar.

In order words, Helene.

That made more sense. She would have known that the team would have needed the uplink to return to the Virtual Realm and rescue Manar. She'd nipped that plan in the bud before they even realized it was a problem. Without the neural uplink, CJ had no way of returning to the Virtual Realm, and Manar would remain at Helene's mercy until she decided to release him, or worse. For everyone else, that would have been the end of it. However, CJ had worked closely with Manar while the genius designed the neural uplink. Because of what he'd learned from Manar and from the Virtual Realm, CJ was more than confident he could replicate the technology.

All he needed was enough time.

He texted Bethany that their plan would have to be delayed a few days, and then he sent another one to his brother, updating him on the missing uplink. After that, CJ rushed down to his room, collected his tools, returned to Manar's office, and locked himself inside.

CJ took a seat on the chair. For the first time that day, he deliberately allowed his thoughts to spiral.

DJ LEAPED AWAY FROM KARLA, breathing hard. The redhead let him go. Although she was breathing normally, DJ thought he could make out a light sheen of sweat on her forehead. He grinned, wanting to believe a small part of her now-deeping sneer was pride in disguise.

"A few more of these, and I might actually be able to repay you for all these bruises." He stretched, and then winced as over a dozen sore spots protested the treatment. A few bones popped. The sound echoed through the empty gym.

Karla snorted. "It is good to have such hope. Maybe it will push you to move faster than a sloth."

DJ chuckled. "It's just a matter of time."

Karla didn't say anything to that. She couldn't, not when they both knew it was the truth. It'd only been a few days since they'd started this training, but DJ was almost twice his former top speed. He hadn't managed to hit her yet—or even touch her clothes—but he'd gotten better at anticipating her attacks. Even more importantly, he'd started developing his own unique fighting style that made the most of his strengths. He'd been using Karla's techniques ever since the nanites powered him up, but that just made it easier for the redhead to trounce him up and down the gym floor. Even with his new style in the beginning stages, Karla had to work more to get hits in.

Relatively, at least. She still had a tendency to cheat and accelerate when she got too impatient.

"Should we call it a day?" he asked.

Karla gave a single nod. "There is something you need to see," the redhead responded.

"Oh?" DJ straightened from his stretch, and his nanites went to work on his sore muscles. Over the last few days, Karla had taught him that the nanites could heal anything that wasn't severely damaged. The effect wasn't instant, but DJ would recover several times faster than normal. Small wounds and bruises that might have healed in a few days would be fixed in one. Sore muscles from torture disguised as a workout would need only a few minutes. "Where are we headed?"

Several days ago, he'd offered to get Karla a room at the headquarters. In response, she'd knocked him in the ribs. DJ still didn't know what about his offer had triggered her crazy, but he guessed he was about to find out.

Karla simply sheathed her knives and started walking out of the gym. They rode the elevator down in silence. It was the middle of the day, so the ground floor was packed. Some of them were staff of Sparta, but the majority were guests trying to get to the upper floors.

All of them stopped when DJ and Karla stepped into the room. It didn't happen all at once. Someone would glance up and catch his eye, then nudge their friend, who also glanced over and drew the attention of others, and on and on.

DJ sighed. It'd been a little over two weeks since Tyra had attacked Sparta. It wasn't nearly enough time for the rumors about him to die down. Most of the public knew him as one of the principal defenders in the attack and the reason that the headquarters hadn't fallen, even when the numbers said it should have.

The Sparta staff knew a little more. Their eyes were filled with respect and admiration but also disbelief and just a hint of fear.

DJ didn't know how to deal with it. Most times, he stayed in his room, except when he was with Karla at the gym or when he went down to Manar's office to give his brother some food.

All of it was ruined now, though, as Karla strutted ahead, glaring at everyone who looked at her. Her open hostility drew attention away from him, at least until he saw Karla's fingers inching toward her sides, demanding he interfere.

"Why were those people staring at you?" Karla asked, after DJ had hurried her out of the building. It was snowing, and everyone on the street was bundled up in sweaters under jackets. DJ was still wearing his damp gym shirt. But the cold didn't touch him.

DJ sighed. "I had to use my new abilities during the attack on Sparta. A bunch of people saw. Word spread and got exaggerated in the spreading."

Karla nodded as if she understood. And hell, she probably did. She'd already admitted she wasn't shy about hiding what she could do. Such an attitude meant that, eventually, people would take notice.

She turned into an alley and started jogging at a pace that was faster than most runners could sustain for long. DJ sighed but followed easily. There wasn't anyone in the alley, so it wasn't like there was any risk of being seen. *At least she's not being an idiot about it*, he thought.

"People are fascinated by things they do not understand," Karla said. "Then they become afraid and break those things."

DJ didn't say anything because he didn't know how to deal with Karla when she was actually being thoughtful and not a crazy psychopath. And she was right. People became incredibly stupid about things they didn't understand. DJ's nanites, and what he could do with them, fell smack-dab into that category. Right now he was lucky. CJ had erased the tapes immediately after the battle, and Olsen and Christy had been downplaying the stories from the guards as figments of adrenaline-induced hysteria—confusion in the chaos of the battle. But obviously that wasn't going to hold for long. DJ didn't doubt that he'd have to use his abilities in public again before the whole thing with Helene was settled.

DJ didn't have a problem keeping up, even after they maintained the pace for over ten minutes. A part of him celebrated the fact that a year ago he would have been gasping for breath in half that time. They stuck to the backroads and alleys for the most part, jumping over fences and walls and scaling buildings when they reached a dead end. The first time they reached the end of an alley network, Karla turned into a blur and ran out into the street. She moved so fast that DJ could barely see her. Normal people definitely couldn't. Even cameras wouldn't have been able to pick her up. He hesitated for a second, sighed, and followed her. DJ couldn't match her speed, but he was more than fast enough to breeze through the traffic without being seen.

The next network of alleys was too narrow to run through, made worse by all the garbage bags and broken crates lying around. Karla growled the second time she almost tripped on something, but she still scaled a wall with the ease of a cockroach. DJ watched as she climbed for a few feet, then kicked off the wall to grab an air conditioner vent, jumped to the opposite wall, kicked off *that*, and then somehow shimmed up the wall until she got to the edge and flipped herself over it.

DJ deflated. He could scale walls, sure. That was basic Marine stuff. But they used specialized climbing gear. Shit, even a grappling hook would have helped here. What kind of fool climbed a wall in 2043 with their bare hands?

Karla leaned over the edge of the roof and glared down at him. DJ sighed. *I guess the me kind of fool.* He scanned the alleyway for anything he to aid him. The ground was filled with broken bottles, empty, rotten wooden crates, and garbage bags that occasionally made questionable noises. DJ sighed once more as he made his way to the same wall Karla had used.

It was easy to find her handholds and easier than he'd expected to pull himself up using them. DJ wasn't as ripped as some bodybuilders, but he was pretty up there in weight, especially after the nanites enhanced his bone density and muscles. Still, there wasn't much strain on his fingers as he pulled himself up the wall, switching from handhold to handhold. Eventually he got to the point where Karla had parkoured the rest of the way up. *No, thanks,* he thought, sticking to handholds and slowly pulling himself up until he reached the roof.

Karla was sharpening her daggers when he got there. Fortunately, all she did was glare at him before continuing. Unfortunately, the parkour lessons weren't over. The rooftops were wider than the alleys. Somehow they were more annoying to transverse.

At least for DJ.

Karla easily jumped over the air vents and skylights that dotted the roofs. She used the chimneys and pipes as handholds, not even noticing the sloping or uneven roofs. Her movements were smooth, casual, and entirely efficient. She kept the same pace as she had when they were taking the alleys. DJ, meanwhile, bumbled his way through the obstacles with just slightly more grace than an elephant. Where Karla vaulted over or went through obstacles, DJ went around. Where she ignored the slippery terrain or kept her balance through sheer momentum, DJ slowed down so he didn't trip. He spent so much energy trying not to fall that, for the first time, he started noticing the strain catching up to him. That slowed him down even more.

Eventually Karla noticed his difficulty and slowed her pace. But even then, the distance between them steadily increased from one rooftop to two, then to the point that he could only barely see her in the distance. DJ followed as best he could, moving in a straight line even when he could no longer see her. Several minutes passed. DJ was starting to consider turning back. Karla had obviously lost her patience and left him. More than likely, even if DJ *did* catch up, she'd just get pissed and attack him.

A whistle on the wind made him turn around, just in time to find the business end of a knife heading for his face. DJ crouched without thought, and the knife sailed over his head. He punched out. Karla easily kicked his fist away. DJ rolled backward to create some distance between them, but the redhead didn't follow.

She snarled at him instead. "You are pathetic. Are you so scared of death?"

"Who the fuck isn't?" DJ retorted instinctively. The bulk of his mind was still trying to figure out how she'd gotten behind him. She must have made a wide arc so DJ didn't see her. Maybe she'd dropped down to the street level and then run back? Either way, it showed how slow he must have been moving.

"Good," Karla nodded. DJ felt a chill run down his spine. She pointed over the edge of the roof with one of her daggers. "If you fall, you will not die. You have only passed the first threshold. You might break a bone, but most likely not." She pointed the dagger at him, and her scowl turned into a wicked smile. "However, my babies will rend your flesh and saw through your bones with one swipe. Choose."

DJ gaped. "Choose what, you psycho? What the hell are you—"

Karla lunged at him.

Motherf—

DJ jumped backward, narrowly avoiding having his throat slit. Karla pulled back. She was slow, slower than him, but just by a bit. Immediately, DJ understood what she was doing, and he let loose every curse word he'd ever learned. He turned around, showing Karla his back—and when he wasn't immediately stabbed, it confirmed what he'd guessed.

She's fucking with me, he growled internally. Karla—rightly so—thought that DJ was moving so slowly because he was afraid of falling off and breaking his neck. So she had given him a choice: He could move fast enough to risk tripping and *maybe* breaking something, or he could continue to move slowly and get killed by her. DJ wasn't sure he believed he wasn't going to break a bone if he fell, and he was sure she wasn't going to kill him. However, there was no doubt in his mind that she would leave a few scars to teach him a lesson. He must have taken too long to start because Karla growled. In the same second, a line of fire burned its way across his back.

That was all the motivation that DJ needed.

The first few rooftops were hell. DJ moved as fast as he could, but each new line Karla added to his back told him he wasn't moving fast enough. But he *couldn't* move faster. Parkour required *flexibility* and *agility,* words that no one would ever attribute to DJ.

Karla growled again. "You're pathetic."

"What the fuck do you want from me?" DJ growled back. "I'm not a fucking gymnast or some bullshit stunt guy."

"No. You are better than those people. You just think too much." She punctuated her statements by adding another scar to his growing collection. DJ almost turned around and attacked her. He was *this* close. But as pissed as he was, he was used to her method of training. "It is why you are pathetic."

DJ seethed but didn't say anything. He would prove her wrong.

Who the fuck is she to call me pathetic or say I think too much? What sort of insult even is that?

DJ sped up. She always did that. She insulted him for no reason. In a week, he'd gone from barely being able to see her attacks to being able to anticipate them and even react instinctively. Sure, she slowed down for his benefit, but DJ knew that his progress was impressive. Would it kill her to say that once in a while?

No, she would rather insult him. DJ vaulted over a chimney. He stumbled on his landing but picked up his speed just in time to avoid being sliced open again. Sometimes he thought the only reason Karla had agreed to train him was to cut him whenever she wanted. She'd said she got antsy whenever she stayed without killing something for too long. And DJ knew for a fact she hadn't killed anything in a week. Maybe that's why she was taking it out on him.

DJ slipped, but he just sped up. His momentum carried him to the edge of the roof where he jumped to the next. His legs easily took the impact even without him needing to crouch. But some idiot had decided to start a vegetable garden in the middle of winter. It probably would have been merciful for DJ to run through it, but he jumped over it instead and then vaulted over a satellite dish. Because the snow reduced his visibility, DJ didn't see the HVAC unit until he was almost on top of it. Without thinking, he rolled over it. A knife stabbed through the metal where he'd just been. DJ fumed but increased his pace. Instinctively, his feet made micro-adjustments with each step until his tread was just as secure as if he were running on the ground.

"Left," Karla barked when he reached the edge of the roof. DJ ran across the thin ledge until he was close enough to jump across. Although it was a leap of close to ten feet, he cleared it easily and continued on. The next hour continued like that, with Karla yelling out directions every few minutes. Eventually, after several minutes of her being unable to get him, Karla started running alongside him. When DJ sped up, the redhead simply laughed, easily keeping pace.

At some point, after two hours of running, Karla jumped off the building without a word. DJ leaped after her without thinking and tried to grab her. For his troubles, he got two new scratches across his knuckles. The redhead landed easily on her feet, whereas DJ had to tuck and roll. He bounced to his feet immediately, frantically patting himself down. But there was nothing. He could feel a few bruises, but that was the worst of it. DJ stared up at the building. It was just a two-story apartment, but that was still about twenty feet. He had just fallen from it and was standing with nothing more than bruises.

"Now you begin to understand," Karla muttered beside him.

Yeah, he did.

They continued without a word, following alleyways and backroads like before. DJ had been able to keep pace with Karla before. He was still able to, even though she'd noticeably increased her speed. The only time he fell behind was when they, rather conspicuously, ran across the East River bridge. Karla barked out a location and sped off in a blur. DJ followed as fast as he could. While it wasn't much faster than his current speed, he was confident it was fast enough that no one would be able to make out his face.

They rendezvoused somewhere in Queens. By the time he got there, Karla was tapping her feet impatiently, snarling at anyone who came close. DJ made her wait several minutes while he caught his breath. Though they'd been running full tilt for close to three hours, Karla still looked like she'd just gone out for a jog, whereas DJ was bent over, hands on his knees, panting like a dog in the heat.

He straightened after a while and flicked the sweat off his forehead. *How long until I'm able to do that?* he wondered, glancing at her. That allowed him to see a faint glimmer of approval in her eyes. It was gone in the next second. But it was enough to have DJ grinning like a fool when they started up again. It didn't take long before he was out of steam again. Fortunately, they ran for only a few blocks before scaling another building.

Karla ran to the edge of the rooftop and perched on it like a bat. DJ caught up to her at a more moderate pace. He stopped behind her, trying to keep his breathing under control.

Without looking at him, she nodded at the building across the street. "That is our target." The target was a rundown factory that looked one stiff breeze away from tipping over.

"Okay … what am I looking at?"

"Several class A and B drones escaped here after you and your team rebuffed their attack on—"

"Wait. You were there?" DJ asked, incredulously. "And you didn't think to help out?"

"It was your test to pass or fail."

"Son of a—" DJ pinched the bridge of his nose. *It doesn't matter*, he told himself. *It doesn't matter. It's done now.* "What are these classes you mentioned?"

"The drones fall into three categories," Karla explained. "You are most familiar with class A. They are the smallest and make up the bulk of the AI's army. Class B drones are the largest, heavily armored. Class C drones fall between the other two in size. They carry and distribute the AI picospores."

"In that case, there were both class A and B drones during the attack." DJ frowned. "You're saying some of them escaped after being hit with the frequency generator? And they came here?"

Karla nodded. "Your law enforcement tried to carry them off, but they were too slow. Most of the drones rebooted in time to escape. They split off into several groups and in several directions. I could follow only one." She nodded again at the factory.

"Okay … I think I'm all caught up now. So what're you thinking?"

"The factory is one of the AI's drone production depots. We are going to destroy it."

"What? No! That's a dumb idea. Even if only a portion of the drones are in there, that's probably still hundreds of them," DJ reasoned. "Plus there's a chance Tyra is also there. If she is, we're going to get creamed. But even if she isn't we're still going to get creamed … just less."

Karla stood, and DJ immediately knew he'd said the wrong thing. "You think that she would defeat me?"

"Of course not," DJ backtracked immediately. "I'm just saying that there's no need to take such a risk. You said the drones all split off into different groups, right? That means the drones in the factory are just *part* of Helene's army. Sure, we can probably take it out, but it's not going to really do anything to her since she probably has a dozen other depots."

Karla snarled. "Then we will destroy those ones as well."

"Sure," DJ agreed, "but to what end?"

"No," Karla scowled, turning to face him, daggers first. "You are afraid that this woman, this *Tyra*, is stronger than I am, that I would lose to her."

"What? No! Where the hell did you get that?"

Karla spat on the ground. "You think that I am weak. Just like he did." She drew herself up to her full height. "I will prove you wrong."

And with that, she jumped off the building.

DJ rushed to the edge and watched her quickly descending form. *Fuck.*

CHAPTER

71

DECEMBER 2043

SPARTA HEADQUARTERS, NEW YORK

CJ CAME BACK TO HIMSELF SLOWLY as he put the finishing touches on the new neural uplink. He blinked, looking down at the device in his hand.

It's done? It's done!

He let out a breath, leaning back against the chair. On top of the table, the uplink glowed happily out of its sides. CJ had kept its original design, so it still looked like a pair of headphones, but everything inside was all him.

He'd duplicated Manar's feat.

CJ calmed himself before his excitement turned him into a block of wood. It was only an achievement if it worked. The original neural uplink had worked as a brain analyzer that examined the average frequencies of a person's brain, translating the results into codes that could be programmed and then uploaded onto the internet.

CJ needed to test out only the first part. He placed the headphones over his ears and connected one of the wires to the computer on the table. One side of the computer screen showed the graph readings from the uplink. The other side translated those readings into codes.

Perfect, CJ thought. He leaned back. All the exhaustion he'd ignored over the last few days had finally caught up to him. *How long have I been here?* The table and floor were littered with plastic wrap and plates. He knew he'd been eating, even though he couldn't remember precisely when and what.

He yawned. He should probably go to bed. He'd been awake for several days. His body was practically begging him for rest. But even if he lay down for several hours, CJ knew he wasn't going to sleep. He was too excited. He was *so* close.

He sent a text to Bethany and then left Manar's office for the first time in days. The guards outside looked at him with confusion but didn't say anything. CJ made his way to the elevator—which was blessedly empty—and pushed the button for Hermione's floor. His excitement had taken a backseat to nerves, which CJ had spent most of his life dealing with.

He pushed open the door to the lab. Hermione was still working, which he'd expected. She rarely ever took a break, at least of her own volition. When Ndidi was around, she would force Hermione outside at least once a week. CJ knew his brother had tried doing the same thing once or twice. But Hermione brushed off anyone else who tried to get her out of the lab.

Hopefully not everyone, he thought. Hermione hadn't noticed him yet even though CJ wasn't trying to be particularly quiet. She was bent over a microscope, peering at whatever was on the slide. A moment later, she made a frustrated huff and then transferred the slide to the room's nanoscope and inputted a command. A small screen ejected itself from the nanoscope and displayed the calibrations that the AI algorithm made in real time. Hermione stared at the image for a minute and then compared it to whatever she saw in the textbook's worth of notes arranged around her.

CJ cleared his throat, moved closer, and cleared his throat louder since she didn't respond the first time. The third time, Hermione jumped, looking startled. "CJ," she breathed in relief. Then her eyes turned angry. "Where the hell have you been? DJ said that *both* of us have to find a way to counter the new picospores. But I've been working on it *by myself* for close to a week, even though I hit a dead-end months ago." CJ flinched and tried to respond, but she wasn't done. "I looked everywhere for you. No one seemed to know where you were except your brother, and *he* seems to have disappeared too. Does it run in the family or something?"

He waited, but Hermione just looked at him with an expectant expression. "Um," CJ said hesitantly, "it does not. And I … uh … don't know where my brother is, but I was in Manar's office, working on … um … an idea that might help bring him back."

That took the wind out of her sails. "Oh," she said, deflating. "Well, how'd it go?"

CJ scratched his head. "I'm still … um … working on it. It looks feasible. You said you needed my help with something?"

"Desperately," Hermione said. "I have been analyzing the small amount of picospores we managed to extract from some of the Dead Eyes that attacked us a few weeks ago. I do not understand a thing. And I am losing my mind over it. The basic structure of the spores is the same. However, Helene has …"

CJ stood beside her and bent over some of her notes. While he acted as though he was listening to her explanation, most of his mind was drowning in anticipation. *Where is she?* If he were a dog, his ears would have been upright and pointed at the door, while the rest of his head stared straight ahead at Hermione, who was gesturing in frustration at the nanoscope. CJ stared at the screen absentmindedly.

Suddenly, his eyes widened. "Are … uh … are they replicating themselves?"

"Right? *Right?* I'm not just going crazy. They're building new spores from a drop of blood."

How is this even possible? CJ thought. He moved closer to the screen. The image was blurry—the picospores were smaller, so the nanoscope AI algorithm couldn't properly calibrate the image. But even then, what CJ was seeing shouldn't have been possible. The picospores—several million of them—swam in a medium of blood, which they tore apart to build more versions of themselves.

The process was slow. CJ was sure there were a lot of things he was missing. Nevertheless, it was happening right in front of his eyes.

"Ndidi … um … spoke about this," CJ muttered.

"Yeah, she said Helene did something similar. But that was with nanites creating picospores. That was fantastical enough. I could somehow wrap my head around it. But now picospores are synthesizing other picospores? That is so far out of their design I can't even fathom how Helene did that. Do you know what this means? What could it mean? Do you understand what it could do?"

Of course, CJ did. Probably not as much as Hermione, but enough. And even that was scary. Synthesizing or replicating themselves using a host's microelements—that was how viruses reproduced. And the picospores were doing that too.

Hermione was pacing, her arms wrapped around her head. Now that she had someone to talk to, the panic she'd been holding back was checked. "Now you can see why I've been losing my mind. If this got out … I mean, if she found a way to mass-produce this. What am I talking about? She's already mass-producing it. But to what end? Is she trying to start an apocalypse?"

"No," CJ muttered, oddly numb. "She's trying to … uh … take over the world."

A knock on the door interrupted whatever Hermione was going to say. Bethany poked her head in.

"Bethany," Hermione breathed. CJ felt as though he'd been dunked in cold water. In the span of a few minutes, he'd forgotten the entire reason he'd come to the lab. Hermione stared at her sister. She took a step toward the door and then stopped. Her hands dropped to her sides and then immediately went to her hair, picking away the strands that were strewn across her face. She dusted herself off and attempted to straighten her rumpled clothes.

For her part, Bethany wasn't any better. She was tense enough that she could have been mistaken for a block of ice.

CJ immediately felt guilty. Both sisters hadn't seen each other for several months, and it was obvious that neither of them knew how to handle it. Bethany might not have been ready to talk to her sister, but she'd agreed to because CJ had selfishly asked her to without considering how it might affect her.

"H-hey, sis," Bethany replied, trying an awkward smile. "Can I … uh … talk to you?"

Hermione brightened. "Sure, of course. We can ta—"

"In … um … private?" Bethany cut in.

CJ had already turned back to the nanoscope and pretended to be engrossed in the picospores shown on the screen, but he could feel Hermione's gaze on him.

"Um, sure," she said. "We can talk outside."

CJ didn't turn back—he didn't move until he heard the door open and close and then the sisters faintly talking on the other side.

He immediately sprang into action. It was easy to find the different spore extraction tanks, but it took him a minute to locate the memory of Hermione explaining which tank contained which version of the picospores. Bethany had been kidnapped during Mayday, but when Helene had controlled her, she hadn't shown any of the obvious signs of the first and second spore iterations. That meant that Helene had inoculated her with only the third batch of the spores which was stored … *there.*

CJ made his way toward the tank, picking up the mini-tank on his way. He shot frequent looks at the door. He didn't know how long Bethany would be able to keep Hermione distracted, but if he wasn't done by then, CJ doubted he would ever get another chance. His brother would never let him out of his sight. Fortunately, CJ had planned out his movements extensively in his mind.

He dropped the mini-tank beside the larger tank and connected the two. There were billions of spores within the spore extraction tank. It was impossible to know which ones had been Bethany's, so CJ transferred them all into the mini-tank and carried it back to the counter, where he hooked it up to a computer. He took out a flash drive from his pocket and plugged it into one of the ports. A second later, the monitor showed a progress bar as the search program he'd placed in the drive executed.

The program finished. Another progress bar replaced it, this time showing the search completion rate. CJ watched it for a moment and then opened another tab on the computer to activate another program.

DJ's worry—along with Bethany's, Hermione's, and everyone else's—was that, by injecting the picospores within himself, CJ would be opening himself up to Helene's control. He knew that he was being impatient and reckless. But he wasn't an idiot. The risks could be planned for and minimized as long as he put enough thought into his plan.

And CJ had put *a lot* of thought into this.

The search completion rate had just hit 20 percent when the other program finished. CJ opened it immediately, took a moment to review it, and then started editing it. It was the program he'd created when they'd been trying to use the picospores to find Tyra Chityothin. CJ had designed it to systematically take control of groups of spores, erase their original commands so that they didn't self-destruct, and then attack another group. The end goal was to trace the spores' connections to their source. However, that wasn't CJ's goal today.

All he needed was the first part: taking control of the spores.

Time flew by as CJ cut out everything from the code that wasn't needed. Several times he had to stop and ground himself so he didn't spiral and lose sense of the world. Allowing that to happen probably would have made him go faster, but he needed to be aware in case the sisters came back early.

A few minutes later, CJ inputted the last few keystrokes just as the program finished its search. Several groups of spores were highlighted on the monitor. He isolated those groups and ran the edited program through them. Another progress bar came up, this time tracking how much of the group his program had taken control of. CJ couldn't start the next part until this was completed.

Now all he could do was wait.

CHAPTER

72

DECEMBER 2043
SPARTA HEADQUARTERS, NEW YORK

BETHANY LOOKED AT HER SISTER OUT of the corner of her eye. It was the first time she had seen her in months. She didn't know why, but she'd expected something to have changed since their last argument. But Hermione still looked the same: tired, frazzled, and hopped up on too much coffee.

The nervousness is new though, Bethany thought somewhat hypocritically; she was drowning in the same emotion, so much so that every time she moved, she half expected to hear creaks in her joints. A part of her regretted agreeing to this. She obviously wasn't ready for this conversation. But it was a small part. While she didn't necessarily agree with CJ's decision, she respected it. She felt that it was her duty to help where she could to see that he achieved his dream.

That was what she'd wanted for herself.

"Hey," Hermione said finally. Her voice was soft, hesitant as if she knew she had to say something but not what. That was fine. Bethany didn't know what to say either. "How've you been?"

"Good," Bethany replied. "The attack … um … was rough. Fortunately, the isolation chamber was originally a safe room, so we didn't have to move. That … um … that made it easier. The major problem was keeping everyone calm with the crowd and the noise. But we managed. And I … uh … I finally managed to get through to Tabitha."

Tabitha had been one of Bethany's closest friends when they'd all been held by Helene. Unfortunately she was one of those that had been affected after Helene's defeat. Since then, she'd been unresponsive to everything Bethany had tried. However, she'd finally gotten through to her during the attack.

"That's awesome." Hermione smiled. It was an awkward smile, the type that adults gave to kids when they wanted to pretend they were listening even though their minds were elsewhere. Bethany had gotten a lot of those as a child. She wondered if Hermione even remembered who Tabitha was. "Not the attack, of course. That was terrifying. But the thing about Tabitha. It shows she's improving, right? What else has been happening?"

Bethany told her. It wasn't a lot. She spent most of her days in the isolation chamber. That didn't allow for much variety in her schedule. Bethany could have summarized her last few months in a few words. And she wanted to. Hermione didn't care anyway. She was just trying to be nice. Her job was to keep her sister distracted while CJ did his thing inside.

Bethany went into as much detail as she could. Her story was filled with several pauses while Bethany tried to find the right word in her mind or locate the right memory. Apart from her conversation with CJ, Bethany hadn't spoken so much in months. This made her stuttering worse than normal.

"W-what have you … um … been up to?" she asked when she couldn't think of anything else to say. "I … uh … I heard that Helene is back somehow. What's … um … up with that?"

Hermione sighed. "She's not so much back as she never left. We just thought that she did because that's what she wanted us to think, and that's what we wanted to believe."

Bethany knew this already since CJ had told her. But she still arranged her face into a frown and asked, "What … um … do you mean?"

Hermione spent the next ten minutes explaining everything that had happened over the past few months while Bethany tried her best to mimic the emotions she felt when CJ had told her the first time.

"It sounds like … um … you have been working hard," Bethany said when she was done. "You … uh … need to rest. You have bags under your eyes."

"You're probably right," Hermione breathed out. "Lately I've been feeling like I'm losing my mind." Her eyes widened, and she stared at Bethany in horror. When Bethany realized why, it immediately made her angry. She could deal with her sister's condescension, but she couldn't deal with her pity or with Hermione looking at her as if she were made of glass.

Bethany glared at her sister. "This is … um … why we don't talk anymore. Because … uh … because, you still treat me like I'm something delicate … like … like I'm going to break with every small thing. Do you … um … know how demeaning that is?"

"Bethany, that's not—"

"Yes, it is," Bethany insisted. "Just now, you thought that … um … that I would be offended by what you said. I passed that stage ages ago, Hermione, but … um … you wouldn't know that, because you … uh … weren't there, were you?"

"Bethany …"

"I … um … don't regret it, you know," Bethany continued.

Hermione tensed.

CHAPTER

73

DECEMBER 2043

SPARTA HEADQUARTERS,
NEW YORK

CJ HAD HIS HANDS ON THE KEYBOARD the moment the progress bar hit a hundred percent. The spores had been fully converted—reprogrammed by him with upgraded defenses to prevent Helene from reclaiming control. If she wanted to regain control, she'd have to break through both individual and collective layers of protection. It was CJ's job to make sure that wasn't possible. He took a deep breath. His fingers had become stiff while he was waiting. CJ flexed them absentmindedly while reviewing the code structure for the picospores.

He'd seen them several times over the years. Each time he was able to understand just a bit more of what Helene had done. After he'd come back from the Virtual Realm, however, the wool over his eyes had been removed. CJ now had no difficulty reading Helene's codes. It was what had allowed him to develop a program to take control of the spores in the first place—something that he wasn't sure even Manar could have done before they'd gone to the Virtual Realm.

CJ pushed the thought aside as his fingers flew over the keyboard. The code sequence for one spore was identical to that of the entire group, so any changes he made would apply to all of them. His task now was to edit the code and eliminate any footholds Helene could exploit to break back in. It wasn't easy—Helene had planted traps, loopholes, and redundancies everywhere—but CJ's deep familiarity with her methods gave him an edge. Even more importantly, CJ had greatly advanced his skills after returning from the Virtual Realm, making him far better equipped to deal with her sabotage.

Whenever he thought about his time there, CJ generally focused on how his experiences had forced him to create, or maybe reveal, a version of himself that he hadn't even known had existed: someone with a little more backbone and determination, someone with the ability to take care of himself without help.

But even so, the entire Virtual Realm had been a goldmine for advancing his knowledge. CJ had never actually had the time to study the things he'd seen. But just passively observing and interacting with the different tapestries that made up the Virtual Realm had opened his mind in ways he hadn't even realized until he'd returned. It'd taken his skill to a level that was previously exclusive to Manar and Helene.

In a lot of ways, CJ had been reborn in the Virtual Realm. Maybe that was why it'd hit him so hard when he'd learned that it was all a ploy by Helene. Even if it was, that didn't diminish what CJ had gained while there. If anything, it was the AI's mistake.

And CJ would prove that—by surpassing her.

His fingers flew over the keyboard in a blur, cutting out everything that might be linked to Helene. Some of the traps were obvious and had probably been put there by the AI to draw attention from the more subtle loopholes. He cut out both easily. Helene had tied some traps to core areas within the sequence. CJ couldn't delete those without risking the code's integrity. For that, he created new sequences entirely and replaced the trapped sections with his own.

Several times CJ had to catch himself before he got lost in his work. With his flow broken, he slowed down. Despite that, it took him only a few minutes to complete his edits. CJ took a break, leaning back against the chair. The new code was spread out in front of him. He scrutinized it. His code was far simpler than the original, and he was sure he'd cut out several of the spore's abilities. But that was fine. He needed them to do only one thing: make him normal.

CJ spent a moment reviewing the changes before moving on to building the code's defenses.

In the Virtual Realm, CJ's go-to defense had been the nullification aura, which negated and eliminated anything he deemed offensive. Even just standing within the aura was enough to slowly destroy some programs. Unfortunately, the nullification aura had come from the orb. As much as CJ would have liked to imbue that ability into the spores, he couldn't.

Still, CJ had spent months with the orb. When he wasn't fighting for his survival, the bulk of his time had been spent analyzing the web of codes that made up the orb and each of its abilities. He wouldn't be able to replicate the nullification aura, but that didn't mean that CJ wouldn't be able to create something similar.

He cracked his knuckles.

CHAPTER

74

"WHAT DON'T YOU REGRET?" Hermione asked. Bethany narrowed her eyes. They both knew Hermione understood what she was talking about. But she was going to make Bethany say it. That was fine. Bethany would spell it out if that was what it took to get it through her sister's head.

"I … um … d-don't regret r-removing … uh … the p-picospores." Her anger made her stutter more, so Bethany slowed down her words. "It was … um … t-the best decision … uh … that I have ever made. H-Helene—"

"Jesus Christ! Listen to yourself, Bethany," Hermione snapped. "You're stuttering like you're having a seizure."

"I've … um … *a-always* s-s-stuttered, Hermione," Bethany countered. The angrier she got, the worse her stuttering became. Bethany took a deep breath and tried to calm herself down. There was no reason for her to be angry anyway. She'd known that this was how her sister would react. Maybe she'd thought that enough time had passed. Bethany shook her head. "I've … um … b-been s-stuttering since I was a child. Did … uh … did y-you hate me then?"

Hermione flinched like she'd been slapped. "What the hell are you even saying? Of course I didn't hate you. And I don't hate you now. You're my sister, for Christ's sake."

"If you … um … if y-you accepted me then, why … uh … can you not a-accept me now?" Bethany asked softly. It was a question Bethany had wanted to ask for a while. Growing up, Hermione had always been loving and understanding about Bethany being on the autism spectrum. Why had that changed?

Bethany held her breath while she waited for the answer.

"Because I don't understand it," Hermione replied after a pause, just as softly. "I don't understand why you would choose the stuttering and the memory gaps and the stigma over a life where you didn't have to go through all of that."

"Um … H-Helene—"

"I know," Hermione said, staring at her. "I *know* that Helene used the picospores to control you. I know that it was invasive and traumatic. I know that I would probably never be able to understand what you went through. But," she said, taking Bethany's hands, "we are going to defeat Helene. It's going to happen, sis. And when we do, the picospores are going to be safe. I'm going to create a set just for you. I've already studied how Helene cured you the first time, and I'm sure that I can—"

Bethany pulled her hands away. Her face was tense and, thus, expressionless. Bethany was glad for that. She didn't want to show Hermione how much her words had hurt her. She spoke slowly so she wouldn't stumble over her words. "Um … I will admit that … my initial reason for extracting … the picospores from myself was … because I couldn't bear … the thought of Helene using them against me again. But it didn't … take me long to realize that … that reason took a back seat to … uh … a much greater one."

Bethany met her sister's eyes. "Um … I don't need to be *cured*. Because there's … nothing wrong with me. Everything you mentioned, everything hardship that you listed, they … are a part of me. They … have shaped me throughout my life. They're … not symptoms of a disease … to be cured. They are *me*.

I thought … um … you would understand that, but I know now that you … uh … never will."

Hermione called after her. But Bethany was already walking away. She heard the laboratory door open and turned to see CJ stepping out of the room. He stopped when he saw Hermione in front of the door and said something to her. Bethany turned the corner. She'd completely forgotten she was supposed to keep her sister distracted. Fortunately, she'd bought enough time anyway.

CJ should have gotten what he wanted. Hopefully his brother would be more understanding about his choice than Hermione had been about hers.

CHAPTER

75

CJ LEFT HERMIONE STARING empty-eyed into the air. It was obvious the conversation with Bethany hadn't gone well. Usually CJ would have felt guilty for his role in it. But at the moment, he was buffeted by other emotions that took priority: joy, excitement, anxiety, and fear. The combination made it difficult to walk. Fortunately, Hermione was too distracted to notice.

The walk back to Manar's office passed like a drug-filled illusion as CJ tried to feel the picospores in his blood. He flipped his pass card to the guards in front of Manar's office and locked the door behind him. He didn't *feel* any different, but he knew the spores needed some time to acclimatize to his system before they started working on their commands.

It was only a matter of time.

CJ stared at the equipment set up around the room. He cocked his head in thought. If he had a few hours to kill, could he spend them in the Virtual Realm?

It would be best for him to get the lay of the land so he could prepare for a deep dive. CJ spent the next few minutes rechecking the equipment. Finally, he lay down on the couch and placed the neural uplink over his head.

He took a breath.

And then switched it on.

EPILOGUE

THE NIGHT WAS QUIET. Far too quiet for a city that never sleeps. But these days no one wanted to be out when the sun went down. Liz Polova didn't know how to feel about that. She hadn't realized how much she'd gotten used to the noise until it was gone.

Not that it mattered. She parried the attack from Chloe and leaped backward, creating an opening for her sister to—

Liz froze for a moment, shaking her head. Chloe used the hesitation to close in with a strike aimed at the spot where Liz was going to land. Liz brought her own daggers low to block the attack and then slid to the left so that Chloe would be able to pincer—

Liz tensed once more and then forcefully pushed past the lapse. When she attacked, Chloe drew back. Chloe attacked, and Liz either evaded, forcing an opening that no one was there to take. Their spar continued for another half hour, during which Liz tried to force herself from habits that she'd spent a lifetime developing.

José stood somewhere in the darkness that surrounded the improvised sparring ring. Liz could feel the weight of his disapproving gaze. It was always disapproving these days, no matter what Liz did or how hard she tried to please him.

She hesitated once more when she waited to take advantage of an attack her sister would have made. She felt José's glare press in. Idly, Liz noticed that his judgment had lost the effect it'd once had on her; she didn't jump to his commands like a dog.

He'd made her abandon her sister.

Liz suppressed the spark of anger before it could fully form. She forced herself to focus on the bout. With her full attention, Liz stopped making the mistakes that had plagued her all night. But that created its own, unique problems. It had been a few weeks since Liz had finally outstripped Chloe in speed. That, combined with Liz's superior strength and reflexes, meant Chloe was no longer a match for her in a head-on fight.

It should have been something to be proud of. She and Karla had been aiming for the day they could defeat Chloe since they'd held their first blades. But the victory tasted sour. Something was missing.

At some point, the relative quiet of the night was broken by the sound of José's phone ringing. Liz sighed, and she and Chloe disengaged. It'd only been a week since they'd moved here. The hounds were getting closer. Her eyes roved over the room until she found her things already packed.

José's phone rang again. Liz finally realized it hadn't beeped with an alert; this was an actual phone call. Without a word, Chloe and Liz spread out across the unfinished building, checking all the entrances. The sweep took less than a minute. José's phone was still ringing when they came back.

Liz shook her head at her father, signaling that she hadn't seen anyone. José narrowed his eyes but finally picked up the call, putting it on speaker.

DJ's voice filled the room. "*I was afraid your paranoid ass wasn't going to pick up,*" he said. Liz could almost picture the grin on his face. "*Good thing you did though, 'cause we need to meet. I'm thinking lunch? You free?*"

"I thought I made myself clear the last time we spoke, Darren Kojak," José growled, making his irritation clear. "My family and I will not be joining your pathetic war against Helene."

"No, yeah, you made that clear as glass. That's why you separated your daughter from her twin sister and all that, right? Dick move, by the way. I'm not sure I ever said that."

Liz held her breath. Her whole body tensed, readying itself to flee in case her father went on a rampage. José controlled himself at the last minute. "Did you call because you were tired of living?" he hissed.

"I called because I figured you deserved to know that you messed your daughter up so much that she charged into one of Helene's drone production facilities headfirst and without a plan, all to prove a point."

Liz was beside her father before she realized she'd moved. She almost snatched the phone away from him before returning to her senses. "Explain yourself," she told DJ. "What happened to my sister?"

"Oh, Liz? I've told you all I know. She told me she'd followed some of Helene's drones down to a factory in Queens and brought me there so we could both destroy it. I said that was a stupid idea. She claimed I thought she was weak or something, so she charged into the place to prove a point. That was several days ago. I've been waiting outside, and she hasn't come back out."

Liz started to reply. But José spoke, his voice harsh. "Your deceitful attempts to involve us in your mess are pathetic. Do you think we're fools, that we would come running because of some tale you have spun?"

"I don't give a flying fuck what you believe. This was a heads-up kind of call, 'cause I figured you deserved to know. Do with the info what you want."

The line went dead.

José stared at the phone in his hand, anger wafting off him like steam. Liz knew she was in danger standing so close to him in his current mood. But she didn't care. She continued staring at him, begging him with her eyes. But when her father finally calmed himself, he spared her only a disdainful glance and walked toward the center of the room where Chloe was.

"Pack your things," he said, crushing the phone. "We'll move to the next safe house."

"And Karla?" Chloe asked. "DJ might be annoying as hell, but he wouldn't have gone through the stress of tracking us down just to lie—"

"Karla," José said, staring down Chloe, "made her choice. Now she must bear the consequences."

Chloe frowned and then glanced at Liz. But Liz was already gone, blurring to the nearest exit.

She'd abandoned her sister once. She wasn't going to do so again.

DECEMBER 2043
SOMEWHERE IN THE VIRTUAL REALM

Manar grimaced as he turned the corner. He scanned the walls, searching for the mark he would have left if he'd passed that way before. It was important since every inch of the place looked the same. The marks were the only way he knew he wasn't walking around in circles.

He couldn't afford that.

Manar scanned the walls thoroughly and sighed in relief when he couldn't find anything. Small blessing! Now he could add more to his mental map. He still hadn't found an exit, but he was certain he was almost done combing the building. He was going to stumble upon the way out sooner or later.

Manar was hoping on sooner. It was difficult to track the passage of time in the Virtual Realm—even harder when one had spent most of their time trapped in a cage and the rest wandering about a labyrinthine building. It had been over a month by his estimation, but it could have been anywhere from three months to half a year.

Manar had spent a lot of time in that cage before he'd figured out how to break out.

Manar shook himself out of his thoughts and focused on the wall again. He needed to mark it in order to track his progress. He squinted at the blank surface until he made out the sequences of ones and zeros that made up the wall.

Manar studied the sequence for several moments, moving from one individual code to the general tapestry. Once he was sure he understood it, he reached out and *shifted* a sequence downward. It was a relatively simple adjustment, but it still took all of his focus. Panting, he watched a small crack form on the wall in front of him. It was faint, relatively minor, but the imperfection stood out in the flawless construction of everything else.

An eternity ago, Manar could have done the same thing without lifting a finger—with just a glance in fact. But that was when he still had access to his body. Manar had his suspicions about why he'd lost that connection. They only pushed him to move faster.

Manar turned back and stared as if he would be able to peer through the walls and several hallways to a room where a gigantic timer ticked down to the end of the world.

He needed to get out here and tell them. He was running out of time.

Everyone was.

ACKNOWLEDGMENTS

MY COMPLETION OF THIS PROJECT could not have been accomplished without the coaching and support of the beta readers, editors, and critics that I've met on this journey. My heartfelt thanks to everyone.

- Alex Kempsell
- Davida De La Harpe Golden
- Deborah G Lynn
- Jennifer Moy
- Jesse Winter
- Nathan Goyer
- Paul Goat Allen
- Tasneem Ali
- Victoria and Richard Wolf

And, to my caring, loving, and supportive family. I cannot express enough thanks to my family for their continued support and encouragement throughout this project. Please bear with me until I wrap up this five-book series.